THE HAUNTING
OF BARRY ALLEN

ALSO AVAILABLE FROM
TITAN BOOKS:

ARROW: VENGEANCE
by Oscar Balderrama and Lauren Certo

And continuing from
FLASH: THE HAUNTING OF BARRY ALLEN:

ARROW: GENERATION OF VIPERS
by Clay and Susan Griffith (March 2017)

THE FLASH™

THE HAUNTING OF BARRY ALLEN

Clay Griffith and Susan Griffith

TITAN BOOKS

THE FLASH: THE HAUNTING OF BARRY ALLEN
Print edition ISBN: 9781785651410
E-book edition ISBN: 9781785651427

Published by Titan Books
A division of Titan Publishing Group Ltd
144 Southwark St, London SE1 0UP

First edition: November 2016
10 9 8 7 6 5 4 3 2

TIBO37513

Visit our website: www.titanbooks.com

A CIP catalogue record for this title is available from the British Library

Printed and bound in the United States.

1

My name is Barry Allen and I am the fastest man alive. I solve my problems by running faster. Always faster…

Running is a solitary experience. Even in a crowded marathon, a runner's world shrinks with each pounding foot, each carefully controlled beat of the heart, every steady draw of breath.

At least that's what Barry believed. It's not like he was ever on a track team. Most of his life, the only time he'd run was when he was late—which was often.

Then he was struck by lightning, *literally*, and he became more than Barry Allen. He became the Flash, and he learned a lot more about running, particularly running at unnaturally high speeds. He also learned that he never ran just to run. The Flash ran to help people, because that's what a hero did.

Even so, he could achieve his own coveted runner's

high, and disappear. Everything around him melted away, and Barry was alone with his speed. It became his sanctuary.

Except when Cisco Ramon and the S.T.A.R Labs team buzzed in his ear.

"Barry! We have a four-seventy on highway sixty-four near mile marker one oh three."

Every word crackled with eagerness.

"A forgery? On a highway?"

"Four-fifteen," Caitlin Snow interrupted calmly. "Reckless driver."

"Auto transport rig." Cisco lost none of his excitement. "It's carrying a bunch of vintage Corvettes."

"How do you *still* not know the police codes?" Caitlin demanded.

"Not my fault!"

As the friendly bickering continued, regardless of the fact that the audio feed was still live, the Flash pushed up his speed, veering toward the east side of Central City. The world slipped past. At this velocity everything appeared to stand absolutely still, and he focused tightly on the narrow corridor ahead as he darted back and forth and over and under any obstacles in his path.

Within seconds he spotted the careening vehicle.

A massive trailer truck loaded with eight cars swerved across the center of a busy six-lane highway, traffic clustered loosely all around. The rig hit the median rail and bounced high into the air. The chains and straps holding cars snapped, sending shiny Corvettes tumbling into the air like out-of-control missiles.

Tires screeched as drivers swerved and reacted in desperation.

The Flash poured it on and lightning flickered around him, sparking everything with a living glow. The sounds of the disaster echoed oddly. The decibels dropped to a low-pitched hum.

Seven of the cars on the highway were about to smash into other vehicles or be crushed by flying Corvettes. If that happened, more would follow.

A man in his fifties jerked the steering wheel so hard the right-side wheels of his Audi came off the ground. The Flash pulled alongside, and his hand vibrated the locked door, shifting the mechanism. As the car began tilting, he pulled it open, unfastened the seatbelt, and pulled the driver out, depositing the man on a grassy shoulder as his car completed its flip and slid along the pavement on its roof, sending out cascades of sparks.

The driver's hands were still outstretched, as if gripping the steering wheel.

Yet another car spun toward the massive wheels of the trailer. It was a model that had one of those defective airbags announced on the news. He didn't want to find out if it would fail. The Flash pulled an elderly lady from behind the wheel…

…when suddenly his speed force wavered.

For just a nanosecond.

A sudden twinge gripped him, as if time blinked for a moment. He let go of the woman, leaving her suspended above the pavement.

What the...

Then as if it had been his imagination, it was gone. Instantly he reached out, grabbing the woman just before she connected with the highway. He left her on the same shoulder of the road. Another instant trip into the chaos brought the truck driver to safety. He reeked of liquor.

Four more cars, four impacts averted. That left only one last vehicle, and there were at least eight seconds before the little economy car was crushed to a pancake. Plenty of time.

He was at the car in one.

Through the window, a woman's terrified face greeted him, frozen in place. Her arm stretched to protect the small boy in the back seat, who looked confused and frightened at the same time, slowly beginning to comprehend the danger, staring at his mom. Reaching for her.

One of the Corvettes tumbled straight for the little car, and the woman tried to swerve. She wouldn't make it. A meticulously restored cherry-red '65 model hovered just inches from smashing through her windshield. It moved slowly, but with inexorable certainty. The Flash moved his head a centimeter to avoid the Corvette's side mirror.

Six seconds.

He had an eternity to study the passengers. The only things moving were sparks of red electricity. The woman looked familiar for some reason. She was young, too young to die, yet he could see in her eyes that she recognized her fate. Seconds from the end and her only thought was to reach for her son.

Resolve sang in the Flash as he vibrated his hand through the door lock and sprung it open. He worked quickly to pull them both from the car as the Corvette's hood crept closer, pressing into the windshield with aching slowness. The glass cracked gradually, as if a spider was slowly spinning a web. The boy's lips moved by minuscule degrees. Barry made out the word. The boy called out for his mother, one last time.

Four seconds.

The Flash grabbed both the mother and son, their bodies pliable as they hung in suspended time. He had to pay attention when interacting with people who weren't moving at his speed. If he gripped them wrong, the friction might leave terrible burns, or he could easily rip off an arm if in his heroic zeal he exerted too much pressure.

He could kill the people he attempted to save.

Wrapping up the boy with his left arm, the Flash pulled the woman close on his right before placing a foot on the car's fender. The trunk began to lift into the air as the Corvette's impact gradually shoved the front end into the pavement.

Three seconds.

The Flash propelled himself across the road, bending to duck under the rig itself as it tipped onto its side. He stopped just for an instant at a metallic blue sports car well out of the way of the truck or its flying cargo. It barreled toward the rear of a braking vehicle. The driver couldn't react in time.

Shifting his grip on the woman, the Flash let go of her for a moment. She hung in the speed force, her expression just starting to alter from terror to surprise as she sensed something changing. He used that time to open the door and press the man's foot hard down onto the brake pedal. Then his arm wrapped around the woman once again and he was off.

One second.

The Flash skidded to a halt on the small patch of grass. The world jolted to its normal pace. Keeping his grip on the boy, he set the woman gently on the ground, holding her for a moment to steady her on her feet as her perceptions shifted.

The hum disappeared and the air filled with the impacts of cars and an explosion of twisted metal. People screamed and ducked as the now empty vehicles collided. Barry felt the small boy's hand clutch at him. The man in the blue sports car slammed on his brakes just in time. Cars behind the chaos screeched to a halt in a burn of rubber.

The speed of the events rocked the woman on her heels. She croaked out one word.

"Dean."

"He's here. He's safe." The Flash shifted the boy from his arms to hers. She let out a short sob, wrapping her son in a tight embrace. It took her a moment to grasp the reality of what happened, now that her son was in her arms.

She looked up and recognized the scarlet costume. The boy responded quicker, his eyes wide.

"It's the Flash!" That air of awe and admiration never got old.

"You're a very lucky kid." He certainly didn't mean the car accident. He smiled warmly at the mother.

"You saved him," the mother gasped out. "Thank you."

"You're welcome. Are you all right?"

"That doesn't matter." She pressed her son's head against her face.

The Flash laid a hand on the boy's arm. "You stay here and take care of your mom."

Then he was gone as he sped around the crash site, ensuring everyone was safe and making sure fires were out. By then, emergency vehicles wailed in the distance. He stopped again by Dean and his mother. The woman appeared to have recovered. Barry finally recognized her. She worked at the coffee shop he usually visited, C.C. Jitters. Her name was Lily.

"You two still doing all right?" he asked.

The woman appeared stunned.

The boy nodded fiercely. He looked to be about ten years old. The narrowness of his escape hadn't processed yet, and hopefully it never would. Seeing the Flash had shoved everything else to the side at least for the moment. To him, this was an adventure.

"I can't wait to tell my friends I met you!" Dean put his hands on his head as if his brain would explode with excitement. The Flash wished he had something to offer the kid. Searching the ground, he found a small piece of wood and picked it up. Vibrating his finger rapidly, he used the friction to burn his name into the wood, and then held it out.

The boy clutched it like it was a golden ticket.

Lily blushed under the Flash's gaze.

"I don't know how to thank you."

The Flash gave her a warm smile, gently nodding. "You already did." The fire trucks arrived, and he turned toward the emergency personnel who began running toward the crash with first-aid kits and oxygen tanks. He recognized Captain Sandoval, who gave him a thumbs up as the men spread out to attend the shocked and wounded.

Lifting a hand to wave, the Flash sped off.

"No casualties," he announced over his suit comm link. "Well, unless you count the Corvettes."

"Corvettes? Nooooo," came the dismal wail.

"Cars can be replaced," Caitlin stated.

"Not vintage Corvettes," Cisco protested. "You wouldn't understand."

Barry could picture the roll of her eyes even as he zipped away.

"Are you coming in?" she asked the Flash.

"Maybe later, guys," he replied. "I've got to catch up on some work, and then I've got dinner plans."

2

The West house had been Barry's home since he was eleven. Since the terrible night his mother, Nora Allen, was murdered and his father, Henry, was arrested for the crime. Convicted and sent to prison.

Barry had been cast adrift.

Joe West had taken him in and given Barry everything he needed—a sanctuary, understanding, space, and most of all, unconditional love. Joe had also provided the boundaries that a kid needed, even though Barry challenged them at times.

The Wests weren't rich. Joe didn't make a lot of money on a cop's salary. There were long hours when he wasn't home… but Iris was. Joe's daughter. Being the same age, Barry and Iris had formed a solidarity. Her friendship had allowed him to remain a child, even through the life-shaping events that had shattered his world.

The house was small but, as with most bungalows, the design gave the illusion of space. Family mementoes dotted the shelves. Hues of browns and yellows gave it warmth that seeped into Barry as he entered through the front door.

Pots clattered in the kitchen. Iris was home. Something smelled wonderful. As he walked in, her slender frame was bent over the oven door from which the delectable aroma came. She turned toward him.

"What's for dinner?" Barry stepped up next to her, taking a deep sniff.

"Chicken parmesan." A natural smile flashed wide across her face as she slipped on an oven mitt.

"My favorite!"

She cast him a curious sidelong glance. "You say that about every meal."

"I've never said that about quiche."

Her sweet laugh filled the room as she pulled out three full trays of baked chicken breasts heaped with decadent red sauce and oozing mozzarella cheese. Barry's belly gurgled at the sight. His elevated metabolism needed refueling. Even though her hands were full, he gave her an elated sideways hug.

"You are the best!"

"They had a sale at the market, and I figured you'd be hungry after all the running around you did."

"You saw it?"

"I was sent to cover the story, but you'd already darted off before I could get an interview." Iris waved a tray under his nose. "I thought maybe I could snag one tonight, after dinner."

"Done!" Barry exclaimed, reaching for the cupboards to collect plates. "Is Joe going to make it home in time for dinner?"

"He texted me he was on his way, as long as he doesn't get called back in for some emergency." She frowned. "I'd like at least *one* family meal where none of us are running off in the middle of it."

As Barry moved to set the table, the front door opened.

"You made it."

Joe West closed the door behind him and smiled. He set his keys and wallet on the side table. "I could say the same about you." There was a spring in his step as he walked over and clapped an arm around Barry. "Good to have you home for dinner. Even better that I don't have to cook it."

Though Barry and Joe were the same height—just over six feet tall—Joe was broader and more muscular than his wiry foster son. His tie was loose, and he had a perpetually rumpled look about him. There was a softness in his deep voice and a gentleness in his eyes.

"You're in a good mood," Barry said.

"It was a good day today," Joe replied cryptically, and he didn't stop grinning. Barry's curiosity was piqued.

"Promotion? Pay raise? A vacation?"

"I'll tell you over dinner."

Before Barry could press, Iris came into the dining room wearing oven mitts and carrying a baking tray filled with steaming chicken. Her face lit up at the sight of her father.

"Hi, Dad," she said. "Go get changed. We'll have everything ready by the time you come down."

The detective's grin broadened. "Won't take me but a minute." The big man pulled his badge and service revolver and headed for the stairs. "I want at least three of those so don't let Barry get a head start!" he said over his shoulder as he reached the landing.

Iris shook her head. "Some things never change."

"Hey, I wasn't always the Flash," Barry protested. "It's not my fault I have a crazy metabolism to maintain."

"No, but even when you were a kid, the two of you always competed at mealtimes. I was lucky to get table scraps—it's a wonder I didn't starve."

"Well, you've always been a little thin."

Iris raised an eyebrow, and he shut up.

"Go get the garlic bread and the salad, would you?" she said. Grateful for the change in subject, Barry slipped past her to do as he had been instructed. On his way back he helped himself to a couple of slices. Either Iris didn't notice, or she was all too used to his table manners.

There was a creak of the stairs and Joe came back down, wearing jeans and a white shirt. As he settled himself at the head of the table, his face still held a broad grin. Iris and Barry took their own seats to either side.

"I like this," he said. "It's been a while since we all sat around the table at the same time."

"Without something interrupting us, you mean," Barry said with a sheepish grin. Joe nodded. He then pinned Iris with an accusatory eye.

"You didn't turn off the phones, did you?"

Iris gave a small snort of exasperation as she dished out the meal, piling four cutlets onto his plate.

"It crossed my mind, but no."

"So what's with you, Joe?" Barry demanded. "What happened today that's got you so happy?"

"You say that like it's strange," Joe replied with mock indignation, reaching for his food. "As a general rule, I'm a happy kind of guy. Aren't I?" When no one answered, he dug into his meal, continuing to talk between bites.

"I delivered a baby."

"No way!" Barry let out an incredulous laugh. "Where?"

"In the middle of a supermarket. We were there for a robbery report, but in all of the excitement a woman went into full-on delivery mode. Just like on television." He paused and looked up. "Got to admit, I was scared to death. I've never done anything like that before." He glanced at Iris. "When you were born, they let me cut the cord and hold you, but that was all. The doctors did all the heavy lifting."

"What was it?" Iris rested her chin on her palms.

"A boy." His warm gaze found Barry. "A beautiful baby boy. The way he stared at me. The gratitude of his parents. Those little hands." A glimmer of moisture reflected in the big man's eyes.

Barry understood completely. He felt that same

sort of high every moment as the Flash. Sometimes it took him to heights that made coming down almost impossible. Not that he really wanted to.

"I don't get to experience something like that every day," Joe confessed. "Too much cruelty in my line of work. But on days like today, I wouldn't want to do anything else."

"I know what you mean," Iris said. "For all the crime stories I have to write at the *Picture News*, all the corrupt politicians we've got, all it takes is one story— about an ordinary person doing something amazing— to make me love my job all over again."

"To a family of heroes," Barry announced with mock pretension, and he lifted his glass. Then he winked at Iris before looking over at Joe. "And I think we know who gets the credit."

Iris smiled at her father. "We were brought up right." Joe scoffed, reaching for garlic toast. "No, really," she said. "You always taught us how important it is to think about others, rather than just ourselves."

"You'd have both turned out fine," he replied. "And, Barry, you were headed in the right direction before I even came into the picture."

Barry shrugged. "Sure, but when you *did* come into the picture, I could've easily turned into a bitter kid. Without you, Joe, we might not have the Flash. I might've become a sociopath, like most of the other metas we run into."

"I find it hard to picture you as a super-villain,"

Iris said, and she grinned. "You're way too much of a nerd."

"Nerds turn evil," Joe said. "Look at… what's his name… Hartley Rathaway. What's Cisco call him? The Pied Piper."

Barry shook his head. "He isn't a nerd. *Cisco* is a nerd. Hartley Rathaway is an honest-to-god evil genius." He pointed with his fork. "Let's face it, most every villain, nerd or not, could've used a Joe West in their life."

"Or at least a good swift boot in their rear," Joe muttered. He regarded Barry with a hint of a smile. "I hear you had a great day, too. Saw the footage. That was some rescue you pulled off."

"All in a day's work," Barry muttered as he speared some more cutlets and piled them onto his empty plate. He shifted, embarrassed to be in the spotlight, and wolfed down the chicken.

"You're the only one who can do that kind of work, Barry." Joe patted Barry's hand against the table. "You both make an old man proud."

3

Early the next morning, the Flash wove through the streets of Central City, bound for his home away from home.

S.T.A.R. Labs had been the billion-dollar brainchild of Dr. Harrison Wells, successful scientist and entrepreneur, a man of theory and practice. Throughout his school days, Barry followed Wells's career, standing in awe of what the man accomplished.

The crown jewel of the research center was the particle accelerator. Intended as a source of limitless energy, it was promoted as the doorway to a future of ease and plenty, the key to an onrushing golden age. Unfortunately the key broke off in the lock.

During its maiden test, the accelerator ruptured, creating an artificial thundercloud and sending a wave of strange dark matter rippling across Central City. While most men and women remained unaffected, a percentage of the population had their DNA twisted, causing them to transform, to become something unprecedented.

These *metahumans* became the true harbingers of the future. Some could fly. Others could channel terrible energies through their minds and bodies. Yet others could alter their physical forms, morphing into substances that were far from flesh and blood.

The transformations left physical, mental, and psychological scars. Many of these new men and women were warped by the experience, striking out in fear, anger, and greed. Some remained content to seek profit, while others sought to exert their influence over persons they saw as weak and vulnerable.

One metahuman used his powers to oppose them.

The night the particle accelerator exploded, the wave of dark matter engulfed Barry Allen in his forensic laboratory at Central City Police Headquarters, just as he was struck by lightning. The result was a coma.

Nine months later, he woke.

To a great extent Central City had healed from the cataclysm, though S.T.A.R. Labs remained a husk, maintained by the slimmest of skeleton crews. As Barry attempted to rejoin the world, he discovered how much he had changed, and sought answers at the source of the phenomena.

Arriving at S.T.A.R. Labs, the Flash roared through the doors of that once-great scientific coliseum and wound his way through the hallways, skidding to a halt in the main control room, dubbed the Cortex.

Cisco Ramon and Dr. Caitlin Snow looked up from their work and smiled from inside the blizzard of paper that went airborne with the Flash's entrance. These two were all that was left of the great congress of geniuses gathered by Harrison Wells.

Barry pulled back his red cowl and plucked the floating sheets from the air faster than the eye could follow. He hastily piled them on a countertop and turned to face his friends, a sheepish grin splitting his boyish features.

Cisco tipped a greeting with his giant soda cup from Big Belly Burgers. Short with a round face and long dark hair shoved behind his ears, he looked more like an intern than a full-blown mechanical engineer. His t-shirt read ASK ME ABOUT ABSOLUTELY ANYTHING AT ALL.

The burger scent wafted across the nearly sterile control room, and Barry's stomach growled. Even the quick jaunt to the lab made his body crave food. His eyes locked on the large pile of French fries on the semicircular workstation next to Cisco. He grabbed a handful and shoved them in his mouth, enjoying the salty jolt. Cisco didn't even blink.

"Did you guys notice anything odd with me yesterday?" Barry asked.

"Odd?" Caitlin stopped smiling. Even when she appeared happy, there was something pensive about the young, brown-haired bio-engineer. Her eyes were distant, even haunted. Though she was loath to admit it, it was as if she was waiting for the world to disappoint. Given her tragic history, such an outlook seemed entirely too justifiable.

"What do you mean?" Cisco asked, his endless curiosity piqued. "Oh, and please... have some fries."

"Thanks," Barry said as he chewed. "Not sure. A little hiccup? A glitch in the readings?" He walked over to stand next to them.

"A glitch?" Caitlin frowned and swung back into a chair at her computer station. Fingers rippled over the keyboard. "What does that mean? A glitch in what?"

Cisco leaned close to Barry's suit, inspecting the raised lightning bolt emblem on the chest that contained micro-sensors. His voice was concerned.

"Did you break our suit?"

Barry reached around him to gather the last of the fries.

"No."

"Thank God." Cisco narrowed his eyes as Barry shoved the fries into his mouth. "Then what are you talking about?"

"I'm not sure." Barry fished a cheeseburger out of the greasy bag on the table. As he peeled back the wrapper, he said, "That's why I'm asking. Just like a... a *blink*." He frowned in contemplation, mirroring Caitlin's expression. "A nanosecond of... something. I just felt a tug in my speed. I think."

Caitlin scanned multiple readouts on her screen,

biological data that was steadily collected by the sensors in the Flash suit, and transmitted to S.T.A.R. Labs. "There's nothing abnormal registering now. Heart rate slightly elevated. Blood pressure fine." She switched to another screen. "Your speed was constant yesterday, so far as I can tell. Do you feel sick?"

"No, I feel great." Barry shook his head and polished off the cheeseburger. "That burger needed pickles though."

Cisco wadded up the empty bag and hook shot it toward a garbage can.

He missed.

"I don't like pickles."

Caitlin turned from the screen to Barry, her gaze probing.

"Are you sure?"

"I should know whether I like pickles or not."

"Not that." Caitlin waved him away. "Barry, are you sure about what you experienced? Can you describe it more clearly?"

"Forget about it." Barry laughed, and wished he hadn't said anything. He didn't really know *what* he'd felt, or even if it was real. More likely it was his imagination—a side effect of the adrenaline rush. "It's never happened before. Just a glitch, like I said. Maybe a piece of a Corvette nicked me, and it didn't register." He looked at Cisco. "So only one burger?"

"I didn't know I was feeding the multitudes," Cisco replied wryly. "Maybe you could go buy another one…

and one for me, while you're at it."

"You're on." Barry welcomed a quick jaunt to Big Belly Burger. "It's fun, running through the drive-thru."

Caitlin raised her hand. "Could you do something for me?"

"You want a milkshake?"

"No. Well, yes, but first could you do a stint on the treadmill? I want to run a few tests."

"Caitlin, really, don't worry."

"I *am* worrying, Barry," she protested, her voice becoming firm. "Anytime something odd happens, we *have* to pay attention. So just… run. Please. I want to establish a baseline." When he saw how serious she was, Barry relented.

"Okay." He started toward the side chamber where his industrial-strength treadmill sat.

"Wait," Caitlin called out. "It would be better to duplicate external conditions. You can run the Pipeline."

Cisco logged his computer into the server she was using, and they began setting the parameters in the suit. Clearly outnumbered, Barry sighed and headed out the door at a normal walk, working his way down to the vast circular tunnel that ran the perimeter of S.T.A.R. Labs. It had been built to house the particle accelerator equipment, similar to its more famous counterpart in Switzerland. Later it had been retrofitted into a makeshift prison to hold metahumans who could not be left on the streets to prey on innocent people. Now it was dark and quiet.

Deserted. Technically endless.

Entering the tunnel, Barry switched on the lights, casting stark shadows over an array of equipment, revealing gaping holes where devices had been removed. He touched the lightning bolt-shaped earpiece on the side of his head.

"You guys ready?"

"Ready when you are," Caitlin replied.

Barry waved at the camera mounted high on the wall, and bolted.

As he hit a steady pace, Caitlin's voice came into his ears.

"Bring it up to Mach point four-five. That's the maximum speed you reached during the rescue on the highway."

The Flash ran easily, passing 300 mph without effort. Though he was moving at unbelievable speed, his surroundings were utterly calm.

"A little faster, Barry," she instructed. "Come to Mach point five."

The Flash chuckled with excitement, and kicked it up. He could see the fringes of the lightning crackling off the suit now, and the familiar sensation began to course through him. The tunnel ahead grew even clearer as he ran past the same spot every few seconds. Over and over and over.

"Hold that pace." Caitlin was in full analysis mode. "We'll monitor your vitals. Let us know if you feel anything. Anything, Barry," she repeated sternly.

"I will," he promised. "All good so far." The Flash settled in, hardly noticing his arms and legs pumping. Electricity crackled. A straight run like this was easier than maneuvering at high speed, dealing with foreign objects like flying cars.

His mind wandered, and he frowned at the memory of a little boy, frozen in the speed force, staring at his mom in terror, not afraid for himself but for her. And there was his mother, reaching out, unaware of anything except her son's danger.

"Okay, Barry," Caitlin's voice crackled, "slow down now."

Her words didn't register. He went faster, instead, pushed himself harder. He might need another microsecond to save the next Lily and Dean. Step after step fell with mesmerizing precision. The cold walls of the Pipeline started to stretch and lose clarity on the edges. Blood pounded in his ears.

A crimson shape rose up on Barry's right side. He turned and saw his father, Henry Allen, in a Flash suit. The scarlet-clad figure matched him stride for stride, even though he was heavier and older. The suit looked strange, soft and molded.

Barry looked the other speedster in the eyes and realized it *wasn't* his father. It was him. It was Barry, only older. The face was thicker and worn with deep creases along the mouth. The eyes were the same ones Barry had seen in the mirror his whole life, only tired and… something else.

The older Flash reached out, and opened his mouth to speak.

Barry flinched, and found himself tumbling. The harsh lights of the tunnel suddenly flew all around him. Solid blows landed on Barry's shoulders and back and legs. The world whirled around him.

His hands flew out, slapping helplessly off hard surfaces.

He bounced and rolled and slammed into a wall. Caromed off the steel across the tunnel floor and impacted the opposite wall. His breath pounded from his chest. His body slid around in a full circle and he found himself staring up at the shadowy curve of the tunnel ceiling.

Noises roared in Barry's ears, and only now did he realize they were voices. Caitlin and Cisco called out in alarm.

"Barry! What happened?" Caitlin said. "Talk to me. Answer me!"

"Are you all right?" Cisco added. "I'm on my way down!"

"I'm fine." Barry lay still. His chest rose and fell, but not because he was out of breath. His heart pounded. He didn't move, trying to recall what he had seen. "I just tripped."

"Tripped?" Caitlin exclaimed. "You don't trip."

Barry sat up. He leaned back against the solid wall, pulling off his cowl. Then he stiffened in alarm.

"I think I ghosted." Barry looked up and down the

tunnel, searching for some sign of temporal change.

"Ghosted?" Caitlin responded. "You mean time travel? No, Barry. You weren't moving nearly fast enough. And there's no sign of tachyon elevation."

"But I saw myself," he said. "When I time travel, I can see images of myself. What time is it? What day?"

"It's only a few minutes after you went down there."

"*What day?*"

"Barry, it's the same day," she insisted. "You didn't time travel."

Footfalls pounded in the distance and a shape appeared around the curve of the Pipeline. Cisco gasped for breath, sheened with sweat, and staggered up to where Barry sat on the floor. He stopped and bent at the waist, hands on his knees. His mouth opened and closed, but he couldn't speak. Barry looked up, and waited.

"Are you...?" Cisco finally rasped. "Are you... are you...?"

"Am I okay?" Barry replied. "Yes. Are you? Sit down. Catch your breath, man."

Cisco nodded and ran a hand through his straight black hair. He leaned heavily on the wall, sliding down, sucking air into his lungs. Barry got to his feet and put a comforting hand on his shoulder.

"Breathe. I'm good."

"What does a heart attack feel like? Like this? Probably like this. I'm glad you ate my cheeseburger now. Thank you. I'd be dead right now if I ate all that grease."

Barry again peered into the dim expanse of the tunnel.

"I think I ghosted, but Caitlin says it's impossible."

Cisco regarded him quizzically with his face flushed. He scrabbled for his phone, checked it, and held up the screen for Barry to see the display.

"Well, not unless you returned to the *exact* moment you left, and that's never happened before." His gaze shifted to far away, and he added, "It also means we could all be time travelling all the time." Cisco's mouth opened in an amazed circle as Barry helped him to his feet. "Oh, man, I just blew my own mind!" They moved toward the nearest exit, their footsteps echoing in the emptiness.

"I'm pretty sure I saw myself," Barry said.

"Maybe it was a speed mirage. Some kind of image sticking to your retinas."

Barry shrugged. "Maybe. It's possible. I'll admit my mind was wandering a little." He shook his head. "But the Flash I saw down here wasn't a mirror image."

"No? How did you look?"

"Older. Much older. And I looked scared, Cisco.

"I looked really, really scared."

4

Caitlin's worried expression met Barry and Cisco as they entered the Cortex. So did a blinking light on Cisco's computer screen.

"Are you all right?" Her eyes studied him critically. Shifting into her physician persona, she came forward to examine him.

"I'm fine," Barry assured her. "I lost concentration."

"Okay, now *that's* strange," Cisco remarked as the blinking light caught his eye. He rushed toward his workstation. Barry joined him, and leaned over Cisco's shoulder. He squinted at the monitor.

"What's strange?"

"Tornado," Cisco said. "Right in the heart of downtown."

Barry looked at another monitor showing the view outside.

"It's a clear day."

"Hence the 'strange.'" Cisco called up a city traffic

camera. A dark spinning mass ripped across a crowded boulevard, debris and broken branches lifting into the air.

"Actually," Caitlin commented behind them as she made her way back to her own bank of computers, "tornados can occur near the trailing edge of thunderstorms. It's not uncommon to see clear, sunlit skies behind them."

"Except there's literally no thunderstorms," Cisco informed them, checking the weather radar on a monitor to his left. He played the keyboards like a maestro. "Nothing. Nada. There's like zero percent chance for one to develop." He shot them a meaningful glance. "But I'll bet there's a one hundred percent chance of Weather Wizard."

The Flash rolled his eyes. Mark Mardon was one of their least favorite metahuman psychopaths.

"Where's the wand?" he asked.

Cisco moved to a lit display case on one side of the control room, and pulled out a metal cylinder the size of a heavy flashlight, similar in shape, about the length of an arm, but with a claw at one end. Cisco had fashioned it during a previous encounter, to prevent Mardon from using his power by metabolizing the free electrons in the atmosphere. He handed it to the Flash.

"I expect this back in pristine condition, young man."

Barry hooked it onto his belt. "We'll see."

Caitlin pursed her lips as she observed Barry's most recent bio readouts.

"Maybe you should—" she began.

"Okay, I'm out," Barry announced, and he was gone, leaving her to sigh with annoyance.

"—wait until we collect more data," she continued over the comm link. He could hear the worry in her voice.

"It's downtown by the waterfront," he replied. "Too many people are there. We can't wait." Even as he said it, he approached his target, so he put the strange glitch out of his mind. They would figure it out. They *always* figured it out.

Time to focus, he thought to himself. *Time to run fast, and save lives.*

The wind blew fiercely and debris filled the air. As he jerked to a stop, Barry put an arm up to protect his eyes. He peered down the street.

There it is. The rotating cloud had a snakelike form extending to the ground. Rain fell hard onto the pavement in a drenching gush. Papers, sticks, leaves, and dirt flew everywhere as the tail of the tornado scoured a nearby park down to the bare soil. A car tumbled down the street and a tree twisted off its trunk with a wrenching *crack*.

"I'm reading sustained winds of more than 120 miles per hour," Caitlin informed him.

"That's slow," the Flash replied.

"Only to you," Cisco pointed out.

The storm roared toward the River Financial Center

where well-dressed people regularly crowded upscale cafes, having their business lunches. The region around Central City was no stranger to tornados— natural and otherwise—so as the twister drew close, people were already moving. A few stood gaping at the impossibility of the deadly squall that had appeared out of the blue.

The Flash darted this way and that, shouting at them to get to shelter. As they complied, he turned to face the oncoming column of air. It was one thing to watch a tornado on a nature program, yet another to stand at its destructive feet and feel the raw power circulating inside it. From afar, such phenomena were hypnotic and amazing.

Up close, they would kill.

The rain hit, and water fell in sheets. The cloud mutated rapidly, drawing up more and more debris. Its muscular core rotated nearly overhead now, and the merciless force wrenched windows from frames amid a hail of shattered glass. It lifted the roof off a cafe.

The Flash darted forward, his speed protecting him from the force of the wind, racing around the appendage that tethered the twister to the ground. If he could cut off the tornado's connection to the earth, then the storm cloud would just fly by overhead without continuing to inflict its terrible damage.

The world blurred past as he ran around and around the funnel, moving *against* its natural spin. Finally, he felt the tornado's momentum slow. With its energy draining, the tail of the storm ceased gouging the ground, and lifted up. Once contact was severed, the results were immediate and the Flash watched as the cloud rose up into the sky.

Remnants of the carnage drifted to the ground in a shower of shingles, leaves, and heavy branches. The rotating cloud lifted high enough to pass over the financial center, then it faded to mere gusts. Blue sky appeared, shining through. His sigh of relief was audible even over the cheer of the crowd.

Checking for anyone who might be hurt, the Flash smiled and reached down to help a shaken man to his feet. The tight grip of gratitude on his arm spoke volumes, and as the man stared back, there again was that look. Sheer appreciation echoed in every gesture and expression. The feeling it gave rippled through Barry. He needed no other reward.

"Crisis averted," he said into his mic, causing the man to shoot him an odd look.

"Don't count your chickens," Cisco replied. "There's another tornado forming on Canal Street!"

"Another one?"

"Holy smoke!" Cisco exclaimed. "It's an F5."

Bracing himself, the Flash raced off again.

He reached the other twister just as it swept through a parking lot. People trapped there by the cyclone fence struggled through the fierce winds as cars began to shift like toys on a table. The Flash darted over hoods and car roofs to grab the helpless, trapped bystanders before they were crushed.

Within moments he had deposited them all in the relative safety of a nearby lobby. The muffled roar of the storm grew louder as it advanced relentlessly on a cluster of buildings.

"Stay under cover," he told them as he turned back toward the door. The tornado sucked up massive amounts of debris like an out-of-control vacuum. Its base stretched to cover half a city block.

"I don't think cutting off the connection is going to be enough with this one." As he stepped outside, he had to shout to be heard over the roar. He gauged his chances, and the debris began to pelt down, bouncing off of his protective uniform. "It has way too much energy."

The great behemoth of a storm lumbered toward him as if Goliath had finally spotted young David. The funnel crashed into the roof of the venerable old Central City Keystone Bank. The corner of the marble edifice gave way, and the hundred-year-old oak trees surrounding the building simply snapped. The unearthly roar grew steadily louder.

The Flash began to circle the tornado, running in the same direction as its spin. It was the only way he could remain on his feet. He could tell from the unyielding power of the storm that he wouldn't be able to disconnect it from the ground, nor draft this beast off its course.

"Guys," he said into the mic. "Any ideas? I won't be able to hold this thing steady for long. It's all I can do to stay on the ground."

"Barry, in order for a tornado to sustain itself, it needs two things," Cisco said. "A warm updraft, and a cold downdraft."

"Can I cool the updraft?"

"No. In fact, by running around the tornado you're adding energy to it. However, if you can warm the downdraft, that could rob the storm of its energy. It would help if you could fly."

"Yeah, if only." Barry looked up at the roiling monstrosity that disappeared into low black clouds. "Wait a minute. I've got an idea."

He stopped running.

Thunderous winds seized him and he rose into the air. The Flash bounced off a hunk of wreckage, landing with his feet, propelling himself upward. Leaping from one shattered piece of the bank to another, climbing the massive wall of wind.

Something slammed into the Flash's head and he staggered, continuing to career from one object to the next. A barrage of five-inch-diameter hailstones pelted him. He couldn't dodge so he put his head down and plowed through. As his speed increased, so did the impacts, but they weren't penetrating the suit or his flesh.

Already he couldn't see the ground. Black, swirling clouds and lightning surrounded him, sparking jagged bolts across the crowded sky every few seconds. High above the city, he started to run against the wind. Leaping from object to object, like crossing a roaring river on slippery stones.

The lightning that lit the clouds joined the bolts roiling off of the Flash to fill the sky. The more he ran, the more white-hot energy crackled in the air. He dodged the brittle flashes of lightning pouring from the storm while trailing his own bright streaks of electricity.

On he ran, burning through the sky, warming the cold air aloft. Tightly focused, he saw nothing but his next footstep, the next piece of rubble that was his path as he raced about the crown of the storm. The din of the tornado was lost in the roar of his own speed.

Abruptly a piece of wreckage dropped under his foot. The wind was losing its power, and with it the ability to keep the debris airborne. Stones and girders and sheets of metal spiraled downward. Barry had to follow, weaving his way down through the crashing rubble.

He redirected what he could on the way, unable to stop the deluge of wood, metal and bricks that pelted the ground. The trapped contents of the faltering tornado fell with thundering force as he reached the sidewalk. The Flash sidestepped a plummeting tree that stabbed six feet into the dirt next to him.

"Scratch… another one." Barry's breath came hard as he skidded to a stop. Leaning over his knees, he sucked in as much air as his straining lungs would permit.

"Are you all right?" Caitlin asked.

"Just peachy," he gasped.

"Those two dissipated pretty quickly," Cisco mused.

"That seemed *quick* to you?"

"Be careful, Barry," Caitlin said. "Weather Wizard has got to be around."

"So far nothing," the Flash said, "and Mardon likes to take credit." He straightened and stretched out a sore shoulder.

"Yeah, he has a flair for being a drama queen," Cisco agreed.

"No demands. No drama. No Weather Wizard." The Flash looked around. "One of the tornados tore up the Central City Keystone Bank pretty badly, but Mardon isn't robbing it. That seems weird for him."

People emerged from indoors, gaping at the storm damage. With a thumbs up the Flash assured them it was safe, and then raced off to conduct a high-speed search of all the buildings the tornados had struck, stopping to help injured or shell-shocked people. He pulled people from the rubble of the CCK Bank, and shuttled several to the hospital while the emergency crews were still distant sirens.

"You recovered yet?"

He was shaking hands with a doctor at the emergency room, and refusing the offer of an examination, when Cisco's voice vibrated in his ear.

"Recovered from what?" Barry asked glibly. Before Cisco could answer, he added, "I feel great. I don't just *talk* about the weather, I *do something* about it."

"Well, time to do something about crime. There's been a break-in at the Natural Sciences Museum."

"There's no sign of metahuman activity there," Caitlin added. "The police are responding."

"I better go then…"

The Flash was already on his way.

"…since I work for the police."

5

The classical gray Central City Natural Sciences Museum sported a translucent dome on top. Through the glass, the spread wings of a pterodactyl could be seen from the street. The main doors stood open.

Speeding through the various wings, the Flash saw shocking incidents of vandalism, but there was no crime in progress. Upstairs and down, each room told the same sad story. Glass display cases shattered. Relics and artifacts smashed on the floor. It broke his heart.

He made another circuit searching for signs of entry—smashed windows or forced doors. There were none. Only one person was present, a young man sitting at a desk talking on the phone. The man looked shell-shocked.

Sirens sounded outside, and the Flash went to meet Joe West, who approached with his badge displayed on his belt and a notepad already in his hand. Joe's furrowing brows pulled his entire face into a frown.

His gaze centered on the fading bruises still visible under the mask.

"Hey, Flash," he said. "Good job with the tornados downtown. Could've been a major disaster. You look like you've been in a helluva fight. Was it Weather Wizard?"

"No, these bruises came from a hailstorm in one of the tornados," the Flash replied with a grin. "I didn't see Mardon, but it had to be him."

"That's just great." Joe nodded toward the museum. "So what's the story here?"

"The place is wrecked." The Flash rubbed the back of his head and gave a heavy sigh. "So much stuff destroyed. It's sad."

"You see anyone inside?"

"Yeah, there's one guy in the administrative offices. He looks pretty stunned by everything. I suspect he made the call to the police. The museum is closed today, so there are no visitors. Whoever did the damage is long gone." Uniformed officers began gathering around them, and Joe turned.

"Let's sweep the building. Be aware, one male subject inside. Apparently unarmed, but use caution." A couple of the officers drew sidearms and entered. Joe and the Flash followed them. "Who the hell would want to destroy a museum? Steal something, yes, but just wreak havoc? Where's the sense in that?"

"I can't even imagine what we've lost here." The Flash shook his head sadly, stepping cautiously through a collection of fossils that had been smashed to unrecognizable fragments.

Joe scowled. "I'm going to need Barry Allen on this," he said.

The Flash nodded. "I'm sure he'll be here."

"Never doubted it."

"Well, it looks like you have this under control. Good luck, Detective." With that, the Flash darted away.

Barry walked into the museum, carrying an equipment bag across his shoulder.

"Hey! I got the call. Sounds like a mess."

"I'm always amazed at how fast you do that," Joe said quietly. "How can you enjoy life at that speed?"

"There's something to be said for taking it slow," Barry replied, "but I don't remember it."

"One of these days, I'm taking you and Iris on a vacation where we do absolutely nothing."

Barry smirked. "You know, I'd like that." A police officer approached with the young man from the office.

"Detective West," the cop said, "this is Peter Stingle. He's the guy who called this in to nine-one-one. He works here."

"I-I'm an intern," Peter corrected in a stammering voice. He was thin, about eighteen years old, pale and shaken. "I'm only an intern. I just came in to arrange some insects." He looked at Joe, nearly in tears. "I do insects. Arrange the collection. That's what I do."

Joe signaled the uniformed cop to move on, and

flipped open his notepad.

"So give me the story, Mr. Stingle."

"So I came in to arrange insects and…" He waved his arms around. "This."

"This?" Joe eyed the kid. "So this was just here when you walked in?"

"Yes, sir."

"There was nobody else around?"

"No, sir," Stingle said. "The m-museum is closed today. That's why I came in to arrange the insects."

"What about the alarm?"

"Th-there wasn't one. The door was unlocked when I arrived. That's when I knew something was wrong. When I w-went to check, the alarm was already off."

Stingle was shaking now. Barry had done his share of nerve-wracking internships. To be at the center of something like this must be terrifying. He felt bad for the kid.

"So you can turn off the alarms?" Joe asked sharply.

"Y-yes, sir," Peter stammered.

Joe covered a frown of annoyance, but he had to rule the kid out as a suspect so he continued his questioning.

"Did you see anyone here?"

"I didn't really look." Stingle looked down at his shoes. "I didn't want to run into the r-robber. I went to the office and called Dr. Larson."

"Who's he?" Joe asked.

Barry provided the answer. "Hugo Larson. He's the museum director."

"Yes!" Peter nodded vigorously. "I c-called him, but couldn't get an answer. So I called the police, and then I tried to call Dr. Larson again, and then the police came, and now I'm talking to you."

Joe pointed up at a camera mounted on the wall. "Let's have a look at the security footage."

Peter swallowed hard. "It's turned off."

"How do you know that?"

"The monitors are in the office, where I was. W-when I first came in and saw all this, I thought I'd check around the museum to see if anyone was here. I didn't want to run into some kind of robber. But the feeds from the cameras were blank. Someone had turned them off."

"Someone?" Joe said. "Do *you* have the ability to turn off the cameras, too?"

"Sure."

Barry shook his head. This kid didn't even realize what Joe was hinting at, which made Barry pretty sure he had nothing to do with this. The security system was switched off and the doors were unlocked. No sign of forced entry. It could've been an inside job, but Peter Stingle seemed an unlikely suspect.

Either that, or he should win an Oscar.

Joe waved over a uniform cop. "Mr. Stingle, go with this officer and contact someone on the museum staff. If you still can't reach the director, call someone else. We need them down here." He turned to address the cop. "Get the address of the director, and send a unit over there to bring him here." He glanced at Stingle again. "Okay?"

"Sure." Peter rubbed his forehead, and he looked at Barry. "I just wanted to arrange insects. You know?"

"I do know." Barry smiled to comfort the kid, who walked away with the police officer. "I think you're on the right track, Joe. It definitely looks like an inside job. There was no evidence of forced entry. But I don't think it was that kid. He just wants to, you know, arrange insects. He's no criminal."

"We'll see," Joe replied. "Wouldn't be the first time some harmless young kid snapped under pressure."

Barry hefted his crime scene kit.

"Well, let me get to work."

It was two hours later when a disgruntled Joe squatted next to Barry as he was dusting a display case for fingerprints. Barry looked up, surprised that the time had passed so quickly.

Several people stood nearby in a shocked clutch— various members of the museum staff who had been summoned. The director wasn't among them, however.

"Kid was right," Joe said. "Security cameras shut off, and erased back twenty-four hours. And you were right, too—no forced entry that we can see. We've got some of the staff in now, but it's going to take time before they'll know if anything was stolen."

"Looks more and more like an inside job," Barry commented.

"Yeah," Joe muttered. "Any luck with the fingerprints?"

"Yes and no." Barry sat back on his heels. "Museums are notorious for grubby hands. Especially a hands-on, interactive museum like this one."

"Well, maybe we'll get lucky with one of them."

"Our best bets are those." He pointed to some red smears.

"We've got bloodstains," Joe said with excitement.

Barry nodded. "Yeah. Looks like whoever did this cut their hands in the process of breaking displays."

Joe leaned in closer. "We'll check all these museum guys for cuts," he murmured.

A uniformed officer came running up.

"Detective West, we have a body."

Joe and Barry both stood.

"Who?" Barry asked.

"Where?" Joe demanded.

"The director of the museum," the cop answered. "The black-and-white sent to his home found him dead."

"Damn." Joe shot Barry a glance.

They pulled up to a moderate split-level house in the suburbs, the home of Dr. Hugo Larson. It was one of those neighborhoods where violent crime seemed like a remote concept. Neighbors stood in yards and on sidewalks, holding a cup of coffee or a dog's leash, staring in shock at the police cars and flashing blue lights gathered around one particular house.

Another detective met Joe and Barry at the front door.

"Joe," he said. "Allen. The deceased is a male in his late sixties. Identified as Dr. Hugo Larson. He lives here alone. Wife deceased. He has two adult children, but they reside in Midway City."

"Cause of death?" Joe asked quickly.

"None apparent."

The interior of the house looked as simple as the outside. On most every surface knickknacks and photographs crowded neatly. It didn't look as if a crime had been committed here—until they reached the living room.

A body slumped on an olive-green couch. The man wore dress pants and shoes. His white shirt was open at the neck, revealing part of his chest. Draped over a chair nearby were a suit coat and a necktie. He looked as if he had come in from work and sat down to relax.

Barry frowned. "That is Hugo Larson, all right," he said. "What a shame. He was a brilliant guy. A renowned expert in geochemistry."

"You mean like rocks?"

"Yes." Barry smiled at Joe. "Like rocks. He could've made a fortune working for one of the oil companies, but he preferred running a museum and teaching." He put down his forensics kit, pulled on a new set of latex gloves, then knelt next to the body to get a good look. The face had a bluish tint. The tongue was swollen and distended. It was familiar, horrifyingly familiar.

"Check his hands," Joe said. Barry gave him a disappointed glance and lifted Larson's right hand, turning it palm up.

"Yeah." He sighed. "Glass fragments and blood. His hands are cut."

"Like someone who'd smashed some glass cases," Joe said without gloating.

"It doesn't make sense." Barry looked up. "I mean, Dr. Larson is one of the sweetest men I've ever met. He wouldn't have done it. He *loved* his work. He was passionate about discovery and preservation."

"Evidence doesn't lie."

Barry examined the man's hands closer. "There's something else." He pulled out a lens and studied Larson's palm. "There's some dark particulate matter here. Fragments of something."

"Of what?"

"I don't know." Barry took some samples.

"How did he die?" Joe asked, studying the dead man's face.

"My first guess is that he succumbed to histotoxic hypoxia. There are signs of petechiae. Small hemorrhages in the eyes and on his skin."

"Is that a bruise on his chest?"

Barry gently moved the dead man's shirt aside. "I don't think it is. Looks more like ecchymosis."

Joe waited for the explanation.

"When veins lose oxygen, they turn blue. When someone asphyxiates, more oxygen is depleted and a dark discoloration of the skin and tissue develops. Cyanosis. I can't be sure until I get autopsy results." Barry stared at the body, lost in thought. "Joe, don't you remember the Darbinyan crime family murders?"

"Kyle Nimbus?" Joe replied. "The Mist? You're saying the Mist killed this man?"

"I don't know," Barry admitted. "There are plenty of other reasons for a body to present with cyanosis like this. It could be something else. We'll find out when I get the blood toxicology report back. If it shows hydrogen cyanide, we'll know. Nimbus is the only meta we know of who can transform himself into a cloud of poison gas—and his victims look just like Dr. Larson does."

Joe's face remained grave. "That's two possible metas today. Weather Wizard and the Mist. Is it a coincidence?" He jabbed his pen at Barry with a warning look. "If they're working together, they'll be out to get the Flash."

"And you," Barry reminded him. Both Mark Mardon and Kyle Nimbus held a grudge against Joe, and both had tried to kill him in the past. Joe had shot and killed Mardon's brother, a murderer himself, and he had been the arresting officer who put Nimbus in the death house. Both Mardon and Nimbus had transformed into terrifying metahumans, but that hadn't kept them from retaining all their very human hatreds, and deep-seated desires for revenge.

"I'll finish up here," he added. "Hopefully I can find

enough evidence to make some sense of all this."

Joe patted him on the shoulder and gave a forced smile, his thoughts already miles away. Barry watched him exit the house. Even with all the burdens the man carried on his shoulders every day, he never once slouched. He always stood tall. The thought of adding to that burden, telling him about the glitches and hallucinations, well, now just wasn't the time. It would have to wait, and in the meantime, he'd focus on trying to get ahead of the game.

He'd turn in his report, then send a copy to S.T.A.R. Labs. Maybe if all of them put their heads together, they'd find a way to keep Joe safe—and the rest of the city, too.

6

Shawna Baez stared over the water at the colorful sunset sky. She stood at a long wall of glass, her favorite spot in this massive home that sat on a bluff high above the huge lake north of Central City. How wonderful it would be to own this house, and live here in its space and comfort, she thought.

Rustling sounds interrupted the calm sunset. Men muttered and argued behind Shawna. She groaned quietly. She recognized again the telltale noises of precious gemstones scraping across an expensive marble tabletop

"Wait a minute, Mardon," a voice snarled. "That diamond is worth three of the lousy emeralds in this mirror. You think you can cheat me?"

Shawna tried to ignore yet another growling complaint from Kyle Nimbus. And she didn't want to hear the angry retort from Mark Mardon.

"You idiot! That mirror is Babylonian. It's worth twice this diamond."

Unfortunately Shawna could see the reflection of the two men in the glass. Kyle Nimbus, the Mist, held a jewel-encrusted mirror in his hand. He was a grim, dark-featured scar of a man who made her nervous. His bald head gave him the look of a hardened prisoner—which he was. Or had been, before the particle accelerator explosion ripped through him at the very moment he had been receiving the state-mandated lethal injection.

Now he was a metahuman, and a vile one.

The other man was more presentable. In fact, quite handsome. Mark Mardon, the Weather Wizard. He spoke well and came across as a man of some accomplishment. He didn't *look* like an obvious criminal. His metahuman powers allowed him to control the weather. He could wield lightning and raise rain and control the winds.

He was a man of limited intelligence, however, which meant that Mardon wielded those nearly godlike powers like a bully. It was a shame, really, because Mardon didn't seem like a complete failure as a human.

Which brought her back to Nimbus.

Shawna looked at herself in the reflection, her face deeply shadowed in the fading sunlight. Dark skin and dark hair. Smart. Street smart, anyway, yet she was stuck with men like Nimbus and Mardon. How had it become her lot in life?

She became a metahuman that same night, given the power to teleport herself instantaneously anywhere she could see. Still, she couldn't blink herself out of her own life. Even with the particle accelerator explosion, she was trapped in a life with hustlers. She could have done so much more, and should have been living in a house like this.

Instead she was broke and desperate.

Kyle Nimbus jarred her out of her reverie by tossing the jewel-encrusted mirror on the table like so much junk. It landed with an alarming *thunk*.

"I don't want it," he said. "Where do I find a Babylonian pawnshop? What the hell's a Babylonian? I don't want a mirror."

"I can see why *you* wouldn't want one," Shawna muttered.

Mardon snickered, but Nimbus flew to his feet.

"Don't cross me, girl," he bellowed. "You know what I can do."

Shawna did know, and it was unpleasant—even horrifying. Her skin crawled at the very thought of Nimbus shifting from a normal man to a disgusting cloud of toxic mist. Even in a world of metahumans, that was unnatural.

She gave Nimbus a slow, calm stare before turning back to the sliver of orange over the water. The calm was gone, but she continued to stare at the fading sunset anyway.

Mardon laughed. "She doesn't seem scared."

"Well she should be." Nimbus lunged across the room toward her.

Instantly she was standing outside on the terrace. The chilly air slapped her. She turned to see Nimbus with his hands against the glass, glaring at her through the reflection of the now-purple sky. He pounded on the thick pane, shouting angrily at her, the sound mercifully muffled.

Shawna looked at a spot inside the room near the sofa…

…and then she was standing there. The air snapped around her as she rematerialized next to a table with an ornate chess set. Mardon twitched and looked up at her, grinning again, amused by the way she punked Nimbus. The dark-eyed murderer whirled around, glaring. His features began to waver.

His face clouded and turned gray.

"Stop it!" a voice said from the door. Two men entered, one of them pointing angrily at the quarrel across the room.

Nimbus halted his transformation. Mardon stood, electricity flaring from his fingers, pretending he had been ready to leap to Shawna's defense. She just rolled her eyes. She didn't need his help—not even against a thug like Nimbus.

One of the new arrivals glared in annoyance.

Young and refined, a born Ivy League genius, Hartley Rathaway had an intensity that made him seem as if he was always struggling to keep anger in check. His pale features came off as bookish—the dictionary picture of a scientist. There was a reservoir of resentment in him, and of entitlement.

His extraordinary relationship with sound waves made him a metahuman. He wore strange high-tech gauntlets, and carried an irregularly shaped rock about the size of a softball. It was another piece of the loot from the museum, and the only thing Rathaway seemed to care about. It glittered with crystals protruding from its surface.

"And try not to wreck this house," he said. "It belongs to an old colleague who is in Europe for an extended stay, and he doesn't know we're here."

Alongside Rathaway walked a forgettable man named Roy Bivolo, a hatchet-faced weasel with greasy hair and dark sunglasses. His metahuman power imposed uncontrollable rage—and perhaps other emotions—on his unwitting victims. He was the type of self-absorbed loser Shawna passed on the street countless times every day.

Rathaway looked at Shawna. "Don't touch that chessboard, please."

She felt a ripple of irritation. Again, however, she stayed quiet, shot him a dirty look, and merely clasped her hands behind her back.

"Thank you," he said succinctly. He kept watching her, though, as if he didn't trust her to keep her fingers to herself. "We're ready to make our next move."

"Good." Mardon returned to his seat and stretched out his long legs. "When do we stomp the Flash?"

"I'm for that," Nimbus chimed in.

"All in time." Rathaway strolled over to the chessboard. He wore a cheap gray hoodie, a peculiar affectation, perhaps meant to make him seem more *street* and less millennial. Positioning himself between Shawna and the board, he removed his glasses and studied the game pieces. "We're playing a more complicated game than just, er, 'stomping the Flash.' Never fear. We will put an end to his speedster days, but we want more, don't we?"

"Yeah," Mardon said. "There's a cop I want dead, too."

"Yeah," Nimbus echoed enthusiastically. "Joe West needs to die."

Rathaway exhaled impatiently. "Gentlemen, by the time we're done, we'll have all of our collective grievances sorted out. The Flash will fall. Your police detective will die, and Central City will be split wide open like an overripe fruit."

"That's nice and all, but I want money." Bivolo stood impassively, with his black sunglasses hiding any emotion. "I don't care about revenge or cops or rotten fruit. I want cash. Lots of it."

"Money isn't a problem, Bivolo," Rathaway replied. "I've already made all of you rich with the museum job—and there will be more."

"Me and Nimbus pulled the museum job." Bivolo snorted. "You weren't there."

"Yes." Rathaway put a finger lightly on the top of a white pawn. "And you didn't need to kill Dr. Larson, either. Perhaps you won't get so… overenthusiastic in the future." He looked up at Bivolo. "If you want money, Roy, you'll have more than you can spend in a lifetime." He started to lift the pawn.

"I wouldn't." Shawna eyed the board over Rathaway's shoulder. He was making a stupid move.

Rathaway bristled at her, showing a rare flash of rage before suppressing it and trying to paste a look of curiosity on his reddening face.

"Excuse me?"

Shawna pointed at the board. "If you take the pawn," she said, "it's the wrong move. Look at their knight. Your bishop. And… mate."

"I sincerely doubt that you…" Rathaway trailed off and narrowed his eyes as he looked again at the board. Slowly he replaced the pawn in its original spot. "Oh. I see." He glanced back at her with a mixture of surprise and admiration. "I didn't know you played."

"I used to watch my grandfather. In the park when I was a little girl." Shawna turned away and cranked up her accent, "You know, in between collectin' welfare and cleanin' the houses in your neighborhood." With that she crouched in front of the fireplace, hands stretched out to the flames.

"Hey!" Mardon called. "Can we forget about play time here? What's our next move?"

"What? Oh, yes." Rathaway pulled his attention from the board. "We will continue to hammer the city's infrastructure, robbing its citizens of their sense of safety. We're going to create a new normal in Central City, making it a place where no one believes in the security of authority. Everyone will feel as if the rug has been pulled out from under their world.

"Then they will pay," he added. "Mardon, you and Bivolo will wreak some special havoc, as is your wont."

Mardon grinned savagely. "And when the Flash shows—"

"You do *nothing*," Rathaway cut him off. He tried hard to look firm and authoritative, but there was still something too prep school about him, and he didn't quite pull it off. "You will withdraw. That's where Ms. Baez enters the picture."

Mardon squinted. "But I'm gonna—"

"No! Ms. Baez can teleport you faster than even the Flash can move," he continued. "We will strike and move, over and over, until the city is weary and near a standstill. Then we will enter the endgame." His eyes flicked toward the chessboard, and Shawna, causing her a slight smile.

"Whatever." Kyle Nimbus shrugged. "That's all well and good, but I want the Flash and Joe West dead. And soon."

Rathaway took off his glasses and rubbed his eyes in frustration.

"I warn you, don't endanger my carefully laid plans by engaging the Flash." He put the glasses back on. "I don't need you mucking up the works with some moronic misstep."

Nimbus tilted his head, looking like a dog preparing to strike.

"You calling me stupid?" he growled. "I'm pretty sick of your Little Lord Fauntleroy bullcrap. I'm the most powerful one here. You *need* me... but I don't need you." Nimbus stepped toward Rathaway, who didn't flinch. "And I don't like you."

Shawna gave Rathaway credit for standing his ground; Nimbus was a monster, and an easy killer.

Rathaway's voice stayed calm. He studied the chessboard as he spoke.

"You have your uses," he said, "but don't oversell yourself. We could lose you more easily than anyone else here." He glanced up with a new sense of casual menace that gave Shawna a little jolt. "Very easily."

Nimbus clenched his fists. "I could kill everyone in this room without breaking a sweat. One thought from me and you'd be dead!"

Rathaway purposefully lifted a different white pawn and moved it.

"If it requires a thought from you, then we're all safe."

Emitting an animalistic growl, Nimbus started to lose his shape. Limbs twisted. Fingers elongated and curled. He grew green, then bubbled and boiled like smoke. The man was gone, replaced by a writhing cloud of rancid mist. Tendrils snaked across the room toward Rathaway.

Mardon yelped and dove out of the way.

Shawna vanished from her spot at the fireplace and reappeared at the window, next to Bivolo. She noticed that Mardon didn't pretend to come to her defense now that Nimbus was in full mist form. It was every man for himself. That concept had been hammered into her when her lousy boyfriend had left her to be captured by the Flash, even after she had risked her life breaking him out of prison.

Every man for *herself*.

She was fine with that rule.

Rathaway held out his gloved hands, one of them still holding the crystalline rock. His face tightened with concentration—or maybe it was fear—as the mist swirled toward him.

"Oh, well." Bivolo grunted with mild disappointment. "There goes the gig. Back to stick-ups." He and Mardon stood their ground—neither was going to intervene. They both watched to see what would happen.

She had never seen Nimbus work, but she knew what he could do. She expected the cloud to sweep over Rathaway, causing him to grasp his throat and choke and crumple to the floor.

Then the mist *stopped*.

Slight vibrations began coming from the floor.

Rathaway smiled. "It's no good, Nimbus," he said. "You'd better pull yourself together while you still can."

The mist quivered like the switching of a mad cat's tail. The shape slowly coalesced into a recognizable human form. Body. Arms. Legs. Head… and finally the face. Fury and confusion etched across his features, Nimbus staggered against Rathaway, and nearly fell.

"What did you do?" he croaked.

Rathaway gave a smug purse of his lips and held out his hands, still clad in the science-fiction gloves.

"With my sonic gauntlets, I can agitate your molecules when you're in a vapor state. If I were to keep doing it, you would boil away to nothing." He scanned each of the other three metahumans in the room, wordless, but clearly implying that he could do similar destruction to them all, should it become necessary.

Shawna laughed. The look on Nimbus's face was hilarious. From murderous villain to frustrated little boy. Mardon and Bivolo were on their heels, too, unsure what Rathaway was capable of accomplishing. None of *them* could've stood up to Nimbus—their only choice would have been to run. Yet Rathaway had stood and defeated the poisonous monster, without even breaking a sweat.

"Okay, okay." Mardon gave a nervous chuckle. "We're good. We're friends again. We're all after the same thing—enough money to enjoy our golden years, and no Flash to wreck them."

"Exactly." Rathaway removed his glasses again and wiped the lenses with the hem of his hoodie. He peered through them before slipping them carefully onto his face. He aimed a conciliatory nod toward the sulking Nimbus.

"Friends."

Outside, only a faint tinge of purple hugged the bottom rim of the clouds. Shawna could put up with these idiots long enough to get rich and buy a house like this one. She had no love for this town. It had beaten her down over the years. So what if she took some of their money? She deserved it, and the powers that be would just print more. Soon she'd be able to go anywhere in the world.

Anywhere but Central City.

7

Barry pressed his eye to the microscope. He hunched over the table, and the pressure of the metal against his eyebrow and cheek comforted him.

He'd spent many happy hours as a boy, staring through the lens of a microscope at slides with hair or compound eyes or skin cells. This feeling took him back to the safety of his bedroom with his posters and books, so he always felt relaxed in his workspace at the Central City Police Department. It also gave him a purpose, and a sense of accomplishment. Even when Captain Singh would barge in demanding some report that was overdue, Barry stayed calm because this was a place of science. He understood how it worked.

Barry had always dreamed of being a scientist. He had gone into criminal science purposefully, because he had made a childhood promise that he would solve his mother's murder and free his father from prison. He would never forget that terrible night as an eleven-year-old, watching strange red and yellow streaks flying around his living room. The uncanny blurs circled his mother, who signaled desperately to young Barry to keep back and stay out of danger, even as she was being murdered by something he couldn't understand.

There had been a human face in the midst of the lightning. He had seen the impossible, and from that day forward he had been driven to unravel what was considered unknowable. In fact, Barry eventually solved the murder, but not with his science. It wasn't until the Flash was created that the truth became known, and the killer had paid for his cowardly act.

Barry shook his mind off those terrible memories and returned gratefully to the microscope. The predictability of scientific research comforted him, and always had. While other kids fantasized about scoring the winning touchdown in the Super Bowl, or nailing the last-second basket to clinch a championship, Barry wanted to unlock the secrets of the universe.

"What are you smiling about?"

Joe West stood in the doorway.

"Oh, nothing. Just science stuff. You know me."

"I do know you." Joe tapped his wristwatch. "You're working pretty late. Hugo Larson?"

"Yeah." The smile abruptly faded. There was nothing pleasant about this case. "Our suspicions were correct. I found traces of hydrogen cyanide— something that couldn't have occurred naturally. It must've been the Mist who killed him."

"I've been interviewing Larson's family and colleagues. The guy was a model citizen. There's no connection between Larson and Nimbus. Anything weird from the museum scene?"

"Well, *weird* is relative, but I turned up a lot of fingerprints, as you'd expect from a public museum. However, most of the broken artifacts only had Dr. Larson's prints on them. I also identified his prints all over the smashed displays, and all the blood spots we found were his. With those cuts on his hands, and the evidence we found on his body and clothes, it's hard not to assume that it was Dr. Larson who was the vandal."

"Any good ideas why?"

"No traces of narcotics, or intoxicants of any kind in his body," Barry replied. "No evidence he was under the influence of any foreign substances, and there was nothing in his home to suggest extortion—or any connection with metahumans."

Joe took a deep breath. "Barry, you saw that museum. We're not talking about a broken coffee mug. That place was torn up, exhibits smashed, artifacts broken. It took time and effort. That was an act of rage, but nobody I talked to today said Larson was anything other than a genuinely nice man who never even raised his voice. So you know what that means."

"Unfortunately, yes," Barry replied soberly. "Roy Bivolo, otherwise known as Prism." He felt as if he'd just bitten into something bitter.

"Believe me, I don't want to go there either," Joe

said. "That would explain the rage, and it's the third metahuman we've got in the mix. As if we don't have enough trouble already."

"But why?" Barry looked back into the microscope, because it was clear and understandable. It never irritated or confounded him. "What's Bivolo's angle in forcing poor Dr. Larson to wreck his own museum? And why would Bivolo be working with Nimbus?" He looked up again, unable to escape reality.

"Money," Joe replied. "The place wasn't just trashed—things were missing. We don't have a complete inventory yet, but there's valuable stuff they can't locate. First and foremost, Bivolo is a thief."

"Yet he's always stolen cash," Barry countered. "Museum goods seem like a lot of trouble for a guy like that. It doesn't add up."

"I have to agree with you, but we've got to go with what we've got. We've rousted some of the most active fences in the city, and let them know what we're looking for. We've sent alerts across the country, asking various agencies to keep an eye out for unusual objects coming onto the black market. Once we get a list of what's actually missing from the museum, we'll know better what to look for." He nodded toward the microscope. "Did you get any leads on that stuff on Larson's hands?"

"It looked like iron oxide, but it wasn't quite right. I sent a sample over to S.T.A.R. Labs for Caitlin to check. I'll let you know when I get something." Footsteps at the door heralded the arrival of the solid, dark-haired Captain Singh, wearing his usual harried expression. He carried a file in his hand.

"I'm not the only one working late, I see."

Barry stood up. "Just trying to process the material from the Hugo Larson murder. I should have a report to you tomorrow morning. We think our prime suspects are Kyle Nimbus and Roy Bivolo. It's the motive we're not too clear on."

"You just supply the facts, Allen. We pay other guys to come up with motives." Singh offered Joe a surprisingly understanding look. "Hey, Joe, if Kyle Nimbus is around, maybe we should put a unit on your house?"

Joe laughed. "No, sir, that would just mean risking more lives. Don't worry, I can handle myself."

"I'm sure you can, Detective, but if you need anything, let me know." Singh waited, as if he wanted to say something else, but then just turned to leave the lab, shooting Barry a look over his shoulder. "First thing in the morning, Allen."

"Yes, sir." Barry watched the captain walk out.

Joe stared out the window, where the lights of Central City blazed.

"He's got a point, Joe," Barry said. "Both Mardon and Nimbus hate you. Maybe you should leave town for a while."

"Not gonna happen." Joe gave a stern, disapproving look, as welcoming eyes turned hard and challenging.

"Who do you think you're talking to?"

"Okay, okay. I'm sorry." Barry held his hands up in surrender.

Joe's expression softened. "It's not me I'm worried about," he said. "I just don't want those thugs hurting anyone else. Including you."

Barry nodded, and leaned back. "Hey, you know what this means?" he said brightly. "We've both got arch-enemies! How many other fathers and sons can share something like that?"

"I think I'd rather just go to a ball game."

A phone chirped and both Barry and Joe reacted.

"Mine," Barry said. "Yo, what's up, Cisco?"

"Barry, there's a fire at the riverfront."

"Location?"

"Warehouse near the main depot. They're requesting hazmat units. There's chemical storage in danger."

"I'm on my way." Barry looked at Joe, who signaled for him to go.

The industrial riverfront was thick with gas and oil depots, and a small city's worth of warehouses. The bright lights of storage facilities lit the night, but there was a different glow too. As the Flash came closer he saw the fire, orange and licking the sky. On the other side of a heavy chain-link fence, flames were consuming a large warehouse.

Several men dressed in coveralls stood at the open

gate. They watched the fire, each of them with a phone in his hand. Distant sirens blared from various directions, signaling numerous fire engines en route.

The Flash streaked through the gate past the workmen. He raced into the burning warehouse. The huge building took up half a normal city block and one end of it was entirely consumed in flames. He roared through the dark space searching for anyone who may have been injured by the fire or succumbed to the smoke. Spotting no one, he went back outside and zipped around the shipping yard, moving between warehouses and equipment shacks, looking for people to move out of harm's way.

As he raced back between the burning warehouse and the quay on the river, there was a loud *crack*. The Flash lost control and slammed into a forklift, careening onto the asphalt. Steam drifted off his chest. He felt numb.

This wasn't a glitch.

He'd been hit by lightning.

A faint tingle rippled through him, so he quickly rolled to the side just as another bolt of lightning snapped the ground where he'd been lying. He came to his feet and raced away, narrowly avoiding another strike.

"Come on, Flash," a familiar voice shouted, "you're not a fireman. You should stop sticking your nose in. In fact—" Mark Mardon stood high on the prow of a small freighter tied up at the quay. He raised his hands, and bolts of lightning seared through the air and crashed against two smaller warehouses on the far side of the yard. The roofs exploded and instantly flames shot upward. "—let's give them *more* to do."

"Barry," Cisco reported in his ear. "We're reading micro-bursts of low pressure near your location. It's got to be Weather Wizard."

"I can confirm that," the Flash moaned. He steadied himself on rubbery legs and pulled the weather wand from his belt. He had to get close to use it. He took off for the freighter, up the gangplank, and climbed the steps to the forecastle, reaching the spot where Mardon stood.

Or *had* stood. Weather Wizard was gone.

The Flash looked around frantically, expecting an attack. He quickly searched overhead, recalling that Mardon could alter air pressure and lift himself off the ground. But the Flash stood alone on the deck of the ship. Mardon had impressive powers, but he couldn't move that fast.

Could he?

8

Fire trucks arrived on the scene, and emergency personnel began setting up inside the fenced-in yard. Heavy sprays of water arced toward the fire. Three men in bulky protective suits, silhouetted in spotlights, manhandled hoses off a yellow hazmat tanker stationed close to the burning warehouse.

The Flash streaked off the ship through the artificial downpour, heading toward the fire captain. Captain Sandoval perched on the running board of his fire engine, holding the radio transceiver in one hand and a clipboard in the other. A gas mask hung from his neck, and he shouted directions to his men. Brutal heat washed over them all, but no one hesitated to move toward the flames.

None of them had metahuman abilities.

"Captain Sandoval," the Flash shouted over the roar of the trucks' geysers, "I'm going to create a vortex, and snuff the flames out."

"No. I've got a hazmat team in the warehouse now foaming it down." Sandoval grimaced and held up a clipboard with its soaked pages. "This one is bad. We don't know half of the chemicals in there yet. So don't run around the fire—we can't afford any updrafts spreading potential hazardous waste." He stared hard toward the fiery warehouse. "Who the heck are those guys?"

Two unidentified figures appeared from around the corner of the warehouse. It was hard to make them out in the glaring mix of night, spotlights, and the haze of water in the air. They appeared to wear no protective clothing, and entered the warehouse where the yellow-suited hazmat crew had gone with the foam hoses. As quickly as they had appeared, they were gone.

"I'll get them." The Flash made sure the weather wand was secured, and took off through the drenching spray. He entered the warehouse and stopped next to the three-man hazmat team, skidding slightly in the mixture of water and foam that spread across the ground.

Unbearable heat washed over him. To his left, on the distant side of the vast building, sheets of fire undulated along the wall up to the ceiling. Black smoke boiled through the space, but the Flash could see to the far right what appeared to be a huge mound of foam. Fire retardant covered a large stack of chemical containers.

There was no sign of the two civilians. He started to question one of the hazmat crew when the fireman swung a thick-gloved fist at his chin. Instinctively the Flash dodged, catching a glimpse of sheer anger through the plastic face shield.

What the hell?

"Hey, wait a minute!" he said aloud. "I'm here to help."

A second yellow-suited man leapt for him, but he just sidestepped, sending the fellow into his partner. The two firemen fell to the ground, and began pounding awkwardly on each other. Protective cowls muffled their angry shouts.

Prism.

Something hit the Flash from behind, and slammed him off his feet. A billowing stream enveloped him, and he saw the third hazmat crewman shooting foam in his direction. The powerful jet sent his prone body tumbling across the floor.

The Flash struggled to his feet in the sludge, slipping and sliding, fighting for traction. He ducked and the stream of froth flew over his back. He raced forward, seizing the nozzle and pulling it out of the fireman's hands. He quickly looped it around the struggling figure and used it to drag the man out of the choking warehouse. Then he returned to the smoky interior, where he found the other two hazmat crewmen still wrestling.

Grabbing handfuls of yellow suit, he hauled them all the way to the main fire engine. There he searched for Captain Sandoval. But the firemen around the trucks, with their black slickers and yellow fluorescent stripes, were moving in odd jerky motions, made stranger by the flickering light of the inferno. They were flailing wildly, and crashing into one another.

They were fighting.

That confirmed it. One of the people the Flash had seen walking into the warehouse must've been Roy Bivolo. Yet as quickly as he had appeared, he was nowhere to be found.

"Flash!" Cisco again. "Status!"

"I'm good," Barry reported. "Nothing my rapid healing can't handle. But Prism is here."

Caitlin said, "You mean Rainbow Raider?"

Cisco snorted into his mic.

"Listen," Barry interrupted, "Bivolo's affected a lot of the firemen down here. Somehow he got to them all without me running into him, but I've got to separate them, and quickly. Call the CCFD and get new units down here."

"I'm on it," Cisco said.

At that moment the north end of the burning warehouse collapsed in a spray of flaming debris. The fire rippled along the structure toward the south end where the chemicals were stored.

"Flash!"

Barry whirled around to see Iris running toward him, dashing between fire trucks. She sidestepped two angry men who were choking each other, staring at them in amazement. He ran to her and leaned close.

"Iris. What are you doing here?" he said. "And why are you wearing pajama bottoms and *slippers*?"

"I'm a reporter, and it's the middle of the night."

Defiant, as usual, but then her eyes widened in horror. "What happened to you?"

The Flash looked down. He was partially covered in foam, browned like meringue, and his costume was scorched and torn.

"It's been a really long night," he admitted.

"Right. There are police and new CCFD units on the way."

"Good, but they won't get here in time. Warn them to watch out for Bivolo." The Flash flexed his hands.

"What are you going to do?" Iris took pictures while she talked.

"That warehouse is full of toxic and explosive chemicals. I'm going to move them all out of the way."

Then he was gone.

Black smoke filled the interior of the warehouse. Floor to ceiling. The Flash maneuvered by memory, and found the towering pile of foamed containers. An aluminum rack fifteen feet high and twenty feet deep dominated the wall. The shelves held countless blue barrels, each about four feet high and a foot in diameter. Four barrels were shrink-wrapped together in thick plastic, stacked on wooden pallets.

The Flash tested one of the pallets, but it was too heavy. He vibrated his hand and cut through the wrap. A single barrel weighed about fifty pounds. He lifted one and carried it out, then returned for another. And another. And another.

A red streak stretched continuously between the warehouse and a spot in the yard as far as possible from any of the flames. As the foam-covered rack inside emptied, a pile of blue barrels outside rose as if by magic.

Police officers came rushing through the gate, moving to restrain the rage-filled firefighters. Joe took command, directing them where they were needed, while Iris stood fearlessly next to a fire engine, camera in hand, drenched in water. Pajama bottoms were visible below the hem of her overcoat, fur-topped slippers on her sodden feet.

Each time he returned for another blue barrel, the fire had moved closer. Since he could see its progress, the Flash knew he had to be slowing down as fatigue dragged his steps. But he couldn't stop. Too many people expected to go home to families after their shifts. None of them deserved to get hurt.

To say nothing of the many people around them in the city who could be injured by an explosion, or harmed by toxic fumes drifting in the smoky air. Even Joe and Iris were out there, putting themselves in harm's way. Barry was the only one who could prevent that harm. He was the only one who could save them.

But he had to run faster.

As he hefted another barrel, his vision blurred briefly. He staggered and caught himself against the metal rack. The barrel crashed to the floor and he froze, terrified that it might rupture. Nothing seemed to leak, though.

There was a strange noise, and he looked over his shoulder. A red form appeared through the smoke. It was *him* again. The same Flash he had seen while running at S.T.A.R. Labs. His older self stopped a few feet away and paused, hands on hips, gasping for breath as if he was unused to running. A thin trickle of blood dribbled from his nose.

This time he spoke.

"Barry, they're all depending on you. They're going to die if you don't save them. You're the Flash. You *chose* this job."

He wanted to race over, to help his doppelganger—the one who looked *so* much like his father—but he had to get those last few barrels out of the burning warehouse. In the end, there really wasn't a choice. He tore his eyes off the image of his older self, standing there bleeding, and turned to the rack.

Then he froze.

A man sat on the barrel Barry had dropped. The figure leaned forward, relaxed, forearms on knees. Unaffected by the heat of the approaching inferno. Sharp features and dark hair. He smiled.

"Hi, Flash. How's it going?" The man looked around. "Not too well, huh?"

"Danton Black?" Barry said. "Multiplex? You're *dead*. Aren't you?"

"You should know," the man replied. "After all, you were there when I plunged to my death. You were there watching me fall."

The memory flared.

"I tried to save you."

Black shook his head and vibrated…

…and there were two of him. He quivered again, and three more copies appeared. They all stared with an accusing smile.

"You can't win them all, Flash," Black said. "I was one of the first metahumans you ever faced, and you beat me. My compliments."

"I didn't want you to die."

Black continued to throw off replicas of himself, one after another. Motionless men in featureless black.

"Have you gotten any better, Flash?" Black said from the middle of the growing mob. "How many people will you have to look at and say, 'I didn't want you to die.' Have you learned anything?"

The army of stiff cold bodies pressed against the Flash. The countless empty men stretched back into the darkness, filling the warehouse. Barry tried to shift, but he was trapped by the press. He pushed back, straining to shove them away. The bodies imprisoned him, unyielding, a sea of figures crushing him with their very existence.

He couldn't breathe.

"Barry!"

His throat tightened in the acrid air. He was suffocating.

"Barry!"

Hands pressed against the sides of his face and he saw

a terrified Iris. His lungs opened and he drew in a deep breath, then coughed it out violently, doubling over.

He looked toward the barrel where Black had been sitting, but there was no sign of him. The older Flash was gone, as well.

Iris coughed, fighting to breathe.

"You were just standing there, like you were frozen. I had to—" She coughed and winced from the heat that Barry suddenly felt.

He heard the crunching sound of the blaze. Sheets of flames swelled overhead and long streams of fire dripped down around them. Blue barrels still rested on the metal rack surrounded by fiery debris.

Iris's knees gave out. He grabbed her, raced outside, and deposited her near the main engine. Then he returned to the warehouse and began to ferry the last barrels out. He felt as if he was barely moving, limbs stiff. He could hardly draw breath. Still, he didn't think of anything but running.

No Black. No Mardon or Bivolo.

Just moving objects from one place to another. Barrel after barrel until finally he was down to two.

The Flash lifted them both with great effort and lumbered toward the entry. A loud crack ripped the air above him. A large metal beam fell, trailing flames and wreckage. Exhausted as he was, he could only watch as it dropped heavily in front of him. He gagged for air. Smoke and fire surrounded him. He coughed and couldn't think straight.

Something cold knocked him back. A geyser of foam settled over the flaming beam, pushing down the fire. Through the smoke, the Flash saw two figures at the warehouse entry. Joe West and Captain Sandoval. They manhandled the heavy hose, swinging it back and forth to create a frothy corridor.

"Run! This way!" Joe waved his arm.

The Flash hefted the two barrels and started forward. He slipped in the foam, but kept going. The white stream rained cold droplets around him. He climbed over the smoldering beam. When he reached the two men, they dropped the hose. Captain Sandoval and several others had to wrestle the barrels out of his stiff hands. Joe slid his shoulder under Barry's arm, and helped him away from the fire.

The Flash sat hard on the step of a fire truck. Firemen stood around in confusion. Some were in handcuffs, demanding to be released. Sirens wailed closer in the background.

Joe knelt in front of the Flash and stared into his eyes. Iris crowded close behind. He tried to smile.

"I'm fine, Detective," he said, his voice hoarse. "Or I will be. Hurray for accelerated healing."

Joe lowered his head in relief, and patted him on the knee.

"Yeah. Fast. You do everything fast," he murmured. "Like rushing me to an early grave, son, I swear." Abruptly Joe's phone rang, and he pulled it out. "Cisco? Yeah, he's right here." He looked at Barry.

"Your communications link must be down. Cisco and Caitlin are going nuts."

"I'm sure they are. Tell them I'm fine." Barry laughed, and caught Iris's stern glare. "Suits can be fixed."

Iris still didn't laugh. He reached to take her hand, and she squeezed his back.

9

Shawna Baez stared at the chessboard. Half the pieces were off the board, and the game was moving into the final phase.

She and Rathaway had played two games already. In the beginning he was glib. When she won the first game, he turned serious and didn't speak a word during the second one, which he won. Despite the close contest, her mind wandered with growing disinterest, and she knew that unless he made a stupid mistake, he would win this one, as well.

He knew it too, and he began to relax.

Rathaway's glass of wine sat untouched, as it had for all three games, while Shawna had nearly finished the rest of the bottle. No matter how much she tried to study the board, or lubricate herself with wine, she couldn't stop envisioning the Flash at the fire. She had teleported in, then taken Mardon and Roy Bivolo up to an apartment balcony high above the mayhem.

Mardon and Bivolo chuckled and gave play-by-play commentary as if they were watching a football game. But Shawna just saw the Flash working his tail off to help people, putting himself on the line to save others. She'd finally tired of it and teleported them out.

When they made it back to the house, she went to collapse from exhaustion, leaving them to gripe about missing the big finish.

But there had been no big finish. When she woke, she learned that Flash had prevented the chemical explosion. She was quietly smug about it as both Mardon and Bivolo complained bitterly. Strangely enough, Rathaway didn't seem to care.

"What do you think, Shawna?" Rathaway didn't look up.

"About what?" she responded, picking up the wine.

"About the mission," he said without a hint of emotion in his voice. "How did it go last night? From your point of view."

She stiffened with the wine glass at her lips. Without knowing what he was looking for, she was hesitant to answer. Was he asking her to snitch? She wasn't comfortable with that—even with guys as creepy as Weather Wizard and Prism.

Rathaway must have sensed her hesitation. "From an operational standpoint," he said, and he smiled reassuringly. "Did everything go as planned?"

"Sure."

He sat back. "You don't trust me, do you?"

Shawna gulped wine. "Why should I?"

"We're a team. All of us."

"Do you trust any of those other guys?"

Rathaway laughed. "Oh God, no, but I understand them. Nimbus, for example, seems like a loner, but he's actually an eager teammate. He used to be an enforcer for the Darbinyan crime family, but they turned on him. *That's* why he killed them—because he felt excluded. He's liable to wander off, due to lack of concentration, but he badly wants to be part of the group.

"Now Mark Mardon, the Weather Wizard, wants to be in charge," he continued. "He spent years of his life looking out for his younger brother, Clyde. So he thinks of himself as a benevolent dictator. He wants to be the guy you would thank, for telling you what to do."

"So *is* he in charge?" Shawna shifted her bishop.

"No, but as long as he thinks he has the chance, he'll stay." Rathaway studied the board anew. "Now Bivolo I don't quite grasp. He may be as simple as wanting money. There doesn't seem to be much ambition behind those sunglasses. I don't spare him much attention."

"And me?"

Rathaway paused thoughtfully. "You want money, too, but you want it so you can live better. You want a degree of comfort and elegance in your life. Perhaps you've never experienced it before, I don't know. You also want to believe in people. You *want* to trust me, and I hope you will—because I trust you."

Her eyes flicked up to him. She had visions of her old boyfriend, street thief Clay Parker, with his promises that they'd go off and spend the rest of their lives together. *"Just trust me, baby,"* he would say, and she had.

That she was free now had nothing to do with him. When the metahumans broke out of S.T.A.R. Labs, Shawna had looked for Clay, but he had left town. Left her behind again. Now Rathaway was trying to convince her that she could trust him to watch her back.

She'd heard it before.

"Why should I believe you?" Shawna set her glass noisily on the table.

"Because I have no advantage in lying to you," he replied. "You're the key to our success. I can admit that without reservation. Without your power, Flash would pick off all of them, one by one." Rathaway leaned forward. "Besides, you're the only one here who's a decent person. Mardon and Bivolo and Nimbus are animals. If I don't keep them in check, they'll run wild."

"Then why are you working with them?" she pressed. "They don't seem like your types."

"No, they're not." He smiled again. "Although Mardon has a savage pretty-boy thing going on."

Shawna paused in confusion before laughing with a wicked conspiratorial glee. "That's not what I meant, but you're right."

Rathaway gave her a sly glance and whispered, "Frankly, they make my skin crawl, but I need them.

And if you think about it, in a sad way, they *are* my type. That's yet another reason to hate Harrison Wells."

"Harrison Wells? Isn't that guy dead? What's he got to do with it?"

"Everything. We are all metahumans. That's what they call us. *Meta*human. You. Me. Those three brutes with whom we work. All of us are tied together by a bond created by Dr. Harrison Wells on the night the particle accelerator exploded. Now I'm forced to live with people I once would've crossed the street to avoid."

Shawna's face flushed with anger.

"Like me, you mean?" she hissed. "People who didn't have a trust fund so they could go to a good school."

Rathaway sat back in his chair and stared at the window across the room. White seagulls rose and fell in the late afternoon sun. Either he hadn't heard her comment, or didn't care. He shook his head slowly.

"Every day I wear special earplugs, because without them, my senses would be bombarded by every vibration in the world. I would be lying on the floor screaming in agony. Even with them, I am in constant pain. All thanks to Dr. Harrison Wells and his toadies like Cisco Ramon and Caitlin Snow, both of whom are still living off the corpse of S.T.A.R. Labs." His voice rising, he tapped the arms of his chair. "I warned him. I told Wells that the particle accelerator would fail. He didn't listen. In fact, he fired me. He threatened to ruin me if I talked. I was right and he ruined me anyway," Rathaway shouted. "He ruined me anyway! He ruined *everything*!"

Shawna pushed back in alarm. Rathaway was always distant, and mildly disengaged. Never like this. But if he was telling the truth, was truly in constant pain, she could understand his rage.

"I'm sorry. I didn't know."

"None of that matters any longer. The past is the past." Rathaway drew in a calming breath. "We're all connected, Shawna. We are all outcasts. You've been tossed into that miserable dungeon under S.T.A.R. Labs, just like I have. They can't handle us in the real world, so they treat us like mad dogs. They're afraid of us.

"But eventually they'll decide the only safe choice is to kill us." He gazed directly into her eyes with an exciting energy. "They can't get that chance, Shawna. *I won't let them.*"

"Are you going to kill the Flash?"

Rathaway twisted his head, surprised by her question. It pleased her to have unsettled him even just a little. When he replied, his voice cracked with emotion.

"Yes. Probably."

Shawna winced.

"I won't do it lightly." Rathaway took a drink of wine, as if to steel himself. "The Flash is just a tool of our persecution. He's the weapon Harrison Wells built to erase his mistakes—us. Although Dr. Wells is gone now, his Flash will never stop. He's like a horrible wind-up soldier." He leaned in again. "Don't you see? None of us is safe while he's around. I want you to be safe, Shawna. You deserve it."

Abruptly he returned his attention to the chessboard.

There was a pain in him that she recognized and understood. Her life had been crowded with phonies and operators and poseurs, but for all of his ego, Rathaway felt legit. His eyes shone with the assuredness of intellect. Shawna craved the feeling of someone having her back, someone capable and smart. She wanted to believe him, believe *in* him.

She had never thought about the metahumans as a group, even a family of sorts. The Flash had dumped them all in prison, like locking children in their rooms. Children who couldn't be trusted. On the other hand, Rathaway trusted her. He understood her. He valued her intelligence, playing chess and asking her opinions.

He moved his knight and Shawna took an involuntary breath. He made a mistake. A big one. He was distracted and vulnerable. She felt bad for him. Still, she instinctively reached for her bishop to drop the hammer. Then she stopped.

"Are you sure?" she asked.

"Always. Do your worst."

Shawna slid the bishop over and watched the realization dawn on him. She tried not to smile, but failed.

"I resign." He raised an eyebrow and reached out to flick over his king with a clatter. "Well done."

"I have a secret weapon," she said. "You still think of me as a girl you'd cross the street to avoid."

"You may be right." Rathaway stood. "But I believe I've finally estimated you accurately. Thank you for the games, Shawna, and the company. I hope we'll play again." He nodded to her, and left the room.

Rathaway was a different sort of man. He hadn't made any excuses about losing to her. He hadn't claimed she'd just gotten lucky. He hadn't leered or made crude remarks, as if she expected them because she was pretty. He hadn't bullied or belittled her.

Shawna sat back. The distant sound of gulls and the long autumn sunlight gave her the illusion that she was on vacation at the lake. A strange sense of comfort seeped into her, and she felt at home for the first time in a long time.

1 0

Barry flinched at Iris's stern gaze the moment he entered C.C. Jitters. He knew that look. The famous "Iris ire." She'd taken an isolated corner booth, the better to strike.

So much for a quiet coffee. He placed his order with the barista, whom he suddenly recognized.

"You're Lily, right?" He smiled at her. It warmed Barry to see her again. "The one I saw you on the news."

She nodded, working the espresso machine.

"I am," she admitted. "You're Barry. I've seen you with Iris." She waved at Iris whose frown broke a moment to lift a hand in greeting. Lily leaned in toward Barry. "She looks pissed," she murmured conspiratorially. "At you?"

"Yeah." Barry gave a small sigh. "Better make it a double espresso. I may need it."

Lily chuckled. "Absolutely."

"How are you doing, by the way?"

She looked up from her work. "We're fine. Thanks. I barely remember any of it actually. It seems like a dream. I got sick of seeing myself on the news, but thanks to the tornados and fires and all the flooding rain, my little wreck has gone off the news cycle. But I'm so grateful to the Flash. I know we wouldn't be here today without him."

Barry tried not to blush. "How's your son handling it all?"

She laughed. "Are you kidding? He's in seventh heaven. All he talks about is the Flash." She looked around the cafe. "He's around here somewhere. Teacher's workday today, so they let him hang out here with me. Be warned. He'll probably show you his autograph. He sleeps with it."

"I'll consider myself warned." Barry laughed, taking the hot cup she handed him. Then steeling himself, he went over to Iris. "Hey."

"Hey," she said quietly.

That was never a good sign.

"I'm not late, am I?" He looked at his wristwatch, the one that had belonged to Joe's father. He showed the watch face to Iris to prove he was pretty close to being on time. "I'm sorry," he said. "I know you're busy at the paper, with all the stuff going on in town." She gave him the distended jaw and narrowed eyes. "I'm in trouble, aren't I? You're in your *serious talk* booth, where people can't overhear us."

"If you're talking about last night, then yes, you

might be in trouble." Iris leaned forward so they could speak quietly together. "What happened to you at the fire? You were muttering about Multiplex. I asked Caitlin, and she said that he's still dead."

Barry offered a sheepish shrug. "Probably the smoke inhalation. I was just muddled by the fumes."

"Oh, don't give me that, Barry. I know you too well. Caitlin said you had an earlier… episode, she called it." She pinned him with her gaze. "What's going on? Why haven't you told us?"

"To be truthful, I'm not sure *what* it is," he admitted. "The first time we kind of dismissed it—well, I did. Now after the warehouse, it looks like it might be something more. I was going to tell you both. You and Joe. Honest. You just sort of beat me to it."

Her mouth remained a thin line. "We should have been the first ones you told."

"I know. You should have," he agreed, "but Joe's looked so worn out lately. I didn't want to add to it, you know? Especially without knowing what *it* was."

"He'd feel the same way regardless," she insisted, "and so do I. We're family. We're your first line of defense." She sat back. Her anger spent, it was replaced with worry. "So what is *it*? What's going on with you?"

Barry searched for an answer. "I'm not sure. A couple of times, I've seen things—people—when I run. I saw a version of myself. Older, like really old. And I don't age well, let me tell you." When she didn't laugh, he sighed and continued.

"In these episodes, I show up and warn myself. That is, the older version of me is warning me, telling me to run faster. Like Dr. Wells used to do. 'Run, Barry, run!'" He shrugged, knowing how crazy it sounded. "Then this last time, Multiplex showed up, reminding me how I let him die. Like I needed any help to feel bad about that."

"What else did he tell you?"

"That I can't save everyone, even with my speed. Then he tried to bury me under a wave of his duplicates."

"When I saw you in that warehouse, you were frozen in place. Just staring at nothing. And you were blurry, almost like I could see through you."

"How long did it last?"

"Just a few seconds. It was hard to tell."

Barry swirled his coffee. "It seemed a lot longer."

"Any idea what's causing it?"

"I wish I knew." Barry shrugged. "Caitlin's been running tests on me, and she can't detect anything. But she will."

Iris leaned forward. "What does it feel like when it happens?"

"Like a tug. Like something breaks, and lets go." He thought about it. "It's almost like I'm free falling for a split second." Barry rubbed his face in frustration. "Maybe it's just a side effect of being the Flash, coming up after all this time. Maybe I'm stressing out my metahuman healing factor. All this stuff I do has to put a huge strain on my body." He sipped coffee and thought about adding, *And my mind*.

The worried expression on Iris's face made him feel awful. This was why he didn't want to say anything, but it felt cleansing to put his scattered thoughts into words, to get it out just to see if it made sense.

"Barry, maybe you're pushing yourself too hard," she suggested. "Maybe you need to take a break."

Barry laughed. "Joe said he wanted us to take a vacation."

"Really? That's a wonderful idea. Although we should pick the place, otherwise he might take us fishing. He thinks you like it."

Barry rubbed his chin. "It's not my vacation of choice. How about skiing?"

Iris lit up. "Ooh. *Now* you're talking!"

A familiar high-pitched voice caught Barry's attention. A little boy appeared nearby. It was Dean, and he was showing his autographed wooden plaque to some strangers who gave him a smile. Barry stared as Dean acted out the animated story of his adventure with the Flash, much to the amusement of the young couple who hadn't known the boy existed just a few moments ago.

Next he raced over to the booth shared by Barry and Iris, his face lit up with an excited grin, shoving the tattered shard of plywood in Iris's hands.

"Look! It's from the Flash," Dean said a little bit too loudly. "He saved me! The Flash is the greatest. He saved me and my mom from a big car crash. He came running in and no one could even see him, but I could. I could see him. He smiled at me and pulled us out of our car that got all crunched up. *Wham!* It got smashed, but the Flash was like *zoom* and *whoosh* all around, and the cars were flying everywhere." The boy's words tumbled from his mouth.

"Wow." Iris bent toward the boy. "That sounds amazing."

"Dean." Lily came from behind the counter, weaving through tables. She took her son by the shoulder. "It's time for you to stop bothering people now. Why don't you go sit in the break room and color?"

"It's all right." Barry grinned. "He isn't bothering us."

Lily smiled gratefully. "He gets a little excited about the Flash."

"I love the Flash!" Dean said emphatically. "He's going to be my dad! The Flash will be the best dad ever, because he'll always be there when you need him."

Iris handed the plaque to Barry. He dutifully studied the rough etching and gave the autographed wood back to Dean, smiling gently at the boy.

"Pretty cool," he said. "You and the Flash are pals, huh?"

"Yes! He might come to our house for Christmas." Dean posed in a runner's stance for a second before racing off to show his plaque to another customer. "Whoosh!"

Lily rolled her eyes and returned to the counter.

Barry stared after the boy, a smile on his face. "And that's why vacations can't happen."

Iris rested her cheek on her palm. "I know."

"Plus now I have to eat two Christmas dinners."

"Like that's a problem for you."

"Hey, maybe I could do it." Barry looked at Iris with a bright glint in his eyes. "Maybe the Flash really could show up on Christmas for Dean."

"Why don't you pull your own sleigh while you're at it? Hand out presents to all the good little boys and girls?" She paused, then added, "Oh, wait. There's already a guy in a red suit, and that's his gig."

Barry grabbed a napkin and a pen. "I wonder how long it would take me to visit every home on Earth?"

"You're actually considering it, aren't you?"

"Not yet," he answered. "For the moment it's purely speculative."

Iris picked up her purse.

"Sure it is."

1 1

Barry stood with arms crossed, staring at his costume. It was on a mannequin in the Cortex, where it rested between missions. That Flash figure greeted him every time he entered the laboratory. It was like he was waiting for himself, quiet and immobile. It reminded him of the Future Flash he had been seeing.

Him, but not him.

He wondered if Oliver Queen ever had these dissociative moments. Oliver versus Green Arrow. Probably not. He seemed pretty well buttoned up, and he'd been at it longer.

Barry turned away from the dummy Flash to face his friends. Cisco and Caitlin sat in their usual spots behind the semicircular control board.

"Okay," he said, "so we've got Weather Wizard, Prism, and the Mist."

Caitlin kept typing. "I think it's a good bet that Shawna Baez is with them."

"Peekaboo!" Cisco exclaimed. "I was hoping she'd come back."

"Why?" Barry asked him with a wan smile.

"She's the type of villain who just needs the love of a good man to turn her from the dark side." His eyes took on a faraway look, and he rested his chin in his palms.

"Are you that good man?"

"Heck yeah!" Cisco smoothed his t-shirt, and the dancing chromosomes it sported. "I'm like a sexy Yoda. With me, there is no try, there is only do."

"Or do not," Caitlin muttered with the hint of a smile on her lips.

Cisco glowered at her. "Your lack of faith disturbs me."

"So, Caitlin…" Barry began to pace. "Why do you think Peekaboo is with them?"

She leaned on the control panel. "There's no way Mardon and Bivolo could've disappeared like they did without you finding a trace of them. You're fast, Barry, but they slipped away from you just like that." She snapped her fingers. "Like they—"

"Teleported," Barry finished the thought with an accepting nod. "That makes sense. So four metahumans working together… to do what? They pulled that museum caper and killed Dr. Larson. Mardon has created weather disasters all over town, plus the warehouse fire. But what's the point of it? Except for the museum, they haven't stolen anything. They haven't killed anyone else, luckily. But it's so frustrating. I'm just chasing from crime to crime. I can't get my hands on the bad guys. There's got to be a master plan to all this. Right?"

"Probably." Cisco stared at his monitor with agitation. "I've been running my tracking algorithms based on reported sightings of our villains, but it hasn't come up with anything significant—which is weird, because normally I'm really smart."

"Well, I'm sure Cisco will come up with something, like the super-genius he is." Caitlin smirked. "However, I'm actually more worried about the cause of your glitches, Barry."

He looked up at the immobile Flash mannequin again. "Maybe the glitches are caused by some sort of psychic attack from another metahuman we haven't seen yet."

"We can't be sure of anything until we eliminate it," she said, and she fell on her keyboard, typing with a vengeance. Then she studied the lines of data on her screen. "These are your bio-readings from the warehouse fire last night. There are no signs of the sort of brain activity that would show up if you were under psychic stress. Whatever is going on with you, it isn't a psychic attack."

"Good," Joe's voice echoed as he entered the Cortex with Iris at his side. "So at least we don't have to worry about Grodd."

Iris came over to Barry. "I filled Dad in. Hope you don't mind." Her expression told him it wouldn't matter if he did.

"No, of course not." Barry gave her arm a comforting squeeze. "I should have told him before. We don't have secrets."

"Damn straight," Joe agreed, eyebrow raised.

"Listen, I know it's easier to suspect a metahuman attack or invader from another dimension," Iris said, "but it still seems more likely that the root of your problem is good old-fashioned stress."

Cisco spread his hands dramatically. "You mean instead of a mind-controlling gorilla? Why, what's so strange about that?"

Barry laughed, then turned serious.

"Look, I appreciate the thought, Iris," he said, "but I'm just not that stressed. You know me. I'm cool. I'm *cooly* cool."

"Oh yeah, the king of chill." Iris eyed him evenly. "Says the guy who was seriously considering running to every house on Earth this Christmas. Does that strike you as normal?"

"Normal? No," Cisco said, then he gave Barry a thumbs up. "Awesome? Yes!"

Barry grinned. "I know, right?" He dug into his pockets and retrieved a wad of napkins. He handed them to Cisco, who unfolded the mess and began to study the complex formulae scribbled there. As he did, Barry turned back to Iris.

"And even if I wasn't relaxed, which I totally am, there are still four metahuman criminals running amok. They've got to be our top priority. Once we've tracked

them down, then we can talk about rest and relaxation."
He shot Joe a look. "Iris and I decided on skiing."

Joe gave back a disapproving frown. "Slick move
there, Bar—changing the subject, but we'll let it go.
This time." He pulled several folded sheets of paper
from his coat pocket. "I've got the inventory from the
museum, so we have a list of what was stolen, and
what was destroyed."

Barry zipped over and took the papers, leafing
through them at hyper-speed.

"Most of the museum's precious stones were
taken," he murmured as he scanned the pages. "A few
of the older artifacts. And—oh wow!" He held up a
page. "The Singing Meteorite."

"No way!" Cisco scrambled around the console and
snatched away the page. "I didn't know it was still in
Central City, much less at the museum."

"What the hell are you talking about now?" Joe
demanded.

A boyish grin appeared on Barry's face. "The
Singing Meteorite was discovered in Africa ten years
ago, by Dr. William Coolidge. It has a totally unique
crystalline structure."

"They said you could hear it," Cisco piped in.
"Coolidge said the meteorite led him to it, by singing."

"He sang to the meteor?" Joe said.

"No, *it* sang to *him*," Barry said. "And it's a
meteorite, because it's already crashed to Earth, while
a meteor is—"

"Focus, Barry." Joe tilted his head. "I know what a meteor is."

"Oh, yeah, right. Sorry. Anyway, he said he could hear it singing, and that's how he found it. It was just lying there, out in a field. Without examining it, you'd have thought it was an ordinary rock."

"Uh-huh." Joe started to speak, then shrugged. "I'd say that's crazy, but I've seen things that make it sound perfectly reasonable."

"He's still out at the observatory!" Cisco was hunched over his monitor again.

"He is?" Barry asked. "I thought he'd retired, or died."

"That's it, Barry," Caitlin said, tapping up new data. "That strange substance on Dr. Larson's hands. It could be—"

"Oh, snap!" Cisco exclaimed. "It's Singing Rock dust! That's why we couldn't identify it. It came from another world!" he added dramatically.

Barry pulled the chemical breakdown up on the screen. "You're right. Those results would be consistent with a meteorite."

"Yo, dude," Cisco said, his eyes wide. "You know what I'm thinking? It's time for a road trip to the creepy observatory on the edge of town, to talk to a crazy old astronomer!"

"Oh, man!" Barry gave Cisco a high five. "Finally, my life is a Hardy Boys book!"

Caitlin furrowed her brow. "You're not going tonight, are you?"

"Sure, why not?" Barry said as he and Cisco exchanged eager glances. "It's not that far out of town."

"An hour, maybe two," Cisco added. "By car. Not by Flash. We can stop at Big Belly Burger for a little road fuel."

"I haven't been to the observatory since third grade." Barry started for the door. "We've got to go—for the sake of the investigation."

"A simple phone call wouldn't work?" Iris leaned against the console with a suspicious cock of her head.

"That's too impersonal." Cisco steamed past Barry, grabbing his arm. "Besides, you wanted Barry to have a rest. This is restful. Just a quiet evening at the observatory. We'll let you know what we find. C'mon, man."

Before anyone could say another word, they were gone.

Joe checked his watch. "Well, I've got to get back to the office to finish up some paperwork, and make some calls before it gets too late."

Iris knew exactly what that meant. Back to work, drink more coffee, finish some work, start more work, forget the time, forget to eat… He wouldn't make it home until the middle of the night.

"Dad, you'll eat dinner, won't you?"

"Dinner? Sure, Iris. I'll find something."

"Dad," she said firmly. "Dinner."

"Yes, honey." Joe waved his hand as he walked out.

Iris prepared to go, then realized she wasn't alone. With a shake of her head, she stepped around the desk to take Caitlin's arm.

"Oh no," she said. "You're not staying here by yourself."

Caitlin's expression reminded Iris of a startled cat.

"But I have work to do."

"Nothing that can't wait until tomorrow," she replied, and she hoped she was right. "We need to take a break while we can. You still have to eat, don't you? You can't do that here." She frowned, then added, "Well, you could, but then you'd have no life, and it would be pathetic." Iris tugged a bit harder, and Caitlin finally stood up. "Everything here is connected, isn't it? You'll know if something comes up. You'll get an alert, right?"

"Yes, but—"

"Look, Barry and Cisco get a road trip, so the least we can do is go to dinner."

"I'm not hungry."

Lord above…

"Look, I'd bet you can't even remember the last time you left this lab," Iris insisted. "At least let's go have a drink then."

Caitlin grimaced and stopped, as if struck by a bad memory.

"I'd rather not."

Iris got her moving again. "All right, how about a workout at the gym? You're a doctor, so you know how bad it is for your health, sitting all day at a desk. And with all the metahumans out there, staying in shape is critical. Besides, it'll be fun to have some company."

Caitlin gave a resigned sigh. "Fine," she said. "I suppose an hour or two won't be bad. I'm at a dead end anyway."

"Sometimes stepping away from your work gives you a new insight," Iris offered.

"True." The petite scientist brightened. "Let me get a change of clothes from the back. Usually I just work out here in the lab."

Iris nodded, followed her back to the locker, and stared at the lone treadmill standing there.

"Girl, I'm going to show you what a real gym can be like."

During the drive across Central City, they had to take several detours because of the washed-out roads. As time dragged on, Caitlin began to fret that she shouldn't have left. Iris stopped listening when she started worrying about a cell culture that might spoil if she didn't check on it.

Finally they pulled into the parking lot of Iris's favorite gym, Fitness Universe. It was crowded but not mobbed—most likely because of the storms. Modern pop music came from hidden speakers, and television screens showed the videos that went with the music. Men and women in skintight outfits occupied a variety of exercise equipment. The majority of them were in the peak of physical condition.

Caitlin's eyes went wide, and she blushed visibly. Her own outfit consisted of yoga pants and a loose-fitting M.I.T. sweatshirt. By contrast, Iris was wearing fashionable tights and a bright pink sports bra with headband to match.

Pulling off her heavy blue sweatshirt, the scientist revealed a t-shirt underneath. Iris stared at it without saying a word.

"What's wrong?" Caitlin asked. "It's been washed. Cisco gave it to me for my birthday."

"I could have guessed," Iris said. "'Let's cuttle.' What's with the squid?"

"They're not squid. They're—"

"Hey." A muscular man who had just stepped off the treadmill regarded her with a confused expression. "They misspelled cuddle."

"No," Caitlin exclaimed, "they're *cuttlefish*."

The man rolled his eyes and walked away.

"It's *scientific*," Caitlin called after him.

"Oh, come on." Iris laughed and grabbed her by the arm. "Those two treadmills are free, and they're side by side. We can talk while we run."

The machines were lined up along a glass balcony overlooking the weight room. As they got the treadmills going and found their paces, Iris noticed Caitlin trying to look everywhere except at the sweating male bodies. She leaned closer to her friend.

"It's okay," she said, loudly enough to be heard over the music. "We may both be single, but we're not dead. There's no law saying we can't appreciate the view."

"I suppose not." Caitlin gave a self-conscious laugh. Her gaze drifted down to the ripped athletes, flexing as they lifted weights. "I guess it's better than staring at a computer monitor all night."

"That's the spirit!"

"You know, I'm glad you forced me to do this." Despite her nervousness, Caitlin's expression had brightened considerably since they got out of the lab.

"Me, too," Iris agreed. "We both work hard, and we deserve a night off." Iris dialed up the workout she'd programmed into her machine, then began to regret it as the ramp started to incline. "Oh, Lord," she panted. Beside her, Caitlin huffed even louder.

"Keep going," Iris urged her.

Though she continued to gasp loudly, Caitlin matched her pace as their legs pumped nearly in unison, keeping pace with the challenging program. After ten minutes of pounding steps, however, she started to falter, slowing down.

"Don't stop!" Iris shouted in encouragement. "Run like Grodd is behind you."

Caitlin's pace increased abruptly, and her expression was so intense, Iris felt a bit guilty. After another five minutes of running, Caitlin put her feet to the side and collapsed over the monitor, clutching it like a drowning woman on a floating log.

Iris's program ended and she stepped off, leaning against her knees, sucking for air.

"I think I'm going to be sick," she confessed.

"I forgot to look at all the pretty men," Caitlin lamented.

Iris laughed through her pain, reaching for a bottle of water and handing one over. Caitlin took it gratefully and swallowed half of it in one long gulp. She looked back, her face bright with sweat.

"How does Barry make this look so damned easy?"

"I hate him," Iris wheezed.

Now Caitlin laughed. "Me, too. No one should not have to work out like this, and certainly not every day. It's not fair."

"Even the Green Arrow has to use the gym."

Caitlin offered a mischievous grin. "Felicity Smoak told me she watches him work out. He has abs that are ungodly."

"Maybe we need to go visit her in Star City."

"Road trip for the ladies," Caitlin declared.

"I'm in." Iris finally straightened and moved away from the machine so someone else could use it. Caitlin followed suit. She placed the empty water bottle in a nearby recycling bin.

"I'm still thirsty."

"There's a juice bar. Let's get something refreshing. We deserve it."

They showered and changed before heading for the small stand near the entrance to the gym. There they joined the other young professionals clustered together around the whirring blenders.

Neither of them could make up their minds, so they let the juice barista surprise them. It wasn't the smartest move. What they got were two drinks, one dark green and the other a dark red. They clinked their glasses together in a halfhearted toast and took a sip.

Both girls grimaced.

"Oh, God, is that beets?" Caitlin nearly gagged.

Iris barely choked down a few swallows. She stared at the green pulpy contents and then looked back up at Caitlin.

"Barry had like fifteen chicken cutlets the other night for dinner."

Caitlin let out a whelp of frustration. "I hate him!"

"Buffet at Steak Corral?" Iris suggested. She was hungry now, and it wasn't for a kale smoothie.

"Oh, Lord, yes!" A smile finally emerged from Caitlin as she slammed her still-full glass on the counter. The two women made a quick exit, laughing arm in arm.

1 2

Not far from Central City a spur of mountains rose, undeveloped and still relatively isolated. The S.T.A.R. Labs van raced up the switchback road, kicking out gravel. Headlights played over merciless rock faces and then empty voids, back and forth as Cisco gleefully wrestled the wheel.

Barry clutched the dashboard, and dug his toes through the insoles of his black sneakers. The van skidded at the edge of a crevasse before veering back to the rutted dirt track, and he slammed against the door.

"Could you slow down?" he rasped. "We're not exactly in a Formula One race." He was appreciative to Cisco for a couple of hours of mindless chitchat about video games and movies, and whether Bigfoot could live in these mountains. He was grateful that Cisco hadn't asked about the glitches and the blurring episodes. Even so, gratitude only went so far. Barry didn't want to die in a fiery crash.

The van swept through another turn and the headlights caught a white shape looming ahead as they emerged onto an open area devoid of trees. Cut into the side of the peak was an old-fashioned dome observatory. Compared to the great observatories like Palomar, this one wasn't impressive at all—perhaps sixty feet high compared to Palomar's one hundred and thirty-five. The once-white dome was mottled because of lost panels, and in some spots the structure's framework was visible.

The van ground to a halt and dust rose through the beams. Barry pushed open the squeaking van door and dropped to the rocky ground.

"I can't believe he lives here."

Cutting the engine, Cisco turned off the headlights. He stepped out to join Barry. The only sounds were the ticking of the cooling motor and their soft breathing.

"Cue the wolf howls," Cisco muttered. "Perfect place for a weirdo like Coolidge." They crunched across the hard dirt toward a door. Barry knocked.

"When you say he's a weirdo, what do you mean?"

"Well, he doesn't like people knocking on his door for one thing. That's clear enough."

"Why do you say that?"

Cisco pointed over Barry's shoulder. About fifty feet away, a man stood in the shadows aiming a shotgun at them. Barry tensed, but didn't act for fear of spooking the man. He wasn't worried about himself, but anytime guns went off it was unpredictable. He didn't want to take a chance that Cisco might be hit.

"Dr. Coolidge? Hi. We'd like to talk to you."

The man didn't budge. Neither did the gun.

"Did we catch you on your way out?" Cisco asked. Barry smiled nervously, and willed his friend to suppress the snark.

"We just want to talk to you," he said.

The shotgun shifted higher, and the man's hand tightened on the grip.

"Whoa!" Barry held out his hands. "We're scientists, too. We work for S.T.A.R. Labs. My name is Barry Allen."

Cisco opened his jacket to show his S.T.A.R. Labs t-shirt.

"That's not really proof," Barry whispered. "Anyone can buy those."

"They can?"

"Sure. I've seen them online."

"Nice try," the gunman snapped. "S.T.A.R. Labs closed after the particle accelerator exploded." He gestured with the firearm. "So what do you want?"

Barry kept his hands out. "We want to talk about the Singing Meteorite."

"Why?" Coolidge demanded. "You think I took it?"

"No." Barry was surprised at that. "The police know who took it. We know who killed Dr. Larson."

"I haven't seen anything on the news about an arrest."

"It's complicated. They're metahumans."

"Oh. Those things." The man lowered the shotgun.

Cisco breathed out in relief. "Don't tell me—let me guess," he said. "The gun wasn't even loaded, right?"

"Wrong. What do you want to know about the meteorite, Mr. Allen?" He stepped out of the shadows so that his features were visible. He was an older man, likely sixty-five or seventy. He looked exhausted. His gray hair was thin and flying in all directions, and his beard untrimmed. He wore baggy corduroy pants and a thick cardigan complete with leather elbow patches. The only part of his ensemble that didn't scream "professor emeritus" was the shotgun. He squinted at Cisco.

"You're Francisco Ramon, aren't you?"

Cisco gasped. "How do you know that?"

"I've seen you before. Twice. You were at a session of the National Science Foundation seven years ago, and you asked a question about the feasibility of smelting operations in space."

Cisco put a hand to his mouth. "I did! I didn't even remember that. But wait, you weren't on that panel, were you?"

"I was in the audience, and I have a good memory. Later Harrison Wells introduced me to you at a S.T.A.R. Labs reception, where I was eventually asked to leave."

"Now *that* I do remember," Cisco acknowledged. "To be fair, you were pretty drunk."

"Yes, I was. I had five cocktails and three crab puffs. An unwise ratio. Would you both like to come inside?" Coolidge shuffled to the door and twisted the handle. It was unlocked.

While it was a chilly October outside, the air inside the observatory was frigid. The space was dim, with only two bare incandescent bulbs burning in shadeless floor lamps. A dilapidated control panel made of steel and aluminum took up half of the circular wall. Holes and slots gaped open with wires hanging where dials and readouts had once been housed. Old-fashioned blackboards and corkboards covered the rest of the wall, along with framed photographs of celestial objects.

Piles of paper and ancient three-ring binders littered countertops and desks the color of institutional olive drab. An impressive telescope dominated the middle of the jumbled space. It was currently aimed at the inky slot in the open dome where several bright stars were visible. A tracking motor kept the dome and telescope locked on a target, and the background hum was audible.

"That is a thirty-inch Cassegrain reflector," Coolidge announced. "When this observatory was built, it was the third largest reflecting telescope in the United States."

Cisco bobbed his head in genuine respect. "It's a classic."

"Yes," the astronomer said without enthusiasm. "Like a pyramid or Stonehenge." He leaned his shotgun haphazardly against the wall.

Cisco pointed at the eyepiece. "May I?"

Coolidge extended his hand, then walked over to a decades-old coffee maker and checked an empty glass pot.

"Want some coffee?" he asked. "Most people find it cold in here."

"Sure." Barry waited behind Cisco for a chance to look through the telescope, as he had done years ago when he was a schoolboy. The astronomer shook ground coffee out of a can into a filter, without measuring. He poured water into the coffee maker, ignoring the fact that half of it leaked out the back and dripped to the floor.

"Mr. Ramon, you are looking at Object Six Two Five A two. It is a rogue asteroid. If it were to collide with Earth, all life would cease to exist within twenty-four hours."

Cisco straightened. "Is that going to happen?"

"It is not." Coolidge dropped a towel to the floor and pushed it around with his foot, mopping up the puddle that had formed.

"Whew! That was a close one." Cisco dragged his arm over his forehead in a burlesque show of relief, and then laughed. "Am I right?"

"Hm." Coolidge peered curiously at the engineer. "Wells told me that you were one of the finest minds he ever knew, or you could be, in any case. I have to assume he knew what he was talking about."

Cisco stiffened and his voice cracked. "He said that?"

The astronomer kicked the wet towel under a desk. "Yes, but he tended to be smitten with his protégés. Until he wasn't." Coolidge wandered the work floor until he'd found three mugs, and returned to wait by the gurgling coffee maker. "So what do you want to know about the meteorite?"

"Well," Barry began, "it was the most unique object stolen from the Central City Museum. Its value is more scientific than monetary. So we're wondering, is there something about it that a metahuman would want, badly enough to kill for it?"

"I have no idea," Coolidge said flatly. "Is there anything else, or have you come all the way up the mountain for naught?"

Barry and Cisco stood silently for a moment.

"Um… could we maybe take a few more minutes to explore the possibilities?"

"You can take all the time you want, Mr. Allen." Coolidge poured three cups of coffee. "I'm not sure why you need to waste my time to do it."

"If we could, let's talk about your claim that the meteorite *sang*."

"It's not a claim. It's a fact."

"I'm not disputing it, but do you have any idea *why* the meteorite sang?"

"It possessed… possesses a unique crystalline structure. Dr. Larson told me he had never seen crystals formed quite that way. He theorized that they exhibited extraordinary potential for energy storage. Claimed he'd find a way to tap into that potential." Coolidge grunted. "That's why I sold the thing to him in the first place. What a waste."

"How did you find the meteorite?" Cisco asked.

"I tracked its approach to Earth, calculated where it would impact. And then I went and got it."

"Really?" Barry exclaimed more incredulously than he intended. "I mean, even NASA can't pinpoint that sort of thing."

"NASA can't do a lot of things," Coolidge growled.

"So you first heard it sing in Africa?"

"No." He jerked his head toward the open dome. "Up there."

"You heard it in space?" Barry asked. "You must've had excellent equipment." A thought struck him. "Could you track it now?"

"No." The astronomer held up two fingers. "First, the meteorite hasn't sung since I found it in Africa. And second, I don't have those instruments any longer. I sold them in order to buy food."

With a scowl Coolidge set down his coffee, and picked some fuzz off his dirty sweater. He stroked his beard, seeming to realize it was badly unkempt. Finally he leaned against a metal desk, recalling the easy pose of an academic giving a lecture. But his hands tightened on the edge. Knuckles grew white.

He took a long breath. "By the time I was your age, Mr. Allen, I had won the International Astronomical Society Man-of-the-Year. I had rejected offers from nearly every major scientific organization in this country. Just a few months before I found the meteorite, I turned down six figures to build and direct a state-of-the-art research station. And now I have only this.

That meteorite ruined my career. 'Dr. Coolidge and his singing rock from outer space.'"

Barry stuffed his hands in his pockets. Cisco was already eyeing the door… and the shotgun.

"All right, Doctor," Barry said. "I'm sorry to have disturbed you. Thank you for your time."

"Fine." Coolidge slumped down on a stool. "Go." They set down the coffee cups and walked toward the door.

"Would you like to hear it?" the astronomer asked quietly.

Together they stopped, and turned.

"Hear it?" Barry responded. "Hear the meteorite? I thought it was silent now."

"It is, but I have recordings." His voice had an odd, faraway sound. "Would you like to hear them?"

The two young men looked at each other, shotgun forgotten.

"Yes!"

"I have them here." The astronomer straightened with new energy, and walked over to a desk. He yanked open a drawer and peered in, digging noisily through the contents. "I could've sworn it was here." He began the looting of every drawer in the desk, then all around the observatory, cursing louder with each passing moment.

Papers. Pencils. Power cords. Staplers. Calculators. Slide rules. All came out in piles. Then stacks of CDs and flash drives in all shapes and sizes. Portable hard drives, and eventually a huge collection of 5.25 diskettes.

"It's like a museum," Cisco whispered. "I'll bet good money he starts pulling out boxes of punch cards." Finally Coolidge held up an old storage brick of some sort, and squinted at the label.

"This is probably it," he muttered. "I only have one copy left." He grabbed a huge tangle of cords and went to one of the control panels. He inspected the connectors on the nest of cables, holding each of them up to a socket in the panel, before tossing them aside.

"Ah-hah!" Coolidge slipped a cable connector into the odd socket with an audible click. Then he linked that cable to another and then to some sort of adapter that looked as if it should've come with a wall-mounted hand vacuum.

"There." Finally it all plugged into the small hard drive. The astronomer punched a thick yellow button on the control panel, and twisted a dial. Then he gestured for them to approach. "Here. Listen."

A squalling static filled the air, loud enough almost to be painful. Barry waited for it to pass and the singing to begin. The static continued. When he saw Coolidge listening intently, almost rapturously, realization set in. He looked to see if Cisco was getting anything more out of it.

A bewildered face showed that he wasn't.

"Well?" Coolidge shouted over the noise.

"I can't really make anything out," Barry called out hesitantly.

The astronomer turned up the volume. "I don't have the equipment needed to separate out the layers for you," he said, "but you hear it, don't you?"

Barry leaned into the sound, trying to pick out undertones, but he heard nothing but a single, screeching, headache-inducing note. Coolidge looked beyond Barry and he punched the button to silence the roar.

"I hear it," a voice said from behind. "Clearly."

Barry spun and looked past the telescope. Hartley Rathaway lounged in the open door. The villain known as Pied Piper wore his dark pullover with a hood obscuring his features.

"It's a beautiful recording, Dr. Coolidge." Rathaway smiled broadly as he raised his hands to reveal his destructive sonic gauntlets. "I simply must have it."

"Who the hell are you?" Coolidge moved across the observatory floor toward the shotgun.

Rathaway kept smiling, but his eyes narrowed. The air in front of his gauntlets rippled. The shotgun shook and broke into pieces. Coolidge glared toward the door.

Rathaway pulled his hood back.

"Now do you recognize me?"

"Nope. Should I?"

"What? I heard you talking before." Rathaway jabbed a finger at Cisco. "You remembered *him*! Yet I was Harrison Wells's right hand at S.T.A.R. Labs. Hartley Rathaway." He paused for effect.

Coolidge shook his head. "Doesn't ring a bell."

Cisco laughed.

Rathaway scowled. "You shut up! What are you doing here anyway? Running errands for the Flash?"

"Don't be jealous, Hartley." Cisco inched toward

the control panel where the hard drive lay on a pile of cables. "You just have one of those forgettable faces. And careers."

Vibrations rumbled through the concrete floor. Barry tensed, ready to act. Protecting his identity wouldn't be a consideration, if it came to protecting Cisco or Dr. Coolidge. Then a second figure appeared from the darkness. Shawna Baez. Her eyes darted attentively around the observatory, taking in everyone, and searching for others, most likely checking for signs of the Flash. Satisfied, she leaned forward over Rathaway's shoulder.

"Let's get it and go," she hissed. "He's probably around somewhere."

Rathaway shrugged her back. "Dr. Coolidge, I'll take that recording."

"I don't think so," the old astronomer responded.

Rathaway strolled in with a snide grin while Shawna stayed at the door, peering out nervously into the night. He placed one of his gloved hands on the thick white barrel of the telescope, then faced Coolidge.

"I want you to walk over to that counter and bring me the recording. I want you to hand it to me. If you don't, I will destroy your telescope. Maybe *then* you'll remember my name."

"I wouldn't give you the time of day," Coolidge replied.

Barry studied the layout of the observatory. While Rathaway had more raw destructive power at his command, *and* he was a huge jerk, Peekaboo was the first priority. She'd been the key to keeping the metas out of his reach. Once he took her out of the equation, catching the others would be much simpler.

The lights. If he could knock out the two weak bulbs that lit the observatory, it might be too dark for her to teleport—at least temporarily.

"Just take the thing, Hartley!" Shawna called out nervously from the door. "Let's go before the Flash shows up."

"No!" Rathaway shouted back. "I want him to place it in my hand." He sent a hard shock through the telescope. The sound of cracking glass rang through the observatory. Coolidge let out a hoarse bellow and rushed Rathaway, swinging wildly. The hooded man grabbed the old man, but still took a solid shot to the jaw.

Rathaway snarled and sent out a shock wave.

Coolidge's mouth flew open, and he shook violently.

"Cisco, run!" Barry snatched up a nearby floor lamp, pulling the cord from the wall. He swung the solid brass pole like a bat. It hit Rathaway with a crack, shattering the bulb.

Shawna appeared beside the desk. Her hand fell on the pile of cables. There was nothing on top of them.

Cisco ran with the hard drive, ducking under the telescope.

Barry dragged Coolidge out of Rathaway's grip. His arm vibrated just from the contact. As he pushed the astronomer out of the way, Rathaway quickly recovered and put a hand on Barry's chest, sending power thundering into him. Pain stabbed his head and his limbs went numb.

Cisco paused in his flight and gathered up the long cable trailing behind the hard drive. He looped it over Rathaway's head, tightened it, and pulled hard, catching Rathaway by surprise and dragging him off his feet.

Barry stumbled away, breathing hard, his vision blurred. He dropped to one knee.

Suddenly Shawna teleported next to Cisco. She grabbed the hard drive, but he shouted in alarm and clutched it tight against his chest. They both vanished...

...and reappeared across the observatory. Wide-eyed with shock, Cisco kept his grip on the drive. The two disappeared again. They showed up in yet another spot, still grappling. Cisco screeched in alarm, but he didn't give up the goods.

And they were gone again.

When they reappeared, Cisco gasped, "Wait!"

Peekaboo paused. Frantically Cisco kicked over the other floor lamp that stood nearby. It teetered and fell to the concrete. The bulb smashed and the observatory plunged into darkness.

"No!" Shawna cried.

Barry whirled toward where Rathaway had been standing, but the room spun. He was still dizzy from the sonic attack. By the time he had regained his equilibrium, and his eyes began to adjust to the dark, Rathaway had moved.

Powerful vibrations began from behind him. There was the sound of crumbling masonry, shattering glass, and the creaking of agonized metal. The huge white shape of the telescope fell toward Coolidge and Barry. Trusting the darkness to cover his actions he moved to Coolidge's side, kneeling, scooping the man up, and streaking away just as the giant telescope crashed onto the cement floor where they had been. It rang like a cathedral bell.

Barry deposited the senseless astronomer safely behind one of the metal desks. As his vision grew even more accustomed to the dark, Barry saw a faint shape outlined against the pale wall. Pied Piper pointed his gloves blindly, each sonic blast shuddering the building. Large cracks appeared in the plaster.

Rathaway gestured in his direction, and Barry dodged a random blast, but then a wave of force slammed into him, crushing him against the wall. Blood pounded in his ears. He couldn't focus.

He couldn't move.

"Stop it!" Shawna cried out. "If you hit the hard drive, you'll wreck it!" There was a scuffling, which meant she was still struggling with Cisco.

The vibrations ceased immediately, leaving Barry to fight for breath as he slumped to the floor, gritting his teeth. Grinding pain let him know ribs were broken.

Rathaway scrambled to where Shawna had Cisco doubled over in a hammerlock. Cisco reared up, butting him in the head with an audible *crack*, knocking him away. Shawna cursed, distracted by Rathaway's shout of pain. Cisco broke free and legged for the door.

Barry fought onto his knees, as the pain and nausea subsided. His friend stood silhouetted in the gray rectangle of the door. Unfortunately that provided Peekaboo with enough light to maneuver. She appeared outside, Cisco whirled, and she punched him square in the nose.

He flew off his feet and hit the concrete so hard his breath whooshed out. Shawna stomped on his stomach, bending over to tear the hard drive out of his hands.

"Hartley! Let's go!" She backed away from the door and Rathaway staggered after her, stepping heavily on Cisco as he passed.

Barry took a deep breath and prepared to run after them when another sickening wave washed over him. Thick vibrations tore through the observatory. The heavy sheets of metal covering the dome rustled and filled the air with a sound akin to thunder. Chunks of plaster and cinder block began to fall.

Barry shoved a desk aside and grabbed the astronomer by the collar. He hefted the dead weight and ran for the door, reversing course to avoid something metal that fell in front of him, dodging rivets that popped into the air like bullets, and spinning to avoid twisting girders that crashed from the roof.

He leapt over Cisco to carry Coolidge into the cold night air. Settling the astronomer against the side of the van, he raced back. The dome of the observatory sagged with a groan. Cisco floundered insensibly on the floor just as a long steel beam detached from the dome and hurtled down toward him. Barry grabbed the engineer and dragged him out before the jagged girder crashed to the floor.

Leaving Cisco next to the insensible astronomer, he made a quick search of the area, but didn't find Rathaway and Shawna. That wasn't surprising. They had what they'd come for, and had no interest in lingering.

Barry returned to the van and crouched next to Cisco. His head throbbed and his vision sparked as if he had a migraine. Across the open lot, the observatory wrenched itself into a ruin, piece by piece.

Cisco groaned and tried to sit up. He took his hand away from his face to reveal a bloody nose and eyes that were already starting to bruise. Barry whistled at the damage. Cisco touched his nose and winced.

"Oh, man," he said. "She beat me like a rented mule."

"Your nose doesn't look broken."

"Oh, great—yeah, I guess that's somet'ing." Cisco held his head back and pressed fingers on either side of his nose to stop the bleeding. "I got my clock cleaned by *Peekaboo*. I might want to change her name now to Valkyrie or the One-Punch Wonder."

"It's okay, buddy," Barry said. "I've been hit by her, too. She packs quite a wallop."

"I'm not sure this helps the prospects of me and Ms. Baez becoming man and wife." Barry gave a painful laugh and turned to inspect Coolidge.

"He looks like he'll be okay, but we should get him to a hospital."

"I'd suggest a heavy sedative before anyone tells him what happened to his observatory," Cisco said wryly.

Barry dragged himself to his feet, and then helped Cisco up.

"He definitely won't like that." They lifted Coolidge by the shoulders and ankles, lugging him around the rear of the van.

"I'm not happy to see Hartley Rathaway involved."

"Me either," Barry agreed. "Don't we still have his old sonic gauntlets at S.T.A.R. Labs?"

"Yeah. He must've made new ones. Better ones." It looked as if every word hurt when he spoke, but he didn't let that stop him.

"It explains a lot. When you combine his smarts with Peekaboo's powers, I'll bet that's why you haven't been able to find the metas using your tracking algorithms. He's using her power to move his pieces around in a mathematically random fashion. Man, he's smart."

"And a major league jerk. I'm the guy he tricked into letting him out of his cell at S.T.A.R. Labs when we had him captured before. Plus, he just hates me."

"Well, you did replace him as Dr. Wells's right-hand man." Barry shoved equipment aside in the rear of the van and they positioned the astronomer as comfortably as possible. "Rathaway's the type who holds a grudge."

"Oh, he preserves grudges like tar pits preserve

mammoths. What do you think he wants with the Singing Meteorite?"

"I wish I knew." Barry covered Coolidge with several blankets. The dust from the collapsed observatory was clearing in the mountain breeze. "Nothing he's involved in can be good."

The senseless destruction over the previous days made more sense now that they knew the Pied Piper was involved. He was brilliant and tactical, and had to be running the show. Whereas Mardon and Nimbus had seemed to be causing random havoc, it had to be part of a larger plan.

Barry wondered if Rathaway had anything to do with the glitches in his powers. Could they have been a side effect, caused by the vibratory waves? Probably not—he hadn't experienced any of the symptoms while facing his foe in the observatory.

When Cisco slid into the driver's seat, Barry saw him more clearly in the dome light. His face was covered with blood and his eyes were already purple. Barry hissed with concern.

"Oh, man. Are you sure you can manage? Maybe I should drive."

Cisco waved him off.

"Please. I've been punched harder by scarier girls."

Barry laughed, which made his head hurt again. He put a hand briefly on Cisco's arm, and then climbed into the back to sit next to Dr. Coolidge.

14

Iris reached for her coffee on the desk. It was cold. With a sigh she took a few sips of it anyway, then scanned the information on her screen. Grumbling, she typed in a new search parameter.

She and Caitlin had stayed out later than she'd planned. They'd had a lot more to talk about than she'd thought, but it was worth it. Still, Iris had dragged herself out of bed and come into the office early. The bullpen area at the Central City Picture News would normally be nearly empty this time of day, but the ongoing metahuman-spawned disasters were putting pressure on the press. The drone of light chitchat and clicking keyboards surrounded her.

Since the day they discovered that Kyle Nimbus and Mark Mardon were back in town, Iris had been hunting. The thought of monsters like that in the same city as her dad made her gut twist into a knot. It was Nimbus particularly who scared her; he seemed inhuman and completely unpredictable.

Everyone was looking for the rogues. Where Caitlin and Cisco's methodologies focused on cameras, police reports, and predictive modeling, she employed a far simpler approach.

Social media.

On the Internet, people talked and millions listened. Every day. Somewhere out there, someone had seen Kyle Nimbus or the Mist. Iris herself had tracked the Flash, even before she knew he was Barry, using social media. She would find Nimbus, too. Her father's life depended on it.

Iris no longer maintained a blog dedicated to the Flash, but countless others did. His fandom had grown by leaps and bounds once he'd come out of the shadows. People became obsessed with him, or his villains, and that type of obsession could be used to her advantage.

Her father was a detective, and Iris had always wanted to join the force. She knew investigative procedure, and while she didn't have direct access to the police data banks, she knew what would lead her to Nimbus.

Contacts. Family. Relationships.

Iris had found a lead that had some potential. She came across a dive bar that Nimbus had used as a home away from home in his pre-metahuman days. Given his continued obsession with her father, Iris suspected that there were other things he couldn't let go of. And even if he hadn't frequented the place in a while, someone there might be able to give her some information.

She debated calling Caitlin to go with her, but decided against it. As a precaution she texted Barry where she was going, so he'd know where to search if she went missing.

A sudden gale blew her hair about wildly. Loose papers and napkins went flying, as well.

"Flash!"

Her co-workers looked up, and the murmur increased, but no one was particularly surprised. It wasn't the first time Barry had been there in his costumed persona. She had a reputation as the newspaper's Flash expert—it had been what got her the job.

"Iris, what are you doing?" He stood in front of her, arms crossed and looking perturbed. Folks around them ducked under their desks to retrieve papers that had blown onto the floor.

"Protecting my family." She gathered her purse and moved around him toward the door.

He stepped back in her way. "By risking your life?"

"You do it every day," she said simply.

"That's different. *I'm* different."

"Yes, but I'm not looking for a fight. I'm just following up a lead. Keeping tabs."

"Tabs?"

"On the Mist. Making sure he doesn't show up anywhere near… my dad."

"That's what I'm doing," he countered. "You don't need to—"

"Even you can't watch Joe West every minute. You need help." He opened his mouth, and Iris held up a hand. "You can argue all you want, but I'm not just sitting on my ass waiting for everyone else to play their parts while I do nothing." She pushed her way out the door and started down the sidewalk.

"All right, but I'm coming with you."

She sighed and lowered her voice. "You're overtaxed as it is. This is supposed to help you, so you have one less thing on your plate."

He shot her a boyish grin. "I'm never too busy to hang with you, Iris. Come on. This'll give me time to recharge. We can grab breakfast burritos on the way."

Laughing gently, Iris said, "Okay, I surrender, but when we get there, fade into the background. I'll get more on my own." She headed for her car while the Flash raced away. By the time she was opening the driver's-side door, Barry was slipping his uniform under the back seat.

Andru's Bar and Pool Hall sat on a corner between a motel that had seen the 1950s *Sputnik 1* launch and a pawnshop that looked no larger than their living room. As they drove past a desolate strip of abandoned warehouses, traffic was thin. The pouring rain had sent most people off the streets, otherwise Iris suspected there would be more unsavory types milling about outside. Unfortunately, that meant they were probably inside. The place where you could loiter the cheapest.

The downpour started up again as they parked the car and walked half a block to the bar, bent against the rain. When they reached the door Barry opened it like a gentleman. Iris wasn't sure what kind of message that sent to those within. A lady who needed doors opened for her, or a lady who held some power and respect.

She had to make sure it was the latter.

Three men stood around a pool table inside, along with a bartender—an older woman who wiped down the bar with a cloth. She looked more menacing than her few customers.

One of them sported a long scar down his cheek. He sunk a ball in a corner pocket. The other two stared at the newcomers—no doubt they saw a couple of suburban kids who came off as hipsters looking for dive bar authenticity. Well, they had certainly found it.

Shaking the water from their coats, Iris and Barry went straight for the bar.

"Scotch," Iris demanded. "Neat."

Barry looked shocked. "It's like nine o'clock in the morning."

The bartender gave him an exasperated glare before slamming a glass down in front of her and sloshing in a dram. Iris took a sip and gave a nod at the quality. It wasn't half bad, considering the location.

"You two seem a little out of place," the woman

muttered as she scanned them from head to toe. "Did the school bus break down?"

Barry laughed too loudly. "Actually we're looking for somebody."

The bartender pulled back. Iris could see her already shutting down. They had to do something, and quickly.

"We're looking for a murderer," she said.

The bartender looked doubtful, but she didn't move any further away.

"That's a little heavy for this time of day."

Barry leaned on the bar. "It's a heavy life."

Oh my Lord, Iris thought, but she kept quiet.

The woman grunted a laugh and looked at her. "So who did this guy murder?"

"Judge Howard, and most of the Darbinyan crime family."

The woman paled. "You're talking about Kyle Nimbus."

Iris nodded. "He used to come here, right?"

"You've done your homework, little girl. Yeah, he *used* to come in here, but not anymore." The bartender returned to her work, turning away and focusing on wiping smudged glasses.

"Did he ever talk to you?" Barry asked, keeping an eye on the other patrons.

"Honey, everyone talks to me."

Iris leaned forward. "Did he ever mention—"

"No."

"We're willing to pay for the—" Iris tried.

The woman slammed a glass heavily on the bar.

"If you're feeling suicidal, you can talk to Hap over there. He may know something, and be stupid enough to tell you." She bobbed her head toward the man playing pool. The one with the scar.

Of course, Iris mused. The man was taller than Barry and three times as wide in the shoulders. From his sullen expression, he didn't look to be in a talkative mood.

"Thank you." Iris stuffed a few twenties into the empty tip jar. Barry reached out and took her arm as she moved toward Hap.

"Why don't you let me handle this one?"

"Because you annoyed the bartender," she said.

"I'm not good with women."

"Well, that's the honest truth."

Barry gave her a sour look, so she waved him on. "Just remember that he has a pool cue… and a scar."

He tried to put a hard look on his clean-cut face, and failed. Iris watched him swagger over to the pool table, or at least it looked like a swagger. Either that or he was getting ready to bust out into a dance routine.

Hap didn't even look up. Barry circled the pool table once, cutting into the man's line of sight. The man's eyes narrowed in anger.

"If you got any body bags in your car, you might want to get 'em," the bartender said. "They're going to eat that boy alive."

Iris turned and smiled. "Well, they'll try."

1 5

"I just asked if you'd seen him!" Barry scurried around the far side of the table from the angry man with the scar who brandished a pool cue.

"Ain't no damned business of yours," the man growled. "Do I look like a damned fool? You don't go against Kyle Nimbus just 'cause someone asks politely."

Iris hesitated. Barry could handle these guys in a fight, but she still needed information. So she spoke loudly enough to be heard across the room.

"How about for money?"

The man turned toward her, his eyes widening a bit. It was as if he hadn't noticed her before. He folded his arms around the cue stick.

"You got my attention."

"We just want to know if you've seen him recently and where," she said. "It's… personal, and you'll be paid well."

"Personal? You know he's a stone cold killer, don't

cha?" At her irritated expression, Hap laughed. "I guess you do. Tell you what, sweetheart. You beat me at pool, and we'll have a chat." He looked her up and down in a way she didn't much like.

"It's a deal," Iris said. Barry's expression was priceless. He came over to her.

"What are you doing?" he whispered. "Do you even know how to play pool?"

"Not at all. But I know the Flash."

She went to the wall rack and picked out a cue. They all looked alike to her, but she tested a few for show. Finally she chose one and came back to the table. Her hands shook, and she tried to still them.

"Nine ball." Hap grinned at the other guys who had gathered. "I'll give you the break, just to be a good sport, little lady. If you can run the table, I might be more talkative."

"What if I lose?"

"We'll just cross that bridge when we come to it."

Iris nodded, feeling a lump in her throat. One of Hap's pals racked the balls in a tight diamond shape with the nine in the middle. Everyone was watching— even the bartender stopped her work. Iris struggled to maintain her confidence. This was for her father.

Suddenly her nerves quieted.

Chalking up her cue, she bent to line up her shot. The crack of the break sounded loud in the nearly empty bar. The colored balls flew around the stained felt, scattering wide, which was good. The one ball sat in a fair position. She didn't dare miss. One slip-up and a hustler like this guy would clear the table easily. She'd never get a second chance.

Iris glanced up at Barry and he winked at her. She positioned herself over the table, pulled the stick back, and exhaled, striking the ball as her breath stilled. She sank the first ball cleanly and almost laughed with surprise. The second and third balls slipped into their pockets with ease.

She sent the four ball spinning off course, and she knew she was in trouble. She almost shouted. Suddenly it curved over the table in a wide arc and dropped down into its pocket almost as if it had a mind of its own.

"Whoop!" she said, hoisting her cue.

"What the hell was that?" Hap twisted his cue in his rough hands.

Barry grinned casually. "That was her certified backsliding swing shot."

"Looked like cheating to me."

"That, sir," Barry said formally, "was skill."

"Damn lucky," Hap muttered.

Yes, it was, Iris thought, and she smiled. Barry toasted her with her own drink and took a sip, then almost gagged. Hap's face turned redder as his anger started to grow, realizing something was off, but not able to figure out what.

Iris moved on to the five ball. Again her nerves got the best of her, and she missed the mark. That didn't stop the cue ball from ricocheting off the rail with more momentum than it should have had. It careened off rail after rail until it struck the five again, driving it into the pocket.

"What the hell?" Hap let out a furious yell. "No way that you had enough power to make that shot!"

"Blind man's bluff."

Hap glared at Barry. "Shut up. I'm talking to the slip here."

She shrugged, unaffected by his bluster.

Barry regarded her. "Clear the table."

Iris couldn't help an impish grin this time as she closed her eyes and struck the cue ball, sending it rolling. The six, the seven… Every time a ball looked as if it was going astray, it would suddenly curve toward the proper target. When the second to last ball slipped into the pocket, Hap exploded. He snatched her cue out of her hands, and examined it closely.

"The stick came from your own rack," Barry pointed out.

"You still coulda done something to it. No one puts that kind of crazy spin on a ball—'specially not a girl."

"That's not true, and you know it," Iris said, crossing her arms.

"She's just that good," Barry insisted.

"If she's that good, why haven't I heard of her?" Hap slapped the stick back into her hands.

"Just finish the game, Hap," the bartender groused, "and stop your whining."

"You shut up, Doris!" Hap snarled.

Iris walked around the table, sizing up her last shot. She drew the stick back through her fingers. Off to the right, Hap bumped into a small table, sending drinks crashing to the floor. The shattering of glass caused Iris to jump as she shot and the cue ball went wild, completely missing its target. She held her breath.

Abruptly the white ball spun around the table, making full use of the wide space. It careened off the rail five times before slamming into the nine. Then the yellow-striped ball began its own dance, smacking the edge continuously until the angle was just right and it found its home in the pocket.

We won!

Hap slammed his hand down in a rage. Barry handed Iris back her drink, placing himself between her and her furious opponent.

"She won," Barry said. "Now pay up."

"She cheated!" Hap bellowed.

"Hells bells, Hap!" Doris shouted from behind the bar. "I was watching the whole time, and I didn't see nobody do nothing out of the ordinary."

"She had to be cheating, Doris!" the big man insisted.

"Just tell her what she wants to know."

"Like hell," Hap snarled, his voice a growl in his chest. He moved toward Iris, lifting his cue stick, the one he had never gotten a chance to use.

Barry moved, too. Or at least he must have. Suddenly Hap's cue stick bent forward, then snapped back, straight into his forehead. He went flying backward. Blood gushed out of a newly opened cut.

The other men came forward. Neither of them were as large as Hap, but that didn't make them harmless. One got tangled in Iris's cue stick, and fell at her feet, slamming his head against the side of the table. The other went down heavily, as well, his feet slipping in spilled beer.

It was like watching the Three Stooges, Iris thought with a suppressed chuckle. Doris had no such reserve. She threw back her head and howled in laughter.

Barry stood over Hap as the man hunched, holding his bleeding forehead.

"Don't even think of laying a hand on her."

"All right! All right!" Hap held up a red hand.

"Where is Kyle Nimbus?" Iris took a step closer. Any hint of humor disappeared. "What's he up to?"

"I don't know. He don't tell me his schedule, but he's probably around for the same thing he's been after for months now. The head of that cop who sent him up. That dude's as good as dead." Iris didn't bother responding. It would be wasted breath.

"When's the last time he was around?"

"Word is he was over in Danville, buying beer at Cardy's Mart. He used to live over that way."

"When was this?"

"Coupla nights ago, I think. That's all I know." He looked at her through slitted, bloodshot eyes. "Now give me what I'm owed."

Iris tossed him a hundred-dollar bill. Barry took her by the arm and steered her out the door. She lifted a hand to wave at Doris behind the bar.

"Hell, girl, you made a boring day a lot more interesting," the woman called out. "Good luck."

Once outside, they bent into the rain-streaked wind and hustled for the car, in case the pool toughs decided to come looking for payback. Jumping in, Iris peeled out with a squeal of tires. The windshield wipers slapped full tilt, but she could still barely see through the curtain of water.

"It's really coming down."

"Danville," Barry mused. "I've been through there a dozen times already in the last few days. I never saw him."

"Well, now we've got a specific place to check out."

"Yeah, Cardy's Mart. I'll head over there and see what I can find." He shook his head. "And no, you're not coming. Not if there's a chance Nimbus is in the area."

Iris's mouth twisted with a touch of ire. "Wasn't going to ask. I'm going back to the office. I've had some search programs running all morning. They're bound to have come up with something by now."

"Keep me posted on what you find out." He scanned the area around them. "Drop me off at the next corner." By the time they got there, he was the Flash.

"Be careful," Iris told him.

"You, too." And with that, he was gone.

She put the car into drive and headed back to City Center.

* * *

The office bustled with activity. A couple of her co-workers asked her if she'd learned anything from the Flash, but she remained noncommittal, and they backed off.

New reports came in from all over the city about flooding, power outages, and trees down across roads. Mayor Bellows scheduled a press conference for that evening, and everyone tried to surmise what the mayor would say about the developing disaster.

Iris's computer woke with a shake of her mouse. The screen held the results of the past few hours, but it would take a while to go through it all. She got started, digging through the numerous tweets, blog posts, and snapshots. She sent a few tweets and offered comments of her own, asking for help.

A text popped up on her phone. It was from Barry. He hadn't found Nimbus. She cursed and went back to what she was doing.

Hours passed and she started to form a clearer view of Nimbus's habits. Sometimes he was seen at a bar, other times on the street. Either as a cloud or the creepy man he was when he wasn't toxic. Sure enough, Iris uncovered sightings that put him near Cardy's Mart in Danville, just last night. From that, she focused her search and slowly followed a trail that led west.

The mayor's address began, and her co-workers crowded around the monitors set on the office walls.

It was already seven o'clock. Iris had barely moved since returning from the dive bar. Mayor Bellows tried to appear confident, but failed. He assured the people that the metahuman assaults would not last much longer. Decisive steps were being taken to safeguard the people of Central City. The crowd at the paper mocked the promises.

Iris returned her focus to her own social media feeds. The voices and views of thousands of citizens echoed across Central City, and she listened. It was one of those people who sent the information she was looking for.

A grainy photo that could've been a green cloud drifting past an alley. Something looked familiar. A shock rippled through her. She recognized the neighborhood next to her own. She zoomed in on the time stamp.

It had been taken five minutes earlier.

Her hand fumbled for her phone.

"Barry! He's going after Dad!"

1 6

Joe returned home to a dark, empty house. Neither of the kids was home.

Between his day job and his off-hours activities, it was a wonder if Barry got any rest at all. The kid was going to run himself ragged—that was his nature. Barry liked to claim that his parents or even Joe had instilled in him an unflagging sense of duty, but Joe knew better.

That was all Barry.

Maybe it stemmed from losing a parent. Joe had spent endless hours with him since the night his mother died, talking it through with the boy, the teenager, and the man. Barry claimed to understand that it hadn't been his fault, but while his mind might have come to accept the fact, his heart was another matter. A kernel of self-doubt always resonated.

Joe let out a gentle breath of frustration. Grief wasn't something to push past. There was no sense running away from it, because it would just follow. There was no expiration date on grieving. It became a part of you, and you had to make room for it or you would forever feel it inside you, like an invader. That was grief. He didn't know if Barry had made it to that point, and if he hadn't, Joe didn't know how to help.

Other than to be there for him.

He set his keys and his wallet on the foyer stand, hating the utter stillness of the house. Maybe they needed a cat or a dog, something to greet him when he came home. Given the crazy hours all of them kept, though, any pet would be left alone for much of the day. That wouldn't be fair to the animal.

Putting the thought aside, Joe headed for the kitchen to see if there was anything left for dinner. He should have stopped on the way home, picked up some take-out, but he'd been too tired.

Bending to peer into the refrigerator, he saw that all of the chicken cutlets were gone. Luckily there was still some sauce in the jar. With a little bit of pasta, that would make a quick meal that didn't require a lot of work.

He set water boiling on the stove and went upstairs to change. In the bedroom he didn't bother to turn on a light—there was plenty from the street. He yanked his holster off his belt, set it on the dresser, and reached for his badge. Then, in the stillness, he heard a soft creak on the stairs.

The door hadn't opened and closed, so most likely it was Barry, moving too fast for the ear to track. Joe turned, expecting to see the kid standing right there, grinning as usual.

But it wasn't Barry.

It was Kyle Nimbus.

"Detective West," the bald man said, dark shadows obscuring most of him as he stood in the bedroom door. "I've been waiting a long time for this."

Joe tensed at the appearance of the murderer in his house, freezing for an instant before his training kicked in.

"Sorry to have made you wait, Nimbus," Joe said. "I'm afraid I'll have to keep disappointing you, though." He stepped closer to the dresser and his hand shot out for the weapon that sat there.

"Oh, but you won't." Nimbus's lips curved into a vindictive smirk of victory. "I'm going to turn this crappy little bedroom into your very own gas chamber."

As Joe grabbed for his gun, the Mist dissolved into a green cloud of hydrogen cyanide. Firing two rounds, he realized the futility and flung himself on the other side of the bed, away from the billowing poison. He grabbed the edges of the bed sheet and he pulled it across in front of him, using it like a sail to disperse the cloud as much as possible as it moved toward him.

Nimbus couldn't hold his gaseous shape for long, which meant he was beatable if Joe could keep away from him. Still tendrils of smoke reached out. Joe punched the remote control for the ceiling fan, kicking it up into high speed. There wasn't enough spin to drive Nimbus away altogether, but it caused just enough dispersal for Joe to make a mad dash for the bedroom door.

He held his breath, dove over the bed, and ran through the haze.

Nimbus gathered himself and followed on the detective's heels. The writhing mass cascaded over the stairs in an effort to cut Joe off down below. The poison fell to the floor as if it had sudden weight, and then lifted, coalescing back into human form. The bald man's malevolent smirk made Joe's blood run cold.

He lifted his gun and fired. The bullet grazed Nimbus before it shattered a lamp across the room. He transformed and tendrils of smoke coiled again, swelling and reaching out.

The Flash's heart hammered as he veered down the street where he had played as a kid. Everything appeared serene, but he knew better. His house came into view. Through the front window he saw frantic motion, and an ominous dark green cloud filling in the foyer. Joe was barely visible just beyond it.

"Nimbus is here!" Flash shouted into his cowl mic. He didn't slow, and rammed the door with his shoulder, vibrating just enough to weaken the hinges. The heavy wooden panel flew off the jamb and straight through Nimbus, dispersing him.

Joe leapt to the side, rolled on the floor, and came up with his gun at the ready. The mist coalesced again, gathering in the doorway. The Flash zipped past to stand alongside Joe.

"That's enough, Nimbus!" he shouted.

"Not even close." The mist again took on human form. "Not by half. I'll have my revenge, and you're not going to stop me!" Leaping forward with a vicious growl, he devolved again into a cloud, sending it streaking toward the Flash and Joe.

But they weren't there.

Coming to a stop outside and down the block, the Flash reached out to steady Joe, who staggered a bit.

"Are you okay?" he asked. "Did you inhale any of it?"

"I don't think so." Joe shook his head. "How did you know?"

"Iris tracked him."

"I told her not—"

"She saved your life."

Joe stopped. "I'll thank her tonight." He smiled. "Right now, go get that psychopath before he hurts somebody."

"Water is heavier than gas." It was Cisco, his voice in Barry's ear. "Is there a water line nearby?" As he said it, Nimbus came running out through the open doorway, spotted them, and headed in their direction, a dark but solid form in the night.

Without a word the Flash moved to a red fire hydrant and vibrated the cap on the street side, spinning it off onto the pavement with a metallic *thud*. With blurring fingers, he spun the heavy bolt on top, sending a rush of water into the street.

Nimbus laughed. "Fat lotta good that's gonna do you, genius." He transformed again and green fumes billowed out, increasing in size.

The Flash thrust his arm out and spun it so fast it became a blur. Using the motion to direct it precisely, he turned the gusher into a wide-dispersal, high-speed spray that enveloped the entire cyanide cloud. Taking a page from the firefighters at the chemical fire, he used the driving force of the spray to batter Nimbus to the ground.

The thug reformed, becoming human. As he staggered the Flash pulled his arm out of the stream. This was his chance to take down the Mist. One solid hit was all he needed.

Joe moved toward Nimbus as well, running with his gun drawn.

A red blur streaked past, skidding through the cascading water to collapse with a pained grunt on the road near the hydrant, sliding several feet on the hard asphalt. The figure on the ground was...

Him. Again.

His older self pushed himself up onto his hands and knees. He looked up, blood smeared across his face.

"Run, Barry. He's coming."

A heavy grunt sounded from behind and the Flash turned. The gush had expanded, becoming a curtain of water and the shadow of something large lurked behind it. The huge shape roared from the darkness. Barry didn't have time to react. Brutally strong hands grasped his throat and pulled him forward. Small yellow eyes glared at him as a thin-lipped mouth opened to reveal long, pointed teeth.

Grodd!

The huge ape grunted, his voice like rough gravel.

"*Flash.*" Grodd's lips didn't move. "*You won't run now.*" The monstrous creature communicated through telepathy granted to him through horrifying experimentation, combined with the effects of the particle accelerator explosion.

The Flash took hold of the gorilla's forearms. They were like tree trunks and he couldn't budge them. He struggled to look down for the other Flash, but couldn't find him.

Abruptly he flew upward. Grodd lifted him over his hairy head and with a savage roar threw the Flash down the street. Careening through the air, the Flash spun his hands in tight circles, trying to create a vortex that would prevent him from crashing, and keep him away from the rampaging meta-ape. It didn't work.

His head cracked against a hard surface, and he collapsed into a shallow pool of water. A hard blow struck him and his vision darkened. In a panic, the Flash tried to focus. He couldn't leave Joe alone to face Grodd and Nimbus. He fought to stand on wobbly knees.

His vision returned and he recognized the slime-covered walls and a familiar cold stink of the sewer.

How?

A crashing blow landed on the back of his head,

and he smashed into the wall. His head bounced on the concrete and he collapsed to his knees in the fetid water. Thick fingers touched the Flash's shoulders.

Instantly he moved, slipping inside the giant outstretched hands, and his fists blurred red, pounding against dark fur. Blinding force battered the Flash to the ground again. He hit something soft, wondering if he was feeling his own bones being pulverized.

He forced his head to the side, and to his astonishment, he saw green. Beyond the huge bulk of Grodd stood trees, thick and lush. Shafts of dewy sunlight streamed from the deep forest canopy above. The gorilla settled heavily on his knuckles and looked around. He huffed gently.

"*Flash.*" Grodd's face was close to Barry's ear. The gorilla's stinking breath was hot and acrid. "*Stop running.*"

The Flash had to strike while he could. He pushed himself up, but Grodd's massive foot pressed onto Barry's back and shoved him down onto the damp ground. A powerful hand grasped his head and drove it into the mud, the taste of thick loam filling his mouth and throat.

He couldn't breathe. He desperately pushed back, frantic to find the air, but his face went deeper into the earth. Blackness surrounded him.

1 7

Joe ran as fast as he could. The kid had Nimbus on the ropes. The Flash's body vibrated. Lightning crawled over him, the electric spiders of energy that lived inside the speed force. They appeared almost alive as they moved.

He was a bright red blur that crackled with furious energy.

Only a few feet away, Kyle Nimbus stared in terror. Water drenched him, and he scrambled hastily to his feet. Joe fired his gun as a warning, then pointed it directly at the murderer.

"That's it, Flash!" he shouted. "Take him down!"

Spinning without hesitation, Nimbus raced down the street, ducking between parked cars. Another couple of shots, and Nimbus stumbled, but then Joe stopped, unwilling to put his neighbors at risk of being struck by a random bullet. The Flash could snatch him up without using lethal force.

But no red streak roared past Joe in pursuit of Nimbus.

Nothing.

Turning, he found the Flash frozen in place, his right arm pulled back as if arrested in the process of throwing a punch. His body vibrated so wildly that Joe couldn't even make out the features of the face he knew so well. Water from the hydrant passed through him as if he were a beam of scarlet light.

Joe could see his house through Barry's body.

Pocketing his gun, he moved to grab Barry by the shoulders, but his fingers closed on empty air. Thinking he had missed, he tried again. No. His hands were visible *inside* the blurry shape.

Horror washed over Joe, a helpless dread that rippled through him. Then he realized that his fingers were tingling, and *painfully*. He pulled his hands back, and the burning sensation stopped.

He stood helpless in the frigid cascade of water.

"Flash!" he shouted, hoping to get his attention. For a moment he had almost called him by name. Despite the danger, people were peering out windows and standing on porches.

Still Barry didn't react.

"Flash! Can you hear me? It's Joe!"

There! A subtle shift occurred, ever faint, but Joe took it as a sign that Barry was trying to come back.

"Fight! Don't give up!"

The blurring slowed, and suddenly he could see

eyes, wide and panicked. He grabbed Barry's face in both hands, and it was solid. Immediately his hands went numb, but he didn't let go.

"Slow it down," he said softly. The vibrations ceased, and the costumed form collapsed against Joe, who grabbed tighter, holding him upright.

"What… happened?" Barry gasped, clutching Joe's arms.

"I was about to ask you the same thing." Joe tried to guide him away from the hydrant that was drenching both of them in a cascading roar. He aimed for the house, wanting to get them both inside, away from prying eyes. He'd sort out an explanation later.

"Are you all right? Barry!" Joe heard frantic voices shouting over the Flash's comm. "What's going on?"

The Flash pulled back from Joe.

"Grodd," he said. "It was Grodd. Didn't you see him?" He looked around, confused.

"Here?" Joe frowned, and shook his head. "No. Grodd wasn't here. It was just you, me, and Nimbus."

"But I saw him," Barry insisted. "And the other Flash. The older one." He looked around helplessly.

"They weren't here, son," Joe replied. "It was just you. You froze up." He tried not to show panic. "I couldn't touch you."

"Grodd had me prisoner," Barry muttered. "In the sewer, and then in a jungle. He was crushing me."

"Look for yourself," Joe said. "There aren't any wounds." They stepped through the broken doorway.

"You were imagining it. You've been here the whole time."

"That can't be." Barry shoved his cowl back as he was led into the living room. Joe took his shoulder in a firm grip.

"Son, listen to me. You didn't go anywhere. You were here the whole time."

Barry's expression shifted from confusion to realization.

"It happened again." Barry looked utterly pale. "Just like at the warehouse fire. With Iris. Oh, damn..."

Joe guided him to the sofa. "Here. Sit down."

"What happened to Nimbus?"

"He took off. I'm guessing the water must've hurt him when he was in gaseous form. Plus I think I shot him when he was human. Unfortunately, it didn't take him down."

Barry sank into the sofa with a deep breath.

"We were lucky he ran," he said. "While I blurred out, he could've gone after you again."

"Well, he didn't." Joe walked over to where the door lay in the middle of the floor. "But this isn't about me anymore. What happened to you out there?" He propped the door in its frame, spotting a couple of folks in the street in front of the house. He heard sirens in the distance.

"Whatever it was, we'll fix it," Barry answered. "Caitlin and Cisco will figure out what to do."

"You can't be so easygoing about it, Bar." Joe turned to face him. "If you were a normal kid and you were sick, at least we'd be able to figure out what you had and then we'd have an idea what to do. But if something is going wrong with your power, there's no path to follow."

Barry opened his mouth to reply when Iris burst in, shoving the shattered front door onto the floor with a crash.

"Dad!" she said, stepping back with surprise. "Barry!" Then she propelled herself toward them.

"Iris, we're okay." Joe let his daughter crash against him, and he took her in his arms.

"When I saw that Nimbus was nearby—"

"It's all right." Joe let Iris go to where Barry sat on the couch. "We're both fine."

Barry smiled at her. "Nice work," he said. "If it wasn't for you, I'd have been too late." Then he paused. "There's something else, though…"

Iris studied Barry's expression. "It happened again, didn't it? I can see it in your eyes."

"Yeah." Joe picked up his wallet and keys from the debris in the foyer. "We're going to S.T.A.R. Labs. I want Caitlin to look at you."

"Let me fix the door first." Barry came to his feet, pulling up his cowl.

"Barry, I don't want you—" Joe hadn't even finished when the door was back in place, not quite good as new but solid.

"—to use your speed till we know what's wrong." The Flash stood in the foyer, moving the door back and forth and looking smug. Then he turned to face them.

"I'll meet you at S.T.A.R. Labs."

"What happens if you blur on the way?" Joe argued. "We won't know where you are."

"Cisco can track my route." Into the comm, he said, "Right?"

"Roger that," Cisco said.

"Besides, I have to leave as the Flash, and you have to be here when the police arrive," Barry said. "Don't worry. I'll meet you at the lab."

"We'll see you there," Iris said, settling the matter before Joe could protest further. Her arm snaked through her father's.

Joe knew when he was licked. "Fine. Just be careful."

"Thank you for your assistance, Detective West," the Flash called out, stepping onto the porch. Sirens could be heard in the distance. He darted away, pausing at the still-open hydrant and shutting it off. Then he disappeared into the night.

Joe shook his head, leaning against the doorframe.

"How long is that boy going to pretend nothing is wrong?"

"I know." Iris sighed, and then studied her father. "Are you all right?"

"Yeah, why shouldn't I be?"

"Well, you *were* just attacked by a metahuman?"

Joe bobbed his head. "Oh yeah," he said. "I'm good." He turned and headed back inside. "Come on, let's get ready. I'll call dispatch and let them know the black-

and-whites don't need to bother. Then we can head over to S.T.A.R. Labs. I want to hear what Caitlin says."

He stopped, and kissed Iris on the cheek.

"Thanks for whatever you did to warn Barry about Nimbus. It was probably dangerous, so don't tell me about it right now, but I appreciate it."

"You're welcome, Dad."

By the time they arrived, Caitlin already had Barry sitting on her diagnostic bed with his long legs dangling over the side. His chest was bare, sensors were stuck to his body, and her monitor was processing the information.

Joe paced back and forth as she drew blood, while Barry gave Joe a reassuring smile. Iris stood off to the side with her arms folded across her chest. Her tremendous patience was a constant annoyance to Joe. Even when she was younger, nothing ever seemed to faze her. Not exams, not the news… not even the loss of her mother. Iris just focused on the moment, and always met it head on.

While Joe was a nervous wreck, she remained a pillar of calmed assurance.

Caitlin, on the other hand, wore an intense expression as she went from one task to the next.

"We'll see if there are traces in your blood," she said.

"Traces of what?" Joe came closer.

"Well, this soon after the latest event, I'm hoping it will have left some sort of marker." Caitlin took the vials of blood to a workstation against the wall and dropped them into the centrifuge. "Some indication of a chemical imbalance or foreign agent."

"And if not?" Joe asked anxiously.

"I'm going to run a CAT scan and MRI." Caitlin offered a reassuring smile at Joe. "I'll find the answer, Detective West. I promise."

Joe nodded. "I know, Doctor. It's just that we know so little about Barry's speed—all we've got are guesses."

Caitlin stopped and stared at him.

"I don't make guesses," she said.

Joe shook his head apologetically. "I don't mean that. I just, I mean—"

"What he's trying to say," Barry interjected, "is that studying a metahuman involves brand new science. We have a limited data set."

"That's what makes it kind of exciting." Cisco swept in with a tray of sub sandwiches. "It's frontier science—this is the wild, wild west... so to speak."

"This is my son we're talking about," Joe growled. "It's not *exciting*. We have got to do better. We have to learn faster."

Taken aback, Cisco offered an apologetic shrug as he handed the sandwiches to Barry.

"Thanks, Cisco, you're a life saver," Barry exclaimed, taking the platter and digging in. "I'm starving."

"Little wonder," Caitlin said. "Your reserves are dramatically depleted."

"Reserves?" Joe watched Barry devour his first sub. Even without superspeed, he ate like a starving wolf.

"Barry's metabolism burns at an extreme rate," Caitlin explained, "which is why he's always hungry after he taps into the speed force. At the moment, he appears to be running on empty."

"Why would that be?" Barry said through a mouthful of roast beef. "It all happened pretty quickly, and I've taken lots worse beatings before. I was worried about Joe, so that added to the stress, I guess."

"Hmm." Caitlin studied the data stream on her screen. "It must be these glitches—or the *blur*, if you prefer—consuming your energy. And the rate is pretty alarming."

Cisco examined some of the readouts. His usual happy countenance was replaced with a frown.

"Seriously," he agreed. "He's like got nothing in the tank. How are you even awake?"

"Too hungry to sleep," Barry confessed. "I could use some more sandwiches. Or maybe some pizzas? I could eat like a dozen or so pies."

"Whatever you like, Barry." Caitlin nodded to Cisco, but Iris stepped in.

"I can order them. You two keep working." She grabbed her credit card and smartphone, and shot Barry a look. "You just stay where you are."

"Hey, I feel fine," Barry insisted as he unwrapped another sandwich. "Really."

"Maybe," Caitlin said, but she didn't sound convinced.

Joe sighed, taking Barry by the shoulder. "Don't fight it, Bar. We've got you outnumbered."

18

"What were you *doing*, Nimbus?" Mardon demanded. "Rathaway told you to stay away from Joe West." He glared over a glass of bourbon. "Besides, I want a piece of him, too."

Nimbus poured another drink for himself. He slumped in a chair, sullen and angry. He rubbed his bald head with rough hands and muttered.

"Mind your own business," he growled.

Roy Bivolo sat at the table, too. He chuckled while leaning back, amused by the two criminals snarling at each other.

"Rathaway's going to have your head," he said with barely disguised glee.

Shawna, on the other hand, ignored the bickering while she searched a cabinet for something to eat. She opened a jar of peanut butter only to find that it had been scraped clean. She shoved it back in the cupboard and continued her search.

The stockpile of groceries they'd stored up at the beginning of the caper was running low. A mound of dirty dishes filled the sink, the marble countertops were stained and covered with used pots, and the trash overflowed onto the expensive tile floor. She'd spent time lying low with petty criminals before, and was reminded that men, left to themselves, were content to live like animals.

If they think I'm going to clean this up, they can screw themselves. Behind an empty box of cereal she discovered a protein bar, lying forgotten, so she pounced on it.

Mardon yanked the bottle away from Nimbus. "What gives you the right to take out West, all by your lonesome? It's my brother he killed."

"Your brother, and *me*," Nimbus growled. "He put me in the gas chamber."

"Crap, will you let that go?" Mardon said. "You got out. And besides, you deserved it. You killed like what, ten guys?"

Nimbus clutched the edges of what had once been a beautiful mahogany table, now gouged and stained and burned.

"What do you know?" he said darkly. "I ought to let you see what it feels like—to have nothing to breathe but poison gas. You start to cough, and choke, and then you can't draw a breath. You just sit there, completely aware, knowing you're going to die."

Wham! Shawna slammed the cabinet.

"So why didn't you kill this West guy, if you're so stone cold?" she growled. When Nimbus and Mardon stared at her like an unwelcome interruption, she crossed her arms in defiance. "You two sit around and brag how badass you are, but you can't take out one cop. Sounds pretty lame to me."

Nimbus glared. "You don't know how it was. I woulda had West, but the Flash showed up."

Bivolo angled his head toward Shawna. "What do you know about anything, girl?" he asked. "Without a man to back you up, you might want to keep your nose out of things that don't involve you." He sneered toward the Mist. "The Flash showed up. And Nimbus got scared. End of story."

She raised her eyebrows.

He's doing this just to mess with them.

"You'll want to keep your nose out of *my* business, Bivolo," she said flatly. "I could teleport you out to the middle of the lake and just leave you there. Next time you call me *girl*, that's exactly what I'll do. Got it?"

Mardon scoffed, "The Flash? I could've had him at the warehouse fire. He was in my sights."

"Sure you could," Bivolo spat. "You've had your shot at the Flash, and got nothing."

Shawna laughed. "Without me, you wouldn't be here to gripe," she said. "The Flash would've shown up, carried out a bunch of dangerous chemicals, put out the fire, signed autographs for a buncha orphans, and still had time to drop you bums off in prison."

Nimbus growled like an animal. "Nobody's ever going to put me in a cell again," he said. "You hear that? I'll kill anybody who tries."

Mardon rolled his eyes. "So what did the Flash do to keep you from offing West?"

Nimbus started to answer, then he stopped and seemed to be thinking.

That's gotta hurt, Shawna thought wryly.

"He... uh... he did this thing I never saw before." That piqued her interest.

"What was it?" Shawna pressed.

Again Nimbus rubbed his ratlike head.

"He was all... *blurry*. You know. Blurry."

"He does that a lot," she said. "And then what?"

"And then? Well, he kinda... he was like almost transparent. Just standing there like he was building up all kinds of power. Like a wrestler coming off the top rope."

"Yeah?" Mardon squinted suspiciously. "So what did he do? How did he beat you?"

Nimbus looked from Mardon to Shawna to Bivolo, as if searching for sympathy. They all stared silently. His mouth hung open.

"I... uh... I wasn't about to find out."

"You left?" Bivolo barked. "You *ran*?"

Shawna snorted. "The fearsome Mist. You're so scared of the Flash you just split. So he didn't *do* anything?"

"He was going to!" Nimbus protested, his words slurred. "You weren't there. None of you! You didn't see him. He was ready to drop some kind of superspeed vortex lightning punch, or something like that."

Mardon sat there, wide-eyed, and looked at Bivolo. Suddenly both men broke out in laughter. Shawna couldn't help herself, and joined in with a chuckle that suddenly burst into a deep guffaw. Before she knew it, she was doubled over at the waist, laughing so hard she couldn't stand straight.

Nimbus pushed back from the table, fuming.

Bivolo stood up with his fist raised. "A superspeed vortex lightning punch!" He then turned slowly and drove his fist toward Mardon, inch by inch, until the knuckles gently touched his chin. Mardon threw himself backward out of his seat in slow motion.

Shawna laughed harder, nearly losing her footing as Mardon rolled against the wall with make-believe force. He looked up from his spot, sprawled on the floor.

"Great plan, Mist—running away before the Flash even does anything. You've really taken Rathaway to heart."

Nimbus sat quivering with rage. His features grew indistinct and went a sickly green.

"Nimbus!" Hartley Rathaway shouted from the kitchen door. "Don't."

The Mist's features fused again, and his color returned to normal. Rathaway peered curiously at Mardon on the floor before turning back to him.

"Despite my direct orders," he said, "you went after Detective West."

"Orders?" Nimbus snarled. "I don't take orders. You're not my boss."

"Actually I am. As long as you're on this team, you will do as I say. Do I have to teach you another lesson?"

"As long as you're under my roof, young man..." Mardon stood up with a smirk. "...you'll live by my rules."

Rathaway regarded Weather Wizard coldly.

"Essentially, yes," he said, looking angry at being mocked. "There's nothing funny about this. Nothing funny at all. Your incompetence could have derailed all of my careful plans."

Shawna snickered. "Yeah, one good superspeed vortex lightning punch and it's game over."

"This isn't a joke, Shawna," Rathaway scolded.

She drew back, annoyed with his attitude. "I know that, Rathaway, but come on—no harm, no foul." She leaned against the counter.

"Yeah, she's right." Mardon moved to the table to stand near Nimbus. "Lighten the hell up. I should've done the same thing, going after Joe West, but Nimbus had the guts to do it."

Rathaway frowned. "You *won't* do the same thing. You will do as I say, if you want to be rich." He paused, then continued. "We're entering a new phase of the operation, and it's essential that we work together. We're going to ramp up the pressure on Central City."

"What's the point?" Bivolo raised both hands dismissively. "How's this going to make us rich? We're not stealing anything, not since the museum. We're not making any demands. We're not taking out the Flash. What kind of two-bit scam are we running here?"

"The smart kind." Rathaway narrowed his eyes. "The kind none of you have ever been involved in before."

Bivolo just cursed and turned away. Mardon shook his head and actually slapped a friendly hand on the Mist's shoulder.

"C'mon, Nimbus—let's do our drinking elsewhere."

Nimbus's head jerked up. "Yeah, sure," he said. "This kitchen stinks, and it ain't the dirty dishes."

Rathaway stood aside from the door. "Tomorrow morning at eight. Be here to prepare for the next phase."

Mardon picked up the bottle of bourbon.

"Sure thing, but if we're not here, Hartley, you be sure to wait for us." He grabbed several glasses between his fingers, and said with an upper-class flourish, "Mr. Bivolo? Ms. Baez? Drinks on the veranda."

Bivolo rose without comment and joined the other two men as they walked out. As they passed Rathaway, Nimbus stopped and turned.

"You gotta sleep sometime."

Mardon laughed deep. "Nah, not Hartley. He stays up twenty-four seven, being smart."

Shawna hesitated. She had no real desire to hang with these guys, but she liked the sympathy Mardon had displayed. Looking at Rathaway, she was surprised to see a faint smile on his lips.

Well, I'll be damned.

He had played them. He turned a group of bickering

malcontents into drinking buddies. Most likely he was playing her, too. Knowing that gave her an advantage the others didn't have. She knew she could play chess with Rathaway whenever she wished.

For the moment, however, she felt like she wanted to be a part of the gang. So she pushed off the cluttered counter, and followed the guys out.

"Traffic alert on the City Center Bridge."

"Hang on. I'm doing another building check." The Flash completed the run-through of every room in a ten-story apartment building. It had been a long day of chasing disasters, after the stressful night of the Mist's attack on Joe. This was the fourth lightning fire he had addressed today. Weather Wizard had been busy, but the Flash still hadn't found him at any of the scenes.

He carried the weather wand with him most of the time now, in case he encountered Mardon in person again.

Content that the building was empty of people, the Flash ran down the stairs and halted on the sidewalk amid coiled hoses and pooling water. He gave fire and rescue crews a thumbs up. A group of people gathered outside the cordoned area.

"When are you going to stop all this, Flash?" one shouted.

"My business is underwater!" another yelled.

"What are we supposed to do?" a third demanded.

"I'm sorry." The Flash held up his hands apologetically. "I'm doing everything I can."

"Get those metahumans, and put them behind bars!" It wasn't so much a cheer as an angry order.

"I will. I promise," he said. "I have to go. I'm sorry." He touched his comm. "What sort of traffic alert?"

"Not sure," Cisco said, "but this isn't a fender bender."

"Okay, on my way." The Flash streaked south.

A river with several bridges stretching across it bisected Central City. The most important one ran from City Center to the crowded residential and business district of Lawrence Hills. It was always busy, and frequently gridlocked. However, the problem wasn't rush hour.

Cars littered the bridge, crumpled and battered, some moving and some not. Smoke filled the air. Horns blared. Voices shouted. Doors were flung open and people fought in the middle of the highway.

The Flash sighed. Prism was here.

He raced into the melee, quickly pulling aside two men wrestling on the yellow line just before they were crushed beneath the tires of a sedan spewing steam from under its hood. He weaved through traffic, slipping cars into neutral, taking car keys through open windows, and removing the odd lug wrench from angry hands.

A black Hummer roared past, nearly clipping

him. The Flash caught up to the massive SUV, racing up onto its roof. He clutched the luggage rack and dropped his face into the driver's-side window. The driver furiously texted with both hands and steered the monster vehicle with his knees.

"Hey!" the Flash shouted. "Stop texting, and hit the brakes!"

"Shut up!" the man bellowed back. "I'm going to miss the matinee!" At that the Flash gripped the doorframe and reached inside. He pulled the phone from the driver's grip and lobbed it over the side of the bridge.

"Hey, you jerk!" Finally the driver stomped on the brakes, causing the Flash to seize the rack to prevent being catapulted over the hood. The Hummer skidded to a screeching stop. "That was my phone!"

The Flash dropped to the ground. The driver, scarlet-faced with rage, yanked open the glove compartment and drew out a handgun. The Flash delivered a sharp blow to the center of the steering wheel. The airbag exploded outward with a bang, and slammed the guy back against the plush leather seat. He grunted and sat stunned, covered in white dust.

The Flash wrenched the pistol away, and it joined the cell phone in the river far below.

Another car roared past. The Flash raced after it and put a vibrating hand through a rear tire, causing the sedan to flop to a harmless crawl before it could slam into a pile of vehicles that blocked most of the lanes.

From the middle of the bridge, the Flash spotted a familiar figure halfway toward the far end. Roy Bivolo strolled away from him, down the center lane with his arms wide, catching the eyes of oncoming drivers. When cars passed, they immediately accelerated or veered into their neighbors. Drivers screamed out of their windows and leaned on their horns.

The Flash took off toward him, but didn't make it far. Stopping several more collisions, he finally pulled a flailing woman free of her out-of-control car and set her on her feet, just so she could try to kick him. Dodging easily, he turned back toward Bivolo, who was only twenty yards away. The next wave of oncoming cars waited at a red light.

"Bivolo!" the Flash shouted. He touched a small switch on the left side of his cowl. Colored lenses slid down to cover his eyes. A gift from Cisco. The lenses fired color sequences into Barry's retinas, thus blocking Bivolo's power to spark an emotional response in anyone who looked him in the eye. Unfortunately the lenses hadn't been tested.

When Prism spun to face the Flash, Barry reacted out of habit and looked down to avoid eye contact. The lenses flashed colors in quick succession. The effect was slightly nauseating.

"What's the matter, Flash?" Prism called out. "Can't stand the sight of me? Come on. Run on down here. See if you can do it without looking me in the eye."

The Flash took a deep breath and lifted his head.

He stared straight into Bivolo's eyes. The world tinted with red, orange, yellow, green, blue, and purple hues. Bivolo grinned—

—and the Flash grinned back.

Bivolo stiffened, and glanced up toward the bridge tower. The Flash streaked toward him and landed a solid punch. Bivolo flew off his feet, bouncing on the pavement. Barry wasn't a violent person by nature, but he still found it very satisfying to finally get his knuckles on one of the bad guys.

"Okay, Prism. Time's up." The Flash walked leisurely toward him where he lay in the road, rubbing his jaw. "You've only got one trick, and it's not working. I guess your super-villain days are over."

Bivolo lifted his arm.

A black haze appeared next to him. Shawna Baez stood there. Glancing up, she grabbed Bivolo's hand, and they were gone.

The Flash looked up in the direction Peekaboo had glanced. High above the deck, the two metas clutched precariously to a tower platform. The fastest way to reach them was a suspension cable.

Jumping on the narrow steel coil, the Flash ran up the slope toward the tower's platform, where he found Bivolo and Shawna, looking terrified. The wind battered them on their narrow perch. When the Flash neared, a whoosh of smoke appeared again.

He was alone.

The two materialized down on the bridge just as

another wave of traffic approached. The Flash raced back down the steel cable and came within an inch of seizing Bivolo before he vanished again, leaving behind the sound of metal crunching and squealing tires.

Through a wasteland of scattered cars, a pickup truck rammed the front end of a small economy model and shoved it toward the side of the bridge. Despite its smoking brakes, the small vehicle crashed against the railing. The woman at the wheel screamed—not in fear but in anger. The truck just revved its powerful engine and smashed the car over the rail, sending it into the air.

"Guys, I got a car over the side of the bridge," Barry called into his mic. "I'm going to get her." He shot past the truck, stopping to grab the keys and pitch them away. Bolting through the crushed railing, he ran along a girder, then plunged down a support beam and out onto the surface of the river. He sped along the water until he saw the small blue car, seeming to hang in the air above him.

He circled beneath the car, running around and around on the surface, creating an updraft that slowed the vehicle's fall. The rising air drew water with it, and a spout lifted into the sky. He had to regulate his speed carefully to prevent a hard cannon of water from slamming against the underside of the car.

The waterspout struck the vehicle, bouncing it upright and level. The Flash slowed down so the spout would begin to drop, lowering the car with it.

He grinned to himself, pleased with his makeshift elevator, until he saw that the car's windows were open and the geyser was flooding it. The woman at the wheel thrashed, trying to escape the water that was drenching her.

With the car only fifteen feet above the river, he dropped his speed again and let the updraft weaken. His feet lost traction, causing him to stumble. The geyser collapsed and brought the car down. The Flash threw himself out of the way, but the edge of the undercarriage caught his right arm and a knife of pain shot through him, making him cry out.

The blow pushed him under the water. Above his head, the car splashed into the river and bobbed like a foundering boat. The Flash broke the surface with a gasping breath.

"Barry, are you all right?" Caitlin asked in his ear.

"I-I think I broke my arm," he gritted. "By the way, how long does it take a car to sink?" He swam awkwardly for the passenger's side. Pain shot through him every time he moved his right arm.

"Too many variables. There's no set rule for it," Cisco replied.

"How is the driver?" Caitlin asked. "Can she get out on her own?"

The Flash bobbed next to the open passenger window. The driver was stunned, but seemed uninjured. She showed no cuts on her face; there was no blood.

"Ma'am, can you hear me?" he called. "Are you all right?"

She looked at him with a blank expression. She appeared to be about forty and in good physical shape. The river water sluiced into the car through the window, already coming up to her abdomen. She was sinking quickly.

He swiftly swam around to the driver's side. As the water began to lap at her neck, she jerked frantically at her seatbelt. She pulled it away from her chest and tried to struggle out, but it only snapped back tighter. Her breath turned ragged. She was either going to hyperventilate, or swallow a lot of water.

The Flash pressed his hands against the door and vibrated. Unexpectedly, the force propelled him through the water away from the car. He swam back. The driver started shouting for help. The Flash held onto the car with one hand and shattered the lock with the other.

The water slapped at their jawlines. The driver pressed against the roof of the car, trying to stay in open air.

"Ma'am!" the Flash said firmly. "I need you to take a deep breath. You'll be fine, but take a deep breath." Her panicked eyes latched onto his. She sucked in a lungful of air. He smiled. "Take a deep breath. I'm going to—"

The river swallowed them.

Barry hadn't taken a breath himself. He could

surface again, but he couldn't let the driver think he was abandoning her. With his lungs already tight, he grasped the door. The sinking car had a weird bulky weight. Bracing one foot on the frame, he wrenched the door open. The driver tried to surge out, but her seatbelt still held her.

The Flash wedged himself between her thrashing body and the steering wheel. She clawed at his back, trying to use him for leverage to push herself away. Even in the daylight, it was dark under the surface. His chest was on fire, and grinding pain shot through his body. He had to use his left arm to feel along the edge of the seat for the safety belt release.

He touched the metal latch, and pressed.

Nothing happened.

"Barry, what's going on?" Caitlin said urgently.

He tugged on the belt, trying to force it loose, then seized it in his left hand and vibrated. At last the metal buckle came apart in his hand.

The Flash pushed himself back. The seatbelt still threatened to tangle him and the driver, who sat motionless now. Her dark hair floated around her face. His own vision sparked and dimmed. Limbs turned sleepy and thick, but he still took her by the shoulders, pulling her out of the car.

He wondered which way was up.

In the dark, he made out the roof of the car and trusted that it was still oriented correctly. He kicked away and swam, holding the driver tight against his chest with his searing right arm. He didn't know if he was going in the right direction. He didn't know if he was using his speed. He should have been at the surface by now.

His vision dimmed. Barry fought to keep his mouth closed, to suppress the savage urge to draw in a deep breath.

Kick. Trust in the direction.

Just another second. Keep kicking.

His face hit a wave of cold. Light surrounded him. He hesitated to breathe because he didn't trust it. He saw what looked like the bridge and the skyline of Central City.

Throwing open his mouth he dragged in a rasping breath. The woman flopped helplessly against him. He angled her face out of the water. Her eyes were rolled up and her lips were blue. The Flash clutched her to his chest and swam for the shore, kicking up a violent wake, as if a speedboat was roaring across the river.

"Are you all right?" Caitlin cried. "What's going on?"

But he couldn't manage to speak yet. Soon his legs scraped the bottom. With a shock of pain, he carried the woman out of the water onto a rocky area under one of the bridge's great steel pilings.

"Barry! Answer me!"

His legs wobbled and he dropped to his knees next to the sodden woman. He couldn't find a heartbeat.

"She's not breathing. I've got to do CPR."

"Couldn't you get her to a hospital faster?" Caitlin asked.

"Can't carry her. I've got a broken arm, and I can barely walk. No time to wait."

"Barry, do you have enough control? If you try chest compression, you could shatter bone."

"She's going to die if I don't do something." The Flash put a hand to her slack face. "Hang on, I've got an idea." With one hand, he pulled her closer to the girder. Then he tensed, as if preparing to run, but he stayed locked in place. Power surged up through his body. Nerves fired. Muscles filled. Energy crackled into his system. The air sparked.

"Barry," Caitlin said, "lightning could kill her, too."

He didn't respond. If he did nothing, she would die. This was his best bet. The power roared through him, threatening to escape his weakened control. Crackling energy popped off his arms and legs. It was going to burst out, whether he wanted it to or not.

Reaching out, he grabbed the steel strut. A ripple of lightning coursed down his arm and into the rusty piling with a deafening crack. At the same time, he held his right hand over the woman's chest. Spiders of electricity arced from his fingertips into her body. She spasmed off the ground, held in a white-hot glow. Her eyes flew open. When she fell back into the gravel, her mouth parted and she spit up water.

Barry dropped beside her, and heard her take several quick breaths before she coughed into a regular rhythm. She let her head fall to the side and her eyes met his. She blinked and closed her eyes. He took her wrist, and found a steady pulse.

"She's alive," he muttered. "Send an EMS team to our location."

"They're already on the way," Cisco said. "Good work, doctor." A moment later he added, "It looks like Prism is gone."

"It's just as well," the Flash replied, "because I can't move."

2 0

Barry jerked awake, and found himself in the corner of the Cortex. The lights were always at the same level, so he didn't know if it was night or day. He remained still, pondering why he was sitting on the floor. Two blankets lay draped over him. He stretched his legs out in front of him. They were red.

He was wearing the Flash suit.

The sound of gently tapping keys and the constant background hum seeped into his hearing.

I should get up, he thought. When he moved, he only saw one hand. *Oh my God! I've lost an arm!*

Then he saw his right limb restrained in a sling, and everything swept back into place. The car in the river. His broken arm. Flexing his fingers, he didn't feel any sharp pain. He reached up to pull the sling off over his head. His muscles ached, and he groaned.

A chair squeaked. "Barry? You awake?" It was Cisco.

"Yeah." Barry pushed himself to his feet as his friend rushed to help him. He stood, gingerly testing his limits. A bit weak, but even that was slowly passing. "How long have I been out?"

"Not long enough." Cisco steadied Barry, watching him carefully before stepping back. "Five hours. You came back from the bridge, Caitlin took blood and put your arm in a sling. Then you sat down in the corner and went out like a light."

"So you left me lying on the floor?"

Cisco shrugged guiltily. "We were afraid that if we woke you, you'd rush out again." The young man's expression held actual worry.

"Five hours is too long for me to be out of action." Barry tested his right arm. Stiff, but pain free. He went to the main computers, moving slowly. "Where do I need to be?"

"Nowhere right now," Cisco insisted. "Just chill, man. I haven't logged any meta activity in hours. Nothing since you came back from the bridge." Then he grinned and held up a small cylinder about five inches long. "This might make you happy—it's a working prototype for an anti-Prism strobe, a portable version of the color sequencer we used on you when he whammied you last time. This little beauty should reverse the rage effect in anyone he's already hit."

"That could be really useful," Barry said. "Do we have a couple hundred of them?"

"I wish. This is our only one, and we don't know yet

if it works. You have to be pretty close to the victim for it to be effective."

"At this rate, I'm going to need a backpack to carry all my anti-villain gear. I remember when being fast was enough." Barry bent backward, stretching his spine. "Where's Caitlin?"

"In the medical lab working on your tests."

"Has she slept at all in the last few days?"

"I don't know, but I'd bet she hasn't." Cisco moved back into the bright lights of his workstation, and Barry winced at the sight of his swollen nose and eyes, still bruised purple.

"What about you? You still look like hell."

"Gee, thanks," Cisco said. "I'm fine. Really. We Ramons are a handsome but strong people. Don't worry about me."

"Okay." Barry rubbed his hands together. "Well, while the metas are napping, I'll take over Caitlin's lab work so she can get some rest. I wouldn't mind some relaxing science, moving at normal human speed, with a minimum of punching."

As he turned to leave, Caitlin came walking down the ramp from the med lab. She carried a thick stack of papers and a tablet. Dark circles rested beneath her eyes. Deep creases hung along her mouth. Her clothes were disheveled, and she had tied her hair up in a hasty bun that was coming undone. When she saw Barry, she straightened with alarm.

"What are you doing?" she asked quickly. "How's

your arm? I didn't tell you to take the sling off."

"It's fine." Barry waved his right arm vigorously, causing Caitlin to freeze in terror. "See?"

"Stop it!" she scolded loudly. "Stop doing things. For once. Why do you always have to *do* things?"

He offered a worried smile. "I'm sorry. I am fine though." When her eyes flicked to the papers she held in her hand, he added, "Aren't I?"

She took a deep breath. "I'd prefer to wait before we discuss this."

"Wait for what?" A knot started to form in his stomach.

"For us, I think." Joe's voice came from the door as he and Iris entered. They were both a little out of breath, as if they had rushed over. They regarded Caitlin before pinning Barry with pained looks.

"You called Joe and Iris?" Barry tensed. "You found something. What is it? Just tell me."

Caitlin plugged in the tablet and swiped the screen a few times. Around the room, screens flared to life with a video that showed quivering blood cells. They looked normal, if a little hyperactive.

"Barry, these are your erythrocytes, from a blood sample I took six months ago, and retained for reference."

He watched the screen. "They look fine. What am I missing?"

"Nothing. These do look perfectly fine." She tapped the tablet, and another image appeared. "This is from the blood I took a few hours ago."

In the new image, the red blood cells were moving much faster, careening against one another almost as if on the attack. A yellowish substance seeped through the extracellular matrix between the blood cells. It appeared to be pulsing.

Suddenly a thin lance of yellow pierced one of the healthy cells. The red oval vibrated rapidly, and then blurred out to near invisibility. In an instant the once healthy hemoglobin was replaced by a lifeless, colorless shape. As they all watched, more cells sickened, until finally the entire screen was a yellowish mass.

Barry glanced over his shoulder. Caitlin restarted the loop and he stepped closer to the screen. He'd never seen anything like it, and his scientific mind found it fascinating. He had no idea what the strange fluid could be.

"What the hell is it?" Joe exclaimed. The fear in his voice brought Barry back to reality. He was looking at his own blood, not a random sample or a classroom exercise. He tried to calm his adoptive father by putting the science above the emotion. He crossed his arms and theorized.

"Whatever it is, it's a fluid of some sort."

Caitlin shook her head.

"Actually, it's not," she responded. "It's plasma. Not blood plasma. Plasma."

"Plasma?" Barry signaled her to run it again. "As in one-of-the-four-states-of-matter plasma? How is that possible?"

Caitlin tapped the tablet and the screen changed to a swirling mass—a whirlpool of sorts. A vast wormhole. It spun slowly. Then the camera pulled back to reveal an accretion disc around the mass, and chunks of flotsam flew toward it to join the circling wreckage. The edge of a building was visible in the corner of the screen. A red streak flashed past and surged up toward the swirling black disc, using the flying rubble as stepping stones. The red streak began to roar around the wormhole, creating a fantastic, crackling field of energy.

This was a shot from one of S.T.A.R. Labs's external cameras. It was the huge swirling wormhole that had formed in the sky when the Flash had used Eobard Thawne's time-travel technology to go back to try to save his mother.

Iris and Caitlin shared a glance. That was the day each of them lost the man they loved. Eddie Thawne, Iris's boyfriend, had killed himself in order to wipe Eobard out of the timeline.

On the screen, while the Flash raced in a crackling circle around the wormhole, a fiery trail roared into view, and Caitlin moaned softly. It was Firestorm, a metahuman hero composed of the atomic union of two different men—Dr. Martin Stein and Ronnie Raymond.

Raymond had been Caitlin's husband. Firestorm was enormously powerful, yet when he helped the Flash shut down the wormhole, Ronnie didn't survive the ensuing explosion.

Caitlin's hand snaked out and she tapped the tablet.

On the monitors around the room, the wormhole froze. Barry quickly turned the conversation back toward something she could handle.

"So you're saying the plasma in my blood sample is associated with that temporal anomaly?"

"Yes." Caitlin shook herself, and focused on the lab results. "It has the same signature. You are infected with plasma from the singularity that almost destroyed Central City."

"But why is it in my blood?"

"I don't know. You and Dr. Stein both came into contact with the wormhole, but when I tested his blood, there was nothing like it there."

Joe stepped forward. "You didn't detect it in Barry until now either, but it has to have been there since the wormhole was closed. Why is it just showing up?" His questions almost sounded like accusations.

"You're right." Caitlin remained calm. "The anomalous energy *was* in Barry's blood, ever since… that day. And I never saw it until now."

"But why?" Barry asked, keeping his tone neutral. "The wormhole incident was months ago. I've had blood tests since then, and there's been no wormhole plasma. Why now?"

"That's the question, all right," she agreed. "Something had to have acted as a catalyst, and since you haven't been injected with any unknowns, it had to have come from within your own system. In order to find out what it was, I had to replicate it.

"So I took some of the sample—" She tapped the screen and a shot of normal blood cells appeared again. "—the one from six months ago, and introduced various elements. This is the result." Another tap, and the weird plasma reappeared.

"What did you use?" Barry moved to the desk and started scanning the data.

"Cortisol."

Barry furrowed his brow. "Cortisol?"

"Specifically *your* cortisol, which, like much of your biology, is different from the average person's. I was able to extract a useable amount from the blood and urine samples we have in storage. When the cortisol was introduced into the seemingly healthy blood sample… *voila*." She finished with a flourish, then looked self-conscious.

"Oh, man," Cisco breathed, "that's a fight-or-flight hormone."

"But," Barry countered, "everyone has cortisol in their system, all the time. Including me. I still don't get it—why is this happening now?"

Caitlin leaned against the control panel. "As with any disease, the pathogen—if I can refer to the plasma that way—grows inside the host. Often the host won't experience any symptoms until the disease reaches a point where it impacts normal body functions. You seem to have reached that point."

Iris stared at her.

"Caitlin, it sounds like you're talking about cancer."

2 1

Barry tried to stay calm, and thought he was succeeding until he realized he was flipping pages at superspeed. He cleared his throat, set the lab results back in order, and pretended to stare at the overhead screen.

His heart beat heavily against his chest.

Caitlin bit her lip and held up a cautious hand. "There are words we don't want to use here because Barry's metahuman physiology makes them truly meaningless. We are *not* talking about cancer. All we know is that there is an anomalous substance in Barry's blood, and perhaps other systems of his body. And we know that it is inducing a physiological symptom—the blurring effect. Most likely this plasma is interacting with his use of the speed force. We need to study it, and find a way to remove it."

"Did you test blood samples from before the wormhole occurred?" Barry asked.

"Yes. There is no sign of the plasma in those."

"What *is* cortisol?" Joe asked in frustration. "We're not all chemists here."

Caitlin proceeded again with calm precision. "Cortisol is a hormone that is released in the body in response to signals from a neurotransmitter such as epinephrine. It happens when the human body is under stress. It's very common."

Joe rubbed his face. "If it's caused by stress, it's sure common in me right now."

Barry laughed, moving to Joe's side and putting an arm around the man's shoulders. Joe smiled and placed a hand on the back of Barry's head, suppressing a deep sigh.

Caitlin nodded in sympathy. "I'm sure that's true of all of us."

"But, Caitlin," Barry said, "if this blurring thing is triggered by stress, why isn't it happening all the time? Why aren't I blurring right this second? Because I don't mind telling you, Doctor, I'm a little tense."

"I don't know." Caitlin looked as if she had a bad taste in her mouth. She placed a hand on the stack of lab results, riffling them with her thumb. Despite her professional demeanor, the weight of the unknown dragged down her voice. Having to say she didn't know clearly hurt her. "Apparently it's not that straightforward. There could be a cascade of effects. The spread of the plasma might be keyed to the amount of cortisol in your system, or there may be other hormonal or biochemical interactions I haven't yet discovered. We simply don't have enough data, but I intend to get it."

"Well, there's no time like the present," Barry said. "Let's put it to the test, right now."

Caitlin shook her head. "I don't know…"

"Look, it's a controlled environment," he said. "I'm safe. You're here to watch over me. Come on. Inject me with some epinephrine. That'll stimulate cortisol production."

"There's not enough epinephrine in all the hospitals in Central City to get a reaction out of your metabolism," she replied.

"Then there's only one alternative," he countered. "Use the pure cortisol you synthesized from me."

"I only have a few ounces," she said. "Not enough to make a difference."

"It sounds like you're trying to avoid testing me."

"Oh!" Cisco exclaimed. "We could shoot him."

"Shoot me?" Barry asked. "With what?"

"A gun. Joe's got one." Cisco smiled. "Getting shot at tends to produce a stress reaction. Right?"

Joe crossed his arms. "We're not shooting anybody."

"Wait a minute, Joe." Barry pointed at Cisco like he had a good idea. "It's not like the bullet could hit me. My speed will kick in, and I'll just pluck it out of the air. I've done it a million times. It makes a certain amount of sense."

"It *doesn't* make sense," Joe retorted in a louder voice. "I don't care if you are the Flash. I'm not shooting you."

Iris narrowed her eyes. "It seems a little dangerous,

especially since the whole problem is that your powers are unreliable," she offered. "What if Dad shoots you, and your powers don't kick in?"

"Thank you, baby." Joe kissed Iris on the cheek. "At least *somebody* here has some sense."

Barry frowned. "There has to be something we can do," he said. "It doesn't make sense to put it off until there's a disaster."

"Why don't you run on that treadmill you keep in there?" Joe indicated a glassed-in room off the Cortex.

"Running won't do it." Barry looked over at Caitlin. "Will it?"

"I don't know," she said. "We could give it a try, now that we know what we're looking for. After all, there's no such thing as too much data."

"Then the treadmill it is." As Barry moved toward the machine, Cisco spun his chair back toward the keyboard. He reset the suit's bio-monitors.

"Still think we should've shot him."

Joe gave him a tight glare. "You need to stop that now."

Caitlin activated the monitors in the treadmill room while Barry stepped up on the wide rubber tread, facing the station where she was sitting. This was a special device designed around the unique abilities of the Flash, who would turn any commercial machine into shards of wreckage in just a few seconds.

She gave him the signal to start, and settled back to watch the monitor screen. He started off slowly, his feet pounding as the sliding track started to move. He picked up the pace, hitting fifty miles per hour, and held that for thirty seconds. Then he went to 100 mph for a moment before really bearing down. His arms and legs became blurs, and the hum of the treadmill turned into a high-pitched whine.

Barry's field of focus narrowed. The world hazed on the sides and sharpened straight ahead. He stared directly at Caitlin, but her focus was on the monitor. Her concentration was inspiring, coming so soon after she had been forced to watch the last moments of her husband's life.

Inspiration turned to guilt. She was a world-class research biochemist and physician, yet beneath that purity of intellect, Caitlin fought to suppress her human vulnerability. Barry remembered the pain in her eyes that day after Ronnie disappeared into the maelstrom.

Yet here she sat, concerned entirely for him. He didn't want to be the cause of the anxiety he saw on her face. She seemed so alone with her questions—all of them about him. If only he had saved Ronnie that day, at least she'd have someone to comfort her.

He'd give *anything* to protect her from misery, but instead he only seemed to add to it.

Something red appeared in the hazy corner of his eye.

Barry shifted his line of sight slightly and saw his older self, running alongside. His cheekbones were prominent under the line of the scarlet cowl. He looked exhausted and hollow.

I must be blurring, he realized. But he still saw Caitlin sitting in front of him, frozen at the keyboard, focused on the numbers, interpreting the data.

"Barry," his older self said in a weary echo of his own voice. "You've got to run faster."

"Who are you?"

"*Faster*. It's the only way."

"Why are you here?"

"The plasma is everywhere now. It's growing. It's killing you. You've got to get it out. You know how to do it."

Without noticing, Barry picked up speed, almost as if to run away from his doppelganger.

"You can do it," his shadow said, matching the pace. "You've done it before. Oliver Queen shot you with a tranquilizer, and you burned it out. Alcohol disappears in your system within seconds. You can burn the plasma out, too. Run faster!"

There was truth in that. It made a peculiar sense. His metabolism operated on a rate far beyond normal humans. Alcohol had no effect on him. Medication only lasted for a few seconds. The plasma shouldn't be any different. If he could just run fast enough, he could overwhelm its capacity to replicate, or destabilize its structure. The speed force could be the answer.

"That's it, Barry." His older self nodded to him, looking even thinner. "Run!"

So Barry ran. Lightning whirled around him,

sliding through his body, firing the engine inside him. He ran, driving his legs and arms into pistons so fast they could only be timed by the spinning of electrons. The world lengthened out in front of him, and settled into a quiet hum.

He looked back over his shoulder. A man sat relaxed on the edge of the treadmill, forearms resting on his knees.

"Ronnie?"

"Hey, Barry." Ronnie Raymond gave a friendly nod of his head.

"Wh... what are you doing here?" Barry stopped running, yet the world didn't change around him.

"Relaxing." Ronnie laughed and half turned, leaning back casually. Dark-haired and handsome, young and intense, this was the man Barry had known, albeit briefly. Confident, even cocky. He wore the Firestorm matrix on his chest, and his head and hands were enveloped in nuclear fire.

"We thought you were dead."

"Oh, I am." Ronnie's smile shone out through the flames flickering over his face. "I die a lot, don't I?"

"I'm sorry, Ronnie," Barry said. "I should've saved you, the day of the wormhole."

"It's not your fault, Barry. You did your part, and I did mine. No hard feelings." Abruptly Ronnie stopped smiling. He shifted uncomfortably, as if in pain. The fire around his head started to give off greasy black smoke.

"Caitlin really misses you."

"I miss her, too." He groaned and doubled over. His

face and hands blackened. The nuclear fire began to consume him.

"Oh my God, Ronnie!" Barry said. "What's happening? Tell me how I can help you."

"You can't, Barry," Ronnie said. "You never could. You can't even help yourself." When he looked up, his face was a cracked, skull-like visage. His hands were bones with liquid flesh dripping to sizzle on the floor. "You can't run that fast." His body burst into flame, pouring smoke into the air.

Without warning Caitlin's face appeared in front of him. Barry jerked back in alarm, but she took a relieved breath. Joe, Iris, and Cisco crowded behind her. Barry stood on the treadmill, still in the Flash suit.

"He's back," Caitlin told the others.

"Oh, man." Barry massaged the dull ache in the back of his neck. "How long was it that time?"

Caitlin glanced up at a monitor on the wall. "One minute and twelve seconds. We've got a good battery of bio-readings for me to go through, but come with me now and let me take some blood."

"Man, that was freaky," Cisco said, astonishment in his voice. "You were all see-through. Just standing there like a ghost."

Barry stepped off the treadmill directly over the spot where Ronnie had been sitting. His legs went wobbly, so Joe grabbed him and helped him stand. They slowly followed Caitlin.

"How fast did I go?"

"You were approaching Mach One when you blurred out," she replied. "I had just managed to activate the sonic boom dampener, to stop you from blowing out the windows."

Iris took Barry's other arm. "Did you see your future self?"

"Yeah. He looked even older this time—and really drained."

"Anybody else?" Joe asked. "Like Grodd again?"

Caitlin looked back curiously. He caught her eyes and hesitated.

"No. Nobody else."

She nodded and led them into the examination room.

22

Shawna Baez and Hartley Rathaway appeared suddenly on the soft blue carpet belonging to the mayor of Central City. Mayor Anthony Bellows sat at a large mahogany desk with his tie undone, white shirtsleeves rolled up, and a face ragged with fatigue. He looked up, eyes widening in shock. Two men who sat facing the mayor noticed his reaction and jumped to their feet. They both wore suits and displayed badges.

They reached for their pistols and aimed at Rathaway.

"Don't move, Piper!" the closest one commanded. Shawna recognized him as Detective Joe West. She grabbed Rathaway's hand to teleport back out, but he pulled out of her grip.

"Easy, Detective." Rathaway held up his bare hands to show that he wasn't wearing his vibrational gauntlets. "As you see, I am unarmed—but I'm not unprepared. You wouldn't want to accidentally shoot me."

The second man stared from behind the barrel of his pistol.

"No, we don't want to *accidentally* shoot you," he growled. "Put up your hands, and step away from the woman."

Rathaway sighed with exasperation, pulling his hood back. "You are Captain Singh, I believe. No doubt you have to spout your cop speak, but you'd do well to listen to me before doing anything you'll regret." He glanced at his watch. "You have less than ten minutes before Kyle Nimbus walks into a busy supermarket. He won't be there to buy milk and bread."

"You wouldn't do that." West's eyes tightened with fury. "You're not that man."

"No, I'm not, but Nimbus is. The clock is ticking. The Mist is waiting by the phone, and if he doesn't hear from me within ten minutes, he'll do something very unfortunate. So let's put the guns and the testosterone away, and get down to business."

Mayor Bellows raised his hands. "Captain Singh, Detective West, put your weapons away. This is the mayor's office, not a shooting gallery. Let's listen to what the man has to say."

Both detectives slowly lowered their pistols. West slipped the gun inside his jacket. Captain Singh didn't holster his, but kept it pointed at the floor, finger pressed over the trigger guard. They held their position in front of the desk, keeping themselves between the mayor and Rathaway.

No one paid Shawna any mind, and that bugged her a little. She tried not to smile, though, knowing what she knew. Rathaway would never send Nimbus to kill so many innocent people. It was a complete bluff, but it worked.

Rathaway swept his arm back toward the window, where sunlight streamed into the office. "You see the weather outside? It's a beautiful fall day, and it can stay that way if you'll just see reason."

"Please continue, Mr. Piper."

Rathaway strolled over to the desk, pausing to shove Captain Singh out of the way. He sat in the captain's chair, then he looked back and indicated for Shawna to join him. Hesitating at first, she came forward. West stepped aside and she perched on the edge of his chair. The two policemen stayed close until Rathaway glowered over his shoulder, at which time they moved near the window.

"All right," Rathaway said, "here's the situation, Your Honor. Your city is being taken apart, piece by piece. Your resources are or soon will be at a breaking point. Police. Fire. Rescue. Hospitals. Basic services like water and sewage and transportation are going to fail soon. Don't bother to deny it. I know the truth." He leaned in closer. "You are a week or so away from being the mayor of a failed city, at which point, two things will happen. One, the population will begin to flee. Central City will become blighted, the subject of 'where are they now' documentaries and Internet lists of the once-great cities.

"Or two," he continued, "the federal government will step in to manage the crisis. Your authority will be negated, and you will never get it back because you'll get kicked out with the next election. Along with you will go the interests of all your business and social allies."

"Did you practice that speech?" Mayor Bellows asked. He didn't look particularly impressed, which surprised Shawna.

"You are in no position to be smug," Rathaway replied, a hint of irritation in his voice. "I practiced this part, too. I'm here to give you a third option. You can pay me five hundred million dollars, and repeat that amount each year until I say you can stop. If you do that, the sun will continue to shine on Central City."

"So it's all about money?" The mayor scowled. "That's your villainous plan?"

"Money is a part of it, because money is a part of everything," Rathaway replied coolly. "But this is mainly about winning, and I have won. You need to recognize that there is no place for you to go, and you must concede."

Mayor Bellows took a deep breath. His eyes flicked to the two detectives standing near the window, and then he lowered his gaze to the desktop. When he looked up, he seemed suspiciously calm.

"We don't negotiate with terrorists, Mr. Piper."

"I'm not negotiating," Rathaway responded. "I'm dictating. Five hundred million per year. It's actually quite reasonable, considering the damage I'm doing to your city every day. Some professional sports teams have annual payrolls nearly that high. I'm sure if you go to your major contributors, and the business leaders of Central City, they'll be happy to put that amount together. They understand the cost of doing business."

"Even if I agreed, how do I know you can deliver? Those metahumans are animals." Bellows smiled viciously. "Present company excepted, of course," he said sarcastically.

Shawna ignored the insult because, despite his blanket statement against negotiating, Bellows was negotiating. Typical politician.

Rathaway inspected his fingernails. "You just have to trust that it's in our mutual best interests. Above all, my partners are greedy. Money satisfies them. *Your* partners are greedy. Their top priority will be getting back to business as usual." He crossed his arms and stared across the desk. "What's it going to be?"

"If I say no…"

"Tick tock, Your Honor."

"He's bluffing." Captain Singh brought his pistol to waist level. "I can put him down, and our troubles go away. CCPD will wrap up the other thugs."

Rathaway remained still. "Have fun explaining that to the families of the dead. How you took their loved ones because you felt the need to be a real man." He turned to stare at Singh. "I don't bluff, Captain. I anticipate."

Singh didn't flinch. "Give the word, Your Honor."

"Stop it, Captain." Mayor Bellows leaned forward.

Rathaway smiled. "Very sensible. That's why I came to you privately, so we could find a gentleman's path to agreement. I could just as easily have invaded a television station to announce my fiendish ultimatum, but there's no sense backing you into a corner. I want this deal to happen. I want you to look like the man who saved Central City. The public doesn't need to know how you did it.

"Once you save the city from the terrible metahumans," he continued, "you can be mayor for as long as you like. Or congressman. Or senator." He extended his hand. "A simple handshake, and it all gets better."

The mayor stared hard at Rathaway's hand.

"There's more to it, isn't there?" Detective West said from the window. "Come on, Rathaway. Spill it."

Rathaway laughed, and nodded toward Mayor Bellows.

"Well, yes," he said, pulling his hand back. "Now that he mentions it, there are a couple of addenda." He tilted his head in West's direction. "It's a little awkward to have the detective here, since he's directly… impacted. As part of our agreement, Joe West is to be fired from the police department, and he must leave the city. A couple of my colleagues have a bit of a grudge against him, and his presence makes them uncomfortable."

West chuckled coldly. "I'll give them a nice comfortable spot in Iron Heights."

"There, you see," Rathaway said. "That's needlessly antagonistic. So Detective West must go, and the city's scarlet knight—"

"I don't have any control over the Flash," the mayor interjected. "I don't even know who he is."

"And that's part of the problem, isn't it?" Rathaway replied. "Vigilantes running roughshod over our legal system. Are we living in Star City now? You must do your civic duty, and criminalize the Flash. In fact, putting a bounty on his head would be a nice touch."

"So you can take down the Flash without breaking the law," West said. "Not gonna happen."

"Don't be a sore loser, Detective," Rathaway snapped, and he faced the mayor again. "There's one last thing, and for this you should give me a medal. I want to protect the city from a threat that has nearly destroyed it twice in the recent past. You see, I am one of the founders of S.T.A.R. Labs. As much as Harrison Wells, I created the particle accelerator, and just as I predicted, it failed." Rathaway gripped the arms of his chair. "On the positive side, eventually it led to his death. Now I want S.T.A.R. Labs leveled. No, let me rephrase that—I want to be the one to level S.T.A.R. Labs."

"That's private property, Hartley."

A new voice, Shawna realized with a shock, and she turned.

The Flash leaned against the door, arms crossed, a broad smile on his face.

She leapt to her feet, slapping a hand down on

Rathaway's shoulder. She looked at the window for an escape route. The venetian blinds were shut and Detective West stood with the adjusting wand in his hand. He grinned, pulling a cellphone out of his coat pocket. It was active—he had been broadcasting the meeting to the Flash the whole time.

With no view outside, Shawna was limited to teleporting inside the office. It would be hard to stay away from the Flash for long.

He pushed away from the door in a leisurely manner.

"Anybody here happen to know how many supermarkets there are in Central City? I do, and they're all empty now—no shoppers for the Mist to harm. You're a chess player, aren't you, Hartley? I believe that's check."

Shawna teleported Rathaway across the room. She released him and jumped next to Captain Singh, who was just bringing his gun up. She teleported him beside Mayor Bellows so the muzzle pressed against the mayor's head.

She appeared behind the Flash and wrapped her arms around him, then left him in the corner behind a large fern. The exertion made her vision blur, and she felt lightheaded. Still she popped next to Rathaway and moved him again, just as the Flash zipped toward him. Leaving him behind the mayor, she materialized in front of Joe West.

She put her hands on both sides of his face and

smiled at him. Then he was next to the door. She moved Rathaway yet again as a red blur came toward the mayor's desk. They appeared in front of the window.

She parted the venetian blinds.

Sunlight streamed in. Shawna and Rathaway vanished.

23

Barry's head dipped for the fourth time as he lifted the fork to his mouth. His body needed food, but he was too exhausted to eat. He rubbed at his face, feeling nothing but dried sweat and grit under his hands. Sighing, he attempted to stay focused on the simple act of eating.

It took effort to even chew.

Eight times he made it to his mouth before his eyelids started to droop again. He jerked awake as Caitlin entered the room and plopped a stack of research on the top of her desk a few feet away. For a moment he panicked, wondering if he had blurred. But she didn't seem alarmed.

He tightened his grip on his fork.

"You haven't eaten much," she pointed out.

"I haven't had time," he replied. "Now I don't have the energy. Since we missed Rathaway at the mayor's office, he's really ramped up the attacks. More fires.

More floods. More chaos. We made him mad." He glanced around. "Where's Cisco? We need to talk about strategy."

"He's in the lab, working on a way to shut down the Pied Piper's gauntlets. Don't worry about him right now. You've been running full speed for two days. You've got nothing left in your system, Barry. Eat."

"I will." He looked at the pile of paperwork. "Are those my latest results?"

"Yes."

He reached over to take the top report, but Caitlin pulled the stack out of his reach.

"Just keep eating," she said firmly. "I'll tell you what I've found."

"I can speed read through them."

"And use up the little bit of energy you've got left? Don't be silly. You can look at them later, when you've gotten more zip back into you."

"I am zipless," he admitted. "It'll pass."

"Barry, it isn't just the running around, saving people, and looking for meta-villains. Every time you blur, the plasma grows, and it's not just co-opting red blood cells. It is spreading through other cells too, and it's draining your speed force. The longer it goes on, the longer it will take you to replenish."

"Guess I'll just have to eat faster," he said. "Either that, or give me pie intravenously." He chuckled. Maybe it was the exhaustion making him a little lightheaded.

Caitlin actually paused and put a finger to her chin.

"I was kidding!" Barry exclaimed.

"I *could* give you some boosters—electrolytes, simple proteins. We could use protein shakes, for when you're too tired to even eat." She watched his head dip again. "Like now."

"Look. I'm eating." He lifted his fork to shove in another mouthful.

"I'm serious. You're draining faster than you're replenishing." She rummaged through the folders in front of her. Finally she pulled out an X-ray. "This is the break in your arm from the fight on the bridge." She slid it in front of him. "Taken this morning."

Barry held it up to the light. To his surprise, he could still see a hint of the fracture line. "It's not healed."

"It's healing, but far slower than it should. Under normal circumstances, your bones would have knit completely by now thanks to your metahuman physiology."

Barry frowned and then lifted up his shirt. "I guess that explains this."

Caitlin gave a soft cry.

"Good God, is that a burn?"

"Yeah, left over from the house fire on Livingston Street."

"Damn it, Barry. That was two days ago!"

Caitlin moved toward the med ward. It took her all of two minutes and she was back with some salve and a bandage. Barry stood quietly as she quickly and efficiently took care of the half-healed burn. He hissed as she dabbed some ointment on it. Pain wasn't new to him, but rarely did he have to deal with it for extended periods.

"It'll be all right," he told her. "Don't worry."

She scoffed at him, applying a bandage over the burn.

"This is serious, Barry."

"It's just a burn."

"But it's not healing. It may be minor now, but the next time you get your ribs caved in, or breathe some hydrogen cyanide, you may not come back. You're no longer indestructible."

He smiled at her. "You thought I was indestructible?"

She sighed. "You know what I mean. You're more vulnerable now. You could easily die out there." The expression on her face told Barry where her thoughts were heading.

"No one's going to die." He stood and took her by the shoulders. "Look at me. That's not going to happen."

Caitlin stared at him for a long moment. "It better not."

"I'm getting my second wind," he said, but her dubious expression told him she wasn't buying that for a moment. He returned to the food.

"You really need to take it easy," she said, going back to her papers.

"We both know that's not going to happen until those metas are behind bars. I'll take it easy then. Otherwise, the Flash has to stay on the clock."

"You're always on the clock. If not fighting this

group, then another. It will always be something."

He held up a hand. "I promise, the moment these guys are down, I'm going on vacation. Even if it's fishing with Joe and Iris." That made him grimace.

"I'll believe it when I see it." Caitlin placed her hands on the desk and leaned over them. "I know you, Barry. You're not the vacation type, not when there are people in trouble. That's the problem. You think you can do it all. Just because you can do everything quicker than everyone else, it doesn't mean you can do it all alone."

Barry shrugged. "Well, who can keep up with me?"

"It's not a race, Barry," she argued. "You have to let someone else help you, or you're going to die."

"All of you are helping me," he said, meaning it. "Don't think I don't appreciate it, too. I do. If it weren't for you—"

"I don't mean us. We'll always be here for you."

"Then who?"

"Oliver."

"Oliver Queen?" Barry immediately shook his head. "He's busy. He's the Green Arrow."

"And you're the Flash."

"But he's got his own problems. I'm not going to add to them."

"Excuse me, but you've got an army of metahumans trying to destroy this city. Plus you're experiencing unexplained issues with your power. And yet, even with those problems, if he asked you to lend him a

hand right this second, you'd go. I know you would."
She took a deep breath, and continued. "You don't
have to be alone in this. There is no shame in asking
Oliver for help. You're sick, Barry, and if you keep
pushing like this, we're going to lose you."

He started to protest again, but closed his mouth.
Caitlin was right. Under normal circumstances he
could have handled this. He wasn't worried for
himself, but what if he blurred while he was trying to
save someone? It wouldn't be him that paid the price.

"All right," he said.

Caitlin looked shocked. "What?"

"I said all right. I'll call Oliver."

Caitlin ran over and gave him a fierce hug. "Thank
you!"

"He hasn't said yes, yet," Barry reminded her. "He
may not be able to come."

"He will," she said. "I know he will. Oh, and ask
Felicity to come with him. I'd love to have her help
with the plasma problem."

"She's not a doctor."

"No, but with her computer skills, we could double
our output here in the labs. And I want her analytical
eyes on my data."

"Anybody else?" His eyebrow rose. "John Diggle?
Speedy? How about Deathstroke?"

Caitlin ignored his sarcasm. "I'll leave that to Oliver.
He knows what he's doing."

"I'll call him today." Barry yawned and stared

listlessly at the plate. "Iris will be happy. She loves her some Oliver Queen."

Caitlin gathered her papers against her chest. Her beaming smile, the first ray of hope Barry had seen in her for days, let him know he was making the right decision.

2 4

The next evening, the Flash patrolled the city, as usual. The pouring rain stopped, but not before a lightning-sparked fire took down a tenement used by the homeless. He rescued more than twenty people with the help of the CCFD, then searched the area for Mardon or Bivolo.

Nothing.

City Center traffic was much lighter than it should've been on a normal night. He passed blocks of high rises, dark due to the failing power grid. A number of luxury condos stood empty because of fire damage. The once-bright lights of fashionable restaurants and ritzy clubs remained dark. Rathaway made sure the rich and powerful felt the impact, hoping to ramp up the pressure on the mayor.

The Flash turned a corner and stopped dead.

"Hm," he grunted. "That's weird."

"What is?" Cisco asked, but Barry didn't answer.

Two men in military fatigues sat on the sidewalk with their backs against a light pole. They bent forward with their arms placed awkwardly behind them. The Flash pulled to a stop in front of them.

"Hey, guys. What's up?"

The two soldiers looked up with amazement. "It's him!" one said. "You're the Flash!"

"Yeah. Who are you?"

"I'm Douglas Thomas."

"Okay, hi, but I really meant what are you doing here?"

"I'm Randy Murrow," the second soldier replied. "We're tied up." The Flash peered behind them. Sure enough, their wrists were bound with plastic zip ties.

"Is there a reason why?"

"Our buddies went nuts," Douglas said. "They jumped us, tied us up, and took off with the Humvee. Left us here. We need to get loose and find them."

"Your buddies went nuts?" the Flash asked warily. "What happened?"

"We were on patrol." Douglas twisted to show the unit patch on his shoulder. "We're National Guard. Came in for public safety duty. We were rolling down the street here and a guy flags us down. We pull up and our sergeant starts talking to the guy."

"We were in the back," Randy said. "We didn't see him, just heard a voice."

"Right." Douglas nodded. "No big deal. We've been talking to locals all night. So anyway, after a minute, we hear the sergeant and the other guys—Gephardt and Ramirez—they're talking real mad, shouting and cursing. Next thing we know, they're pulling us out of the back. Dragged us over here and strapped our wrists to this pole."

"Gephardt wanted to shoot us, but they couldn't agree," Randy said. "They ended up just driving off."

The Flash took a deep breath. "Okay, got it. So when you got to town, did anybody brief you on a guy named Roy Bivolo—maybe called him Prism? Did they show you a picture?"

"Naw, man." The two soldiers struggled to look at each other, shaking their heads. "We just rolled off a C-130 about three hours ago, and hit the streets. Orders to keep an eye out for looters or citizens in distress." Douglas leaned forward. "Really, man, wouldja mind? You got a knife or something?"

The Flash reached between them and took a plastic strip between two fingers. He vibrated the first zip tie apart, and then did the second one.

"Man! Cool!" The two soldiers laughed as they massaged their wrists.

The Flash held up a finger to silence them. "Hey, guys," he said to Cisco and Caitlin. "We've got trouble. Bivolo bushwhacked a squad of National Guardsmen." He looked at Douglas. "What kind of weapons were you carrying?"

"We each had an M-16 with grenade launchers for tear gas, and Sergeant Cooley's got a forty-five auto on his belt. The Humvee carries a fitty up top."

"A what?"

"A fitty. A fifty-caliber machine gun."

"Oh." Barry spoke into the comm, "Alert CCPD that there's a heavily armed National Guard vehicle with three soldiers on board, somewhere in the city. They've encountered Prism. I'm going to find them." He looked at the troopers. "Thanks, guys. Gotta run." And he was gone.

The Flash laid down a search grid, and was a red streak racing up and down streets. In his wake, papers scattered, coats fluttered, hats blew away. At major intersections he stopped to listen for the sound of gunfire. Luckily, he just heard cars, horns, and voices.

Turning onto a major avenue, he saw it.

Ahead of him, a desert-tan Humvee rolled through the light traffic. No one manned the machine gun on the roof. He rushed behind the rumbling vehicle, following for another block, then swung out wide and saw three soldiers inside. Two in front, and one in the back seat who had ear buds in and looked to be asleep, with his helmet shoved down over his eyes.

The Flash slipped up to the open driver's window.

"Are you Sergeant Cooley?"

"Gah!" The driver jumped in alarm and turned the wheel hard toward the Flash. The trooper in the passenger's seat jerked, too, fumbling for his rifle beside him. The Flash deftly dodged the heavy vehicle as it squealed into the curb and ground to a halt. Cars swerved around it, blaring their horns.

The Flash stood on the sidewalk, carefully watching the men in the Humvee. They went quickly from frightened to amazed. The passenger woke up, and grinned.

"Holy crap! It's the Flash!" he said, adding ironically, "I wondered if we'd run into him." The driver shoved open the door. He wore the insignia of a first lieutenant.

"Hey, sorry," he said quickly. "Didn't mean to almost run you over. I'm not used to guys running up beside my vehicle when I'm moving. You okay?"

The Flash held up a hand. "I'm fine. I'm looking for a vehicle with a Sergeant Cooley, and two guys named Gephardt and Ramirez. Is that you?"

"No, no Cooley here." The lieutenant ducked back inside. "Anybody know where Cooley is? Or Gephardt or Ramirez?"

The soldier in the back leaned up. "Yeah. Sergeant Cooley is in Bravo two seven."

The lieutenant turned to the Flash. "You're looking for Bravo two seven. We're two four. I can call them for you."

"Yeah, would you see if you can?" The Flash came over to the Humvee while the lieutenant climbed back in and reached for the radio. The other soldiers got out, including two more from the rear of the vehicle, and they gathered around him.

"Can you really run on water?"

"Yeah, when I need to. It's not as easy as it looks, though."

"No way! And up the side of a building?"

"Yeah, sure." The Flash tried to listen to the lieutenant without much success.

"Could you?" One trooper pointed at the high rise across the sidewalk. "Just run up to the top and back?"

"Maybe later. I'm a little busy trying to find these other guys." He pushed closer to the lieutenant. Lights flashed around him, and he realized that the troopers were leaning in with their smartphones to take selfies.

"No luck." The lieutenant tossed the radio back onto the seat. "They didn't answer."

"I had a feeling," the Flash said. "Let your command know to keep an eye out for them, and be careful. They could be dangerous."

"Dangerous?"

"They're under the influence of a metahuman named Roy Bivolo. That'll make them emotionally unstable, and that's a bad combination, given that they're heavily armed."

"Is Bivolo the guy with the cold gun?"

"No, he's—" The Flash stopped and shot him a frustrated frown. "Why didn't they brief you guys—" He was cut off by a distant boom and the asphalt rumbled underfoot.

"I just felt an explosion," he said into his mic. "Are you picking up anything?"

"Just a sec," Cisco replied. There was the sound of

fingers on a keyboard. "Can't tell. We've lost most of the cameras downtown. We're blind in big chunks of the city. Trying other sources."

"Keep me posted," the Flash said, then he turned to the lieutenant. "Keep trying to reach Sergeant Cooley. If you can talk to him, you may be able to calm him down and shake Bivolo's whammy."

Before the officer could reply, the Flash ran up the side of the high rise the soldier had pointed out, ignoring the whoops he heard from behind. Once on the roof, forty stories up, he scanned the cityscape.

There was smoke rising, about five miles north.

Heading in that direction, he quickly arrived at his destination, and swept to the top of a ten-story building. He spotted a Humvee on the street below. Its headlights and forward spotlight shone into a cloud of smoke boiling out from the ground floor. Two soldiers stood watch, M-16s at the ready, while a third trooper manned the heavy machine gun on top.

"Barry," Cisco reported, "I've got your location. That's the Central Plaza Arms on Weisinger. Every unit is full, so there are lots of people inside. One of the occupants is your boss, Captain Singh, there with his husband."

"Bivolo might be targeting him," the Flash responded. "In any case, I need to take out the machine gun first—uh-oh!"

"What?"

One of the soldiers shouted and pointed up at

the Flash. Instantly the machine gun swept upward, barking as it did so.

The Flash launched himself off the side of the apartment building. At his speed, bullets appeared to be plowing through turgid air, each leaving a slow trail of turbulence. As he sped down the brick wall, he could see faces in the windows. People stared out in surprise or curiosity or fear. Many of them had phones in their hands. Some carried small children. Each window was a frozen tableau, ready to become a target zone.

He plucked the first shell from the air just a few feet from the building. Continuing downward, he grabbed another one, then another. The machine gun had created a wide sheet of steel flying toward the face of the building. In the dark and smoke, it was hard to see the bullets in flight, but the Flash had to catch them all before he could go after the gun itself. Just one of the massive slugs could shatter glass or brick or bone.

He snatched three, five, eight, ten. He couldn't hold any more, so he opened his hand. The collection of brass-jacketed shells hung in the air and would eventually drop, doing little or no damage unless someone stood directly underneath them.

Nearer the ground, the bullets were closer to the building. Worse, the smoke billowed thicker, and he strained his eyes to track swirls penetrating the cloud. One shell was just grinding into the brick, while another was partially buried in the wall. He swatted others from the air, feeling the burn against his hand.

Above him, he caught a telltale glint. A glitter of glass. He had missed one on the way down.

The Flash roared back up the side of the building, the bricks hard against his feet. On the eighth floor, a bullet was entering a window. A neat thick-rimmed hole spread around it. The glass itself rippled like water.

Just inside was someone Barry knew well—his supervisor, Captain Singh. The man craned his neck to see the disturbance below, his face a mask of intensity. He held his service pistol in one hand and was talking on his phone at the same time, likely calling for a police response or demanding answers from the National Guard.

He stood less than an inch from the window.

The tip of the bullet already touched his cheek.

The Flash's vision blurred. A surge of panic washed through him. *Not now!* He had made it in time. He had run fast enough. He was right here. He had to focus on the bullet. Like a man with a high fever trying to accomplish a simple task. Ignore the disturbance that tried to rob him of his ability.

Reaching in, he delicately pinched the back end of the shell between his thumb and forefinger. Every ounce of attention went into that one act. He brought it into the speed force with him just as the flesh of the man puckered from the impact. The Flash snatched the bullet back through the hole. Singh's expression didn't change. He had no idea what had just happened, and wouldn't until he noticed the hole in the window, and found the bruise on his cheek.

Abruptly the world began to shimmer and the Flash's vision sparked. He was blurring on the side of a building, high above the unforgiving street. He had to get down. The Flash half fell and half ran toward the street. The impact with the pavement drove the breath from his chest. He bounced and landed hard on his stomach. Remembering the soldiers, he tried to push himself up, but his hands seemed to sink into the concrete.

Through his wavering sight, he watched the machine gun lower toward him. The faint echo of bullets pounded the pavement around him.

"Get up, Barry! Run!" The Future Flash knelt beside him. "You can still save them. You just have to fight."

"I *am* fighting," Barry wheezed. He struggled to get his feet under him, but his muscles responded like lead. He struggled not to flop forward over his trembling arms.

"It's not enough." His future self placed a comforting hand on his back. It reminded Barry of his father. His older face seemed understanding, but terrified. "You know that, Barry," he said. "You can do more."

Barry tried again, but his limbs had gone numb. He felt tears gathering.

"I don't know if I can." Warmth spread down his cheeks. "I'm so tired."

"Flash!"

Barry slowly wrenched his head up to see a shadowy figure atop the Humvee. The mysterious outline stood in the smoke and flaring headlights, his face buried in the darkness of a hood. He carried a bow.

The Green Arrow.

Barry lowered his head and muttered, "Better than Grodd, I guess." He pushed himself up. Two soldiers writhed on the street, wrapped with metal coils. The trooper behind the machine gun slumped unconscious over the side of the turret.

Struggling into a sitting position, Barry wiped his forearm over his wet face. "Okay, I know the drill by now. Let me have it. Tell me I'm not fast enough to save anybody. Tell me I've failed this city. Shoot me with an arrow."

"What?" The gravelly voice came from the dark hood. "Are you injured?" The shadowy figure vaulted from the Humvee and landed in a crouch. He was clad in green leather, with a hood and mask covering much of his face.

Barry furrowed his brow in confusion. He looked around for his future self, but didn't see him. Thick smoke clogged the air. Shards of glass and concrete covered the sidewalk. The two soldiers moaned in pain.

He slapped his hand against the sidewalk. It was solid. He looked up at the familiar eyes shining out of the dark.

"You're real."

Green Arrow narrowed his gaze.

"Did you take a head shot?"

Barry laughed, and looked around. Deep gouges

marred the pavement where he had been lying. The machine gun shells had passed through him while he was blurred.

"No, I'm good. I'm just glad to see you." Just as he extended his hand to shake, and for help standing, Arrow's eyes turned hard and he sprang to his feet. He went for a shaft in his quiver and brought it to his bow.

Barry flinched, throwing his hands over his head.

"I *knew* it! Here it comes!"

The arrow whooshed past Barry's head, followed by a yell of pain from behind. He spun around. The lobby had been blown open, the glass doors and frames shattered by a grenade. In the fading smoke, a man in a uniform with sergeant's stripes flew off his feet with an arrow wedged in his right shoulder. He carried a heavy duffel bag and had a thick tangle of gold chains and jewel necklaces looped around his neck. He fell to the glass-covered floor, and an automatic pistol skittered out of his grip.

He lay bellowing in pain. Barry grimaced.

"Ooh. You shot Sergeant Cooley."

"He'll be fine," Green Arrow growled. "Will you?"

The Flash stumbled to his feet and took the green-gloved hand. It was solid and firm. He offered the archer a relieved grin.

"Better now."

2 5

"Hey! Look who I found." Then Barry stopped. *Why do I even bother?*

As the Flash and the Green Arrow strode into the Cortex, Caitlin and Cisco sat talking to John Diggle and Felicity Smoak. The latter smiled and waved.

"Barry." John nodded. The ex-military man stood six-foot-five, broad-shouldered like a linebacker, enough to make any criminal think twice before angering him. Barry knew him to be an effective fighter, a loyal friend, and a dedicated husband and father. Former bodyguard turned crime fighter. The right hand of the Green Arrow.

Barry threw his arms wide as the second newcomer walked over.

"Felicity, I'm so glad you came."

"Always, Barry." She hugged him enthusiastically, reminding him of a sprite made of pure electricity and intellect. Beneath her open and expressive persona, she had one of the keenest minds in the country, particularly when it came to computer theory and network operations. Her blonde hair was pulled back and her eyes shone out from behind glasses. She broke off the hug and stared hard at his face.

"You have a bruise on your jaw."

"Well, yeah, it's been a little rough around here. So what have they told you—"

"No," Felicity stopped him, gripping him tight. "*You* have a bruise. You. Barry Allen. The Flash. Caitlin said you'd been having problems. Are you okay?"

Caitlin returned to her workstation with the look of a doctor whose unfortunate diagnosis had been verified.

"Told you. It's noticeable."

"I'm fine." Barry put a self-conscious hand to the bruise. It actually hurt to touch. "Or I will be, now that you guys are here."

The Green Arrow pulled back his hood and removed his mask to reveal Oliver Queen, the scion of one of Star City's wealthiest and most powerful families. Or at least they had been—the Queens had fallen on dark times, and he was one of the few who remained alive. Oliver was tall, powerful, and athletic. His face was sculpted and still, his dark hair closely cropped.

Steady, calm eyes regarded the room. Some saw quiet confidence in them, Barry knew, while others found them cold. He hadn't been able to decide. Still, because of that sturdiness, Oliver exuded an intoxicating commanding poise. A hint of violence lurked beneath that, however, as if he was constantly on the verge of lashing out.

"You should've called earlier."

"You guys are just as busy as we are," Barry countered. "With assassins or super soldiers or demons or political campaigns or whatever. Even now I worry that I'm pulling you away from something important."

It surprised him how relieved he felt, though, like seeing a protective big brother. He doubted Oliver felt the same way, but that didn't matter. He was here.

"We always have time, Barry," Oliver said. "Sorry we're late. It was tough getting in. You've got a lot of major roads washed out. Even so, I'm glad I got to you when I did."

"Caitlin told us where to find you," Felicity explained. "A little hack into the National Guard server gave us a situation assessment."

Cisco looked impressed. "Yeah, I was about to do that, too."

"So let's have the details." Oliver set his bow down and removed the quiver from his back. "What's going on?"

"Well, to begin, there's a team of five metahumans trying to blackmail the city," Barry said.

"Anybody we know among the metas?" Oliver asked, but his attention was locked on the bruise. He gave Felicity a quick worried glance.

"Roy Bivolo. Remember him? Prism." On cue, Bivolo's photo appeared on the overhead monitor. "He's the guy that made me crazy that time, when I beat you up."

Oliver furrowed his brow. "You didn't beat me up."

"Well, I did… a little," Barry's voice lilted.

John smirked, but Oliver grunted. "Who else is involved?"

"None that you've met. Shawna Baez."

"Peekaboo," Cisco announced, and he put up her photo.

"That's a cute name," Felicity said. "Like Hello Kitty."

"She's a teleporter," Barry said. "Line-of-sight only, but she can bring passengers with her. She's the reason I haven't been able to get close to any of them."

Oliver's jaw tightened. "We need to take her out first."

"That's what I thought, too!" Barry said, and he grinned. Oliver remained stoic, so he cleared his throat. "Anyway, we also have Mark Mardon."

"Weather Wizard," Cisco added.

Felicity smiled at him. "Let me guess. He controls the weather."

"Yeah, usually he does it on a micro-climate scale," Barry said. "He channels lightning or creates baseball-sized hail. But recently he's been affecting larger areas with heavy rain, tornados, lightning strikes. Big stuff. Lots of damage. Next we have Kyle Nimbus."

"The Mist," Cisco intoned.

"Creepy." Felicity recoiled from the snakelike bald head and sunken eyes.

"Creepy is right," Barry added. "In the annals of bad guys, he's a *bad* guy. He was a mass murderer who gained the ability to transform himself into a cloud of hydrogen cyanide."

"You mean a real cloud?" Felicity looked over the top of her glasses. "He turns himself into a *cloud*?"

"Oh, no way." John glared in disbelief. "Even in Central City, no way a man changes himself into gas."

"Yeah," Barry said. "He physically transmutes his molecules into a cloud of poison gas. He's a nightmare. And finally, Hartley Rathaway."

"Pied Piper," Cisco said.

Felicity studied Rathaway's picture. "Does he play a little flute?"

"No," Cisco answered.

"Does he control rats?"

"No. And *eww*."

Barry sat on the edge of a table. "He's a master of sound and vibrational tech. He's really brilliant. Used to work for Harrison Wells here at S.T.A.R. Labs. He wears special gloves that emit high-energy sound waves. We have an old pair we took off him." He pointed at the high-tech gauntlets sitting on a table. Felicity's eyes lit up and she scurried over to examine them. "I've been blasted by those several times, and I can tell you that you don't want any part of it. The only reason my organs weren't turned to jelly was my metahuman healing factor." Caitlin looked away, which caught Oliver's attention. Barry kept on without comment, "Rathaway's the leader of the gang. He's a skilled tactician. Without him, the other four would've screwed up by now, and we would've gotten them already."

Oliver nodded. "Any idea about their base of operations?"

"No," Cisco said angrily. "I've used every pattern recognition matrix and all of the tracking software we have. There's no discernible repetition that lets us predict where they're going to strike, or estimate where their lair is." When they all stared, he added, "Oh, they have a lair. I'm sure of it."

"Maybe I can help with that," Felicity said. "Do you mind if I go over your data?"

"Music to my ears." Cisco waved a hand over his keyboard. "You're welcome to everything we have. Just say when."

Oliver continued to watch the footage of Rathaway on the monitor. "I'll want full dossiers on all of them, but here are a few ideas. First, Bivolo's powers are in his eyes, right?"

"Yes, he triggers an emotional reaction through the color receptors in the optic nerve."

"So, two options," he said. "Either we don't look at him, or we make it so he can't look at us."

"How?"

Oliver gave Barry a deadpan stare. "I could shoot his eyes out."

"What! No, Oliver, we don't do that in Central City."

"Relax, Barry. I'm joking. We don't do that in Star City either."

"Any more," John muttered.

Oliver shot him a quick glance. "Have you thought about running in and putting a bag over his head?"

"A bag over his head?" Barry laughed, but he realized Oliver was serious. He started to argue, then paused. "Hmm. A bag over his head. That's a really good idea. It's just hard to get to him."

"Right, Peekaboo," Oliver said, and Felicity giggled. "She's a problem. If she requires visual targeting, however, I could hit her in the eyes with some sort of foam to block her vision."

"That could work. Might even work on Bivolo."

"You know, I was thinking," Felicity interjected enthusiastically, "with the Weather Man—"

"Wizard," Cisco corrected.

"Oh, sorry. Wizard. With him, does his power involve exploiting charged atmospheric particles, because if it does—"

Barry spun around and pointed to Cisco, who held up the weather wand.

"You are correct," Cisco announced. "I designed this little baby the last time, to interrupt his connection with atmospheric electrons. And it worked. And it would work this time, too—"

"If you can catch him," Oliver finished the thought.

"Right." Cisco waved the cylinder like a lightsaber.

"Can you arrange an early warning system to ping you when he starts to use his powers?" Felicity asked.

"Yes," Cisco answered. "Can and did. We can detect spikes in atmospheric energy, as well as extreme changes in pressure. By the time Barry gets there, however, Mardon is always gone."

"Again thanks to Peekaboo," Oliver said, and Felicity giggled again. He stared at her and she shrugged. "Now, the Mist—"

Felicity raised a finger. "Oh, I was thinking about creepy gas cloud guy. Hydrogen cyanide is extremely flammable." She looked at Cisco and Caitlin apologetically. "Of course you know that. I'm sure there's some reason you haven't done anything with it."

"Holy flame arrows!" Cisco suddenly leapt to his feet and pointed at Oliver. "You're going to use your flame arrows, aren't you!"

Oliver nodded approvingly. He bent close to Felicity.

"Get some flame arrows," he whispered.

Barry winced. "That's great and all, but we don't want to blow him up. I mean, I *want* to, but we shouldn't."

John leveled the practical look of a soldier at him. "If he's as bad as you say, Barry, we need to take him down before he hurts anyone else."

"I know, but let's look for a middle ground. Stop him from killing without incinerating him. I had good luck dissipating him with water, and forcing him back to his human form."

"Right." Felicity nodded in approval. "Water is heavier than vapor. That would work. We don't have any water arrows, but we can work with the concept."

Oliver took the sonic gauntlets from her and studied them. "And this Rathaway, what does he have without his gloves? A gun? Anything?"

"No weapons, no," Barry said. "He's very persuasive, but on a strictly human level. There's no psychic power. We've taken his gloves away, and that works, until he gets them back or builds new ones. He's smart… but so are we." Barry reached into his belt and pulled out two little capsules. "We came up with our own earplugs that limit the damage his gloves can do. We can give a pair to you, and one to John, too."

"Good," Oliver said. "Anything else?"

"Oh, he's also a giant jerk." Cisco swung his feet off the table. "To prove it, he stole a meteorite. Well, his goons actually stole it, and they killed the museum director."

"He killed someone to steal a meteorite?" Oliver frowned.

"Yeah, the Singing Meteorite," Cisco began.

Felicity beamed. "The Singing Meteorite?" It almost sounded lyrical, the way she said it.

Oliver stared at her. "You've heard of it?"

"Oh sure, it's only the most famous meteorite since… well, it's the most famous meteorite ever."

"And it sings?" John asked.

Cisco quickly explained the history of the meteorite, and of Dr. Coolidge. Felicity huffed, jealous that he and Barry had met the astronomer, and started asking questions about exactly how misanthropic he really was. Oliver interrupted her.

"So what was the reason for stealing this meteor?"

"We're not sure," Barry said. "We know it has

unique vibrational properties, so Rathaway must be searching for a way to weaponize it."

"Maybe this guy just collects sound-related items," John offered. "Don't super-villains do that sort of thing?"

Barry looked doubtful. "Not that I know of. That seems sort of weird."

"*That* seems weird?" John raised his eyebrows higher than a human should be able.

"Okay, let's get the teams on the same page." Oliver tossed John the gauntlets to examine. "I'll want to hit the streets tonight, and wrap up these metas as soon as possible."

"Great," Barry said. "I can't wait to take these guys down. They've hurt too many people already. It's time to give a little back."

"That's what Oliver does," Felicity said proudly. "He figures out the best way to hurt people. Bad people I mean. People who *need* to be hurt. Not just people in general. That would be wrong." Oliver put his arm around her waist and she went silent.

"And while you guys are planning," he said, "I wouldn't mind a cup of coffee. Barry, you have the time?"

Barry grew unexpectedly nervous under the archer's gaze.

"Sure. Yeah. Let's talk."

26

Another storm seemed to be gathering as Barry and Oliver went downtown to police headquarters. Despite the deluge of duties piled on the Flash, Barry Allen had to show up at the office, as well. In fact, his workload had tripled with all the recent events. Some of it was related to the metahuman assaults, but most was common criminals taking advantage of the chaos.

CCPD headquarters was built during the art deco period. It boasted hard edges, geometrical designs, and rich embellishments. Barry found the mathematical symmetry soothing. The gleaming bas-relief in the lobby depicted the Greek gods and proclaimed "Truth, Liberty, Justice." He felt strangely a part of the golden age to which it harkened.

This late at night, the building hummed with activity, but not many civilians were present. Barry waved to familiar faces, all looking exhausted, as he hurried to the elevator and rode to the top floor.

Barry entered his empty laboratory and flipped on the lights, then weaved around columns to stand under the large skylight. He took hold of the dangling chain and pulled, hand over hand. It clanked through pulleys, the skylight parted high overhead, and a dark figure dropped softly to the tile floor. Barry hung onto the chain as Green Arrow looked around.

"It has a Dr. Frankenstein feel," he said.

"Does it?" Barry replied with a grin. "Never thought about it. Kind of fitting though, because this is the exact spot where the Flash was born. It was a dark and stormy night then, too. The lightning struck me right here, just as I was covered by the wave of dark matter from the particle accelerator explosion." He hauled on the chain to reverse it and shut the skylight.

"That's not completely true," he said when he'd finished. "I think the Flash was actually born the night my mom died. That's what made me. The weather was better that night, though."

Green Arrow walked over to the broad windows overlooking Central City, peering out toward the river and S.T.A.R. Labs. The bright lights of the tall buildings around them made the city look serene. Lightning sparking the distant sky spoke otherwise.

Shelves filled with oddly colored chemicals lined the walls. In the middle of the space stood a large rollaway corkboard covered with a map of Central City. All around it sat tables stacked high with paperwork, anchored by large paperweights.

Barry zipped around the room, collating the pages from several different piles. He created a soft windstorm as he ran about, setting a few loose papers fluttering. If anyone saw him from outside, he would appear as a streak of light flickering about the room.

"Didn't we come here to talk?" Oliver remarked, leaning against the window, pushing his hood back. "It's disconcerting, trying to conduct a conversation with a red streak."

"Sorry." Barry stopped, forced to wait for a clunky machine as it whirred before spitting out some paper strips of data. "I'm just in a hurry to get all this finished, before the next crisis." He grabbed a vial from the centrifuge, finding the process too slow. He spun the liquid with his hand, darted over to a workstation, extracted some of the sample, and placed it under a high-powered microscope. "Working keeps my mind off other things, too."

"Yes, I can see that," the archer pointed out. "But you did ask for my help."

Barry stopped again. "You're right." He couldn't prevent a low slump, even though he consciously tried to adjust his body language in front of Oliver. All he really wanted to do was sleep, yet there was too much to do. He went to the coffee maker in the corner, and poured two large cups.

"It's not as good as Jitters," he said apologetically, "but it'll do." Barry yawned as he handed one over. The archer took it, but didn't drink.

"Earlier tonight, on the street," Oliver said, "you acted as if I wasn't real. What was happening there? Is that what you mentioned on the phone?"

"Part of it," Barry confessed, "or I thought it was. Turns out you were real."

"You've been hallucinating?"

"Yeah." Despite the hot cup of coffee in his hands, Barry felt suddenly cold.

"Tell me about it."

Oliver's firm voice and attention gave Barry the resolve to relate the story. All of it—from the Future Flash to the cavalcade of villains. Giant talking gorillas and murderous ghosts, it sounded crazy even to him, when he said it out loud.

"What do you think it means?" Oliver asked. He didn't act as if it was crazy.

"I wish I knew. I don't know if it means anything," Barry admitted. "I don't know where the hallucinations are coming from. If they're coming from inside my head, then I guess I'm telling myself to run faster, because that's all my future self ever says. *'Run faster.'* Maybe since Harrison Wells isn't here to tell me, I have to do it myself."

"Is it working?"

"I don't think so." Barry sat in a rolling chair. "It seems like strange advice, since the plasma inside me is feeding off my speed force, but it's always worked in the past. So maybe I just haven't broken through the barrier I need to overcome."

Green Arrow hadn't moved a muscle since Barry started talking. It was unnerving speaking to a hooded specter. Oliver's eyes shone in the half-light of the laboratory.

"What about the others?" he asked. "The other hallucinations—what do they tell you?"

"What you might expect villains to say. To *stop* running. That I can't do it—whatever 'it' is. I'm not fast enough. I can't save everyone." Barry shrugged.

"Not all are villains, though. Firestorm was a hero. He gave his life to save the city. What did he say?"

Barry thought about that incident. The image of Ronnie, burning to death before his eyes, played out again. He stood up to derail the memory.

"The same thing. That I couldn't save him. Never could." He returned to organizing the files, but at human speed. "I'm telling myself one thing, and others are saying something else." He stopped and peered at the archer. "Strange things can happen when the mind is under stress, right?"

"Absolutely." Oliver turned his head to study the map of Central City. "What does it feel like, this blurring effect? Is there pain?"

Barry struggled to put it into words. "It feels like I'm… *disconnecting* from this reality. Like a sudden glitch, and then I'm speeding up while at a dead stop."

"Like a car engine, revving in neutral?"

"Yeah, but with the wheels off the ground, just trying to make contact, to get some traction."

"Do you know why it's happening?"

"We think we do. Back when I fought Harrison Wells—um, Eobard Thawne, um Reverse Flash. It's complicated—well, months ago we opened a temporal anomaly, a wormhole. While trying to shut it down, apparently I got some of it inside me."

"You have a temporal anomaly inside you." Oliver regarded Barry. The speedster could tell he was struggling to process information that was clearly outside his normal expertise. So he tried to clarify.

"The anomaly was at least partially made up of plasma, and I now have that plasma inside me. Since that day, it's been growing slowly, but recently it reached some sort of critical mass where I began to present symptoms—primarily what I call blurring. Apparently when my system floods with cortisol, it activates the plasma.

"When the plasma is active, I vibrate out of phase with this world. The plasma then feeds off the speed force until I'm drained. And it's draining me faster than I can replenish." He lifted the coffee cup and took a giant gulp.

Oliver rubbed the rough stubble on his chin. He set aside his untouched coffee, and focused on Barry.

"So knowing you, you're handling this by running yourself ragged, trying to fight five meta criminals and keep Central City afloat while rescuing every wet kitten from every tree."

Barry tried to come up with a witty reply.

When he couldn't, he returned to filing papers.

"So what happens if you become totally depleted?" Oliver asked.

"Don't know," Barry said, "but it probably isn't good."

Oliver remained silent for a moment. "Are you dying, Barry?"

At first the only response was the sound of papers, and the squeaking of sneakers on the old wood floor. Barry felt the masked gaze boring into his back, and realized he couldn't file the question into a folder and make it go away. He leaned on a table and took a deep breath.

"I don't know," he said. "We don't know how this thing will progress, because no one has ever seen it before." He turned around to face Oliver, seeking some agreement or comfort from the dark face. "No matter what, I think we'll find a solution. We always have. Why wouldn't we this time?"

Oliver shook his head.

"I know," Barry said. "I let it get away from me."

"No." Oliver looked Barry straight in the eyes. "You've saved a lot of lives, even while you're barely on your feet. What you've done is amazing."

Barry straightened, pulling back his hunched shoulders. For a moment the weight lifted. Oliver's praise was better than any drug Caitlin could pump into him.

"Thank you. That means a lot."

"We'll take down your rogues," Oliver told him, and Barry believed him. "You're not in this alone any longer. John and I will patrol tonight."

"I'll come with you," Barry said quickly, "and show

you the grid pattern I've been—"

Oliver's head tilted with *that* stare.

"Oh." Barry backpedaled. "I mean, I'll go home and rest."

Oliver straightened off the windowsill. "We'll call you if we need backup."

"It's just hard." Barry breathed out a sigh of relief. "You know, stopping?"

"Even we can't be there twenty-four seven."

"Yeah?" Barry said, a hint of a smile playing across his face. "When was the last time you took a vacation?"

The deep furrows of Oliver's brow relaxed, and the tightness of the jaw lessened. His entire face went from hard-edged crime fighter to ordinary friend.

"Well, I once spent a lot of time lounging on a Pacific island. Now that I'm back, I prefer to stay at work." He paused, then added, "I do go away, though. I've taken time to recharge. It helps when you have someone like Felicity pushing you to go, and the fact that I have her with me makes me want to do so."

"I'll swap with you. I'll go with Felicity, and you go fishing with Joe. Probably in the snow or something."

"Spending time with family is a wonderful thing," Oliver replied. "I miss those days."

"Oh, man, I'm sorry, Oliver." Barry winced. "I didn't mean, that is, I shouldn't have… I'm really sorry."

"Don't be. I was making a point. Enjoy the people in your life while you can. You never know when it will change."

Barry sighed miserably. "That's why I feel the need to run all the time. I don't *want* it to change, for anyone. You know, every time I save somebody, even if it's the tenth rescue of my day, it's *their* moment of truth. It's their turning point. I have to be there for every one of them. I have to run fast enough to do that, to do it every time."

He suddenly had a thought that wasn't quite a thought.

A flash of lightning lit across his brain, so fast it couldn't be seen, but as bright as day and vivid for the split second it existed.

"What?" Oliver asked. "What just happened?"

"I don't know." Barry took hold of the chain again. "Something just occurred to me. The first time I noticed even a hint of the blurring was during a routine rescue on the highway. Well, routine for me. Like I said, it was life or death for them. But I saved a woman who was about to die in her car, and I could see in her eyes that she *knew* she was about to die.

"Yet all she could think about was her son in the back seat. She wasn't trying to save herself. She was turning around to help her son. Just like my mom did."

"Your mom?"

"The night she was murdered by Reverse Flash. I was eleven, and I came into the room and saw her in the middle of these streaks of yellow and red lightning. I didn't know then, but it was Reverse Flash and the Flash—me—fighting. Mom couldn't know what it was, just that it was dangerous, and she held out her hand to keep me from running over to her. The only thing she cared about was protecting me." Barry looked at Oliver. "Just like Lily did with her son, Dean. If I hadn't been there, or if I had been a split second slower, that boy would've been just like me. His whole life would've changed in an instant, like a bolt of lightning."

"But you *were* there."

"That time. For that mom and that kid."

Oliver took a long silent moment. "Are you living your life to prevent something that's already happened?"

Barry just clutched a file and stared off into space.

"That's a hard way to go, Barry." Oliver shifted uneasily from one foot to the other. The creak of leather echoed in the high-ceilinged room. "I've lost some good people, people I loved. Tommy Merlyn, both of my parents, and others. I lose count. People who died fighting my war."

"I'm sure that's not true."

"The point is we can't save everyone. We have to learn to soldier on."

"I don't feel like a soldier, but I'll do anything to be sure I don't lose anyone else, no matter what it costs me."

"Not tonight, though." Oliver narrowed his eyes. "I'll cover for you tonight."

"All right." Barry fell heavily into a chair and hung his head. His arms and legs dragged like dead iron. He felt like he could rest for the first time in a very long time. "Thanks."

"My pleasure."

27

Their vacation home was becoming more like a prison. It wasn't just the trash. On a certain level the garbage, the filthy clothes, and the old food all made it feel real, and as long as Shawna could get away from it occasionally, she didn't mind roughing it.

This was getting a little *too* rough, however.

Even the relief that had come from associating with Rathaway had faltered. They hadn't played chess since returning from the observatory. In fact, she rarely saw him at all, though his presence was marked by the weird sounds coming from the makeshift laboratory he'd set up, in what had been an extensive wine cellar. The noises that filtered up set her teeth on edge.

Shawna stood at the large window, enacting her daily ritual of watching the light of the sunrise play over the lake. The once-pristine glass was smudged and filthy. Even the beautiful oranges and yellows reaching up to shatter the darkness couldn't dredge up the comfort it had just a week ago.

Behind her, Mardon snored on the sofa that had gone from a comfortable piece to a stained flop. She heard Bivolo and Nimbus come into the room.

"Is that coffee?" Nimbus croaked. "I need coffee."

In the reflection, his ratlike gaze locked on the steaming cup in her hand. She wasn't supposed to teleport out for coffee, but that hadn't stopped her. There was no coffee in the house, barely any food. No one bothered to restock—except for Nimbus who occasionally brought back beer and liquor.

"You went out," Nimbus growled. "You can't go out. I get yelled at when I go out. Why don't you? It can't be because Rathaway likes you. He'd rather have Mardon." Nimbus chuckled at his juvenile wit.

Shawna drifted down to the corner to be farther away from him.

"You try to kill cops when you go out. Idiot." She slurped her coffee as loud as she could.

"Call me an idiot again!" Nimbus bellowed. "I dare you. One more time. Just one more." Mardon's snoring stopped, and he awoke with a grunt.

Shawna turned and drew her shoulders back. Bivolo waited with a smile on his lips. Before she could speak, however, Mardon rose up from the sofa.

"Will you two shut the hell up! I'm trying to *sleep*." Dark circles rimmed his eyes and his typically chiseled features were sunken and sallow. His hair was unkempt and his beard untrimmed. "I'm working my damn butt off. Is it too much to expect a little peace and quiet? There's a whole damn house to fight in, and you gotta come in here."

Bivolo laughed at that.

Shawna might have felt sorry for Mardon. He had a bad boy style she had always liked. She might have even fallen for him in her younger days.

"You shut up!" she shouted back. "You wanna sleep, go find a room upstairs. There's plenty of them. And what's this 'working your butt off' crap? I carry all you creeps around every day. Without me, the Flash would've slapped all of you like the little girls you are."

Bivolo laughed again, louder this time. Nimbus looked expectantly at Mardon, who only blinked dully before falling back onto the sofa with a groan.

"Yeah," Shawna snarled. "That's what I thought."

The door opened and Rathaway entered, preoccupied and then surprised.

"You're all here? Good." He had papers in his hand—the now-dreaded daily agendas for each of them. He handed everyone a sheet and turned to leave without another word.

Shawna scanned hers with the annoyance of a retail employee finding herself scheduled for the fifth weekend in a row. He had her ferrying Bivolo to three locations today, and the route he'd laid out was grueling. Worse, she'd have to be back by dark to take Mardon out.

"No!" Mardon crumpled the paper, swung his feet

onto the littered rug, and crouched on the edge of the sofa. He massaged his neck and tossed the wadded sheet across the room. "This is it, Rathaway. I'm done with your cute little schedules. I'm done with getting moved around like a piece of furniture. And I'm done with the whole damn operation unless something changes. Right now!"

Nimbus nodded eagerly in agreement, sidling over to stand near Mardon, but not saying anything.

Rathaway exhaled impatiently.

"What now, Mardon?" he demanded. "I don't have time for your tantrums. My work is at an important stage."

Mardon pushed himself up, regaining a little of his old swagger.

"I don't give a rat's ass about your 'work.' You listen to me for a minute. You went to the mayor almost a week ago, and you said he was about to give in, but then the Flash showed up. So we cranked it up. You said that would break him—but it hasn't!

"I come back from a mission and I can barely walk. I'm exhausted, Rathaway. I don't wear gloves to do my work. I control the weather…" He slapped his chest. "…with *this*. It's me. My body. My brain. I can't keep this up, and without me, you got nothing. So I'm gonna make the schedule now. We're gonna change it up."

Rathaway waited silently, not even trying to hide his contempt. Mardon paused as if expecting an argument. When it didn't come, he continued.

"Look, the mayor and his people obviously aren't

afraid of you. They figure you'll just keep playing your game until the Flash saves them. Give him enough time, and he can check every house in Central City. It's crazy he hasn't found us already."

He paused. Rathaway just stood there.

"Yeah, so…" Mardon continued. "We need to remind the mayor who he's dealing with here. We've got to make him hurt."

"Yeah!" Nimbus shouted. "Let's kill the mayor!"

"No." Mardon rolled his eyes. "He's the guy we're bargaining with—the guy with the money. But Bellows will cave, once we show him how much it'll cost to keep stonewalling us. We don't kill him, but we need to kill someone else. Maybe a lot of someone elses."

Nimbus cackled and slapped Mardon on the back. Bivolo perched on the arm of the sofa. He wasn't laughing now, and his emotions were unclear behind his sunglasses.

Shawna looked at Rathaway. Waited for him to say something smart. This was a horrifying idea. He had to put the genie back in the bottle.

With every silent second that passed, she felt perspiration on her neck.

"What do you have in mind?" Rathaway asked.

Shawna breathed hard through her nose, and fought with herself not to get too upset. Not yet. Rathaway was playing them, like he always did. This was another ploy, stringing Mardon along. It had to be.

Mardon showed new confidence. "Well, I had this

idea before, but never got around to it," he said. "You know the Cary Reservoir Dam?"

"Yes," Rathaway replied.

"It's an old dam, and it wouldn't take much to break it. If I drop ten or fifteen inches of rain into the lake, the thing will bust wide open—as long as no one opens the flood gates to relieve the pressure." Mardon stood up, invigorated by his growing influence in the room. "There's an old town in the flood path. It's been there forever, but it's part of Central City now. Mainly poor people. I know. I used to live there." He sneered quietly to himself. "That dam breaks and a couple hundred people might get killed. Plus, the city will lose the power they generate at the dam, and the water from the reservoir. We'll make it bad enough to get the mayor to cave."

Rathaway pursed his lips. "It's just poor people, after all," he said, and he gave a slow nod.

Mardon grinned. "Right. *Now* you understand. We let Bellows know that the next time, it'll be a couple hundred of his rich pals who get it. Just so he knows we're willing to do what it takes."

Rathaway thought for a few seconds.

"Fine," he said. "Do it. Take Bivolo to disrupt any workers who might be around. All I ask is that you work up a timetable, so I can look at it before you go." He held up his hand to stanch any argument. "Just so I can plan the approach, to minimize our exposure. I've kept the heat off up to now, and intend to continue doing so."

"Yeah, all right." Mardon nodded back. So did Bivolo. "But it needs to happen soon. Don't put it off, or we'll go off and run our own operation."

"Agreed," Rathaway said. "The sooner the better."

"No!" Shawna dragged the word out of her gut. "No. I won't do this."

Mardon glanced over his shoulder to look at her with contempt.

"What do you need to do?" he said. "Carry us up, and stand around till we're done. Even for you, that's not much work."

"I won't help you kill hundreds of people!" Shawna yelled, and she looked at Rathaway with pleading eyes. "It's mass murder. You can't let them do this."

"I can." Rathaway stared at her. "I will. And you will help them."

"No. I won't. You can't make me."

"You're right." Rathaway narrowed his eyes and stroked his chin. "I never really thought of that. I can't make you."

Mardon scowled at her. "Skip it. We don't need her. Send Nimbus across town to create a diversion, keep the Flash and the cops busy."

Nimbus grinned. "I can do that."

"But—" Shawna began.

Rathaway looked at her, his face unreadable, before shifting to Mardon.

"Bring me a plan by tonight." He walked out of the room.

Shawna felt her face redden. Rage surged through her body, compounded by a strange sense of embarrassment. She couldn't shake the feeling she was failing, and coiled up in that emotion was the panic of abandonment. They had put her on the outside now.

She started after Rathaway, when she heard Nimbus laughing, causing her to whirl on him.

"You want coffee, you stinking monster? Here!" She raised the heavy mug. Both Mardon and Bivolo ducked out of the way. She hurled it at Nimbus, but he puffed into green gas so it merely passed through and shattered the sunrise behind him into a spider-web of fractured glass.

The three men laughed as she stormed from the room.

2 8

Pleasant weather put everyone in town on edge. Any second, they assumed, a tornado would appear. Or torrential rains would wash cars into the river. Or lightning would set fires. Or hail would smash windows.

It had to happen, Iris mused. It seemed like it happened every day in Central City.

At least Barry had actually slept in his own bed for once, and he desperately needed it. Oliver Queen's arrival had made that possible, and she was grateful.

Her dad sat in on a meeting with Mayor Bellows, and the news from City Hall was grim. No surprise, Central City was suffering massive infrastructure loss. Roads washed out. Bridges collapsed. More than five thousand people who had been evacuated from their homes huddled in shelters. The farmland just outside of the city was impacted, as well. An important wheat crop was going to be ruined, because no one could plant.

Frantic calls from county officials and the governor's

office bombarded the mayor. A few units of the National Guard had arrived for swift-water rescue and public safety, yet they had already been compromised. The federal government wanted to activate FEMA operations in the city.

A call had come in from General Wade Eiling, to propose sending regular army into the city, but the mayor said no. Bellows didn't want his city to fall under military control, but he didn't know how long it'd be before Eiling stopped asking and started ordering.

According to Joe, Bellows was under pressure from city leaders to consider taking Rathaway's buyout. That would have meant forcing her dad out of the police force, as well—an idea that made her blood boil. Joe and Captain Singh managed to argue the mayor back in line, but they had to stop the metas soon, or there was no way the mayor could avoid cutting a deal.

Joe and Barry would be hung out to dry.

Iris suppressed the anger and took a deep breath of the dry air, forcing herself to enjoy the beautiful day. She had several appointments lined up, and a long list of calls to make. Today she was trying to run down former friends, colleagues, and associates of Hartley Rathaway.

Cisco had provided her with a stack of information from the S.T.A.R. Labs databanks, but Iris knew, as a reporter and the daughter of a police officer, that old-fashioned legwork was what paid off. Knocking on doors, making calls, and asking questions sometimes could locate what metadata couldn't touch.

She took her phone to a small city park not far from her office. A cup of coffee and a bagel sat on the bench next to her. Young men played a vigorous game of basketball as if the city around them wasn't under attack. They brought an all-or-nothing intensity to their game, and that comforted Iris. If this game meant the world to those sweating, grunting guys, maybe the world wasn't ending after all.

"Physics Department."

Responding to the answering voice on the phone, Iris said, "Yes, hello. I'd like to speak to Dr. Ronald Savic, please."

"I'm sorry. He is on sabbatical this semester."

"Oh, is he in town?"

"No, he's in Markovia on a lecture fellowship. He's been there since June. I can give you the number of the department there, if you'd like."

Iris took the number and tapped the phone off. Savic had been a S.T.A.R. Labs colleague of Rathaway's who had gone to academia after the particle accelerator explosion. She might follow up with him later, but if he'd been in Markovia since early summer, he wasn't likely to have any useful knowledge concerning Rathaway's recent movements.

She flipped through her thinning list, bit into her bagel, and reached for the coffee.

"Hey."

Shawna Baez was there.

Iris froze.

"You're Iris West, right?"

"Mm-hmm," Iris mumbled through a mouthful of bread, and started to glance around for Shawna's allies—but something in the woman's face held her. She looked sad and a little frightened. Her manner wasn't aggressive. In fact, she appeared more likely to run away than attack.

"You know the Flash, right?"

"Mm-hmm." Iris swallowed. "Yes."

Shawna let out a long breath. She glanced down at the bagel sitting on its crinkled paper.

"You want half a bagel?" Iris asked.

Shawna looked up. "What? Oh, no. Thanks."

Iris took another bite and sat back, crossing her legs. She wanted to appear casual and relaxed—that would calm Shawna, she hoped. This was just a chat on a park bench. Yet she was very aware of the sound of her chewing.

Shawna pulled her heavy sweater tighter and hunched against the chill. Her foot bounced with nervous energy. She stared across the park. Kids swinging. An elderly couple shuffling past, holding hands. The sound of the basketball game filled the air with the slap of sneakers on asphalt, the shouting and laughing of men, and the clang of the ball off the rim.

"I might need to get him a message."

"What sort of message?"

"The kind that saves innocent lives. There are some things I can't live with."

"I can call him now. He can be here in seconds. Literally."

Shawna jerked. "No! Don't."

"Okay, okay. I won't." Iris put her phone on the bench. "There. Don't worry. I won't do anything you don't want me to do."

Shawna gave a weak smile. "I just don't want to be pressured, you know."

"I do. I want this to go however you want it to. You took a big step finding me like this. I appreciate that. Are you sure you don't want the other half of my bagel?"

"I just…" Shawna ran a hand through her hair. "It has to go just right. I'll be in touch before anything happens."

"What's going to happen?"

"I'll call you at the newspaper. And when I do, he better be ready to move fast."

Iris laughed. "That's what he does."

Shawna laughed nervously. "Yeah."

"I'll be waiting for your call."

The girl nodded and vanished so quickly that Iris wondered if she'd imagined the whole conversation. Maybe she was having hallucinations, too. Maybe there was some strange new metahuman in town with weird psychological powers. Then Shawna reappeared and took the half bagel off the paper.

"I skipped breakfast. Thanks." She was gone again.

Iris snatched up her phone and called Barry.

* * *

The rooftop was cold. The weather had stayed chilly all day, but the disasters had taken a break. Iris wished she'd worn a heavier coat against the late afternoon wind. She paced impatiently through the gravel.

Gusts whistled past the wires that ran overhead. It was an older part of town, so phone wires and TV cables were still frequent. She had been there nearly an hour past the time when Shawna asked to meet. Maybe it was a test. Maybe Shawna got cold feet. Maybe one of her comrades found out.

"Anything yet?" It was Barry's voice, through her earpiece.

She almost answered, but remembered how Oliver Queen had told her to avoid speaking. If Shawna was watching from nearby and she saw Iris talking, it would smack of a trap.

"Uhn-uh," she grunted.

It was Oliver who had argued that they should use this opportunity to seize the teleporter, and remove her from Rathaway's arsenal. Iris was surprised how quickly she found her outraged voice. Shawna was trying to do the right thing, and they needed to help her, not betray her. While Oliver remained suspicious, Barry backed Iris.

Joe was less enthused. He didn't like trusting his daughter's safety to the word of a criminal. In the end, however, they'd decided that she would meet Shawna, but they insisted on having observers ready, in case of trouble.

"Shawna picked a good spot for a meet-up," Green Arrow said. "High visibility for her to maneuver and escape, plus wires and obstacles to cut down on the Flash's mobility. If you can, keep her facing the white brick building to the west. I'm in a room on the fourteenth floor, and I'll have a clear field of fire. If I need to hit her with foam, she has to be looking this way."

Iris was about to break her silence to argue.

"No foam until Iris gives the word," Barry said.

"It's her play," Green Arrow replied. He didn't sound happy.

Iris smiled to herself.

"Okay, cool," Barry replied. "How did you find an empty room in the first place? We didn't even know where to look until two hours ago."

"Online search," Felicity said. "Somebody was subletting an empty apartment. They'll never know he was there. John's on another building, inspecting the satellite dishes."

"Yep," John reported. "I've got eyes on Iris, too."

Iris looked around casually, but couldn't see either of them. It felt strange, knowing she was under observation. She wondered if the metas were watching her, too.

This could be a trap for the Flash. Iris didn't know Shawna Baez, and plenty of people could come off sincere whenever they chose. Despite the promise that she'd come alone, Iris was glad to have backup.

Not that she'd had a choice. Her dad would've

handcuffed her to a table if she hadn't agreed.

"Iris."

She spun around, her feet slipping in the gravel. Shawna stood at the edge of the roof. The wary woman flicked her eyes side to side.

"You're alone?"

"Yes." Iris started toward her, but Shawna thrust out her hands. Iris stopped, content to stand her ground. "I'm glad you called."

"I want you to know I'm not a snitch."

"I know."

"In my neighborhood, snitches get stitches. You know?"

"Yeah, I get it."

"But innocent people don't need to be involved. Kids don't need to get hurt."

"I agree. I want to help you stop that from happening."

"I tried to convince them, but they don't listen. Rathaway is so fixated on what he's doing, he doesn't care what the others do. It's not cool anymore."

Iris nodded sympathetically.

Oliver buzzed in her ear. "Maneuver her around. Put your back to the sun. Get her facing west."

Iris wanted to yell at him, but suppressed it. Shawna shot her a strange look.

"You're doing the right thing," Iris said. "You have to draw the line somewhere. Mardon. Bivolo. Nimbus. You're not like them. They're killers. You're not."

Shawna shoved her hands into the pockets of her

sweater, and wrapped herself in thick wool and stared at the rooftop.

"It was just about money before. Money ain't nothing to some people. They won't miss a little bit—they got more. I was gonna get some and take off. Live a life. Have a house, you know. A nice house."

Iris nodded again.

Shawna looked up, a little annoyed. "I bet you got a house, right?"

"I live with my dad. It's a nice house. Small, but nice." Iris bristled and wanted to say, *A police officer doesn't make much, risking his life every day.* She bit back the retort.

"For real? You live with your old man? He's a cop, right? He's the one Mardon and Nimbus hate."

"Yes, that's him." Iris tried to keep her voice from growing cold. She couldn't help but wonder if Shawna had joined in on the conversations, talked about killing her father, maybe even laughed along. She grimly considered wandering to the other side of the roof, putting her back to the west, and signaling Green Arrow to take his shot.

"So you two get along, you and your dad?"

"Yes. We get along," Iris acknowledged. "I love him. He's my father. I'd do anything for him."

Shawna's face changed. She became years younger and looked lost. Something in her innocent expression saddened Iris, and drained her anger. The girl sat down on the raised edge of the rooftop, and let out a tired sigh.

"That's cool. I wish I... That's cool." She lowered her head and scraped her boots through the gravel. "I don't know what to do."

"Yes, you do. You wouldn't be here if you didn't."

"But I'm not a snitch. I can't be."

"You're not a pawn either. Are you?"

Shawna's head jerked up angrily. Iris felt a rush of panic. She had pushed the wrong button. Then she realized Shawna's eyes were focused elsewhere. She was furious at something else.

"No, I'm not." Shawna slapped her knees and stood up. "All right. I'm going to tell you something."

"Wait. Don't you want to talk to the Flash?"

"I want to tell you. I don't trust him. He put me in a cell before, with mirrored walls, so all I had to stare at was myself. That's not right. So I'll tell you, but not him."

"Okay." Iris produced her phone and started the digital recorder. "Can you tell me where Rathaway and his gang are holed up?"

Shawna scowled and clenched her fists. "I told you I ain't no snitch! I won't give them up like that. That's not how it works. But I *will* tell you what they're planning to do. Then it's up to your boy, the Flash, to catch them. And he better run real fast, or a lot of people are gonna die. You know?"

Iris felt cold. "I know."

29

The Flash came to a stop next to Green Arrow, who studied the terrain through small field glasses. They crouched inside a dark overlook shelter at the top of the dam at Cary Reservoir.

From that vantage point they could see the reservoir and the high, curved face of the dam. It was a relatively small one, only two hundred feet from the top to the river that flowed at the bottom of the modest gorge. The floodgates were closed so it was easy to see discolored patches on the concrete face where repairs had been done over the years. Far below a powerhouse squatted amid thick power lines running to steel lattice transmission towers that marched toward Central City.

The Flash cleared his throat, hesitant to interrupt Oliver. The guy was intense even when just looking at stuff. Green Arrow tilted his head to show he was listening.

"I just got back from Joe and Digg," Barry said. They're with the CCPD evacuating the homes along the river, but they won't have much time to get several thousand people out of harm's way. If the dam breaks—"

"Then it won't break," Green Arrow said. "No sign of Mardon or Bivolo. Any word on Nimbus's distraction?"

"No, and we've evacuated and closed the mall that Shawna said was his target. But that won't keep him from going somewhere else."

Green Arrow continued scanning the area without comment.

Barry grew more impatient kneeling among the years of candy wrappers and beer cans in the dilapidated shelter. He was eager to run, to finally have the chance to catch Mardon and Bivolo. He touched the weather wand hanging from his waistband. If Mardon didn't know they were there, this would be his best chance to get close enough to stun him.

Oliver tensed and pointed down. "Bivolo."

Twenty stories below, a figure moved through the shadows of the small parking lot next to the powerhouse. He weaved between three parked cars, and headed toward the door.

The Flash didn't see Mardon with him. "Do you have your goggles?"

Green Arrow held up the bulky eyepieces Cisco had cobbled together.

"You really should wear them," Barry said. "They work."

"The colors affect my balance, and my aim. And they're awkward."

"Hey!" came Cisco's voice in their ears. "I had like thirty minutes max to make those. That's as good as they can be."

"Don't worry," Green Arrow said to Barry. "Bivolo isn't a gorgon. I can look at him—I just can't make eye contact."

Barry replied, "Okay, but if you get whammied and shoot me with an arrow, I'm going to be pissed."

"You'll be more than that." Green Arrow stood and put away the field glasses. Climbing over the rail of the overlook, he shot an arrow at the dam. "Be careful." He kicked off into deep empty space.

Barry nearly shouted in alarm until he saw the thin cable running from the bow to the distant arrow. Green Arrow swung out over the crevasse and landed on the face of the dam. There he ran along the surface, releasing the cable with a whine and dropping rapidly toward the powerhouse. Barry grinned. Without his powers, he'd never have the nerve to do the things Oliver Queen did.

He returned to watching for Mardon. Minutes passed with no hint. No change of any sort. A wet breath of wind hit his face.

"Air pressure just dropped like—" Cisco began.

Powerful rain filled the air around the shelter, and knocked out Cisco's signal. The water struck as if from a giant high-pressure hose. The Flash couldn't see more than a few feet through it.

He ran out of the shelter into the downpour. In a

typical light shower, the Flash could actually run between raindrops as they hung in the air. Here he had to fight through, yet watch where he was going. In this torrent, if he opened his mouth he'd drown.

Working his way along a rickety wooden walkway, he came to the point where it split. One direction continued across the top of the dam, while the other looped off around the reservoir. The dam was only fifty feet away, but it might as well have been on the other side of the planet.

"Hey, guys, can you hear me?"

Nothing but static.

The Flash pounded across the top of the dam, moving with difficulty, expecting Mardon to appear out of the gloom. He reached the west side with no sign. Gushing rivulets of water ran off every surface. Thundering drops pockmarked the ground. He slogged up a rocky hillside, and when he reached a point barely fifty feet from the end of the dam, the skies suddenly cleared.

It was like stepping out of a hard shower. Stars shone overhead. Water ran off him, puddling at his feet.

"Barry!"

"Yeah, I'm here, Cisco," he answered. "Inside Mardon's storm, I can't get a signal. He's positioned it directly over the reservoir. At this rate, it'll flood in a matter of minutes."

"Do you see him?"

"No, but if he's inside that rainstorm, I'll have to

feel around till I find him." He looked back. A cluster of thick black clouds dropped a narrow, solid crush of driving water. It was fed by a strange stream of clouds, flowing in from the south. Mardon was pulling moisture from a distant source and bringing it here, like a river in the air.

The wind picked up, too, whipping in all directions. Water sloshed vigorously onto the banks.

"Oh, no," Barry murmured. "He's using the reservoir like a hammer, shoving the water against the dam." Then a human form floated up through the clouds trailing wisps. The Flash couldn't make out the face, but it had to be Weather Wizard. Mardon was flying and controlling the weather at the same time. He had honed his powers since their last meeting.

Barry hated it when villains did that.

"I see him," he told Cisco, and he felt the wand hanging off his belt. "He's out of range, and he's airborne over the water. There is no way to climb up after him. Any ideas, guys?"

"Can you create a vortex to drain the energy out of the storm?" Caitlin suggested.

"I can't cut off the moisture stream he's created."

"Can you run over the lake's surface, to counter the vibrational energy of his waves?" Cisco offered. "If you can't stop the rain, at least stop him from pounding on the dam."

"I'm afraid any additional vibrations might do more harm than good."

"Mardon's never done anything this intense before," Caitlin noted. "He must be using incredible amounts of energy. He can't keep it up for long."

"He won't have to. The water's already washing over the top of the dam, and the floodgates haven't opened to relieve the pressure."

"Working on it," Green Arrow reported via the comm.

"I need to knock him out of the sky," Barry said, staring at Mardon.

"Lightning bolt him, baby!" Cisco exclaimed.

"Yeah, that could work. I'll give it a shot." With a burst of speed the Flash ran along the side of the lake, back and forth over the smooth grassy slope. His oscillating red streak became a solid red line. Power grew inside him.

He focused entirely on the sensation of the speed. The energy expanded from the faintest awareness to a crackling sensation to thunder straining to break out of his body. Every nerve burned. Abruptly he planted a foot. Pure blinding power galvanized into his right fist. His hand filled with a lightning bolt. He spun and unleashed the streak of raw force into the air.

Mardon lit up in the sky, but it wasn't the Flash's lightning that did it. The man pulled a bolt of his own from the dark roiling clouds. It sizzled down into Mardon and out of his extended arm, arcing toward the ground.

The two bolts collided with a concussive force, and a moment later the wrenching *crack* reached his ears.

The world went white hot. Barry felt himself torn from the ground. He had no sense of direction—only light and heat—and he couldn't see the world. When the blinding white faded, there was only blackness, the cold concrete under his cheek, and the hiss of water boiling from his skin.

The dam rushed past him as Green Arrow rappelled down the rough concrete. Hitting the ground, he rolled, seized an arrow and came up in a crouch ready to fire. He scanned for a target, but saw only three cars, and no movement.

The powerhouse was a large block building with multiple small windows high on the walls. There was one door, which was open—the only way in... for most people. Green Arrow fired a grapple arrow up under the eaves and climbed the wall to the closest window. Layers of dirt obscured his view. He wedged his fingers under the bottom edge and wrenched it up, snapping the struts so the glass swung free.

The building was vibrating, and through the open window, the reason was apparent. Four great turbines thrummed twenty feet below.

Suddenly he felt moisture on his face. Turning back, he saw water drizzling through the air. High above, a slate-gray storm sat directly atop the dam. Though he was only fifty feet from the base of the dam, very little of the rain reached him. By the look of it, however, the downpour might fill the reservoir to overflowing in just a few minutes.

Green Arrow squeezed through the window and hung there to get his bearings. Over the deafening hum of the turbines, he also heard the distinct sound of metal ringing on metal. He dropped to a catwalk that ran around the interior, one story above the floor. It was enclosed in a chain-link screen. On the far wall stood a huge bank of dials and gauges, as well as a control panel. Two men in company coveralls eagerly smashed the instrument board, pounding it with crowbars.

The chain-link screen prevented Green Arrow from taking a shot at the two. Their rage would be Bivolo's doing, so he needed to take them out with the least possible damage.

He started toward them, but the ringing sound of boots on metal heralded the arrival of a third workman, climbing stairs that led up from the ground floor. His uniform identified him as a supervisor. Blocking Oliver's path, he hoisted a huge wrench that looked like it belonged in a cartoon.

The man rushed him and swung the wrench in a vicious arc. Ducking under it, Green Arrow shoved the man against the chain-link. The guy growled, broke free, and lashed out again. Oliver had to do something before a lucky blow connected with his head.

Sidestepping another swing, he felt the wind brush his chin. He grabbed the back of the man's head, bent him forward, and delivered a hard knee to the soft gut.

The man's breath whooshed out and he collapsed to the catwalk, gasping and disabled.

One of the men with crowbars glanced over his shoulder.

"Hey! Robin Hood beat up Tony!"

"Good!" the other guy shouted, and he continued bashing dials, but the first man left his post and came sprinting around the far corner.

From his bandolier, Green Arrow pulled Cisco's device used to defuse Prism's rage effect. He flicked the trigger and it emitted sharp bursts of colored light. The man with the crowbar winced and drew back. He stopped and stared, and Green Arrow landed a solid punch. The crowbar clanged to the catwalk, followed by the man himself.

The final man continued delivering blow after blow to the control panels. Dials shattered. Buttons and toggles hung broken from their housings. Oliver moved closer, held up the device, and whistled sharply to get the man's attention.

"Shut up!" The crowbar came swinging back. It clipped Oliver's hand and batted the device through the chain-link fence, sending it to clatter among the turbines below. The worker never turned from the task at hand.

Green Arrow knelt to hook his bow on the man's ankle, and jerked him down to the catwalk. The man dropped hard, eyes wide and confused. One kick sent the crowbar out of reach, another put his opponent down for the count.

When Oliver stood, he caught a glimpse of a fourth man down on the main floor. Also wearing coveralls, the man lay partially hidden behind one of the huge generators. Green Arrow went to the stairs and slid down, forearms on the railings, feet up. Hitting the cement running, he made for the rumbling turbine, and stopped. The workman struggled to push himself off the floor.

"Are you all right?" Oliver asked.

The man glanced back over his shoulder with glowing red eyes.

This time Oliver felt a raw flush of anger, almost like a surge of pain. His mind flooded instantaneously with tragedies that had been visited on him. The injustices. The lies he had been forced to tell. The deaths he had been unable to prevent. It seemed as if someone was always testing him, always provoking him. The thought filled him with blinding rage.

No, not blinding—because he clearly saw the man standing in front of him. Bivolo was the one who had used innocent men as weapons, not even caring if they died in the process. Green Arrow bent his rage into clean, spotless focus, like staring down a powerful telescopic sight. Prism had the gall to smile in triumph as he strolled past.

"You left those guys alive," Bivolo said, sneering. "Very sloppy. Take care of them."

"Bivolo!" Oliver shouted.

Bivolo stopped, and turned back, his face twisted in

disbelief. "No way," he said. "Maybe you didn't get a good look. I said *kill* them!"

Green Arrow stared deep into the red eyes.

Rage surged, filling him, burning red hot. With slow deliberation, he pulled an arrow, nocked it, and drew back the string.

He lifted it to point directly between Bivolo's eyes.

3 0

"You can't do this," Bivolo said. "Why aren't you enraged?"

"I am," Green Arrow replied coldly. "And my rage is directed at you."

"Oliver!" Felicity's panicked voice shouted in his ear. "What's happening?"

The arrow flew.

It impacted Bivolo's forehead with a sharp crack, sending a grayish foam expanding into the air, to cover his face. The force knocked Bivolo off his feet. As he hit the floor he clawed at the hardening foam, tearing it off in chunks.

Green Arrow fell on him in an instant. He wrestled the man's hands away and kicked him over onto his stomach. Dropping a knee onto the small of his opponent's back, he cinched Bivolo's wrists together with a zip band. He bound the ankles, too, and left him trussed helplessly on the cold floor. The foam was air permeable, so Bivolo wouldn't suffocate.

Green Arrow knelt next to the writhing figure, head down, taking in long breaths, fighting the urge to hurt him.

"Oliver," Felicity said, "are you all right?"

"No," he ground out. Every emotion cried out for Prism's blood, but he held onto his rage as he had done for much of his life. "No, but I've got it under control."

After a few moments he regained his calm, though he had a pounding headache to show for it. Rising to his feet, he climbed back to the catwalk. The three men were moaning. Abruptly the background vibrations were shattered by a high-pitched alarm, and strobe lights from the ceiling. In his ear he heard the conversations again between the Flash and the team at S.T.A.R. Labs.

"He can't keep it up for long," Caitlin said.

"He won't have to," Barry answered. "The water's already washing over the top of the dam, and the floodgates haven't opened to relieve the pressure."

Oliver took calming breaths to fight the lingering pain in his skull.

"Working on it," he said. Oliver helped the closest man to his feet. The supervisor, Tony, was disoriented.

"You're that Arrow guy, aren't you?" he said. "Where's the Flash?"

"What's that alarm?" Oliver demanded.

"It's the overwash alarm." A second man got to his feet. "There's water topping the dam. We need to open the floodgates." When they reached the control panels and broken glass crunched under their feet, Tony groaned. "The switches for the gates are smashed." He eyed several gauges too high up on the wall to have been destroyed. "Oh, crap. I bet we have maybe five minutes before we get operational and structural failure."

"You mean the dam will burst?"

"Yeah, probably."

"Don't you have a backup system?"

The third engineer joined them and rubbed his head, wincing while he scoured the controls, testing buttons and switches to see what still worked.

"On the top of the dam you can trigger a hydraulics release on each of the three gates," Tony said. "Frankly it'll take longer than five minutes to climb up there."

"Tell me exactly what I need to do," Green Arrow said. "I can get up there in time. You three grab that man on the floor, and use the time to get to high ground. Be careful of him—he's dangerous. Whatever you do, don't look him in the eye."

The three men made no move to do as he said. They continued to pry panels off the control board.

"All those people living downriver don't have five minutes to get to high ground," Tony said. "We need to fix it."

"They've already been evacuated," Oliver responded, even though he didn't know that was totally true. The supervisor studied him, and turned back to work.

"Even if that's the case, we're not losing a whole dam on our shift. That looks bad on the resume."

Suddenly a shattering boom rocked the powerhouse. The men looked up expecting water to crash through the roof. The air tingled with electricity. No flood came. The turbines continued to whine.

"What the hell was that?" Tony muttered as he applied a voltage meter to some exposed wires.

"What's wrong?" Oliver said into his mic.

"Barry's down." Felicity's voice was urgent. "Can you respond?"

"Yes," Oliver answered, and then to the engineers, "I'm going up top. The Flash needs me."

The three guys all looked up. "The Flash is here?" Tony exclaimed. "Why didn't you say so? If the Flash needs your help, what are you doing standing around here?"

That actually caused Green Arrow to grin. "You've got three minutes before I trigger the emergency release." He bolted for the stairs and slid down.

"Make it four," Tony replied loudly. "This thing is a mess!"

Outside, Green Arrow returned to the cable dangling from the top of the dam. Hooking it into the bow again, he triggered the recall and ran up the concrete face as the pulley drew in the line. Fast water poured past his boots. He slipped and the wind sent him flying to one side. The ravine below spun far beneath his feet.

He slammed against the concrete, paused to gather his breath, and then started climbing again. Vibrations rumbled under his boots.

Reaching the top, he detached the line, and loaded an explosive arrow. The rain continued to fall, but it wasn't a solid sheet any longer. Breakers crashed against the dam, piling water along the top, threatening to knock him off his feet.

He spotted the Flash awash in the foam. Barry was unconscious, but had wedged face up against one of the hydraulic poles extending from a floodgate assembly. He just as easily could have been washed over the top of the dam into the ravine below, or simply drowned.

Moving to his side, Oliver snapped an ammonia capsule under Barry's nose. His eyes flew open and he splashed awkwardly in the water.

"Easy, easy." Oliver helped him orient himself. Barry focused on Oliver's familiar face, and relaxed. They both stood in the ankle-deep water.

"Did you blur out again?"

"I don't think so. I threw a lightning bolt at Mardon, but he threw one at me at the same time, and they crashed into each other. What are the odds of that?"

"In this line of work, pretty good," Green Arrow replied. "Did you get Mardon?"

"I don't know."

A lightning bolt crackled over their heads. On the west side of the dam, Mardon staggered into view. Electricity flared around him and wind tore at his clothes.

"I mean no," Barry clarified.

Oliver grabbed the Flash's arm and pulled him off the end of the dam. They dropped behind a brick wall just as another bolt seared the air. Barry lay on the sodden ground catching his breath. Oliver peered over the edge of their cover. In the distance, Mardon clutched his right arm as if it was broken.

"He's injured," Green Arrow reported. "Does that wand of yours still work?"

The Flash pulled the metal rod off his belt. Though badly scorched, it hummed to life, only to die again. He inspected it and made a few adjustments. This time it glowed a faint blue. He sighed in relief, but switched it off.

"That lightning strike nearly drained it. It won't survive another one."

"I can create a distraction while you run for him."

Barry shook his head. "I'm not up to speed— not yet. Another lightning bolt, and that'll be all she wrote." He leveled a curious stare at Green Arrow, and handed him the weather wand. "Can you shoot this on an arrow?"

His attention still on Mardon, Oliver took the cylinder. It only weighed about two pounds.

"It's a tough call," he said. "It may be too heavy."

"What if all you have to do is hit him? It doesn't have to be precise."

"Under normal circumstances, I'd give it better than a fifty-fifty chance." Green Arrow hefted the wand in his hand again, and looked around. "But with conditions like this? The wind whipping…"

"What if you didn't have to worry about the wind?"

"What are you thinking?"

The Flash pulled himself up to peer over the top of the brick wall alongside Green Arrow. Mardon remained at the far end of the dam, seventy-five yards away, peering steadily in their direction. He stretched out his arm, and lightning struck a few feet in front of their hiding spot. They both ducked.

"We've got to move now," Barry said. "He's getting stronger."

"And if they don't get those floodgates open, the engineers below estimate five minutes before it starts to crumble."

"When was that?"

"About five minutes ago. What's the plan?"

"You attach the wand to an arrow, I'm going to run straight at Mardon. You fire the arrow behind me. It can draft in my wake through Mardon's interference. At the last second, I'll dodge aside, the arrow will hit him, and the wand will shock the power out of him. Good guys win."

Oliver eyed him suspiciously.

"No, really," Barry said. "It'll work. He'll be focused on me."

"That's what I'm worried about."

"Look, Joe and Digg are down below us with who knows how many others. If this dam breaks, they're going to die. Period. So do you think you can hit Mardon?" Barry wasn't angry. He sounded desperate.

"I can." Oliver reached into a pocket on his tunic and pulled out a small roll of duct tape. Taking a simple razor-tipped arrow, he placed the wand along the shaft, moving it up and back, testing the balance. Finally he tore off some tape and affixed the wand to the arrow. He scowled, looked up, and nodded.

The Flash came up on one knee, still hunched behind the brick wall. He eyed the glinting razor edge.

"That looks sharp."

"It is." Green Arrow drew the string. "Just so you know, this arrow travels at two hundred miles per hour."

"Guess I better hit two hundred and one, then." He took a deep breath. "On three. One. Two. Thr—"

There was nothing but a blur left behind.

Green Arrow popped up over the brick wall and fired.

The arrow flew after the red streak. Lightning flared from Mardon's fingertips, sweeping across the top of the dam, trying to intercept the Flash. It crashed around Oliver, throwing dirt in the air and sending phosphorescent illuminations sparking across the surface of the water.

The Flash froze just a few feet from Mardon.

Green Arrow gaped in horror.

The arrow struck Barry…

…and passed through his body. Yet there was no impact, no blood. The arrow hit Mardon square in the shoulder. The wand flared blue and sparked. Mardon erupted in an electrical storm, his screams audible over the roar of the wind.

The Weather Wizard crumpled to the ground, wreathed in smoke.

Green Arrow vaulted the brick wall and ran out over the top of the water-swept dam. He splashed through water so deep it was hard to see the concrete surface. He couldn't fathom why the Flash was still upright. As he drew closer, he faintly saw the landscape through his friend's body.

Barry was blurring.

Instinctively Oliver reached out for the red shape, and his hand slipped *inside* it. His arm went numb and he jerked back, clutching his tingling limb. The Flash hung there, suspended and intangible, trapped in a stance that should have been impossible to maintain.

The dam shook under Oliver's feet. He looked back, expecting to see huge chunks of concrete calving off into the ravine. In several spots across the expanse of the structure, water frothed up into the air. The flow grew irregular, even as the roar grew louder.

The increased clamor came from below the rim, along its face, but it wasn't a breach. The floodgates had opened. The thundering deluge drowned out all other sounds, while the flow of water around his boots diminished until it was gone. The reservoir's surface dropped beneath the rim. The dam stood intact.

Green Arrow walked to Mardon, who lay in the mud

gasping shallow breaths. Blood seeped from the wound in his shoulder. It wasn't fatal, and Oliver couldn't summon much concern over it. The wand still glowed.

"Oliver?" Felicity called out. "What's happening? We've lost Barry's vitals."

"Mardon and Bivolo are down. Send someone to take them into custody. Report to Detective West that the dam is safe, at least for the moment, but keep people out of the floodplain for now, just in case."

Caitlin asked insistently, "And Barry?"

"He blurred going after Mardon, but he's alive." Oliver gazed back at the shimmering image of Barry Allen. "I think." The Fastest Man Alive was completely still. Not quite in this world. He wondered what Barry was seeing, if anything. As he tried to stare into those young eyes, he expected to find concentration and focus, but saw only the indistinct image of a face.

With a fatigued breath, Oliver sat heavily on the wet ground.

"I'll wait here with him." He studied the unnatural figure of his friend, and said, "Don't worry. The good guys won."

3 1

When Mardon faded out in front of him, Barry thought one of the scattershot lightning bolts made contact. But then he knew. He was blurring!

Mardon grew faint. *No! Why now?* People needed him. He couldn't fail them. Joe and John were in the path of danger.

"Barry!"

As the red blur whooshed past, Barry fell in beside him. The two Flashes ran together.

"Come on," the Future Flash urged, and they bore down. Barry roared into the speed force, feeling power rippling off him like a wake. Their surroundings were indistinct—location meant nothing at this speed.

A tantalizing tingle surged through him. He wanted it to be the speed burning the plasma out. Maybe it would happen this time. He would run fast enough. A quick glance at his older self showed him that the older Flash's suit was smoking from the friction. Barry slowed in alarm.

"Run!" the Future Flash cried. "Don't worry about me!"

He increased the pace again. The other speedster kept up, even though he was clearly in pain. He looked as if he would seize up at any step, tear muscles from the bone and tumble to a horrible stop. His face grew thinner by the second. His eyes went round as if in a bared skull. Barry grabbed his arm and dug his heels into the ground. He dragged them both to a flaming stop.

"What are you doing?" Future Flash gasped, pulling his arm free.

"You're going to die," Barry replied.

"I don't matter!"

"But—"

"*No.*" His older self sank to one knee, breathing hard. "You were close there. You felt it, didn't you? But you stopped."

They were on a concrete stoop. Barry looked around in surprise, feeling a sense of familiarity. It was the front porch of his old home, the house where he lived until he was eleven years old—the house where his mother died. He could smell freshly cut grass. His red boots were covered in green clippings. The mower sat on the sunny lawn in front of him. It was a warm summer morning. He recognized the feel of the air.

Future Flash stood and put a foot on the porch next to Barry. He pulled back his cowl to reveal his bruised, weathered face. Barry gasped at how much he looked like his father. Just as Henry Allen had appeared at his worst moment, when the jury foreman said the word *'guilty.'* His father had turned around to look at young Barry, sitting in the courtroom. Despite the pain, his father tried to give Barry an aura of confidence that almost covered the horrible regret deep in his eyes.

This was the same desolate gaze.

"I'm sorry I stopped." Barry sighed. "I just… you needed help."

"All right. Forget it." His older self laid a heavy hand on his shoulder. The gloves were torn. The flesh underneath was scarred. "We've got time."

"So am I time traveling?" Barry asked. "Are *you*? Do you come from the future or another dimension? Or… what?"

Future Flash smiled, just like Henry Allen, down to the crinkle around the eyes. He stepped up on the porch, offering a hand.

"Come on. Let's go in."

"Wait. Somebody else lives here now."

"We'll always live here."

They went through the front door. It made the same sound as he swung it closed behind them. Barry paused with his hand on the doorknob, feeling the familiar shape. The wood floor of the entryway creaked just right, and made him smile. The furniture sat in the correct places, everything orderly and clean. Nothing was broken. There was no fingerprint powder residue.

No outline of his mother's body on the floor.

Even so, Barry stepped around the spot where she

had died. He saw his basketball sitting against the wall, where it shouldn't have been because "people could trip over it and break their necks." He picked it up. It was his favorite basketball ever. It had developed just the right feel and grain.

He squeezed it between his hands, feeling its hardness—bounced it several times and created that same rubbery ring that should've caused his mother to shout for him to dribble the ball outside. He clutched it to his chest and listened. Nothing.

"That was close," his future self said as they entered the kitchen. He went to the counter and lifted a steaming coffee pot. "Guess she didn't hear you. Coffee?"

Barry could smell it, now that he mentioned it. The kind his dad liked.

"I'm too young. I can't have—" Then he stopped. "Oh yeah. Sure."

"Take your mask off. You don't have to worry about secrets here." When Barry pulled the cowl back, his older self stared with wonder. "Oh, man. Were we ever that young?" He handed over a steaming cup.

Barry set the basketball on the large wicker hamper full of newspapers and magazines, and went to the cabinet. He yelped in triumph and pulled out cookies. Opening the package, he set them on the table and took the cup of coffee. He remembered these cups. Thick and heavy. He loved these cups. Barry crunched into a cookie and sat in a familiar wooden chair. He ran his hand along the edge of the wood.

Future Flash took a cookie. "Chocolate chip? I like oatmeal raisin."

"I do? Since when?"

"Things change." Future Flash lowered himself into the chair where his dad used to sit. He settled slowly, as if he was in pain. He leaned on the table, cradling the steaming mug between red fingers. "Feels good to be home, huh?"

"Yeah." Barry picked up another cookie, and paused. He looked past the sink and out the kitchen window. It was a beautiful sunny day outside. Green leaves fluttered in the breeze. Puffy white clouds slid across the brilliant blue sky. He could smell the house around him. He had forgotten the scent. It filled him with memories and pain. Pictures hung from the refrigerator, and he remembered coloring them as he lay on the floor of his bedroom with a crayon clutched in his careful hand.

His gaze swung to the cookie in his gloved fingers. He studied it as if it was a scientific experiment.

"It's not real, is it? None of this is real." He ate it anyway.

"Real?" Future Flash sat back with a groan and looped his arm over the back of the chair. "Superspeed. Time travel. Talking gorillas. What does *real* mean to us?"

Barry shifted his observation to his older self, looking for faults and glitches. The worn face was so real. The weight on his shoulders. The pain in his eyes.

Future Flash raised an eyebrow. "That wasn't a trick

question, Barry. This isn't some villain's clever ploy to keep you trapped in a dream world."

"So what do you want?" Barry leaned the chair back on two legs, just like he wasn't supposed to, and snatched the basketball again. He started to spin it on the tip of his right index finger. "What exactly do you want me to do, Barry?"

"It's simple. The only thing you can do—run faster. You're the Flash. That's what you do. That's what you've done since the day you woke up in S.T.A.R. Labs. Run faster."

"That's what Harrison Wells used to tell me all the time." Barry kept slapping at the basketball, spinning it faster on his finger. "But he was just using me to get back to his own time. Why should I listen to you, when you tell me the same thing? Particularly since you're not real."

"Harrison Wells might not have been what he seemed, but he was right. If he hadn't pushed you to run faster, you couldn't have saved all the people you have. Our family and friends would probably all be dead now."

"I've heard all that before. I've *said* all that before. To Joe. And Iris. And Caitlin and Cisco." He laughed and took his eyes off the ball. It wobbled on his finger and ricocheted off the wall to skid across the kitchen floor. "Now I'm saying it to myself. I've run out of other people to lecture, I guess."

"Barry, I'm here to help you."

"But who *are* you?"

"I'm you. It's really that simple. I'm you."

"Where am I? What's the purpose of this?" Barry picked up the coffee cup but then slammed it down. "I'm sitting here eating cookies and doing Globetrotter tricks while my family and friends could be dying. Why do you keep pulling me into this world?"

"I'm not pulling you anywhere. Don't blame me. I'm here because of you, not the other way around."

Barry stared directly into his older eyes and saw fear deep inside. Any sense of confidence was pretense. He was terrified of something.

"I don't think you know what you're talking about."

"I'm telling you, this is all because of you."

"Not that. I know this is a hallucination or a dream or something. I don't think I can trust what you say." Barry sat back with a shiver. "I can't trust myself."

"What else do you have? No one else knows what we go through. Are you going to believe someone else, or are you going to believe the Flash?"

Anger flared, and Barry stood up. "Okay, this is stupid. This *isn't* my house. I'm not a little kid anymore. I've got to get back to my world. People are dying!"

"No, *you* are dying." Future Flash sat forward with those serious eyes his father always used. "Barry, you're being eaten up with that plasma from the wormhole. You've got to get it out of you."

"Caitlin is working—"

"Caitlin doesn't understand it. No one can but us."

His older self closed his hands into fists. "If you don't save yourself, nothing else will matter. If there's only one thing you've learned from Harrison Wells—from Reverse Flash—it's that you have to run. That's the only way to solve your problems."

Barry scrubbed at his hair in frustration. He heard a ticking sound and looked at the window. Blowing leaves tapped against the glass. It was dark outside. The summer morning had faded. He went to the sink and peered out. The clouds piled up like a fantastic bastion across the sky. Lightning winked in the coiled recesses of the clouds, popping yellow and purples across the black.

Future Flash joined him at the window. "You need to leave now."

"Why? What's happening?"

"Go, Barry."

"Okay. Let's go."

His older self continued to look out at the storm. "I'm not fast enough, but you are. Or you can be. I can hold him here while you run."

"Who? Run where?" Barry cried. "What's the point in just running?"

The house creaked in the wind. Branches snapped off trees. Objects tumbled through the yard. Trash cans. Lawn furniture. Then pieces of siding and bricks. The grass itself seemed to ripple and pucker before tearing off the ground. Chunks of sidewalk ripped free and flew into the air. Trees lifted, roots pulling out of the soil.

Suddenly everything went calm. Trees toppled back into their holes. Dirt and rocks cascaded to the ground. Dust clouded the air and coated the window.

A doorknob clicked. Barry spun around to face the door across the kitchen. Through the gauzy curtain, he saw a large shape outside.

Future Flash stepped forward, fear lacing his voice. "If you don't run, everyone will die."

"What's out there?" Barry asked.

The door smashed open and a hulking gray shape appeared, sparking with blue electricity. He wore a gray, fleshlike mockery of Barry's Flash costume, his face featureless except for glowing eyes and a strange caul mouth.

"Zoom," Barry whispered.

"Flash." Zoom spoke with his sepulchral voice. He then tilted his head slightly. "Flashes."

Future Flash leapt forward without hesitation, lacing the air with lightning-fast blows. He was a haze of fists, slamming Zoom side to side. Barry watched in amazement as his foe staggered, banging against the doorframe. The monster's knees buckled and he slumped onto the floor of the kitchen. Clawed hands dug into the tile. Future Flash continued to rain punishment. His older self was beating the most dangerous speedster Barry had ever encountered.

From his place on the floor, Zoom looked up slowly at Barry. Black eyes flared blue. He made a strange noise, a rumbling from deep in his chest.

He was laughing.

"You weren't fast enough when you were young." He leapt to his feet, clamping a savage hand around Future Flash's throat. The older man was driven to his knees. "You have no chance when you are old."

Barry latched onto Zoom's powerful arm, trying to free his older self. He felt like he couldn't breathe.

"For God's sake, Barry," Future Flash rasped. "Just run."

"No! I won't leave you."

Zoom flexed his arm, and Future Flash smashed through the kitchen table, scattering chairs and breaking dishes. Zoom raced past Barry, through the house, heading upstairs. In an instant he was back, a gust of wind sending the basketball into motion.

"There." Zoom idly tracked the ball bouncing across the floor. Red blood dripped from his fingers onto the kitchen floor. "More proof?"

Barry knelt next to the motionless older Flash. His gaze shifted upward with dread. Upstairs, where his parents' bedroom was. His blood turned ice cold. This place wasn't real, he fought to convince himself.

"Do you need a reminder?" Zoom held out his stained hands. "Speed won't save you or those you love." Then he was gone.

Barry sprang up and ran after him. He followed the fading trail of blue lightning across town into his other neighborhood. When he arrived at Joe's house, Zoom waited outside the smashed door. Barry charged him, but came to a stop on an empty porch. Zoom vanished down the street.

Barry followed again, knowing their next destination. The Picture News office, and Iris. This was a dream. It had to be a dream. It wasn't his world, but it didn't matter. He was compelled to save those he cared about. Once again he was too slow. When he approached the newspaper building, the front was destroyed, and a blue streak sped away.

Iris had been in there. Was *still* in there.

Zoom headed for S.T.A.R. Labs. Barry slipped into motion without thinking. Rather than following his enemy's track, he veered off and raced to the waterfront. He tore up along the river, leaving a wake of fire and spray. The finlike towers loomed closer. He was off the river and on the grounds. Through the doors. Into the Cortex…

"Caitlin! Cisco!"

There was no response. No one was around. Barry ran through all the offices and labs. Up and down the levels. Through the garage and once around the particle accelerator ring. There was no sign of anyone having been here recently. He returned to the empty Cortex. They weren't here.

"You're wrong, Flash."

A creak came from behind, and Barry whirled around to find Zoom sitting in Caitlin's chair. He hadn't been there before. Had he?

"They *were* here," Zoom growled. "I found them before you arrived."

"No. You couldn't have beaten me."

"While you searched, I went back and brought all the bodies here. Your parents. Your adopted father. The woman you love, and your two friends. All dead."

"No," Barry repeated, almost pleading for this to end, his heart hammering in his chest. The room wavered. He had to put a hand against the wall to stay on his feet.

"Yes. They are all in the Pipeline below." Zoom stretched out his hand, a gnarled finger extended toward the door. "I'll wait while you go to see for yourself. I laid them out for you. A monument to what your speed can accomplish."

"But why?" Barry moaned. Tears welled in his eyes. "It's me you wanted. Why did you have to hurt them?"

Zoom rose and came around the table. He towered over Barry, peering down with his horrible emotionless mask.

"Because unless you see the proof in front of you, you'll never learn."

Barry watched helplessly as the dark hand closed over him.

3 2

"He got both of them." Kyle Nimbus watched live footage from a news chopper flying high above the Cary Reservoir. A horde of inspectors in yellow helmets scurried over the dam. There was a large tent set up on one end, with police officers surrounding it.

The broadcast went back to the studio. File photos of Mardon and Bivolo filled the screen behind the hosts.

"Mardon even takes a good mug shot," Nimbus grumbled. "Anyway, I *knew* Flash had some new power." He shot Shawna an I-told-you-so look. "See? Nobody listens to me, and now we're done."

Shawna didn't say anything. Being alone with Nimbus made her uncomfortable—she missed even the brusque humanity of Mardon as a buffer. Nevertheless, she fought to maintain a bland face. The last thing she wanted was to give off the scent of guilt.

Nimbus hadn't even hinted that he suspected the mission had been compromised from inside. Rathaway hadn't been around since the news broke, so she had no idea what he thought.

She wanted to just teleport, and leave this all behind her. Shawna hated the fact that she cared—cared that even more innocent lives might be placed in jeopardy after this. So she had decided to stay, to bluff it out. Surely the group would break up, now that they'd lost Mardon. He had been their powerhouse.

Soon she'd be able to walk away, without having to look over her shoulder the rest of her life. The only people who knew she'd ratted out Mardon and Bivolo were Iris and the Flash's gang. They wouldn't talk—they were the good guys.

Nimbus picked up the remote to shut off the television, but before he could the face of Joe West came up on the screen. He nearly choked with rage, and turned up the volume.

"—two metahuman criminals attempted to destroy the Cary Reservoir Dam, which would have caused tremendous property damage and put hundreds of innocents at risk. Residents were fortunate enough to evacuate ahead of time. There would have been massive damage to the city's power and water supply.

"The perpetrators were apprehended, their plans thwarted, thanks to the efforts of the Flash and the Green Arrow. These two criminals were members of the gang that has been disrupting life in Central City for the past week or two," he continued. "They are now off the street." He pointed to a reporter who had his hand raised.

"Are the police close to arresting the other members of the gang?"

"We'll get them." West stared into the camera with cold eyes. He thanked the reporter, and hurried off amid more shouted questions.

Nimbus roared from the sofa and grappled with the flat-screen on the wall. Grunting and growling like a rabid dog, he tore it loose and smashed it to the floor. He kicked the wreckage several times for good measure.

"Congratulations, Kyle," Rathaway said as he entered the room. "That will show him."

"Shut up." Nimbus kicked the shattered TV again. "So is this it? Is there any money to split, or has this whole thing been a waste of time?"

"We lost two pieces last night, but we're not finished." Rathaway appeared calm, almost cheerful as he fiddled with his sonic gauntlets. "The game isn't over yet, and we're still in it to win."

"Mardon is gone, stupid!" Nimbus shouted. "What are you going to do to hurt the city now? Talk down to it?"

Rathaway actually laughed. "Very clever. Surprisingly so. But I'm not interested in the city now, Kyle. As the game progresses, the board shrinks and the goals narrow. Nevertheless, they still lead to victory."

"I don't even know what the hell you're talking about anymore."

"I know." Rathaway turned to Shawna. He raised his gloved hand.

Shawna's skin quivered on the back of her neck. At first it was a slight tremor, but suddenly she grew dizzy. The floor and ceiling swam around her. Her stomach churned. She took a step, bumped into a chair. Her feet slapped awkwardly on the floor.

She tried to teleport but her vision flared, and her head seemed about to split open. She couldn't breathe, and after a moment she dropped onto the filthy rug.

Abruptly the pain stopped. She lay gasping for air. Nimbus stood in shock as Rathaway squatted next to her.

"Trust me, Shawna," he whispered, "when I tell you that you can't get away from me. You are mine now, and I will use you as I will."

"What?" Shawna swallowed bile. "What are you saying?"

"I'm saying that you can't teleport away from me. If you do, I will kill you. I don't have to see you, or even be near you. I can trigger another attack like the one you just experienced, and I can do it from anywhere. Anywhere."

"Why are you doing this?" she asked. "We're on the same team."

"Are we?" he replied. "I don't think so. How did the police know to evacuate the people from below that dam? How did Flash and the Green Arrow capture both Mardon and Bivolo? It's as if they had a warning about the attack. Odds are someone squealed."

"Huh?" Nimbus looked from Rathaway to Shawna, at first in surprise, and then anger. "Oh, *that's* it." He began to go green. "You're dead, you stinkin' snitch!"

"Shut up!" Shawna yelled back. "I only wish I'd given them you, too! Flash is too soft, but that Arrow guy would kill you. I hope I'm there to see it."

Nimbus started to drift apart into a cloud, his fading face glaring death at her.

"Kyle!" Rathaway snapped, and he raised his hand. "Stop it—or I will."

Nimbus coalesced back into his human form, and Rathaway continued calmly.

"I need her abilities and I intend to have them." He turned back to peer at her. "Shawna, do you feel this?"

There was a slight tingle in her neck again. She took a sharp breath, gathering her wits, ready to teleport away. She had to try…

"Don't panic!" Rathaway said quickly. "I'm not going to hurt you again. But in the future when you feel that little tingle, that's me calling you—and you'd better come instantly, or it will escalate. Remember, it will happen no matter where you are. I will cause you to experience a cerebral hematoma, and you will die bleeding out of your nose and mouth. Do you understand now?"

She rubbed her hand over the back of her neck and sat up, inching away from him. She still felt queasy. Rathaway offered to help her up, but she ignored him. With difficulty, Shawna climbed to her feet.

"How?"

"The Singing Meteorite. I've always been intrigued by it, studied it years ago, when it was first discovered.

At one time I envisioned using it to create new telecommunication technology at S.T.A.R. Labs. Its physical structure is unique, granting it fascinating vibrational qualities, and the ability to store incredible amounts of energy. When my senses were enhanced, so was my natural connection to the meteorite.

"My extraordinary affinity for sound allows me to sense and calibrate the frequency of the vibrations. I knew I could exploit the resonance qualities inherent to the crystals. First I had to match the meteorite's original emissions, though, and the recordings from the observatory enabled me to do that. I can now channel and exploit its unlimited power.

"In simple terms, think of me as the hydrogen bomb of tuning forks."

Shawna made her way to the glass wall, trying to buy time so she could think of a way to escape.

"There's nowhere for you to go, Shawna." Rathaway grinned like a child. "There are crystal fragments in you. Last night while you were asleep... actually you were annoyingly restless, probably because your conscience was so troubled. So I set up a soothing vibrational wave that sent you off to slumberland, thus enabling me to inject you."

She launched herself at him with a primal cry, but again a searing pain shot through her skull, and she collapsed. She grimaced through clenched teeth.

"I'll kill you!"

"Doubtful." Rathaway regarded her, and the pain

receded. "This is marvelous. My first tests were simple, but you really are quite the masterpiece. I can't wait to use it on those I *really* want to hurt. As metahumans go, I've reached the pinnacle."

He flexed his fingers, and the wall of glass exploded outward. Shawna covered her ears, wishing this would end. She should've left after she gave the information to Iris. She shouldn't have come back. Stupid loyalty. To whom? For what?

Rathaway had fooled her, outsmarted her. She had been seduced by his complete disinterest in her as a woman, and his curiosity about her intelligence.

"It won't matter much longer," she said, and a calm overcame her. "I told the Flash where we are. He should be here any minute."

"Please." Rathaway scowled at her disdainfully. "If you had told him, the Flash and his crime-fighting chums would have been here long ago. No, I doubt they'll ever locate us—not that we'll be here much longer. I have the power I need to do what I've always wanted.

"Get up," he commanded, and he snapped his fingers at Shawna. She almost lunged at him again, but held back.

"What about me?" Nimbus whined. "Where do I go?" Rathaway took a steeling breath, which Shawna recognized as the signal for a lie.

"I want you here with us, Kyle," he said. "You're a part of this team. Before long we'll secure freedom for Mardon and Bivolo, and we'll continue as we have been. Everything is fine. Your future is here."

"Yeah?" Nimbus thought about it for a second. "Wait. You didn't put that junk in me like you did her, did you?"

"No, Kyle," Rathaway said. "You I trust."

In that, Shawna couldn't tell if he was lying or not. But Nimbus bobbed his head, obviously relieved.

"Okay then, that's cool."

"And soon, I suspect you'll get the chance you've wanted so badly—to kill your friend, Detective Joe West. How does that sound?"

Nimbus grinned ghoulishly. "Yeah? That sounds great." He flopped into a chair and extended the remote toward the bare wall where the TV had been. He looked down at the rubble on the floor. "Oh crap."

Rathaway smiled with satisfaction. "Fine," he said. "You two just relax until I need you. Shawna, don't go far." He pointed a finger. "Remember, I can tell." He left the room, followed shortly thereafter by Nimbus, muttering bitterly about having to watch a smaller television.

When the door closed, Shawna was alone. She went to the broken window and stared out. It was a normal day, with the sound of waves lapping the lakeshore far below the bluffs. Birds chirped. A cold October breeze filled the room.

No more storms.

She could've teleported anywhere she wanted. The whole world was open to her, but now she was trapped in this terrible house.

33

Joe West and John Diggle sat huddled over a small lantern. The night held a chill that sank into their bones. Above them, the stars appeared in the sky for a glorious clear night.

Joe's attention, however, was fixed entirely on the blurring image of the Flash, willing him to break free. Joe had called out several times, trying to get him to snap out of it, but to no avail. He couldn't reach him. So the long vigil had begun.

As the hours crept by, the knot in the pit of his gut grew tighter. He reached up to touch the comm in his ear.

"Caitlin, any change yet?"

The young woman's voice came back immediately. "Not yet, Joe," she said. "I'm sorry. I don't get any readings from him when he's blurred, but as soon as I do I'll let you know."

Caitlin sounded tired. She should be resting. Hell, they all should be resting. Oliver patrolled Central

City alone, with maybe an hour of sleep under his belt. Everyone was doing too much.

"All right. Thanks."

Barry's earlier episodes had only lasted a few minutes, and they had left him drained. This one was going on eighteen hours, so there was no telling what it would do to him. As a result they had several electrolyte IVs on hand, to start as soon as they were able to lay hands on him. Anything to give him the boost he would need, before he could slip into shock.

Joe rubbed his face roughly, his cheeks cold despite the heat from the fire.

"He'll be all right," John said, sitting beside him. Joe just nodded.

"We took down two of those metahumans," John continued. "That's two less for all of us to worry about. Gives us some breathing room." John's head bobbed toward the blurry image of the Flash. "Gives *him* some breathing room."

"God knows, he needs it," Joe muttered. "That boy doesn't know the meaning of the word rest. He'll keep going till it kills him."

"Oliver won't let that happen. Trust me. He's got a tranq arrow with Barry's name on it, if he gets too bull-headed."

That brought a smile to Joe's lips. "I'll sign the waiver if need be." He shook his head with frustration. "This Super Hero business is enough to make my hair go white. I don't know how you people do it."

"Well, I'm not the one to ask."

Joe scoffed. "Please. You run with the Green Arrow, and yet still have time to balance a family. You're just as baffling to me as Barry is."

"It's not easy." John shrugged sheepishly. "Every day I have to make a choice. Stay at home and play with my baby girl, or go out and make the world safe for her to live in."

"When you say it like that, the choice is pretty clear." Joe thought about his own career as a police detective, and realized he had been making the same choice for much of his life.

"It was clear." John leaned back and cast his eyes up at the night sky. "Sometimes I'd chuck it all aside just to spend one more hour at home with her, bouncing her on my knee."

"Wait till she wants you to play dolls with her."

John looked dubious. "I'm not sure I do dolls. I'm ex-Army."

Joe laughed. "That won't matter, trust me. You'll be wishing she'd wake up sooner, just so you can play with her."

"I do that now." A wistful expression overcame the big muscular man. "When she's awake, I feel the work calling. But when she's napping, I find myself counting the minutes until she wakes up."

"Welcome to fatherhood," Joe said with a broad grin. "There's something about baby girls that just melts us."

"Amen to that."

"Iris had me playing dress-up ten times a day every time she could. I even answered the door wearing an Easter bonnet. Lucky it was only a neighbor. If it'd been someone from the force, it would still be a story."

"I will *not* be doing that," John stated firmly.

Joe raised an eyebrow. "I'll lay money right now. You'll be wearing makeup and a frock in four years' time."

John waved off that image, laughing. "That's what she has a mother for."

"That's one thing in your favor." Joe's humor faded. "Neither Iris nor Barry had their mothers around. It's the one thing I'll always regret for them."

"They seemed to make out pretty well, even so. You did a good job raising them on your own."

"Thanks. It wasn't easy, particularly with Barry, after all he went through with his mom's death. Iris grew up too fast, too, I think. She had to help take care of Barry when he came to live with us. That boy was so beaten up inside then."

"Good thing he found two people who loved him. It's plain to see."

Joe shrugged. Again his gaze went to the vibrating figure next to them, looking for any sign that the seizure was abating. He couldn't even make out Barry's facial expression—only a hazy image. Lightning ominously crawled over Barry's body. That plasma was inside him, eating away at the speed force. How much longer could he go on before his heart stopped from the strain?

"So you and Nimbus have a past," John said. "What's the deal?"

Joe grimaced. "He's a lunatic. I put him away once. Sent him to the gas chamber, and he deserved to be there. But he escaped and he keeps coming back."

"They always do. In this new world, even dead doesn't mean dead anymore."

"Sounds like you have some experience."

John's expression turned cold. "Yeah. For good and bad."

"In our line of work, making enemies is part of the job." Joe reached for a thermos and poured them both some hot coffee. "Just wish they didn't turn into poison gas clouds."

"True enough." John took the cup gratefully.

Joe let out a frustrated sigh. "I don't worry so much for myself, but for everyone around me. They always go after the ones you love, you know?"

"They can try," John said.

"Yeah, they can try," Joe echoed. He looked at Barry again. "But this…" He took a deep breath. "This I don't know how to fight. I feel so damn helpless."

"You're doing what you can. Being the rock that he needs. Kids make clearer decisions if they feel solid ground beneath their feet."

"What if that's not enough?"

"Then we give them all the encouragement they can stand," John stated firmly. "Whether they like it or not."

Joe grunted. "Never took you for a philosophical sort. Sounds like you've done your share of talking someone down from a ledge. Oliver?"

"Hell, man, Oliver *lives* up on that damn ledge," John said with a harsh laugh. "But I can wax as rhapsodic as a poet, if it gets the job done."

Joe stood and walked over to the shimmering figure.

"I know you're in there, son," he said softly. "Just stop running and come back. We need you here. *I* need you here."

John came to stand next to them. "What happens to him when he's like that?"

"He says he sees things. People from the past, maybe the future." Joe sighed. "Not sure what's filling his head. All I know is the boy carries too much on his shoulders. He's trying too hard to save everyone."

"I'm not a doctor or anything, but this kid has all the symptoms of PTSD."

"Like combat fatigue?"

"Yeah, that's what they used to call it. A lot of soldiers suffer with it during and after wartime, and like it or not, this city is a war zone. It has been for a long time now. Soldiers can't stand on the front lines forever. The more they push themselves, the more they start to make mistakes or get sick. Their bodies and their minds start to work against them."

"It does sort of sound like what's happening," Joe agreed. "Except that weird plasma from the wormhole is inside him, too, so it can't be just psychological."

John shrugged. "Like I said, I'm not a doctor. I can only talk about what I know."

Then Joe froze.

For just a moment, he caught a solid glimpse of Barry's eyes, wide and filled with terror. Then it was gone. He stepped closer and spoke loudly.

"Barry! Can you hear me?" The blur slowed again. "That's it, son!"

"He's coming out of it!" Caitlin called out over the comm. "Heart rate is skyrocketing. Blood pressure is way too high."

Suddenly the Flash stopped.

The blurring ceased and Barry dropped as if he were a puppet whose strings had been cut. Joe reached for him, grabbing him before he fell to the ground.

John raced for the medical supplies, and instantly Joe was glad for the man's military training. Thanks to his years in Afghanistan, the ex-soldier stayed calm and efficient. It grounded Joe, helping him make sure that the emotions boiling inside didn't spiral into panic.

The Flash's arm thrashed, as if he was trying to strike at Joe, but the blow was so weak it barely brushed him.

"It's me, son," he told Barry. "It's all right. You're going to be all right. You blurred, but it's over now." He pulled back the cowl on the red suit.

"Zoom…" It came out as a strangled gasp.

"Zoom's not real," Joe said. "You're back with family." The costumed figure was trembling, and the tremors were becoming more violent by the second.

John wrapped a thermal blanket around him.

"It's bad," Joe said quietly. "This is the worst attack yet."

"His heart rate is slowing," Caitlin said. "Get him back here as quickly as you can."

Joe laid a hand on Barry's cheek. His skin was hot and dry.

"I've seen similar reactions out in the field," John said as he pulled up a uniform sleeve. "He's got way too much adrenalin in his system. Fighting too long and too hard. He's spent."

"Will he be all right?" Joe asked, wanting to hear the answer he needed.

"I'll get him stabilized," John replied. "You bring the van over. Get the heater going."

Joe ran for the van, bringing it closer and opening the vents full bore to get it warmed up inside. He and John bundled Barry into the back seat. Climbing in beside him, Joe remained there holding him close until they finally careened into the parking lot of S.T.A.R. Labs.

3 4

Barry dragged himself back to the waking world, though every part of his body begged him not to. Pain and exhaustion battered him before he even opened his eyes.

The vivid image of Zoom flashed in his thoughts, and he moaned. God, it had been so real. Agony and despair reverberated through him. The thought of all those he held dear, gone in seconds, all because he wasn't fast enough. His hand lifted in a vain attempt to brush the painful memories aside, but it was grabbed in a firm grip.

Barry opened his eyes. Oliver stood beside his bed, looking grim. As always.

"Finally awake. How are you doing?"

He moved, and immediately regretted it. His body was one massive ache.

"Terrible," he groaned.

"Glad you're still with us."

"Me too… I think." Barry managed the barest of grins as he shifted carefully. "I'm not used to healing this slow. What time is it?"

"Late. It'll be dawn soon. Most everyone is asleep, or should be. John is monitoring… the monitors. Your metas have gone to ground for now. We hit them pretty hard." Oliver reached for something beside the bed. He looked profoundly apologetic as he held up another of Caitlin's horrible metabolic shakes. "Here—you're supposed to drink this if you wake up."

Barry grimaced. "I should have stayed unconscious." But he took it. Oliver settled back in the chair next to the bed.

"You did a good job out there," he said. "We took out two of your enemies, and saved a lot of people." Oliver reminded Barry of a general visiting the injured after a hard-won battle. He couldn't deny, though, that the words of praise bolstered him somewhat.

"If it weren't for you and the others, it could have gone badly out there," Barry insisted. "You got Bivolo, and your arrow took out Weather Wizard."

"You're too hard on yourself. We did it together."

The door opened, and Joe, Iris, Caitlin, Cisco, Felicity, and John all rushed in. Though they all looked exhausted to one degree or another, they beamed with excitement as they gathered around the bed. Barry laughed weakly.

"I thought it was three in the morning, and everyone was asleep."

"It was a slumber party, man," Cisco replied. "We were out in the Cortex, making s'mores."

"I hope there's some left. I'm starved."

Caitlin lifted the metabolic shake from the bedside table where Barry had put it, and helpfully handed it back to him.

"Felicity has some good news," she said.

"I could use some." Barry gave the shake a sour glare. "Now more than ever."

Felicity grinned with excitement, but quickly bit her lip to shut it down.

"Well, first of all, this is very tentative so don't get too worked up." She started grinning again. "Something about your temporal anomaly and plasma infection kept digging at my brain. So I went scouring the Palmer Tech files for research projects using those keywords as my starting point. Palmer experimented with wormhole generation and something they called 'plasma-based technology.' I'm trying to get more details. It's not much—not yet, anyway—but it's something."

"At least it's a start," Iris said encouragingly. She leaned in and hugged Barry, which made him wince. Instantly she pulled away. "I'm sorry! Are you in pain?"

"A little bit." He wrapped her in his arms as hard as he could. "This helps. And thanks, Felicity. Hopefully something will come of it, but until it does we can't ignore reality. There's going to be a risk that I'll blur at inopportune times. This last one was the worst yet—you guys probably thought I was gone for good."

"I knew you'd be back, Barry." Joe grinned. "Never had a doubt about it." John shot Joe an approving glance, and Barry wondered what that was about. They all took seats around the room, or found a place to lean.

"Great work up there," John said. "Score two for the good guys."

"Well, it helped that Shawna turned, and trusted Iris enough to give us a lead," Barry said, and he went serious. "Now we need Rathaway."

"We'll get him," Oliver said with an easy confidence that Barry wished he could steal.

"Not if I keep blurring."

Joe handed him a cup of water. "So you saw Zoom this time? That can't have been pleasant."

"No." Barry's voice was barely above a whisper. "He…" Barry stopped. *Killed all of you*, he thought. "… was as nasty as ever," he said.

"So you keep seeing people from your past?" Oliver asked.

"Well, and the future." Barry straightened in the bed despite the pull of sore muscles.

"Like your older self?" Cisco asked. "Was he there?"

"Yeah, he's always there. Giving me advice." Barry rolled his eyes with a smile. "I must think I'm Joe in the future."

"You'll never give advice like me." Joe feigned pride. "Even in the future."

Oliver leaned forward. "Maybe I'm not understanding

this plasma issue. I know Caitlin suspects it's making you hallucinate. Tell me what you're thinking about, just before you blur."

It took Barry a few minutes to put his thoughts into words.

"I feel as if I'm losing."

Oliver frowned. "Control?"

"No. Like… like I won't make it in time. Like I'm about to fail."

"Who do you think you're failing?"

"I don't know." Barry struggled to put into words all those chaotic moments. "The people I'm trying to save, maybe. So I run faster."

"And the blurring is caused by using the speed force?"

"No," Caitlin said. "Barry is infected by a plasma from a singularity. The plasma in his body activates due to specific hormonal activity—we think cortisol— in his system. Once the plasma is active, it hijacks the speed force and causes Barry to blur, which appears to be physical effect of his speed force running wild. And then—for lack of a better concept—as the speed force powers the cells in Barry's body, the plasma feeds off those cells. It's as if cancer infected a body, forcing it to produce sugars, which then fed the cancer." She paused, then added quickly, "But this isn't cancer."

Oliver listened and nodded. "What's the objective of this plasma?"

Caitlin tilted her head in confusion. "It doesn't

have an *objective*. It's not a living thing. It doesn't have consciousness or a desire except to find a host and survive. It's a form of energy. It does what it does, and apparently Barry's speed force is exactly what it needs to sustain itself."

"But you don't blur every time you use your speed," Oliver said.

"No, I don't," Barry answered. "Though there have been times I've felt it about to come on."

"And what did you do?"

"Panic," he answered blithely.

Oliver gave him a stern look.

Barry could only shrug. "I'm not sure really. I didn't *do* anything. Most of the time I'm too busy trying to save someone, or stop someone."

Oliver's expression changed. "Caitlin, this plasma only manifests when Barry is flooded with cortisol."

"Yes."

Oliver rubbed the stubble on his jaw. "Barry, who did you see in your hallucination the first time you blurred?"

"Just me. The older me. That was when I was running the Pipeline here."

"And next?"

"Danton Black. My first real fight as the Flash. He died."

"And next?"

"Grodd."

"The talking ape." John tried to keep the incredulity from his expression. Barry thought he did a reasonably good job.

"Don't mock," Joe said. "He's scary as hell."

"And before all the blurs," Oliver pressed, "you were using your speed to fight or save people?"

"The Danton blur was at the chemical fire on the waterfront. I was trying to keep the firefighters safe. And Iris. She showed up to cover the story. In her pajamas, no less." She glared at him, then gave an embarrassed smile.

Oliver narrowed his eyes. "And with Grodd?"

"That happened at our house when the Mist attacked Joe. But there were other blurs that didn't happen while I was in action. Both here at S.T.A.R. Labs."

"What were you thinking about?"

"I was running. Just running, like I do all the time."

"Think, Barry," Oliver pressed. "What was happening in your head?"

Barry shut his eyes and fought to concentrate, to remember those events. The feelings of racing around the Pipeline.

"My powers had glitched a little the day before, like I told you in my lab, when I pulled a woman out of her car."

"The one who reminded you of your mom, because she was more worried about her son than she was about dying," Oliver noted.

"That's what I was thinking about." He returned Iris's sympathetic squeeze of his hand. "My mom and how I couldn't save her."

"And on the treadmill?" Oliver said quietly.

"Caitlin." Barry looked up at her. She returned the gaze, her eyes growing hazy with unshed tears. "She was sitting there, and I started thinking about how I let Ronnie die. I lived, but Ronnie died because I wasn't fast enough, and Caitlin was alone again."

"And this last time at the dam," Oliver said, "the flood placed all of us in danger. Joe and John were down there. If you didn't stop Mardon, they would die."

"It can't be that," Barry protested. "I'm stressed now, and I'm not blurring."

"It's obviously not *just* stress. There's something else happening inside you. Still, up until now, you've been assuming this is something purely physical."

"Isn't it?" Barry asked. "The plasma is inside me, consuming my cells. That's a scientific fact."

"Yes, it is," Felicity acknowledged, "but that's not what's *triggering* your blurs. It's your emotions. Emotions have their own biology, their own chemical pathways. The mind-body connection is more profound than Western medical science is willing to admit. Oliver has taught me some of that."

"So what are you saying?" Barry scowled.

"Your brain is giving the plasma a way in," Oliver said.

"How? By thinking?"

"No," the archer replied. "By feeling."

"You're saying my emotions are eating me alive?"

"In a way."

"I think Oliver is onto something," Felicity said.

"You care about everything and everyone so deeply, particularly those of us in this room. You have this light inside you that few people possess."

"So I'm my own worst enemy."

"I'm just looking at the evidence." Oliver folded his arms, holding his ground. "I can't say anything about the plasma that's in your system. I don't understand it—that's Caitlin's area of expertise—but it seems reasonable that the blurring incidents are associated with your emotional state, as well."

"So what do I do? Stop having emotions?"

"That's not what he's saying, Barry," Caitlin replied. "We don't totally understand the biochemistry of emotions, but his idea that it's your fear, sparking the plasma to life, actually has merit."

Barry sank back onto the bed. "Well, I can't stop running, and I can't stop how I feel."

"There's no harm in caring for people, Barry," Oliver said, "but like any soldier in a war, you can't let it consume you."

"I've told you before, I'm not a soldier."

"You are," Oliver countered. "You just don't have the discipline of one."

Joe frowned. "He works pretty damn hard at this, you know. He gets the job done. We don't all have to be the grim avenger of the night."

"I wouldn't want him to be, Detective West," Oliver said with a calm stare, "but I think I can offer Barry a few things that might help."

"Like shooting people's eyes out?" Joe snapped.

"Joe!" Barry held up a calming hand. "Take it down a notch."

"No," Oliver said, addressing the detective. "Like taking a tactical breath before acting…" He turned back to Barry. "…and refocusing your mind, so you control your thoughts during a fight. Your mind races like the rest of you. I can help you slow it down, and control your emotions under fire.

"That's something I do understand," he added. "I'm human."

"Well, that hasn't been proven yet," Barry responded, and he grinned, but secretly he relished the calm intensity Oliver maintained.

Oliver's eyebrow rose slowly. "Let's not forget which of us is the *meta*human here."

"Point taken."

Joe rubbed the back of his neck. "Hey look, I'm sorry, Oliver. I don't mean any of that stuff. I'm just a little wound up."

Oliver offered a smile. "Not a problem, Detective. I respect you standing up for your son."

Both Iris and Felicity grunted in agreement.

Barry regarded Oliver. "So you think this tactical breathing thing will help with the blurring?"

"Can't hurt."

"Okay." Barry settled back into the pillow. "And I am a big fan of breathing. I hope to keep doing it for a long time."

3 5

The motorcycle bounced over the rutted road, and Barry hung onto Oliver for dear life. They had been riding for more than an hour, south out of Central City, roaring between fields of brown cornstalks not yet plowed under for winter.

Suddenly Oliver swerved across an open meadow of high grass. He braked among a grove of bare-limbed maples surrounded by a beautiful carpet of bright scarlet leaves. One lone red leaf quivered high above in the skeletal branches. Cutting the motor, he looked around.

"This is good."

Barry groaned as he lifted a stiff leg and slid off the bike. He removed the helmet Oliver made him wear, and had to admit, it was a gorgeous spot. The trees. The knee-high grass. The distant cornstalks.

"What do you hear?" Oliver took the helmet and hung it on the handlebar. Barry snapped to attention, listening for signs of an attack or danger. He spun around, searching for anything odd.

"I don't see anything."

"I said hear. What do you *hear*?"

"Oh." Barry stood quietly. "The wind?"

"No."

"I don't?"

"No. Listen again."

Barry tried once more. "I really think I hear the wind. The branches of the trees, and the corn stalks over there."

"So you don't hear the wind. You hear branches creaking and cornstalks rustling. You can't hear the wind—only where the wind has been."

"Really?" Barry gave him a snide grin. "Is this a one hand clapping thing?"

Oliver unstrapped his bow from the motorcycle. Barry regarded the weapon.

"You're not going to try and shoot me, are you? Cisco tried to suggest that, to test my blurring. Joe nearly shot him instead."

"No, I'm not going to shoot you." Oliver snapped the bow out into form. "Probably." The weapon went from short staff to high-tech compound bow with a flick of his wrist. He drew an arrow from the quiver on the motorcycle. "Do you breathe when you run?"

"Of course." Barry paused, suddenly wondering. "Wait. Do I? Yes, sure I do. I just do it faster than most people. When I'm inside the speed force, physics and biology work a little differently."

"But not *too* differently, because the plasma is linked to hormonal responses. Therefore you need to control your hormones."

"You sound like my junior high principal." Barry laughed.

Oliver's eyes flicked to the bow. Barry straightened reverently, and went silent.

"I'm going to teach you several concepts, and the techniques needed to practice those concepts. Once you master them, I believe this will help with your blurring."

"Today?"

"It's been more than a day since you came out of the blur. We can assume your Pied Piper will make a move soon. We don't have a lot of time."

"How long did it take you to master these techniques?"

"I've been practicing some of them for more than five years and I haven't come close to mastering them yet."

"Well, thanks for the confidence." Barry crooked his mouth in a disbelieving smile. Oliver kicked through the red leaves and into the high grass.

"The purpose of these techniques," he explained, "is to calm your mind when you're about to blur. You need to gain control of your autonomic nervous system. It will allow you to act, but to act with calm and purpose."

"What will it do to the plasma?"

"Don't worry about things you can't control. That's the whole point of this exercise. You need to be in the moment. There will be a time to deal with the plasma, but I'm trying to teach you how to avoid blurring."

"Aren't they related?"

"Yes, but when you're trying to reach the Pied Piper, you can't concern yourself with the connection. You can't worry about saving Joe, or saving me, or running fast enough to save anybody."

"Isn't that the point of being the Flash?"

"Yes, but if you're always thinking about that, it distracts you from *being* the Flash. When a soldier is on the battlefield, he has to remain focused on the moment. In that moment when the bullets are flying, he's only worried about staying alive, and maybe accomplishing his mission. The fact that he's been *trained* to do it allows him to serve his buddies, his unit, and ultimately his country."

Oliver pointed at himself. "But it starts here. Until you're present enough to do what you can do, your purpose is pointless. If you blur because you're panicked about failing someone, you *have* failed."

Easier said than done, Barry thought, but he knew the man was right.

Oliver settled cross-legged in the grass. "Sit there." When Barry joined him, feeling a little silly, Oliver continued, "We are going to practice tactical breathing. Breathe in through your nose to the count of four. Then hold it to the count of four. Then release it through your mouth to the count of four. Then hold to the count of four, before you take another breath." He demonstrated.

"Is that it?" Barry asked. "That's pretty simple, but it can't really work for me. I can run to Star City and back in that amount of time."

"Time means nothing to you. Meditation isn't a factor of time. It's about focus. About the count of four—not the amount of time it takes. The purpose of a breathing exercise is to force your mind to return to the present. Stop thinking about what has happened, or what might happen. Think about what *is* happening." He gestured for Barry to begin.

Barry started to breathe, counting internally. Slowly in. Hold. Out. Hold. Repeat. The October sun warmed his face. Grass brushed against his forearms. Wind rattled the cornstalks. A bird whistled in the distance.

He felt his leg muscles tugging. His ribs ached as his chest filled and emptied. His toes wiggled inside his sneakers. He felt the tips of his fingers brushing his palms. His chest rose and fell.

He really should be looking for Rathaway.

"What just happened?" Oliver asked.

"Nothing. I'm breathing like you said."

"You were, but then your mind went somewhere else. I saw it in your face."

Barry sighed and stood up. "Yeah. I couldn't help thinking about what I need to be doing, instead of sitting in a field meditating."

Oliver regained his feet. "The next time you blur, you might not come back."

"Oh, thanks. *That* calmed me down."

"The point is, there's nothing more important for you at this moment than sitting in a field meditating. You can do this, Barry. You've already done it, but you just don't realize it."

"I have?"

"You said yourself that you've felt the blur coming on, and you managed to hold it off. How?"

Barry thought back to the incident with the bullet and Captain Singh in the window. It had seemed as if he was going to blur then, but he managed to seize the bullet anyway.

"I don't know."

"*Think*. What happened?"

"I had to grab the bullet to keep it from hitting a man." Barry mimicked reaching out with thumb and forefinger, plucking an object out of the air. "I thought I was blurring as I was running in to help him, but I got the bullet anyway."

"Were you thinking about the man, or the bullet?"

"Both. The bullet was going to hit the man. I don't get what you're saying."

"You said when you hit Mardon with lightning at the reservoir, you thought you might blur, but you didn't." Oliver began to swing the bow around his head and shoulders in a series of exercises.

"I know, but then I blurred when I was just running toward him. Is there any chance there isn't a pattern?"

"No. When you were hurling lightning at Mardon, were you thinking about Joe or John? Or were you thinking about the lightning?"

"Well, throwing lightning is tricky. Generating it is one thing, but controlling it takes a lot of focus."

Oliver froze with his bow over his head. He regarded Barry expectantly.

"Focus," Barry repeated, this time with excitement.

"Yes."

"I was focused on the bullet, and on the lightning."

"Yes. Not on the consequences, not on the possibility that you could fail. Only on the task itself."

"I was in the zone, I guess. Is that what you're trying to teach me? That seems easy."

Oliver laughed—a rare sound. "Doesn't it?"

"So I just need to think about… wait, what now? Focus on running? But that feeds the plasma. I still have to move at superspeed."

"Don't get too far away from the moment you just had. Focus is the key, but in your case you can't depend on a bullet or lightning every time you need it. You need to bring your focus with you. You need a trigger. Something that will remind you, when you're about to blur, that you need to stop."

"Stop?"

"Not literally, but stop thinking along one path, and switch to another. Focus. Center. Breathe. Become aware of yourself in the moment. The moment is all that matters. Bring your mind inward. One step after another. That's how a path is formed."

Barry wanted to understand. He wanted to recapture

that light bulb moment he thought he'd just had—until he tried to apply it to the real world. It was just beyond his fingertips. So frustrating. He didn't know if he could think about so many things in the middle of a fight. If someone lost their life because he hesitated, because he stopped to breathe or contemplate, it would destroy him.

"Barry!" Oliver said loudly. "You're overthinking it. You have to give yourself permission to stop. To stop being afraid for everyone, all the time. Do you understand?"

"I understand, but that doesn't mean I can do it."

"I know."

"I realize you want to help me," Barry said. "So I guess you've mastered this not-being-afraid-for-everyone thing?"

Oliver stared at Barry quietly as he nocked the arrow. He turned his torso, keeping his eyes locked on Barry, and fired. The arrow drove into the trunk of a maple tree. Then Barry realized it had pinned the final leaf—as it fluttered toward the ground.

"Well enough," Oliver said.

"Okay, that was impressive. But to be fair, that leaf wasn't attacking anyone you love."

"What was your favorite toy when you were young?" Oliver asked out of the blue.

Barry wondered why, but it wasn't a hard one. "Microscope."

Oliver tilted his head. "Really?"

"Oh, yeah." Barry grinned. "It was so cool. I had

all these slides like a fly's wing and an eyelash and—"

"Okay, here's what I need you to do. When you start to blur, you think of that microscope and how you... loved looking through it?"

"Don't say it like it's a question," Barry protested. "I did love looking through it. I spent hours with that thing. Couldn't wait for the weekend so I could just take time to work with my microscope."

"Hm. Okay. So that's your trigger. Think of that time. That experience. Recreate the focus you brought to that moment. Can you do that?"

"I guess." He paused. "I can."

"Let's practice breathing again, and this time I want you to associate the breathing and the mindfulness with that microscope."

"I can think of something different, if you want."

"No. It's your thing."

"It's just I get the sense you don't like the microscope."

"It's not mine to like or dislike. Let's sit down again and practice breathing techniques."

Both of them settled back into the grass. "Remember your timing. Keep to it. Don't think of anything but your breathing, and your microscope."

They sat quietly, surrounded by the sounds of the meadow and the cornfield. Time passed and Barry began to hear nothing but his own breathing. Amazingly he could feel the pressure of the microscope on his eye, and smell the plastic and steel. He was tempted to reach out and adjust the lens. The comfort and safety of his room surrounded him, the hours of freedom to explore and learn.

"What was your favorite toy?" he asked.

"Probably the Ferrari Testarossa I got for my fifteenth birthday."

More time passed in silence.

"Did I mention my microscope came with its own light bulb?"

"Breathe, Barry, breathe."

"Oh my God!" Iris leaned toward the open car window so cold air could whip over her face. "I forgot how much I love nice weather."

"It's a little chilly, don't you think?" Caitlin clutched her jacket at the neck.

"It's not raining. Or hailing. Or tornadoing." She grinned, but then noticed her companion's trembling fingers. "Cold?"

"No, I'll be okay."

Iris brought the window up. She turned on the heat.

"Sorry. I'm just so happy to see blue sky. I forgot it's fall." Caitlin smiled distantly and stared out the window. "This won't take long. You can get back to work soon."

"I'm not thinking about work." Caitlin checked her phone.

"Expecting a call?"

"No, I've got a sequencer running on Barry's DNA,

and it will send results to me when it's finished."

Iris's fingers went stiff on the steering wheel. "Do you think there's something wrong with his DNA?"

"I don't know," Caitlin admitted somberly. "I don't seem to know anything. No one has ever tried to diagnose a metahuman infected by a temporal plasma. There's *nothing* on WebMD about it."

Iris laughed. "Well, I'm glad you decided to come with me while I do this boring legwork. It's nice to have you here—I get tired of talking to myself, and I don't have a lot of friends. It's kind of hard with the life we lead, you know?"

"I do." Caitlin smiled genuinely. "It is good to get out of the lab for an afternoon, get a little perspective, eat something other than delivery. And it *is* a beautiful day. It's been so nice since Barry and Oliver captured Weather Wizard."

"That was days ago, too, and we still haven't heard anything more from Hartley Rathaway. Do you think he may have left town after we caught Mardon and Bivolo?"

"No." Caitlin was firm. "Hartley doesn't give up. He's always had a chip on his shoulder, and he doesn't like to lose. Whatever he intends to do, he won't stop 'til it's done."

"All the more reason to find his lair, as Cisco calls it." Iris turned left into a small street near Central City University. It was an older neighborhood nestled next to the college, consisting mainly of faculty and student housing.

Caitlin checked her phone again.

"I have to admit, I like having Team Arrow around, because it takes some weight off Barry," she admitted. "Plus, I can be here while Felicity is back at the lab, working with Cisco. There's still hope she can pull off a miracle of some sort with that Palmer Tech research."

"That would be wonderful." Iris wheeled into a cul-de-sac. Cruising slowly around the street, she craned her neck, checking house numbers. "There's the address."

She pulled up to the curb and they got out at a tiny bungalow in need of paint and window screens. Several large plastic garbage cans overflowing with crushed beer cans cluttered the lawn. Cheap beer at that. College student beer.

"Oh my," Caitlin muttered as she kicked past taco wrappers and empty potato-chip bags. "This is a side of college I never encountered."

Iris smiled but stayed silent. They crossed the trash-strewn yard and stepped up on the bare concrete stoop. Iris pressed the doorbell and knocked. Silence. She repeated. And again.

Finally a shuffling noise came from inside.

The door swung open to reveal a bearded young man, maybe twenty. His hair swirled uncontrollably. His eyes bleary slits, he stood in his underwear and mumbled.

"Yeah?"

"Oh. Well, hello." Iris tried not to stare or laugh while Caitlin turned around to face the street. "Hi. Are you Marshall Chen?"

"What?"

"Marshall Chen."

"What?"

Iris and Caitlin exchanged amused looks.

"What is your name?"

"I was sleeping."

"To be fair, it is only three pm," Caitlin offered. "Can we give him a few minutes to collect his thoughts? And his pants."

"*Marshall*," Iris said louder.

The man scrunched his face. "You looking for Marshall?"

"Yes!"

"Are you Amy?"

"No. Is Marshall here?"

"Uh. Maybe." The guy pointed at Caitlin. "Are you Amy?"

"Yes," Iris responded quickly. "She's Amy, and she wants to see Marshall."

The man looked Caitlin up and down. He turned and shouted, "Marshall! Amy!" Then he staggered away from the door, leaving Iris and Caitlin standing there.

After a few minutes, another door opened inside and a new young man came toward the front. He was a little more put together, clean-shaven, wearing both pants and a shirt. He stepped onto the porch and peered out beyond the two women.

"Did you guys see a girl out here?"

"Are you Marshall Chen?"

"Yeah." Marshall looked from Iris to Caitlin. "Wait. Did Amy send two of her friends to break up with me?"

Iris smiled. "We don't know Amy, but I have a few questions for you, if you don't mind. My name is Iris West, and I work for the Central City Picture News."

"Oh yeah?" He scratched through his hair. "I see your site sometimes."

"This is Dr. Caitlin Snow. She works for S.T.A.R. Labs."

"S.T.A.R. Labs?" Marshall brightened and grew more attentive. "For real? I didn't think there *was* a S.T.A.R. Labs anymore. Must be a cool place to work."

Caitlin shrugged and gave a polite smile.

"You work for Dr. Ronald Savic, don't you?" Iris said.

"Yeah. I did. I was an intern for a few semesters."

"Did he ever mention a man named Hartley Rathaway to you?"

"No…" Marshall thought for a second. "Well, yeah. He worked with Dr. Rathaway at S.T.A.R. Labs." He pointed at Caitlin as if for confirmation. "That was years ago before Dr. Savic came to CCU, but he never *really* talked about him. They were in different fields."

Iris exhaled deeply. She was near the end of her list of names. Marshall Chen was a former lab assistant to a former colleague of Hartley Rathaway. That was about as tangential as it got.

After this, she might as well put up flyers with Rathaway's picture, and the headline HAVE YOU SEEN THIS MAN?

"Did you talk to Dr. Savic?" Marshall asked.

"Not yet. He's been in Markovia since June, so I don't think he can help me. But I'll call him."

"He's not in Markovia," Marshall replied. "He didn't go."

"What? The Physics Department told me he went. They gave me a number where I could reach him."

"Really?" Marshall stared at her, his mouth open in annoyance. "Dammit."

"What's wrong?"

"Well, I was set to housesit for him while he was out of the country, but then at the last minute I got a call saying he didn't need me, that he wasn't going."

"Dr. Savic called you?"

"No, it was somebody else. One of his lab guys probably. Man, I really wanted to do it, too."

"Why?"

"Have you seen his house?" Marshall grinned. "It's huge. I mean huge. Out by the lake. Beautiful place. It would've been great. Since I graduated, I haven't been able to find a job, so I just stayed here." The guy in his underwear crossed the living room behind them, clanking through empty beer cans. "If he's in Markovia, I wonder who he got to housesit for him. *Dammit*."

Iris grabbed Caitlin by the arm. "That's where Rathaway is." But Caitlin was already on her phone calling Barry. Quickly extracting the address from Marshall, the two women ran for the car. Before Iris could start it, however, he came rushing toward them.

"Wait! Wait!" He knocked on Caitlin's window. When she rolled it down, he handed her a flash drive.

"What's this?" Caitlin asked.

"It's my CV. My resume. If you guys at S.T.A.R. Labs are hiring, I'd appreciate the opportunity to help you."

"You have already." Caitlin put the flash drive in her pocket as they sped away.

3 7

A waning moon lifted into the night sky. Folk nestled safe in their homes, the day long done. Doors were locked and the streets were empty. Houses that had glowed warm were now dark.

The Flash appeared on a hill two hundred yards from the palatial house overlooking the lake. He was the first one to arrive. Or so he thought. In the darkness crouched a figure. The Flash tensed until he saw the hood and the bow.

"How did you get here ahead of me?" the Flash asked.

"No sign of movement in the house."

The Flash spun around. "Is everyone else here?"

Green Arrow shook his head. "They're five minutes behind me."

"But how did you—?"

Arrow lifted a hand to his ear. "Do we have ID on our targets?"

Felicity's voice crackled. "Satellite imagery shows three heat signatures. Two on the bottom level, one on the third."

"I only see two stories," the Flash remarked.

"Blueprints indicate a wine cellar."

The speedster studied the dark windows. "I wish we knew who was who."

Arrow flicked off his comm. "You're worried about Detective West running into Nimbus."

The Flash flicked his off, as well. "Habit, I guess." He sighed, hating to be so transparent.

"He'll have John with him, and both men are experienced in clearing a house. Focus on your job. Trust everyone else to do theirs."

"I know," the Flash grunted in frustration. "I just wish—"

"No," Green Arrow said, cutting him off. "Detective West is qualified to be here. You need to keep your head. We can't afford to lose you to a blur."

"You won't. This is our shot to end this siege." The determination in his own voice bolstered him, pushing aside his anxiety.

"Good." Green Arrow switched on his comm again, and the Flash followed suit.

"—said, is everything all right?" Caitlin sounded alarmed.

"All good," the Flash told her. "Just a last-minute pep talk."

"Well, don't turn the set off inside the house. Those

earwigs are meant to protect you from Pied Piper's sound waves."

"Gotcha." The Flash shifted back and forth on his feet, eager to start.

"Breathe," Green Arrow told him. "Inhale. Pause. Exhale. Pause." The man spoke so quietly it was like a soft buzz in his ear. The Flash listened as Oliver slowly repeated the mantra a couple of times. His body began to relax. He stopped shifting about.

John announced over the comm that they were in position. Felicity gave them details on the locations of their targets, tagging them to schematics they had acquired beforehand. The Flash nodded to the Green Arrow.

"Let's do this."

Arrow came to his feet. "Spartan, disable the alarms."

"We're on it," John answered via the mic in his stylized helmet that gave him his codename.

"After alarms are disabled, you have the single target on the top floor."

John acknowledged, and a short time later gave the all-clear. The Flash and Green Arrow moved in until they were crouched at the front near the door with their backs against the wall.

The Flash looked expectantly at Green Arrow.

"After you," the archer said.

"Meet you inside," and the Flash was gone. Entering through the front door, he crossed a huge open space on the first floor and went straight for the stairs that led down to the wine cellar. At the bottom, he found aged wines stacked bottle after bottle against the walls.

A heavy table dominated the center of the room, lit by an overhead light. It was covered with a variety of equipment, including a spectrometer, several rotary cutters, and what looked like jeweler's tools. He also noticed crystal shards and chunks of stone, likely what was left of the Singing Meteorite.

Hartley Rathaway leaned into the pool of light, looking far too smug. He wore his sonic gauntlets. As the Flash entered, Shawna took a step back into the shadows.

"Well, look who finally decided to show up to the party," Rathaway sneered. "It turns out our little song bird was a snitch after all."

"I didn't tell them!" Shawna implored. "I don't know how they found us."

The Flash crossed his arms. "I don't know what you're talking about, Rathaway, but you left a trail even a reporter could track."

Rathaway studied him. "I hear you've brought in help. Couldn't handle the job yourself?"

"It just means I get to take out the trash that much faster."

"Ah, the witty comeback." Rathaway clapped his hands. "That must mean you're officially a Super Hero. Congratulations."

"Maybe you shouldn't antagonize the Flash," Shawna suggested.

"It *was* pretty good," the Flash admitted, giving a

small grin, "but that's all I've got. So step away from the table, and let's call this thing over."

"Over?" Rathaway laughed. "My endgame has just begun, you see. All of this has been merely the preamble to my glorious finale."

The Flash groaned. "You got a lot of nerve criticizing my dialogue, what with that cliché monologue you're spouting. I'm already bored."

"Bored, are we?" Rathaway's eyes narrowed. "Then by all means let's begin."

The Flash catapulted himself forward, but suddenly the Pied Piper vanished. Skidding to a stop against the far wall, the speedster sent bottles clanging noisily at the impact. He spun around to see Peekaboo near the stairs, standing beside Rathaway.

Perfect.

He lifted a hand to shield his eyes.

An arrow struck the floor between the two criminals, producing a blast of light. Shawna cried out, blinded and unable to teleport. Green Arrow came down a few steps into the cellar, his bow already nocked with another bolt.

Rathaway cursed and held up his hand. He clutched a device the size of a cigarette lighter, which he pressed with his thumb. The Flash's ears exploded in pain that seemed to come from the earwigs themselves. Oliver also arched backward in agony. Digging his fingers under the edge of his mask, the Flash pulled out the earpieces. The sound stopped, but his ears still rang.

Rathaway grabbed Shawna and shoved past the staggered Green Arrow.

The Flash's metabolism, wonky as it was, eased the trauma from Rathaway's attack. Fumbling along a wall, holding his aching head, he weaved toward Green Arrow. Surprisingly, even without a super power, the archer pulled himself to his feet, his face still pinched with pain.

"Get after them," he grunted.

The Flash nodded and sped up the stairs. He searched through the few large rooms on the main floor. A sizeable back room had a wall of windows facing the lake, all smashed outward. The kitchen was a wreck. Finally he spotted Rathaway and Shawna, almost to the front door.

They were blinking rapidly, and it appeared as if their vision was returning. He only had a few seconds to act. He streaked across the wide floor and grabbed Shawna. Carrying her to what he hoped was a closet, he pushed her inside, closed the door, and jammed it shut.

The Flash turned around. "Give up, Rathaway. It's over."

Rathaway shook his head slowly. "No, I've come too close to let it be spoiled now." He raised his hands.

Green Arrow stepped out from the shadows. The twang of the bowstring sounded as an arrow sped toward the Pied Piper. He still had his hands raised, and a burst of deafening vibrations shattered the shaft. The netting inside the head unfurled and collapsed in a harmless tangle at Rathaway's feet. He let out a laugh.

"A net?" he taunted. "The famed Arrow uses a *net*? Suddenly you're not so scary anymore."

The Flash rushed him, but the master of sound aimed his gloves at the ground and the floor disintegrated between them. The speedster felt his footing give way, and he started to tumble. He leapt for the edge and just managed to grab the crumbled rim. He swung and pulled himself up.

The house trembled on its foundation. The gap in the floor widened, creating a jagged chasm in the center of the large room. Green Arrow staggered, but instead of falling, he spun and fired an arrow that trailed a cable. It slammed into the wall and he slid across the chasm.

Pied Piper reeled to his feet just in time to have Green Arrow's bowstring settle over his head and across his neck. Arrow did a backflip off the wall behind his opponent, pulling the line taut so the wire dug into his throat. Gasping, Rathaway fell back against his captor. He flailed, hands reaching for the agonizing bowstring. His sonic attacks tore into the walls and furniture. Throughout it all, the archer stayed low behind Rathaway's shoulder, gritting his teeth in pain.

The Flash launched himself onto the wall, streaking around the wide gap in the floor toward the combatants. He ripped the gloves off Pied Piper's hands as he passed. Green Arrow unlooped his bow and kicked Rathaway aside. With a single move, he nocked another arrow, pointing it at the villain's head.

Pied Piper coughed and drew in a strangled breath. "You're all... so damn... *physical*."

The Flash held up the sonic gloves. "*Now* it's over, Rathaway. You're powerless, and we've got another set of these to add to the collection."

Rathaway looked at the arrow pointing at his head. He straightened, slowly rubbing his throat.

"You think I'd go through all this without ensuring I'd win?"

"Show me your hands!" Green Arrow barked.

"Happily." Rathaway smiled at the grim man and complied, keeping his palms open to show that he held no device.

As the Flash stepped forward, a burst of sonic vibrations threw them backward. Green Arrow hit hard, making a deep crater in the plaster wall. The Flash flew back into the chasm, barely able to grab onto a broken pipe. He dangled over the side.

"Gloves are out this season," Rathaway growled. "Beneath my skin, I have perfectly harmonized crystals from the meteorite. I don't need gauche artificial means to generate sound waves now. You see, I'm a true metahuman—easily the most powerful one, as well." He strode over to the closet and yanked the door, pulling Peekaboo out.

Green Arrow dragged himself from the debris. Breathing heavily, he drew two arrows from his quiver. One flew toward Shawna, exploding in front of her face. She had time for a startled shout before it was coated in a sticky, porous foam.

The archer let his second arrow fly. The blunt arrow mercilessly slammed Rathaway back and whipped a cable around him. The man's arms were pinned to his sides as he fell. Then Green Arrow scrambled around the ruined floor, clasped the Flash's arm, and hauled the speedster back up.

"That packed a wallop," the Flash muttered.

Green Arrow spun back toward his prey just as sound waves radiated from Rathaway's chest, fraying the steel cord that was holding him. It snapped and dropped in coils at his feet. He gave a furious bellow, and more vibrations emanated from him, focused toward the ceiling. Cracks formed and dust scattered over all of them. The once-beautiful house shook, and then came crashing down.

The Flash looked up to see John and Joe falling through the collapsing ceiling.

3 8

During his time as a police officer, Joe had entered many houses with dangerous people inside, but never quite like this. He and John... Spartan... both wore black tactical uniforms. Spartan had his helmet, and Joe wore a black balaclava with only his eyes showing. Both men wore small breather units over their mouth and nose. They had elected to do without night-vision goggles.

They slipped in through a side door. The only light came from the outside, leaving the world a mix of muddy black and grays. As they crouched, listening for signs of the enemy, John tapped the side of his helmet. Joe suddenly realized he only heard light static in his ear.

Rathaway must have set up sonic interference to block communications.

John signaled them to move out. Finding the stairs easily enough, they headed up with pistols drawn. Joe glanced behind him once and saw a streak of red below.

A sense of relief filled him. The Flash had their backs.

Felicity had pinpointed one of the targets in a room upstairs. Joe could barely make out Spartan's form as they reached the top of the stairs. A long hall stretched out ahead of them. Five doors, three on one side, two on the other. The target had been pinpointed in the last bedroom, but with communications down, they'd need to check every room. The target could have moved, and they wouldn't want a bad guy coming from behind.

Spartan signaled for Joe to take the first door. Joe turned the knob as quietly as possible and eased it open. An open window shade allowed a bit of moonlight inside. The room was empty, the bed still made. A pile of freshly laundered and neatly folded clothes sat on a trunk. The closet stood open, showing hangers draped with shirts and pants. Women's clothes. Shawna's room.

They moved methodically down the hall, silently checking each room. All empty. They finally reached the last bedroom. Joe listened at the closed door, but heard nothing. The gun in his hand lifted as he eased the door open and peered inside. Someone lay sprawled on a bare mattress.

They had found their quarry. Kyle Nimbus. The Mist.

In sleep, the murderer's face held none of its usual contempt and hatred, but he didn't look any less dangerous. Joe signaled John to hold his position. He moved cautiously toward the bed, gun at the ready, until he stood over the vulnerable man.

One shot while Nimbus was in human form, and it would end here tonight. No one would question it. They'd all be relieved. Nimbus had cheated a death sentence before. Joe would just be carrying it out once and for all.

But Joe was a cop. Not a judge, jury, or executioner. His finger slid off the trigger. Instead he pulled out a metal syringe. The tranquilizer would prevent Nimbus from turning into gas. Joe poised the needle right over the sleeping man's arm.

Abruptly he doubled over as the ear buds shot an agonizing squeal of white noise into his brain. It brought him to his knees and he screamed.

Nimbus leapt up. The man's small eyes were black pits as he frantically looked around the room. His gaze settled on Joe, and the rage showed that he immediately recognized the detective.

Joe lifted his pistol and fired, but Nimbus dissipated. The bullets passed harmlessly through him. The cloud lifted up to the ceiling, roiling with seething fury. It dropped toward Joe and encircled him, forming a prison of poison gas. Darker tendrils reached out to pull at his breather, slipping underneath and shoving it to one side. Joe struggled to get to his feet, fighting not to breathe.

Outside in the hall, John shouted. Joe waved him back to keep him out of range of the gas cloud. The madman coiled around, looming large, quickly filling the space of the bedroom.

An all-encompassing blackness crawled inward from the edges of Joe's consciousness. Hunching over, drenched in sweat, he shuddered.

John threw something toward Joe, sending it sailing through Nimbus's incorporeal form. Instinctively he grabbed for it. The long cylinder of a flare landed in his hands. Fighting off the darkness that was caving in, Joe dropped his pistol and fumbled to twist the top of the flare off. It came apart and he desperately attempted to strike one end against the other.

The gas tightened. Joe could feel it pushing against his mouth and into his nose, trying to force its way into his lungs. With a final swipe, Joe ignited the flare. The spark flamed and the end of the cylinder burst into a bright, blinding blaze.

The cloud ignited in a ball of flame. The blast shoved Joe across the room to collide with a dresser. Letting loose an almost inhuman scream, the Mist reformed, trailing dark smoke and his skin charred black. Burnt hands lifted to cover his face.

John rushed in and snatched the metal syringe off the floor. He plunged it into a burnt arm. The scream trailed off, and Nimbus fell face down onto the floor. Joe pulled off the balaclava and coughed violently, his lungs struggling desperately for fresh air.

John grabbed him and pulled him out of the bedroom and into the hallway, where the air was clearer.

"You still with me?"

Joe nodded, wiping his mouth with the back of his hand. John inspected the detective's face.

"Burns look minor, thanks to the tac gear. How's the pain?"

"I'll live. Thanks."

"Any time."

As they started to stand, the floor buckled beneath them.

The Flash saw the plummeting Joe, and felt a rush of terror. Behind him, Green Arrow fired a cable under the falling men. With practiced ease, John reached out and grasped it, catching the narrow lifeline with a hooked arm.

Joe wasn't used to such tactics. He bounced against the line and toppled away, panic and disbelief spreading across his face.

The Flash roared out into empty space, reaching for him. His heart pounded hard in his chest... and then he felt it. The tug at the speed force. Everything accelerated, and suddenly he felt out of control.

Tremors coursed through his body, generating a field of lightning. Small sparks lit his eyes, making the world go in and out of focus. Rathaway's triumphant grin shone just beyond Joe's falling body. The Flash's heartbeat ramped up inside his chest, and the world started to slow.

Green Arrow shouted to him, but his voice was a warbled distortion. The Flash couldn't make out what he was saying, but it reminded him of the lessons. They echoed in his head, but his breath still came in gasps, his thoughts a chaotic tumble.

A shadowy figure raced up beside him.

The world around him went transparent.

No!

He didn't have time for this. It wasn't real. He closed his eyes in a desperate attempt to reassert power over his own body. Finally one conscious memory prevailed.

The microscope.

It represented the methodology of the lab. Even before he became the Flash, painstaking procedure was the path to finding answers. Solving crimes. Bringing justice. Researching. Measuring. Calculating. Discovering. All done at a snail's pace. At human speed. One result after another.

The rushing roar of his blood abated, and he drew a deep breath into his tight chest. The world around him became tangible again. He heard Rathaway, as well as Green Arrow. Joe's falling body started to speed up.

The Flash's hand moved slowly, fingers flexing. His every instinct cried for him to suck in breath after rapid breath, but he kept his focus, trusting Oliver, keeping the rise and fall of his chest steady and rhythmic. One step at a time. Regardless of how many steps he could take in a second. His heart pounded steadily as he stared at Joe's outstretched hand.

Inhale. Pause. Exhale. Pause.

The world snapped back into marvelous clarity. Joe's hand slipped into his, fingers wrapping around his wrist. Joe's weight suddenly pulled the Flash forward. He touched his foot onto the cable Oliver had fixed across the chasm. He focused on planting one foot after another. Feeling the press of his heel on the line, being a part of the real world. A few millisecond tightrope steps and he shoved off, pushing back into full speed, but this time maintaining control.

Joe became weightless, hanging suspended in the speed force. The Flash gathered him in his arms and surged forward, then skidded to a halt on the far side of the pit. Joe regarded him with an amazed expression. Smiling, the speedster turned back to the fight.

Rathaway had Shawna on her feet. His hand shattered her foam mask.

"Take me out now!" he screeched. Most of the walls on the main floor had collapsed, and the rear of the house was visible, with its broken glass wall. Shawna looked that way and suddenly the two vanished.

Debris continued to rain down with a sound like thunder as the house collapsed around the heroes. The ground cracked and split, and the cliff face itself gave way. Tons of rock and soil tumbled into the lake, taking the remnants of the building with it in a terrible avalanche that raised a massive cloud of dust over the once-peaceful neighborhood.

39

Shawna appeared in the opening of an alley with Rathaway at her side. He gasped for breath. She had sped along at the limits of her powers, hoping for... she wasn't sure what she was hoping for. Maybe that he would die—but then she might die too.

Rathaway gave her an angry look. His attention quickly shifted to the vast circular building about two hundred yards away, across a deserted parking lot. S.T.A.R. Labs.

She thought about the people they had left in the crumbling house, about to plunge into the lake. But there was nothing she could do for them now. She had to focus on herself, as always. She had to find a way to get out of this hell she was trapped in.

"Well? This is what you've been waiting for, isn't it? Just destroy it already."

"It's not that simple." Rathaway knelt and put a hand on the asphalt, sending vibrations through her feet. He said, "I helped build that place. It can withstand a hydrogen bomb." He looked up at her. "From the outside."

"So we're going inside?" Shawna twitched at the memory of that terrible mirrored cell, deep in the bowels of the building.

"Yes. They're in there right now." Rathaway stood up, tilting his head as if listening to radio signals. "Dr. Snow. Cisco Ramon. That woman from Green Arrow's team, and another woman I don't recognize. I can hear their desperate communications. They're distracted because they can't reach the Flash and his friends. So our moment is now."

"What about security?"

"Security?" Rathaway laughed. "At S.T.A.R. Labs? Even if they had any, it wouldn't matter." He reached into his coat pocket and pulled out a smartphone—only thicker, and with keys, more like an old calculator. He powered it on and began to tap. "You see, I left a little loophole in the system—but we can only use it once. As much as I hate Cisco Ramon, I know that as soon as he's aware, he'll find a way to plug it."

He paused with his thumb over the button.

"You need to stretch your powers. When I activate the sleeper command, a live, real-time image of the Cortex will appear on this screen. You will teleport us there."

"From a picture?" Shawna wasn't sure she had heard him right. "I can't do that. I have to see the spot itself."

"No, you don't. You can teleport any place you can

see. You will see it, and we will go there."

"But I've never done it before. What if I do something wrong?"

His grim expression told her there would be no arguing. "Are you ready?"

"I don't—"

"Here it comes." Rathaway pressed the key.

The screen lit up with an overhead shot of a clean, high-tech facility. Three people sat at computer stations. There was no sound, but they looked frantic. A fourth person entered the shot. Iris West. Shawna groaned.

She liked Iris.

"Shawna," Rathaway growled, and she stared hard at the screen. She had never teleported this way. She didn't have any connection to the destination. She didn't know how far away it was, only that it was inside S.T.A.R. Labs, but she didn't know where.

He's crazy, she thought. *He's going to get us killed.* But if she refused, he would just kill *her*.

"Shawna. Now."

She cursed under her breath.

Suddenly Shawna knew where the room was located. Her gaze flicked up to the building, and she could actually visualize the space inside. A little thread of attachment slid through space and she felt it anchor where she needed to go.

This might work.

"Do it!" Rathaway shouted.

When she looked back at the screen, she saw one of

the people, a blonde woman with glasses, staring at her computer. She slowly turned around and lifted her eyes directly to the camera Rathaway was using. The woman said something and Cisco looked up, too, gaping at the camera. The woman dove back onto her keyboard.

Here goes… Shawna triggered the teleport as if she was jumping into a cold swimming pool. She saw pixelated lights and darkness. It took longer than normal. Something terrible had happened.

Before she could panic, she stood in a clean, brightly lit room. They were inside S.T.A.R. Labs—at the spot she had seen on the screen.

"I did it!" Shawna shouted.

The people at the computers leapt to their feet. Rathaway walked toward them with his arms spread wide, sweeping his hands before them. They all covered their ears with silent screams of pain, then collapsed moaning to the floor.

"Hello, my colleagues." Rathaway squatted so he could peer under the table at the writhing foursome. "I seem to have forgotten my key card, but I've found my way in."

"You're not… wearing your gauntlets." Panting, Caitlin tried to brush the hair out of her eyes, and only partly succeeded.

"There's nothing I'd love more than to chat, just like our old lunch hours, but, I've got things to do." Rathaway pulled a small plastic tube from his pocket. He popped the lid and slid a crystal into his palm.

Closing his hand around the stone, he concentrated for a few seconds. "Nobody leave this room."

"Or?" Cisco said.

"Or bad things will happen, although no one deserves it more than you." He pulled several more of the plastic containers from his pockets. When Shawna started to follow him out, he put his hand up. "Stay here and watch them. If they try anything, if you teleport out, I'll sense it, and destroy you all."

"Stay here?" Shawna stammered. "But I'm with you."

"Do as I say. They always try something, because they think they're smart." He glared at Cisco, and left the Cortex.

They pinned Shawna with their eyes, but didn't move. She shuffled to the far side of the room, almost comically disengaged, as if she was waiting for a friend to show up. Whispering to each other, they made her very nervous.

After nearly ten minutes of their hushed conversation, she turned suddenly to Iris and whispered, "Look, I'm sorry. I'd like to help you, but I can't. He's got these weird crystals and he's going to use them to blow this place up and kill all of you. He put the crystals in me, so if I don't help him, he'll kill me too."

Iris came around the workstation. "Where's the Flash?" she asked. "Where is everyone who was with him?" Her voice held a near-panicked tremor. Her eyes were wide with fear.

Shawna put a finger to her lips and moved closer.

"You have to be quiet. He can hear everything. Hartley blew the house into the lake and we teleported out."

"Blew the house into the lake?" Iris exchanged frightened glances with the others.

"So what's everyone talking about?" Rathaway reappeared in the doorway. "Why all the whispering?" He eyed Shawna suspiciously.

Felicity's phone buzzed and she leaned over the console. Happiness played across her face.

Caitlin asked eagerly, "What is it?"

"They're alive." When Iris whipped around, Felicity nodded at her with a huge smile. "Yes. Joe too."

Iris put a thankful hand to her head. "What about the Flash?"

Felicity pointed across. "You mean him?"

Rathaway spun about.

The Flash stood in the entrance to the Cortex. His red costume was torn and streaked with dirt. He stared with furious intensity.

"Hartley, I'd really like to punch you several thousand times," he said, breathing deeply. "But if you want to surrender, I'll accept it."

"I don't want to surrender, you idiot." Rathaway started to vibrate. "I want to kill you in the most painful way possible."

4 0

The Flash streaked forward, and just inches from his target he slammed against something he couldn't see. The speedster bounced into the air, crashing back into one of the workstations.

"It worked!" Rathaway laughed with amazement. "A sonic force field! An actual force field."

The Flash shook his head like a boxer knocked to the canvas, and leapt up. He raced for Rathaway, and again caromed off, skidding across the floor to hit the wall with a grunt. He climbed back to his feet. This time he walked across the Cortex holding out his hands, until he touched the barrier in the air. It felt pliable, but when he pushed into it, his hands slowed to a stop.

"What are you doing now?" Rathaway watched with concern.

"I'm betting you can't do more than one thing at a time, Hartley." Red-gloved hands began to vibrate. "And right now, that one thing is your force field. So

I'm going to vibrate through it." Barry knew from the flicker in Rathaway's eyes that he had surmised correctly. If he could penetrate the shield, he might be able to get to Pied Piper and take him down before he could retool to another, more offensive ability.

His hands slipped into the invisible spongy wall, pressing deeper, moving closer to Rathaway's worried face—but then he felt the texture change. His hands were pushed away and a painful shock shot up his arms. Rathaway gave him a smug smile. He was altering the resonance frequency of the field.

The Flash shifted his own frequency and again pushed within inches of Rathaway before the field shoved him back.

"We'll see how long you can keep it up, Hartley." The idea of beating his opponent to the floor became more attractive by the second, and he had to calm himself. "This sort of power is new to you," he continued. "You must be tired already, but it's old hat to me."

"But what if you blur, Barry?"

The Flash jerked his head up.

"Oh yes." Rathaway chuckled. "I've been listening to your team's communications. I know you are Barry Allen, but I couldn't care less. This 'blurring,' however, intrigues me. It must refer to going out of phase in some fashion. Is that what Nimbus saw when he thought you had a new power? You don't, do you, Flash? You have a new weakness.

"So by all means, let's keep playing."

The Flash stepped away from the shimmering force shield. His arms tingled and he flexed his numb fingers. He found himself moving into his tactical breathing. His arms found feeling again. Oliver would be proud.

"Poor Flash." Rathaway grinned in triumph. "All right, it's time for the final act, so to speak. Shawna, come here."

"No."

Rathaway tilted his head. "I said come here."

"No," she repeated, louder this time.

"Don't be an idiot," he growled. "Don't let the Flash trick you into thinking they have a chance. He's wrong—I have no limits. I can kill you with just a thought, and keep my force field up the entire time."

"Then do it!" Shawna shouted. "Just do it and shut the hell up. I'm so sick of you, you smug punk. But remember, I beat you two out of three in chess."

"I let you win because your ego was so fragile."

"Sure you did, you little weasel." She stepped closer, hands on hips, leaning forward with an angry sneer.

"Hey, maybe you should dial it down," Iris said, trying to pull her back.

"Hell no." Shawna tugged her arm away and stepped closer to Rathaway. "Kill me, Hartley, and trap yourself in here. You think you're getting out, with Red standing there waiting to beat you like you owe him money. Are you planning to blow this place up with you still inside? I doubt it. What are you gonna do, smart guy? *What?*" Shawna laughed at him. "That looks like check to me. You got no moves left."

"Then I suppose I have nothing to lose." Rathaway stared at her like death. Suddenly Shawna choked, and doubled over. She clutched her head, staggering. With a strangled cry, she fell to the floor.

"Hartley, no!" Barry ran to the crumpled body. "Don't do this. She has nothing to do with us. Leave her alone."

Nothing in Rathaway's eyes showed that he intended to relent. The Flash charged him, fighting to vibrate through the force shield. Anything to distract the man, force him to refocus his powers.

Iris and Caitlin sprinted to Shawna's side.

"Everybody back away from her." It was Cisco. He was wearing one of Pied Piper's gauntlets, and holding the other. "I'm going to try something."

Iris stretched out her arm. "Give it to me. I'll do it."

"Nah, it's too dangerous. I don't know if it'll work."

"Give it to me! We need you for other things. This is something I can do."

Cisco pulled off the glove and tossed both of them to Iris.

"You wear one and put the other one on Shawna's hand," he explained. "Then hold the two together, establishing a connection. That should create enough resonant resistance to—"

"I don't care about the science." Iris tugged the gauntlet onto her right arm. She pried one of Shawna's palsied hands off the floor.

"N-no, Iris. D-don't," Shawna stammered. "He'll hurt you."

Iris ignored her, jammed the glove on Shawna's hand, and then clasped the gauntleted hands together. Then the air around them shimmered. A deep hum spread. Iris gasped in pain. However, Shawna took a breath of relief, and tightened her grip.

"Iris?" the Flash shouted over his shoulder.

"I'm good." Her trembling frail voice made it sound as if she was speaking through a rotary fan. "We're okay."

He redoubled his attack, vigorously assaulting the force shield, a shadow of red as he cycled through vibrational frequencies. Rathaway stood his ground, but his teeth were clenched. Sweat poured down his face. His eyes locked on the red fingers that slowly inched toward him.

Abruptly he released an eruption of sound. The Flash's head felt as if an axe had cleaved into his skull. His hearing exploded and his vision sparked white. Losing his balance, he staggered back, fighting to stay on his feet.

4 1

When the brightness faded, the Cortex came back into focus. Everyone in the control room lay sprawled around the room. Some were moving, others weren't. The shattering pain abated, and only a thick pounding remained in the Flash's ears.

Rathaway had fled.

He spun around. Iris still held Shawna's hand, and they leaned against each other, stunned. Caitlin propped herself unsteadily against the workstation table, gasping in the aftermath of the burst. Cisco and Felicity slumped over their keyboards, struggling to sit up. He went to each one. They all assured him—with closed eyes or gaping mouths—that they were fine, or would be.

"What was that?" Felicity moaned.

Barry knelt next to Iris, receiving a comforting nod. "He must have accessed the power of the crystals he placed around the facility," he said. "We must've pushed him to his limits."

"He's still here somewhere," Shawna muttered. "He wants to tear this place apart, and now he'll want to kill me, as well. He won't leave until he does both."

"He's not doing either one." The Flash stood. "I'm going after him."

Through the pain, Felicity offered a warning look. "Wait for Oliver and John. They're almost here."

"If we give Rathaway time to recharge, he could blow this place to pieces, and we'll still be inside. I can't wait."

"Actually, you can." Cisco played feverishly on his computer keyboard. The lights dimmed and the tone of the background hum altered. "If I'm right, we've got him. I'm sending resonance pulses through the internal communications and electronic systems. I'm using our own network to weave a sonic shield into the structure of S.T.A.R. Labs. The building itself is now a force screen against sonic or vibrational attacks. It should block his attacks."

"It will now." Felicity typed as if she had superspeed. "I just added a subroutine that will fluctuate your frequencies. That way you won't blow out your system in the first thirty seconds or so."

Cisco nodded approvingly. "Thanks," he said. "Next time, though, could you give me my moment, please?"

The Flash sensed the subtle vibrations around him. They were light, but profound. He smiled in admiration.

"How did you guys figure that out on the fly?"

"On the fly? Please, we've been working on this

ever since we knew Hartley was involved."

Felicity bounced in her chair. "Found him!"

Internal cameras projected an image of Rathaway lurching through the Pipeline, far below. He stopped and pressed his hands against the wall. Suddenly he looked confused, slapping frantically on all the surfaces he could reach, as if feeling for something. They couldn't hear him, but it was clear he was cursing up a blue streak.

Cisco laughed. "That's right, Hartley. You're not the only genius who can do force fields."

Rathaway looked up and saw the camera. He reached into his pocket and produced a crystal, holding it up. He grinned and the crystal glowed. Suddenly strange lines of energy sparked from the crystal's many facets.

"Well, that's weird," Cisco muttered. "I think that's physical sound." Felicity called up other camera views from around the Pipeline. The luminescent energy streams filled the space. Wherever they coalesced, there was a crystal.

The beams glittered around Rathaway, quivering and glowing. Wherever the streaks intertwined, the energy grew more vivid. A massive, indistinct shape appeared. Colorless and undulating as if alive, it filled the space.

"Huh." Cisco stared at the screen. "Okay, I did not see that kind of thing coming."

"What is that?" Barry asked.

"Some sort of simulacrum," Felicity replied. "Made of sound apparently. Amazing."

"This guy…" Cisco shook his head in annoyance, making adjustments to his network. "This guy is a pain. A brilliant fracking pain."

Three men rushed in through the main entrance to the Cortex. Green Arrow and Spartan each held Joe by an arm. They were as disheveled as the Flash, their faces covered in dust and dried blood. Felicity raced to Oliver and Iris enveloped Joe in a worried embrace. John stood alone, with his helmet under one arm and a bemused smirk on his face. Caitlin looked up at him from her seat and gave him a welcoming smile.

Joe saw the bulky sonic gauntlet on his daughter's hand. "What is that? What crazy thing have you been doing?"

Oliver noticed Shawna, slumped in a chair. "Got one. Good. Where's Rathaway?"

The Flash pointed at the monitor. "Pipeline."

"What the hell is that?" John stepped toward a screen and pointed at the wavering mass of energy.

"It's a sonic construct." Cisco continued to type, joined by Caitlin at her own keyboard. "And I'm betting it's coming up here to shut off my brilliant defensive systems by killing us all."

Green Arrow looked at the Flash. "Let's get Rathaway now. Stop him and this… thing goes away."

"I'm ready," the Flash told him.

"Then throw up a schematic of the building," Oliver

said. "I need the layout." Cisco complied, pointing out key aspects of the massive structure.

"We're here at the Cortex. There's the Pipeline below. These are the prison cells. Each cell was specifically modified to match a metahuman's power. We even have one for Rathaway."

"You kept your villains in an abandoned particle accelerator?"

"Where do you keep yours?" Cisco demanded.

"In an underground bunker on a deserted island."

"Well," he said, crossing his arms as if that settled it. "No casting stones then."

The Flash continued to stare at the shots from the Pipeline. The weird sonic manifestation disappeared.

"Wait, it's gone."

A thunderous blow sounded at the main doorway leading out of the accelerator ring. The sonic construct reappeared in another view, pushing against the barrier, and then pounding again... and again.

"I'll go into the Pipeline and get Rathaway," the Flash said. "Oliver, you and John take care of that sonic construct so it can't get up here."

John asked, "What can we do to that thing? It's made of sound."

"Yes," Cisco said, "but from what I can tell, it's corporeal—solid. It looks like Rathaway has the ability to focus sound in a limited space into a physical thing. So that monster can beat its way through the doors despite the vibrational field I built into the building.

But on the other hand, you can probably hit it like it was a person."

"Probably?" John checked the magazine in his pistol.

"Oh, wait!" Felicity went to Iris and took the gauntlet. "Would this help?" She slipped into her seat and made a few quick adjustments. Cisco watched and offered suggestions. After a few moments she handed it over her shoulder to John. "You may be able to disrupt the construct with this, or at least hurt it.

"If it can be hurt," she added quietly.

John stared. "You want me to just walk up and punch it?" He frowned with exasperation. "Great." Abruptly the lights dimmed.

Cisco peered over Caitlin's shoulder.

"Hartley's probing our force shield, and he's got a lot of juice, so he could break it any time. Even if he doesn't, we've only got about five minutes until it burns out the systems, anyway. And then we're vulnerable."

"We'll stop him." Green Arrow headed for the doorway, followed by John. He spared Felicity a long glance, then the two men disappeared.

"Where should I be?" Joe asked.

"Outside with Iris," Barry replied.

"Now wait a minute—"

"There's nothing you can do against these forces. Take Iris and get out. Keep her safe. I'll work better knowing you're out of the danger zone." He turned to Shawna. "You should go, too."

"Why?" She didn't look up. "If he survives, I'm dead no matter where I go."

The Flash started to reply, then thought better of it. He gave a last look at his family and friends, and rushed after Oliver and John. Speeding down to the lowest level, he reached the entrance to the Pipeline before the two men arrived. When they joined him, they all heard deep pounding from the other side of the door.

"You go in first," Green Arrow said, speaking loudly over the din. "Distract that thing long enough for us to get inside, then you head after Rathaway while we handle the construct."

"Don't make it long, though," John said, and he gave the Flash a quick glance. "You won't need more than a few seconds to take him out, right?"

"Right." Barry grinned, backing up a bit. "Cisco, open the door."

"Okay," Cisco replied, "but remember, it's not the fastest door in the west. It'll take around ten seconds to cycle up, and then back down."

"Got it," Green Arrow said. "Go."

The heavy barrier began to rise, revealing a shimmering mass. The Flash ran at the portal and slid under the door like a baseball player going into second. He banged against something solid—the thing's legs maybe—before clambering to his feet. What felt like a heavy clawed hand fell onto his back, grabbing his costume.

Sharp tingling sensations shot through him. He flailed back with an elbow, catching something solid. Blows struck his head and shoulders, knocking him to the side. A loud bang announced an explosion that rocked the large beast.

"Flash, run!" Green Arrow shouted while pulling another shaft.

The Flash shoved against the shimmering sonic mass, clearing a few inches of space. He broke away, and streaked down the long, curved hallway, leaving Arrow and John to handle the invisible monster.

4 2

The Flash vanished, and the door to the Pipeline slid into place behind Green Arrow and John, sealing them in with the construct.

Both men fired, stepping back as they did to buy a little space. The air wavered with each blow, but the creature didn't falter, and moved in their direction.

They had to hold this thing here. If the creature got out of the Pipeline and made it to the upper floor, there would be no way to keep it out of the Cortex. Felicity, Cisco, and Caitlin wouldn't stand a chance. This was the chokepoint.

The weird distortion appeared to flow like water, though it was able to maintain a vague shape. With the fluidity of a cat, it sprang up toward the roof of the tunnel and then twisted, directing its momentum downward. It drove itself onto the Green Arrow, its weight crushing him against the steel.

He coughed blood onto the floor. The thing

swatted him, sending him rolling across the tunnel. It followed, and another blow sent him careening down the Pipeline. Massive footfalls vibrated the steel plates under him. He tried to get a fix on it, to determine where best to strike, but all he could make out was something large and vague, distorting the view of whatever was behind it.

When it drew close, Arrow lashed out with his bow, striking something solid. The creature stumbled sideways, and took damage, but in the dimness of the tunnel, he couldn't track its movements clearly. He cried out as a translucent appendage wrapped itself around him.

Then Spartan's hand with the sonic gauntlet snaked in and seized the glittering appendage. The arm sparked and froze. He pressed his pistol against it and fired. A chunk shattered like crystal, and the shards dissipated into the air.

"Sweet," Spartan muttered and raised the gauntlet to grab it again. This time something slammed him to the ground. The hulking shape loomed, and the air crackled. He threw himself to one side as it ripped jagged gashes in the floor. Pulling himself to his feet, he dodged another blow, staggering away just as the wall was dented.

A way opened for them to slip past. Green Arrow pulled Spartan with him as he ran. With a quick glance over his shoulder, he got the sense of something on four legs, hurtling after them with long arced strides.

The creature gained on them. Following the shimmer and the sound it made, Arrow could vaguely make out that it leapt across the tunnel, bounded off the opposite wall, and landed just ahead of them.

The archer somersaulted over the barely defined mass, his legs tucked in tight to land on the other side. The creature swiped at him, but missed. While it was distracted, Spartan rolled under the beast. A concussive arrow rocked the monster to the side. Green Arrow reached down to swing Spartan to his feet, and they legged it down the hall.

In his peripheral vision, the archer seemed to spot the Flash streaking past him several times, but he couldn't pause. As they gained some breathing space, he pulled four more arrows from his quiver.

"We need a better view of what we're fighting."

"How do you propose we do that?" Spartan panted. "Cover it in paint?"

The sound of the creature pounding after them made them both peer back, but all they saw in the shadows of the passageway was a shimmering shape that filled their view.

"Something like that," Green Arrow muttered. He lifted the bow in a smooth arc and fired the four arrows so quickly it appeared as if they went in the same pull. Each one exploded against the translucence, casting a dark cloud of ash and smoke that clung to the target, slowly revealing a shape.

Its bulbous head shook back and forth, as an

unblinking eye socket turned toward them. Four massive clawed hands dug into the steel plates beneath it.

"Damn," Spartan said. "I liked it better when it was invisible. Do we stand and fight?"

"Head to head, we can't win."

They retreated again, the creature closer now, as an idea formed in Arrow's head.

"Felicity, do you copy?"

Crackling static replied. The lines of visible sound traversing the Pipeline must have been blocking their signal—but he knew video still worked. The team up in the Cortex would be watching, and if they were paying attention, they would know what he was doing. If not, this was going to be a bad idea. A pain began to build in Green Arrow's chest, and he still tasted blood on his lips.

With Spartan racing beside him, he picked through his memory of the building's schematic, trying to remember which cell had been Rathaway's. The cells were set into niches along the outer wall, where the guts of the particle accelerator had been removed. The soot-spotted monster galloped after them on pitch-dark hands.

They finally came to the area where Rathaway had been held, while a prisoner at S.T.A.R. Labs. The cell had been modified to be soundproof, and resistant to vibrations. A short hallway ran down to it.

Cisco must have caught on.

The doors stood open.

Close on their heels, the creature lunged to block

their way. A blow knocked Spartan to the ground. Glittering claws just missed Green Arrow as he leapt, banging into the corner of the hallway, and ricocheting into the open cell. He immediately put his back against the rear wall.

The thing roared at him, pushing into the doorway. The air crackled and the archer's ears rang. The creature raked at him. He spun aside and the wall sparked with a tremendous blow. The thing wriggled in, nearly filling the cell with its intangible bulk. Arrow fought the nauseating pulsations that washed through the small space.

He darted back and forth, searching for room to slip out of the cell, narrowly dodging the claws that struck at him until one of the blows connected, and sent him reeling into the corner. Pain rolled over him, but the thing cried out, as well.

Behind it, Spartan issued another vibrating jolt with his gauntlet. The beast seized up for a second. Spartan's pistol blew a chunk out of its torso.

The beast kicked back, sending the ex-soldier flying away from the cell. Green Arrow shouted as he struggled to his feet. They were terribly out-gunned for this, but the odds didn't matter. He and Spartan would keep going until it ended, one way or the other.

The bellowing construct turned its attention back to the archer and gripped him by the shoulders, lifting him off the floor. Dark claws dug in hard. Arrow shoved his bow into the gaping mouth. Clenching his fists around the bow, he found his last ounce of strength, preventing the jaws from tearing into him. His head nearly split from the incessant pounding. Searing knife-edge agony sliced along his spine. He couldn't hear or see or feel anything.

Green Arrow couldn't take much more. His vision darkened.

"Sh-shut…the door," he gasped.

"Not with you in there!" Spartan replied, stepping forward again, his head bleeding.

"*Shut… it!*"

"Like hell!"

Spartan again thrust his gauntleted hand through the creature's back. It reared in agony as its form disrupted for a moment, dropping its prey to the floor. Green Arrow struggled to hold onto consciousness. He knew none of the people upstairs would seal him inside with the monster. So he rolled weakly onto his right side, clawing for his discarded bow.

The beast worked its massive frame around in the tight space to confront Spartan. It took a lumbering step toward him, and freedom.

With his consciousness fading, Arrow dragged out a shaft and lifted the bow awkwardly. It took precious seconds to nock it and hold it steady. Then the arrow flew. It struck a control panel at the end of the corridor. The panel sparked, and the door to the cell started to close.

"Damn it, Oliver!" Spartan let out a strangled shout as the door slammed shut. His panicked face appeared through the thick Plexiglas. His fists banged against it helplessly.

Green Arrow suddenly felt a rush of cold air and a distant hissing sound. His fingers moved, and cold metal pressed against his cheek. Something touched him. A woman's hazy face rippled into focus.

Peekaboo? They were both trapped inside.

Green Arrow tried to stand.

The creature would be on them again. He had to be ready.

"Stay down!" Her face appeared again. "Can you hear me?"

Green Arrow blinked and fell back. "Look out. It's coming."

"No." John grabbed his arm. "You're out. It's trapped." He pointed at the closed glass and steel door to the cell. They were on the outside. Glimmering air shifted inside.

Oliver slumped. "Hopefully that will hold that thing for another few minutes so the Flash can work." Then the lights went out. The background hum stopped, and the new silence was deafening. The entire structure began to shake.

"There goes Cisco's shield," John said. "We're out of time."

43

The Flash streaked though the Pipeline back to where Rathaway stood, arms outstretched and with bright strings of sound penetrating him. As the speedster came close, he sensed the telltale vibrations put up by the Pied Piper's force shield, and managed to veer off before smashing into it. He slid to a halt, spinning to face his opponent.

"There's no way out of this, Hartley. Just surrender."

"Funny. I was going to say the same thing, except for the surrender part," Rathaway replied. "And I do have a way out. You see, I'm safe inside a protective cocoon, and when Cisco's protection fails, I will destroy S.T.A.R. Labs. Then I will simply walk out through the smoldering walls, stepping over all your bodies."

The Flash started to reply, then thought better of it.

"Wait here," he said, holding up a finger. "I'll be right back." He sped down the Pipeline, past Oliver and John, and then Rathaway again. On he ran, around the circular path, over and over, building speed. By the fourth or fifth transit, Rathaway's expression finally registered his surprise. Four more, and that turned to confusion.

Lightning flared off his body. Power roared up inside him. He strained to contain it even as he generated more. The world narrowed with each step.

Pied Piper began to pour energy into the tunnel. Crushing streams of sound began blasting the Flash, but he didn't dare decelerate. Finally he veered straight toward Rathaway's force field, slamming against it with incredible force. The barrier bowed inward, slowing his forward motion—but he refused to stop. He strained, fighting into the pressure. Bolts of lightning crackled out and over the barrier.

In an instant, the Flash broke through and smashed Rathaway into the wall. Immediately he began to rain down blows. Rathaway tried to cover his head and face, but the Flash grabbed him by the jacket and yanked him to his feet. He pulled back his fist again.

"It's over!" he shouted. Another crashing blow sent Rathaway toppling to the floor. The smaller man looked up with his hands held out. At first the Flash thought he was surrendering.

"It's not over till this place is rubble!" Rathaway shouted.

The Flash took a sledgehammer to the chest. He staggered, crying out in pain. Rathaway laughed.

"I'm more powerful than you now, thanks to the crystals, and I'm going to use that advantage to kill you."

He leveled another blow, sending the speedster tumbling.

Digging his fingers into the seams of the tile floor, the Flash came to a jolting stop. He jumped up, roaring into speed, feeling the vibrations in the air as Rathaway strafed the landscape behind him. Metal shredded into shrapnel and filled the enclosed space. The Flash ran up the wall, and the wave of destruction followed him, cracking spider webs in the pipes and concrete. Light fixtures exploded, sending out a shower of glass.

The Flash crossed the ceiling above, and the thick beam of destruction followed just inches behind his streaking form. He cut a right angle, and then another, and finally a third. Without warning an entire section of steel and concrete dropped on top of the Pied Piper. The debris pummeled him to the floor, piling on top of him, burying him in an avalanche of wreckage.

Sliding down the wall, the Flash came to a stop next to the dusty pile of rubble. He heard faint moans from underneath—Rathaway was still alive. With hands on hips, Barry hunched over, gasping for breath.

Tiny pebbles at his feet began to quiver. Pieces of rubble shifted. A high-pitched screech shot through his head, and he staggered back. The wreckage blasted outward, catching him on the legs and knocking him to the floor. Rathaway struggled to his feet and shook off dust and debris. He looked stunned, blood ran down his face, but his bleary eyes fell angrily on the red-clad figure.

He strode over to kneel beside the Flash.

A knife of sound penetrated Barry's head. He cried out and grabbed Rathaway, grasping his wrists. His arms went numb, but he didn't let go. His ears rang. His ribs throbbed. He tasted blood.

Everything went dark.

Then the Flash realized it wasn't just him. The lights were out. The power was gone. Cisco's protective field had dropped, and the facility was vulnerable now.

Emergency lighting came on. Rathaway grinned with excitement, grabbing the Flash's wrists and pouring screeching vibrations through his bones.

"I've got you. I've got *all* of you now. This is the end for everything Harrison Wells built—and that includes you, Flash."

Barry fought to stay conscious. He had to do *something*. He couldn't strike back—his arms wouldn't move. It couldn't end this way. Down here, alone, with the others depending on him, trusting him to protect them. He had never failed before. Except for Ronnie.

And Eddie.

And his mother.

It felt like he was supposed to think of something. He couldn't remember. His pounding heart echoed in his ears like cracks of thunder. Pain lanced through his head. He had to get Rathaway out of here. That was the key. Remove him from S.T.A.R. Labs.

The Flash was on the verge of blurring. He could feel it. Then it struck him—a desperate plan at best, but he had to try. Instead of fighting it, however, he let the blur happen. Barry forced his hands up and clamped onto Rathaway's neck. He stared into the other man's eyes.

"You're coming with me," the Flash gasped. His body vibrated faster, and Rathaway struggled to break free.

"What are you doing?" he shrieked.

The world melted around them. The images flickered. He knew he had phased. He could almost feel the plasma flaring to life inside him, ripping into his cell walls, hijacking his speed force. He was an insubstantial statue now, incapable of helping anyone—but he might not have to.

Rathaway's face blurred in front of him. It looked the way the others had described it. One way or another, the man was trapped now. He wasn't a threat to anyone. Cisco and the others had time.

Barry blinked and found himself in the lobby of S.T.A.R. Labs. Rathaway wasn't there, and the lobby looked different. Rather than dark and dusty, the walls gleamed bright, clean, and perfect. Banners hung across the space announced the initiation of the particle accelerator project.

THE FUTURE IS COMING FASTER THAN YOU THINK!

Sunlight streamed through the wide glass walls, but he was alone. A red streak raced past the window, cut into the door, and stopped in front of him. The older

Flash bent over, gasping for breath.

"You survived Zoom," Barry exclaimed happily. Then he shook his head, chiding himself. "Or not. You weren't alive in the first place."

"Barry, it's getting worse."

"I don't think so," he replied. "I initiated the blur this time, and I think I can get out of it whenever I want."

"No, you didn't." Future Flash tried to straighten, but couldn't. He went to one knee. "You can't."

"I don't believe what you're telling me," Barry said. "You're a hallucination. You're not real."

His older self looked up. The sense of hurt on his face touched Barry.

"What do you mean?" the older man said.

"We're not really here." Barry waved his arm. "You're not really anywhere, except in my head, but I'm standing in the Pipeline with Hartley Rathaway. We're both vibrating at a very high frequency right now, and we're out of phase. This is a product of my mind trying to deal with a plasma that has infected my body."

"Yes, that's right," the Future Flash acknowledged. "This is all you."

"I know. That's what I mean. It's not real. It's like a fever dream. I can't trust anything I see or hear while I'm blurring."

"I'm not lying to you."

"I don't think you're lying. I just don't think you know what you're talking about. You don't have the answer, because I don't have the answer. You're nothing but me." Barry turned away. "I don't have time for this. I've got to get out of here before someone else shows up." He had to focus on removing himself from the blur. *Ignore the man. Focus on stopping Rathaway.*

"I'm trying to help you, Barry."

"Then tell me how to stop Rathaway."

"You know that already. Just bring him closer to his power source."

"That's real helpful." Barry closed his eyes, trying to concentrate. "But at least this time it wasn't 'run faster.'"

"You won't save anyone if you don't do what I say." Future Flash still labored for breath. His voice became frantic. "You're the Flash. You are the fastest man alive. If you don't run, what are you?"

"I don't want—"

Stop it, Barry chastised himself. *This isn't real. He's just a figment of my imagination. Think about the microscope. Think about anything else.* He had to do something about Rathaway. Render him helpless somehow. The minute they came out of the blur, his opponent would renew his attack. There had to be some way to nullify those crystal shards inside him.

"Barry, please," Future Flash said. "Why don't you believe in me?"

But Barry didn't answer, his attention returning to his hands. Even here, he could feel Rathaway in his grip. A sense of reality in the midst of a dream. He concentrated on that, narrowing his vision. His breathing slowed. He counted his heartbeats as they eased to a rhythmic pace. Everything blurred, except for what was directly in front of him.

Rathaway.

Reality snapped back. He was in the Pipeline, Rathaway frozen in his grip. There was no sign of his older self. His foe drew in a deep, rasping breath. With a massive effort, he shoved the Flash back.

"What the *hell* did you do?" he slurred.

The Flash wasted no time. He pulled back to throw a punch, but even stunned the man anticipated his move. A sonic wave blasted the Flash down the tunnel, hurling him several hundred feet. Slowing to a roll, he tumbled over one of the meteorite crystals. The quivering string of sound still ran from the crystal to its master.

Rathaway screamed in rage, and energy poured out of his body. The walls of S.T.A.R. Labs shook, beginning to crack, and pipes imploded. The Flash only had seconds to do something. Amid this chaos, he had to restore order.

That's it.

Scooping up the quivering crystal, he ran. Following the shimmering lines of power, he found another crystal… and then another. As he ran for the next one, his hands started to sear. The energy burned through his gloves. Leaving the Pipeline, he sped around the facility, following the sonic threads like proverbial breadcrumbs. Finally all the lines of power converged on his hands.

He ran back to the Pipeline and slid to a stop next

to Rathaway. The man's arms stretched out above him. Sweat poured down his face. He had lost his glasses somewhere, but didn't seem to care. All he wanted now was to destroy that which he hated most.

The Flash slipped into the speed force again and began to arrange the crystals around his foe. Pain blossomed as waves of sound vibrated through him. He pushed through the pain, and fixated solely on the complex design that came together in his head.

He created a pattern of linear symmetry, using straight lines to form a curve. Losing himself to the glory of the math, he placed the crystals around his frozen foe, forming lines and angles. When he set the final crystal in place, as if completing the last symbol in a complicated formula, the waves of sound encircled his opponent.

He stopped and watched as Rathaway felt a shift in the power, and his eyes went wide. The crystal array increased the amplitude of the waves, but instead of flowing outward, they bounced back. Vibrations pounded the Piper, and he screamed, thinking it a new assault. Instinctively he continued to use his powers, trying to protect himself, not realizing that the waves that struck him were his own.

The power shook the building to its core. Seeking to contain the destruction, the Flash began to run at superspeed around the crystal formation. He formed a protective vacuum, as well as reinforcing the feedback loop.

The meteorite sang again and its song filled the Pipeline. An ear-shattering symphony of white noise. The crystals vibrated so fast he could barely see them, even at his velocity. They altered their resonance to match the Flash's, so he increased his speed yet again. He lost all sense of place or time, saw vivid colors and heard unidentifiable ringing sounds. The crystals started to glow, and the heat grew intense, searing them both.

Still he maintained the frenzied speed. The pain increased. He wanted to scream, but wouldn't be heard. The light from the crystals filled the world. His eyes saw nothing but white. His consciousness started to vanish.

A series of popping noises filled the tunnel. The crystals imploded, crackling inside the speed barrier. The heat vanished. The Flash slowed, trying desperately to drag enough breath into his rasping lungs. Fearing that he might've killed the Pied Piper, he slowed to a stop, and dropped to one knee.

Rathaway stood like a statue, his mouth hanging open and his expression dazed. He looked down at the Flash and raised a hand, concentrating, trying to inflict some damage. Nothing happened. The crystals in his body had been destroyed, rendering him powerless.

"Where am I?" he said. "The Pipeline? Why?" Rathaway cursed and started to limp away. The Flash tried to get up and follow, but his muscles wouldn't answer him. Then Rathaway stopped, frozen in place.

The Green Arrow stood a few yards away, bow up and a shaft at the ready.

"It's over."

Rathaway appeared as if he wanted to make some comment, but then he simply waved his hand dismissively, and fell back against the wall. He slid to the floor to sit next to his hated foe, wearing an embittered scowl.

"You beat me."

Barry managed a laugh. "Yes."

"Harrison Wells wins again."

44

The Flash ran the streets of Central City. The freedom and the speed felt great.

After the fight, he had spent two full days in the medical bay. Following that came several days of hobbling around Joe's house, with occasional trips into CCPD to work. Caitlin continued to worry about his stunted healing factor, but Barry reassured her that he felt great, considering the beating he had taken.

He weaved almost leisurely through traffic, making the rounds of the areas hardest hit by Rathaway's gang. When he could, he helped push progress by moving stacks of lumber or bags of concrete; anything to assist the recovery. Electricity had been fully restored and a safe, reliable water supply had returned. Rebuilding had begun. Slowly but surely, the city lumbered back to its feet.

The Flash pushed himself and swept up the side of a high rise. Reaching the top, he stopped. The city spread out beneath him and he laughed. His leg muscles burned, but that was to be expected. He actually appreciated the sensation. His heart pounded, too. It would take a few days to get back in fighting trim.

He took a deep breath of the autumn air. Thanks to Oliver, he had the tricks he needed to fight off the blur. That should restrain the growth of the plasma and give Caitlin more time to come up with a permanent solution.

"Barry?"

The Flash spun in surprise at hearing a voice up here. Especially *that* voice. His older self stood across the rooftop. It was impossible. He scanned in all directions. This was still the same roof. The view of Central City hadn't changed. He could see the demolished CCK Bank from here.

Far above, a jet hung frozen in a darkening sky.

This couldn't happen. He wasn't trying to save anyone. There were no stress hormones racing through his system. He hesitated to speak, fearful that he would make it more real.

"You were right, after all." Future Flash took an unsteady step.

Barry visualized the microscope, and his childhood room, desperately seeking the calm. His older self made another palsied movement, struggling toward him.

"I didn't know what to do for you," he continued. "But I do now, though I don't know if it's too late."

Barry closed his eyes.

Breathe. Count. Breathe. Count.

Something touched his arm. He gave a startled gasp, and his eyes flew open. The sky was darker still. His own face stared back. Worn. Sallow. The old eyes were dim and weak.

"I'm sorry, Barry," Future Flash said. A tear trickled down his cheek. "I'm sorry I didn't tell you this sooner. I know how—"

Then he shuddered and stiffened. His mouth wrenched itself open in silent agony. His muscles clenched. Barry heard a humming sound, or a buzzing. A faint motion quivered between him and his older self.

Old knees gave out. Acting on instinct, Barry caught him. The sudden weight dragged them both to the ground. Barry laid him on the hard roof, kneeling over him. The old man tried to reach up, but quickly surrendered to weakness.

The humming sound persisted, and with a terrible shock Barry saw legs behind where his older self had been standing. A man stood there in full view, wearing a yellow version of his own costume. Eobard Thawne, the Reverse Flash. A wide grin split his face. Thawne's right arm was extended, his hand vibrating so quickly it was nearly invisible.

The hand that killed the Future Flash.

Barry leapt to his feet with fists raised. The man in yellow held up his hands, palms out. His uniform stood out vividly in the gloom.

"Easy," he said. "I'm not here to fight, unless you won't have it any other way. Why do you care anyway? He's just a hallucination."

"It was you," Barry snarled through clenched teeth. "It was you all the time. The blurring. The hallucinations. I don't know how you did it, but it had to be you. The plasma infected me the day you opened that wormhole. This was some long-term scheme, wasn't it?"

"No, Barry," Reverse Flash replied. "You still want the easy way out. You want a villain to blame, but this is all you. I'm you, too, in a way." He pulled back his cowl and revealed the face of Harrison Wells, the man Thawne pretended to be for so many years.

"Why do you have his face?" Barry winced, remembering.

"Run, Barry, run."

"You're not Harrison Wells. You're Eobard Thawne. I've seen your real face."

"This is how you'll always see me in your mind. To you, this is my true face. To you, I'll always be Dr. Harrison Wells—the man who made the Flash."

Barry stepped back and looked down. The body of his older self had disappeared. The rooftop held no sign of him. He offered Wells a savage grin.

"Maybe you did, but if you're not real, then what do I care? I'll come out of it in a minute, and you'll be gone."

Reverse Flash took a step closer. He leveled a stare and swung his fist. The blow spun the Flash around and nearly knocked him off his feet. Barry started to respond, but caught himself. He slowly squared his shoulders and worked his jaw back and forth to ease the pain.

"That's nothing," Barry said. "I won't feel it when I come out."

Reverse Flash laughed. "When I say I'm you, I mean it." He inched forward, staring into Barry's eyes. "Look closer."

In that gaze that he knew so well, the one that haunted his nightmares, the Flash saw something different. Deep under the guise of Reverse Flash, of Harrison Wells, there was another presence. Strange. Inhuman. Unknowable but infinitely powerful. Something yellow oozed inside those eyes.

Plasma.

This wasn't Reverse Flash at all. It was the singularity plasma that coiled inside him, eating him alive, given form by Barry's own mind. He had given it the form of the man he hated most. Feared most.

"Oh, God," Barry breathed.

Reverse Flash nodded slowly. "You're too late. I've taken root in your brain and you have given me form. You can't defeat me now. I will have every bit of you, Flash."

"No."

"Oh, yes. You see, this place where we are, it isn't a hallucination. You give it form with your thoughts, but when you blur—as you call it—you are stepping into another dimension. *My* dimension. And soon you won't be able to depart." He raised a hand and turned it palm up. Something glowed in the air, almost like a small lightning storm. "This is your essence, your speed, your soul. I'm slowly siphoning it off. Soon I'll have all of it, and there will be no more of you in your world."

Barry tried to grab the Reverse Flash, but the yellow-garbed figure was instantly across the roof, leaving a cloud of gravel and dust.

"It won't be quite so easy, I'm afraid," the thing said with the voice of Harrison Wells. "The more you use your speed, the more of yourself you lose to me. The only way to get it back is to defeat me." He pulled up his cowl, and grinned.

"So run, Barry, run."

The figure in yellow vanished. A bright trail of yellow stretched through the strangely darkened version of Central City, and disappeared into the distance.

Barry tensed to chase, but suddenly found himself standing in bright sunlight. A chilly breeze swept over the rooftop. He looked up to see the jet trudging across the sky.

The Flash dropped to one knee and struggled to contain his panic.

45

Joe stood at the grill in the small backyard of his house. Normally it would be too chilly to cook out, but this was the last day Oliver, Felicity, and John would be in Central City. With Barry back on his feet, they were heading home to deal with their own crises. So Joe had decided on a barbecue to say thank you and good-bye.

"Looks ready to me." John lounged on the back stoop, beer in hand.

Joe held his hand over the white charcoal briquettes. "Not yet."

"You sure?"

"I don't know how you barbecue in Star City, but here we do it right." Joe pointed the tongs at John who smiled in surrender.

The back door swung open and Cisco came out. "Hey, Joe, what're you waiting for? Throw some meat on the fire, man."

Joe offered a raised eyebrow. "You need to go on back inside."

John tossed Cisco a beer and said, "Here. Don't rush an artiste."

When the door opened again, Oliver emerged, looking impatiently at the grill. Joe instantly gave him a baleful glare.

"Don't even think about it, man." John passed out another beer. "Ra's al Ghul is less controlling over his pit than that guy."

Joe put a hand over the coals, but he didn't really care about the heat or the time. He cared about Barry. He should've been home by now, but Joe wasn't going to worry. Yet. Barry was always late. Maybe he got caught helping someone. That would be typical. He absently stretched his hand over the heat again.

The back door creaked open.

"It's Barry," Felicity said.

Joe grinned and reached for a steak. "*Now* it's time."

"No, Joe," Felicity said in a way that made him turn. "You should come."

The tense look on her face sent a chill through him. The tongs fell to the patio with a clatter, and he raced past the others as they were coming to their feet. He ran through the kitchen and into the living room.

Barry hunched on the sofa. Caitlin and Iris were there.

"What's wrong?" Joe walked toward him, not feeling his legs.

Barry lifted his face. His eyes were haunted, and rimmed with red. He held himself as if exhausted again. Joe's stomach wrenched. He felt sick. That morning, Barry had looked fine, almost his usual self, smiling and confident. Now this?

"I blurred," Barry said simply.

Joe wanted to feel relief. Surely he knew it might happen again, until they had a permanent solution. But something in the way Barry spoke shook him. Joe looked around the room. He needed someone to tell him this wasn't as bad as he feared.

Barry hung his head. "It just… happened. I wasn't running or trying to save anyone. Suddenly I saw Reverse Flash. Eobard Thawne, except he looked like Harrison Wells."

"Oh, that sucks," Cisco murmured.

"It's all right, Barry." Joe knelt and put a strong hand on his arm. "It's not real. You may have to expect these incidents to continue, until we can get that stuff out of you." He looked desperately at Caitlin. "Right?"

"He's right," she said in a voice that should have been more forceful. "It's nothing to worry about."

"This was different," Barry said firmly. "This was worse. Don't you understand? It's *real* now." He looked helplessly up at Oliver, and sat back on the sofa. Touched a new bruise on his jaw. "Wells hit me. In the blur. He hit me and it left a mark. That's never happened before."

"Do you think it could be Thawne behind it all?" Caitlin asked.

"No. It's not him. It's me. It's the plasma in me. It has a life of its own. It's using my thoughts now. It's taking pieces of me." Barry looked at Joe as if something bad had happened at school, and he needed his father to explain it all away. "When it's finished, there won't be any of me left."

Joe fought to keep it under control. "Then we'll try something else. We'll keep trying until it works." He sounded sure, speaking with a confidence he was surprised could escape the fear in his gut. "We'll get it. Don't worry. You hear me? Don't worry."

"We'll figure it out." Caitlin took Barry's arm. "You know that, right?" Cisco added his agreement, along with everyone else in the room. Barry managed a thin smile.

"I know," he said. "Thanks. I know. We've faced worse than this."

Joe knew Cisco was about to say something seriously out of place, so he shot a quick glare over his shoulder that caught the man with his mouth open. He took in Joe's attitude, and slowly closed it.

Barry placed a more convincing smile on his face.

"Sorry to ruin the barbecue."

Joe shushed him dismissively. "You haven't done anything, Barry. It'll take more than that to ruin a West barbecue. You'll feel better once you've eaten one of my steaks."

"Or three," Iris added with a hopeful smile. "You're probably starving by now."

"Yeah. Thanks." Barry nodded. "I'm okay now. It

just shook me up. No harm, no foul. Right?"

Joe stood up. "That's right. You sit here and rest. We'll get you something to drink. I'm going to get busy. Food coming up." He turned, passing Oliver and catching the man's eye. They both went out onto the patio where the grill still smoked. Joe picked up the tongs and stood facing the coals. Oliver waited quietly.

Joe said, "I need your help."

"Detective West, I don't—"

Joe turned around. "Stop, please. I know you're busy, and God knows you have your own troubles." He stopped for a second to collect his emotions. "That boy in there is my son, and he needs help. I know there may—" Joe stopped, feeling his voice catching in his throat. He didn't want to say these words. He tightened his hands into fists. "—there may not be an answer.

"But Barry respects you and draws strength from you, and there aren't many people in the world who have any idea what his life is like. I can only relate so much to him. This crazy life he lives. You two share that. Listen, I know you're not a father—"

Oliver's eyes changed for an instant. Joe tilted his head in realization, but didn't say anything about it. He continued softly.

"I will do *anything* to help that boy. Right now, I need to scream and cry and break things." He pointed at the grill. "But what I'm going to do is cook and make stupid jokes and act like everything is fine, because that's what he needs right now. That's what a father does."

Oliver watched Joe with icy eyes. The man showed so little emotion, it was impossible to know if he could even grasp the depth of what Joe was saying. Green Arrow was so mission-driven, he might not take a job with no sure goal. Usually Joe didn't trust anyone who was so unreadable, but this wasn't about who Joe trusted.

"Detective West," Oliver said quietly, "there's no question that I'll stay. I'll be here as long as Barry needs me. I can help him with the psychology of this problem, while others do the biology. We will find an answer. This world needs the Flash."

Joe released his breath, and a wash of relief filled him. He nodded his thanks, because he couldn't speak at that moment.

The back door swung open and Barry stepped out. He looked better, calmer. His movements were normal and sure. He glanced between Oliver and Joe, and suspicion appeared on his face. He hopped off the stoop and patted Oliver on the back on the way over to Joe. He slipped an arm easily around the man's shoulders.

"I came out here to tell you something else," Barry said quietly. "It's something you may not want to hear."

"What?" Joe's heart started pounding again.

Barry gave him a long, meaningful stare.

"Those coals are ready."

Joe laughed loudly. "You're right." He took a steak and laid it on the grill. A soft hiss greeted them and smoke rose. Joe drew in the smell, that wonderful normal scent. "Oh, and two more things, Oliver."

"What's that, Detective West?"

Joe lifted another piece of beef. "Tell me how you like your steak, and I'll always remember it. And call me Joe, because you're family." He ruffled Barry's hair.

Barry seemed so normal, so relaxed in his sweatshirt, jeans, and sneakers. He gave Joe a genuine smile and went to the stoop. Oliver fished two beers out of the cooler and tossed one over.

"I'm staying on here in Central City, to help you work with the blurring problem," he announced. "I'll figure out a way to make it work."

"There's no reason for that," Barry protested. "You gave me some tricks. I just need to practice them a little more."

"That's exactly why I need to stay. These aren't *tricks*. They're a philosophy, a lifestyle. I'm going to train you like I train myself."

Barry raised his eyebrows. "I'm going to train like you?"

"Yes."

"Can I keep my shirt on?"

"No promises." Oliver twisted the lid off the bottle.

"Oliver! Barry!" The door flew open again, and Felicity rushed out with her phone in her hand. Everyone trailed behind her. "I just got more details on the anomaly research at Palmer Tech."

Barry leapt to his feet. Joe moved to stand beside him. Everyone stared at Felicity.

"This looks good." She scrolled text on her phone.

"A few years back, Palmer designed elements for a device intended to open temporal rifts."

"Why?" Barry asked.

"Energy. They believed they could open rifts and siphon plasma, you know." Felicity waved a finger around Barry, to indicate that he was full of the stuff. "It might be an endless source of energy." She scrolled furiously. "I'll skip the specs for now. Oh, crap. They hit a dead end, though."

"Oh." Barry's shoulders slumped.

"But," Felicity continued with a jolt, eliciting groans from the group, "additional research on temporal rifts was done elsewhere, and with more success, so they say. So this project *could* provide technology that *could* allow us to understand the plasma in your body. And *could* give us a chance to remove it. Note the stress on *could*."

"Oh my God!" Iris shouted. "That's fantastic!"

Barry allowed himself a tentative smile, while Joe grabbed his arm and shook him with a loud laugh.

Felicity followed the text on her phone with intense concentration. Suddenly she stopped and pulled back with a look of dismay. "Oh, crap again. Apparently Count Wallenstein has it."

"Damn," John breathed.

"Who? What?" Cisco looked from one grim face to the other. "Who's this Count Chocula guy?"

"I've never heard of him," Barry said.

"You wouldn't have heard of him unless he wanted you to," Oliver said. "Wallenstein lives high in the mountains of Markovia, surrounded by an army of mercenaries and assassins. He doesn't come out, and anyone who goes in without his permission doesn't come out, either. Half of the world's acts of terror can be laid at his doorstep, in one way or another."

"Okay, that doesn't sound good at all." Barry took a heavy sigh. "What can we do to get this tech, if he has it?"

Oliver gave John a knowing glance, and received a quick look of approval. He smiled at Barry. "We're going to Markovia. We'll break into his castle, and we'll take the tech."

"Break into his castle?" Cisco said slowly.

"We're going to steal it?" Barry laughed. When he realized Oliver was completely serious, he looked at Joe with a crooked grin. "Quite a barbecue."

Joe nodded. "Hell, I don't care if you bomb his castle into dust. I'm just glad to have a solution. Now, let's eat and you can all talk about Markovia." He went back to the grill. "And someone can tell me where the hell it is."

When no one answered, Joe looked over his shoulder. Barry and Oliver had fallen into discussion with the group. From the looks on their faces, they could've been discussing a day at the office or a football game. To ordinary people their world was unfathomable.

At one time, Barry had been an ordinary person, too. It used to surprise Joe to detect Barry's familiar features underneath the scarlet cowl. He couldn't quite grasp that the boy was a Super Hero.

Barry glanced over at Joe with a calming smile and a bob of his chin. In the midst of all this, the boy worried about him. To ease his nervous energy, Joe took a calming breath. He couldn't comprehend what was going on in Barry's head. Looking at him, you'd never know he was facing decisions that could end his life.

He dealt with it the same way he handled scientific problems or threats from metahumans. Joe shook his head in amazement, and drew strength from Barry's easy intensity.

At that moment, Joe couldn't separate the young man he loved from the hero he held in awe. Barry Allen and the Flash were the same man.

The Fastest Man Alive.

ACKNOWLEDGMENTS

Thanks to Nick Landau, Vivian Cheung, Laura Price, Natalie Laverick, Cat Camacho, Miranda Jewess, and Julia Lloyd at Titan Books.

Thanks to Ben Sokolowski, Josh Anderson, Amy Weingartner, Carl Ogawa, Greg Berlanti, Andrew Kreisberg and Marc Guggenheim on the production teams of *The Flash* and *Arrow*, and at Warner Bros.

And thanks especially to Steve Saffel, editor. We learned a lot.

ABOUT THE AUTHORS

Clay and Susan Griffith are married co-authors of novels, short stories, comic books, and television. They were brought together by a single comic book, and they stayed together because of a shared love of heroes, villains, and adventure stories. They are the creators of the Vampire Empire series and the authors of the Crown & Key trilogy.